The
POSSESSION
of
ALBA DÍAZ

ALSO BY ISABEL CAÑAS

The Hacienda
Vampires of El Norte

The
POSSESSION
of
ALBA DÍAZ

ISABEL CAÑAS

Berkley
New York

BERKLEY
An imprint of Penguin Random House LLC
1745 Broadway, New York, NY 10019

Copyright © 2025 by Isabel Cañas
Penguin Random House values and supports copyright. Copyright fuels creativity, encourages diverse voices, promotes free speech, and creates a vibrant culture. Thank you for buying an authorized edition of this book and for complying with copyright laws by not reproducing, scanning, or distributing any part of it in any form without permission. You are supporting writers and allowing Penguin Random House to continue to publish books for every reader. Please note that no part of this book may be used or reproduced in any manner for the purpose of training artificial intelligence technologies or systems.

BERKLEY and the BERKLEY & B colophon are registered trademarks of
Penguin Random House LLC.

Title page art: Woman on stairs © Melinda Nagy / Shutterstock
Book design by Alison Cnockaert

ISBN 9780593641071

Printed in the United States of America

For my story doctor.

Aren't you thrilled that the first book I dedicated solely to you is the grisliest one yet?

But it is a circumstance worthy of much consideration that the wisdom of our Eternal Lord has enriched the most remote parts of the world, inhabited by the most uncivilized people, and has placed there the greatest number of mines that ever existed, in order to invite men to seek out and possess those lands and coincidentally to communicate their religion and the worship of the true God to men who do not know it. . . . Hence we see that the lands in the Indies that are richest in mines and wealth have been those most advanced in the Christian religion in our time; and thus the Lord takes advantage of our desires to serve his sovereign ends. In this regard a wise man once said that what a man does to marry off an ugly daughter is give her a large dowry; this is what God has done with that rugged land, endowing it with great wealth in mines so that whoever wished could find it by this means. Hence there is great abundance of mines in the Indies, mines of every metal: copper, iron, lead, tin, quicksilver, silver, and gold . . .

—José de Acosta,
Historia natural y moral de las Indias (1590)

I

I'D WAGER YOU haven't heard the legend of the Monterrubio mine. Most haven't, especially if they're not from around Mina San Gabriel. It's a rumor, really, whispered from ear to ear, passed from palm to palm like so much silver.

It was an ancient terror, I've heard people say. Or a pagan devil, rising from the dark maw of the mine to devour all in its path. Some say it was a haunting. If you ask me, that's too straightforward. Can you imagine if this were nothing but a ghost story, full of cold drafts and shadows where they oughtn't be, clammy palms and sweaty napes? That's too clean a tale. Too simple.

And this one gets messy.

For they say that Alba Díaz de Bolaños barely survived. They say that when she stumbled down the cathedral steps, she was alive, yes—she was screaming, and all of Zacatecas heard it, their breasts chilled by how shredded and raw her voice was—but her wedding gown and all its silver was slick with blood. Gleaming with it, profane and red as cinnabar, wet as afterbirth.

Some say no one has seen her since.

I have.

And, unlike the storytellers who have mangled these events over the years, I know what happened.

The truth is worse than the stories would have you believe.

I once heard it said that the words themselves are cursed. That the tale, once told, will evaporate like mercury.

I can't know that for certain. Perhaps it will.

So lean in. Listen closely. I won't be repeating myself.

II

Elías

NOT LONG AGO, in a land far from here, Elías Monterrubio found a book of spells. Or perhaps it found him.

In a shadowed corner of a book bazaar, before a stall stacked with manuscripts, he paused. The air around him swam with foreign tongues and the cries of Bosporus gulls and the harsh slant of noon and the smells of men who had traveled far under summer's sun, but at once, all went still. Softness fell around him. Leather-bound and unassuming, as these texts always are, *El Libro de San Cipriano* seemed to reach for him more than he reached for it.

Now, Elías's studies of alchemy had taken him from the familiar spires of Sevilla and the chop of Gibraltar to this far side of the Mediterranean. He was a learned man; he had come across the name before.

Before he foreswore his black craft and turned to God, San Cipriano was a sorcerer omnipotent, the greatest enchanter to ever light a candle and pray. His was not a showy craft, leveling mountains or levitating to impress princes for jewels and coin, but one of quiet incantations. Love was all he wanted, and so love was what he spun spells for. Love was what San Cipriano's followers chanted invocations for, even after the sorcerer left the lies of the occult behind and fixed his attention on the promise of life everlasting.

An alchemist's mind is weights and scales. The romance of transmutation is stripped bare to equations. Charcoal figures scribbled on blank paper. A lingering cough from chemical fumes. Love and its spells, as far as Elías was concerned, were as much a myth as San Cipriano.

But still he paused. Perhaps it was because the title on the first page was written in aljamía, Spanish words in Arabic ligatures, an ancient marriage of his twin mother tongues. That alone was rare. A curiosity. A souvenir from a time long dead.

He bought it. Slipped it into his bag.

And then he forgot about it.

For late that evening, as the call to prayer rippled midsummer's humidity like the gentle strum of an oud, a letter arrived at his workshop.

Your father has returned, it read. *Come.*

MANY WEEKS LATER, Elías cursed himself for taking the bait.

Of course he told himself that he meant to return to Spain anyway. That he had to, on behalf of his circle of scholars. Hadn't they all agreed that it would be easier for Elías to obtain their mercury from Sevilla than for any of them? It was logic, cold as metal. Elías knew Almadén and the black markets of Sevilla intimately. The arrival of his grandfather's letter merely hastened the planning.

And the idea of speaking to his father for the first time in over twenty years? He hated that it drew at him. He hated how much he wanted it. He hated how questions and accusations spiraled themselves deep into his uneasy sleep on the ship that departed the Sea of Marmara's calm waters for the docks of Barcelona.

Why did you stop writing? Why did you never return?

He was cagey and jumpy on the road; he carried his friends' fortune sewn into his clothes. He barely slept. He spoke to no one. All he needed was to make it to Sevilla. Visit the mercury dealers from Almadén and pay his respects to his family. Face his father.

Then he could turn his back on the man like he deserved and return to sea. Before Elías knew it, he would be bound east, praying that no corsairs sank or captured him and the mercury en route to Constantinople. Then life would resume as before. He could bury his father in his mind and never sleep fitfully again.

He knew from years of travel that no trip was ever simple. He did not expect simplicity. Especially not when the sun set over Sevilla's winding streets and he entered the dark, dust-filled house of the Monterrubio patriarch, Juan Arcadio.

Still, when he sat in the drawing room and asked after his father, he did not expect what his grandfather said.

"Victoriano died in the Indies six months ago," Abuelo Arcadio replied flatly.

The drop was dark and sudden. The slam of a door and the profound silence in its wake.

Elías opened his mouth to speak; nothing came out.

He leaned forward to put his head in his hands; no, no, his father couldn't be dead, he had come *all this way*. He stood abruptly, strode three paces to the door, then whirled on his grandfather. He pointed a finger at the old man, a silent accusation before he could find speech.

"You wrote—"

"Don't look at me like that, boy." Abuelo Arcadio waved a

liver-spotted hand dismissively and accepted a glass of sherry from a servant. "There was no dragging you back from your Eastern debauchery without a lie and you know it."

Elías dropped his hand. "*Fuck* you."

His grandfather laughed, broad and unabashed as a sailor. Too throaty and rude for dark-draped drawing rooms. His shoulders shook; sherry swished in the crystal glass, winking cheekily in the candlelight. Abuelo Arcadio laughed with his whole body. That was the way Elías's father laughed.

Used to laugh.

The drop beneath him reopened, and with a sweep of vertigo, he was falling again.

Every accusation, every question spun into brilliant, imaginary arguments as he rolled over on cold, rocky ground beneath the stars; all the weeks of wondering how twenty years had changed his father's face... it was all for nothing.

Six months.

The man was buried and gone. Even if Elías sailed to the Indies tomorrow with nothing but a pickaxe, desperate to exhume the corpse, there would be nothing to find by the time he reached the grave. There was already nothing to find.

"Now that the formalities are out of the way, we can actually talk. Sit." Abuelo Arcadio gestured to the chair Elías had vacated.

He could have walked out the door. Taken the bags of mercury he had purchased on behalf of his friends. Returned to the sea. He had a plan. All he had to do was leave.

All he had ever had to do was leave.

But he hesitated.

That was his inheritance, wasn't it? A bone-deep lust for more, more, *more*. This was what Victoriano Monterrubio had left him in death: no answers, no apologies, only a moment of hesitation. A fatal ripple of curiosity about what more lay twinkling beneath the surface of this meeting.

Abuelo Arcadio would not call for him—lie to him—without good reason. And the only good reasons that existed in this family were reasons that could be molten, forged, and sold.

"What do you want from me?" he asked.

"For you to sit," Abuelo Arcadio said.

He did. Sherry was brought to his side; he refused it wordlessly. Watched his grandfather sip his drink. Waited.

"Victoriano swore to Heraclio that if we bought that mine, all we had to do was drain the flooding," Abuelo Arcadio said. "That there was good ore beneath the waterline. The owner defaulted on his loans and his heir was dead, so we could get it for cheap."

"That is why Tío Heraclio and Carlos left for the Indies." Names attached to faces he had not seen in twenty years or so. Names he had not thought of in just as long.

Abuelo Arcadio tapped the rim of the now-empty glass; it was refilled. "They bought it, they drained it, and they began to dig. Your father was right, for once—the ore is good, but even that is not enough. Ah, Victoriano." A delicate scowl crossed Abuelo Arcadio's face. "He never made a business decision that did not mire this family in debt."

"To whom this time?"

"Criollo merchants. And the Crown." Abuelo Arcadio's voice lowered to a growl over the word. "Taxes! All they want is taxes. The tax on buying mercury for amalgamation is choking us. But Victoriano had a solution for this too."

"Did he now," Elías said. It came out flat. Perhaps he should have accepted the sherry earlier. Unease glimmered in his chest—it was a sense that the ground was shifting under him, like the deck of a ship when the waves grew steep and thick.

Abuelo Arcadio's grin was yellow, stained by years of tobacco. It brought to mind *jackal*. It was not at all kind. "He had whelped a little magician, hadn't he?"

A flush of heat shot through Elías's cheeks. Alchemy was weights and calculations. Alchemy was science. But not to all. To his father's family, he had never been anything more than a charlatan playing with smoke and useless measures. Nothing more than a waste of family money.

"'Summon Elías,' he said," Abuelo Arcadio continued. "'Elías knows mercury.'" He sat back in his chair, gesturing at Elías expansively. "That was the last thing he ever wrote to me. And look what it brought me: a prodigal grandson on my doorstep, laden with bags of mercury. *Tax-free mercury.*"

Smugness becomes few people. Somehow, it suited Abuelo Arcadio, settling over him like the soft, flattering light of sunset.

"Do you know how much silver that mercury can refine?" he asked.

Elías did not reply. He didn't need to. Abuelo Arcadio was already dreaming aloud, the divine power of metal lifting him to his feet and carrying him across the room, where he paced as if he itched with possibility.

"Enough silver to make the mine profitable." It was prayerlike in its reverence. "To save this family from ruin. And then some."

He turned to Elías. His final question was unspoken, but it hung in the air with the presence of a ghost.

"No," Elías said.

"Mulish as ever," Abuelo Arcadio said, with a measure of what some might call grandfatherly affection. It felt a touch closer to condescension. "Heraclio predicted this. You take after your mother, after all."

"She stays out of this." He was on his feet, stung by the lick of a whip.

Eagerness glinted in Abuelo Arcadio's eyes. He had loved baiting Elías when he was a child, for Elías always snapped faster than any of his cousins. Still did, apparently. He did not know which he hated more: Abuelo Arcadio's power over him, or how he let him have that power.

"Victoriano died with an enormous amount of debt in his name. As his only son, it is now yours," Abuelo Arcadio said. "Bring your mercury to Nueva España. Become azoguero in Victoriano's place and refine enough silver to repay the debt. Any silver refined from the mercury that remains will be fifty percent yours."

"That mercury is not mine," Elías said.

"It is in your bags," Abuelo Arcadio said. Again, that jackal smile played across his face. "Is it not?"

The trust on his friends' faces flitted through his mind. How easily they had counted coins into his palms. The way they waved to him from the docks as the ship pulled away. Casually, then returning to their coffee as clouds of gulls rose around them, obscuring them from sight. As if Elías were merely crossing the city and not the Mediterranean. For they knew he would return.

Wouldn't he?

Or was it not possible that he could have perished in a storm, sinking to the bottom of the sea, weighed down by all the coins sewn into his jacket? Was it not possible that he could be captured by corsairs and sold? Or, once he reached Spain, could he not be caught in the act of purchasing mercury on the black market and again condemned to Almadén?

Months would pass. His friends would mourn him as dead. Perhaps even forgive him, one day.

Greed was less a deadly sin than family creed, as inescapable as the name he bore or the way he recognized his father's gestures in his own hands. He swore he was different from his cousins, his uncles, his grandfather. His greed was different. It buried him in tomes and equations and experiments, for it was a lust for knowledge that drove him to seek more. It was a noble greed.

But that much silver...

He could sail to China, or Persia, and live as a scholar prince for the rest of his days. He could turn his back on the Monterrubios, for he would never need them. He could put every sin he had ever committed to his back and become someone new. Unburdened. Free.

"Seventy-five percent," he countered.

"Seventy," said Abuelo Arcadio, extending his right hand to shake.

Elías took it in his. Shook it once and firmly, before he could change his mind. "Done."

AT THE PORT of Cádiz, Elías boarded a galleon in the fleet bound for the setting sun.

After six days at sea, just before they passed las Islas Canarias, a storm struck. For hours, the fleet was tossed across waves higher than a cathedral's spires like pearls cast from a fist. In the hold, crushed against other immigrants as they retched and cried out between repetitions of the rosary, he pulled a small bag of mercury to his chest and shut his eyes, for the darkness he could control was better than the gloom of the hold. He bit his tongue as he and the bodies around him rose with the next wave; breath cracked from his lungs as they were slammed back down against the walls of the hold and mercury struck his chest.

The squall quieted. In the end, it was a miracle only one man died, the sailors agreed as they tied an earthenware jug to the corpse's feet. And of fright, to boot. That was his heart's fault, not the captain's. It was an auspicious start to the crossing, was it not?

Each funereal shot of the cannon over the glassy sea rang in Elías's bones. One, two, three.

They sailed on.

Bile and thirst ravaged his throat. Hunger drew flesh tight as provisions staled and went to rot. The sun rose and beat on his back, on his skull, blistering his nape and the backs of his hands as he tried to read. El Libro de San Cipriano had stowed away among his belongings, still forgotten as he pored over Juan de Cárdenas's *Problemas y secretos maravillosos de las Indias* and studied amalgamation diagrams from José de Acosta's *Historia natural y moral de las Indias*.

His mind bent and folded with each blistering day. He swore he saw his mother in the faces of other passengers. He swore he heard the voices of the dead as he leaned against the side of the ship, enduring the exaggerated rise and fall of the swell—was it not better than being trapped in the airless hold below, among the sweat and chanted prayers and the stench of vomit?—and the punishing blaze of a cloudless sky. Salt spray stung his eyes and lips. Waves beat against the bow. Ghostly fingertips grasped at his shoulders, desperate, as if trying to pull him back from a precipice.

Why are you never content? All you ever do is leave.

The galleon sailed on, into the setting sun, into a horizon turned to molten metal.

FIFTY-FIVE DAYS BROUGHT them to a port called Cartagena, where the fleet split in two. Elías sailed on to Nueva España.

In Veracruz, he stepped foot onto sand. The earth swept up to meet him. He heard the roar of sailors' laughter from the docks as he lurched forward and stumbled, a victim not of seasickness but its inverse.

Palms swayed in a breeze. Clouds swung heavy and low overhead; the air smelled of rain, of wet soil.

Perhaps he felt a first, reluctant curl of forgiveness for his father. For as he looked over his shoulder at the bay, at the galleons docked with their sails slack and exhausted, he knew in his bones that he would never return to Spain.

There was only forward.

And so forward he walked.

Zacatecas
Nuevo Reino de Galicia
Nueva España
ENERO 1765

The land which had been as common to all as the air or the sunlight

Was now marked out with the boundary lines of the wary surveyor.

The affluent earth was not only pressed for the crops and the food

that it owed; men also found their way to its very bowels,

And the wealth which the god had hidden away in the home of the ghosts

By the Styx was mined and dug out, as further incitement to wickedness.

—Ovid, Metamorphoses I.135–140

III

Alba

ALBA SET HER palm on the handle of the confessional door. The wood was smooth, worn and oiled by thousands of penitent fingertips.

She hesitated.

"We shouldn't keep Lucia waiting." Mamá was already halfway to the alcove of Santa Rosa de Lima on the far side of the cathedral, where she always prayed her penance.

They could have arrived punctually at the seamstress's home—or even early—if they had skipped coming to the cathedral altogether. But pointing this out would be of no use. Mamá never skipped daily confession, and so neither did Alba.

She opened the door of the confessional and shut it behind her. Her silk skirts gave a long-suffering sigh as she settled onto the hard wooden kneeler.

"May God, who has enlightened every heart, help you to know your sins and trust in His mercy."

The voice from behind the confessional grate was not one she recognized. Good. A measure of the tightness in her shoulders loosened.

When she was a child, sleepless with anxiety the night before her first confession, Mamá had stroked her hands and assured her that the priests simply heard too many confessions a day to be able to match the sins they absolved to a particular parishioner. Besides, were there not far too many parishioners for them to recognize them by voice in the dark?

Perhaps this was true. The priest might not know it was Alba. But Alba usually knew the priest, and unwrapping any feeling—much less sins and failures—before someone she knew made her want to claw her way out of the dark, stuffy box of the confessional.

She set palm to palm before her, as if to pray. She interlaced her fingers. First one way, then the other. Rose-scented rosary beads clicked and skipped over one another.

The priest cleared his throat.

"Forgive me, Padre, for I have sinned." The phrase could have been one word, accented with a hum of impatience. "It has been"—a matter of hours, really, Mamá made sure of that—"a day since my last confession."

She worried the cuticles of her thumbs. Mamá would slap her hands away if she saw, but here, she was alone. Well, she wasn't, but as the silence stretched long, she could imagine she was.

"Take your time." The priest's voice was low, as soft as a thought. It fell away as quickly as one, as sins crawled out of her mind and crowded into the confessional, heavy and huffing from the effort. Each breath made the air taste staler. Even the traces of church incense had lost their bite, smothered and flattened.

"I think I have blackmailed someone," she burst out.

A shift of clothing from the other side of the grate.

"What do you mean 'you think'?" the priest asked.

"It wasn't on purpose," she said.

It was in self-defense. There had been a battering ram at her gate, one that she had overheard through a locked door:

No Basque families, Papá's voice thundered. Alba could easily envision him wagging a warning finger, whitening brows bristling in firelight. *Think of the Echeverría men—they keep disappearing in El Norte. We cannot take that financial risk now, not when it seems that the bloody Monterrubios have no intention of keeping to their repayment schedule.*

Voices dropped to a murmur. Then—

But who cares for the money when that duke would take her away to Spain! Mamá's voice pitched toward a wail, despairing. *I will not have that, not when there are merchants in Puebla who—*

The world—well, Zacatecas at least—was built on silver. The city would have remained a windblown, sun-bleached outpost if it had not been founded above dark rivers of ore. Silver made the great clock of Alba's world tick with measured, predictable beats: plata passed from purse to purse. Men rose to the heavens or drowned with it tied around their necks.

And women, when they came of age, were bartered away for it.

It was naive to assume she would be exempt. Being Mamá's only daughter, adopted after long years of barrenness, would not spare her from being carved up for purchase at the butcher.

For this was the reality: There were men who would pay Papá for her. She had been at parties and dinners where the long gazes of older men in silks and powdered wigs left thick slime across her skin. She had felt their clammy hands groping her waist during the contradanza, their alcohol-stale breath too close to her face as they tried—and failed—to whisper seductively in her ear.

An ugly daughter, she had heard those same voices whisper. *But a wealthy family.*

Such memories hurtled her back toward a family wedding when she was fourteen, trapped at the wrong end of an impossibly long, dark hall she had wandered down looking for some quiet. A paunchy behemoth of a man barricading her escape. A ringed hand over her mouth, cutting off her scream. Metal pressed hard into her lips and cheeks; the hand reeked of tobacco. A whole body pressed against her, pinning her to the wall—

The hand dropped. The weight lifted. She could gasp for air.

Another drunken male guest had asked in a slurred voice after the location of the chamber pots. The barricade replied. Then vanished.

Alba remained in the hall, back to the wall, panting against the constraints of her corset, heart racing out of time with her pulse. Multicolored sparks exploded silently around the corners of her vision.

She would not faint. If she did, she knew no one would find her. No one would rescue her. She had to compose herself, rearrange her jewelry, and reenter the ballroom alone.

Once the marriage deed passed from hand to hand, a stranger would own her body. Would expect to exploit it for heirs that would inherit their own silver and titles.

Disgust bloomed and spread like a fungus, curling into and rotting her bones.

She was out of time.

One night, she waited until Mamá and Papá had gone to bed, then padded downstairs into Papá's office. She had sleepwalked often as a child; if caught by a servant or parent, she knew exactly how to mime being awoken with a cry of surprise and a bumbling cascade of frightened sobs.

The Persian rugs were plush beneath her bare feet, their designs silvered by the moonlight pouring in through glass windowpanes.

The whole scene seemed touched by the moon's otherworldly lacquer as she fell to her knees before the desk in the corner, then opened the lowest drawer, where she knew Papá kept his most important paperwork.

The Monterrubios owed Papá money. But how much? And was it enough for the shameful plan falling into place in her heart?

"Whom did you blackmail?" the priest asked.

Alba refolded her hands. The rosary had left indentations in her palms; it clicked as she shifted it.

"My fiancé," she said.

Well. Now he was her fiancé. He used to be a boy who hid in the curtains with her at the parties of wealthy mineros.

No one had ever concealed the fact that Alba was adopted. Mamá and Papá were cypresses with fine, pale hair, their eyes the light brown of crisp cones of piloncillo. Alba's hair fell down her back in a slick, black sheet; her eyes were so dark that pupils only seemed distinct from irises in direct sunlight. It didn't matter that she found the arrangement of these features—though severe—pleasing when she saw her own reflection. They were universally decreed ugly.

It's like a dog is staring at you, a cousin had once declared when Alba was six. Then he barked at her and howled in amusement at his own cleverness.

These were the children she avoided when she sought out richly furnished drawing rooms with heavy drapes. One day, she heard the scramble of shoes on the rug and the rough breathing of someone in flight. Curtains reshuffled themselves, then, with a sigh, weight settled next to her. She imagined darkness surrounding the other child. The quiet of thick fabric. The tickle of dust motes that she had come to associate with slowing heartbeats and peace.

"Who's there?" she whispered.

A gasp. "Who're you?"

"Alba."

"Oh." There was palpable relief in the word. "Carlos Monterrubio."

One of the new arrivals from Spain. Music drifted up through the floorboards, muffled by the carpets. The laughter of drunken adults was distant, dreamlike.

"They're playing wedding downstairs," Carlos said. "I *hate* playing wedding." The drapes could not conceal the frustration that pushed his voice close to cracking.

"I know," Alba said. She did not. She was rarely invited to join games. *She's too serious*, the other girls said. But how could she not be acutely aware that the riches surrounding her were not her birthright but a gift of chance, a twist of fate? So Alba studied her Latin and went to Mass and emulated the pious and quiet. She followed Mamá and Papá to the mansions of the merchants of Zacatecas and studied catechism with their daughters. Hers was the one head of black hair among the shades of wheat as they learned to stitch and curtsy and dance. She could never forget it.

"I never want to marry a girl," Carlos said, so softly it was swallowed by the curtains.

"You can hide here until they get bored enough that they'll leave you alone," Alba said softly. "It works for me."

"Thank you."

The silence they sat in forged an alliance. Years passed; the alliance strengthened, quiet and steady. They were each other's shields at gatherings throughout Zacatecas. Even though some of Alba's catechism and embroidery acquaintances tittered over how golden and beautiful Carlos grew, he never attached himself to any of them. He preferred to dance with Alba or not to dance at all.

If men did not want to spend time with women, it was easy—they simply didn't.

It wasn't *fair*.

The priest cleared his throat. "Why would you blackmail your fiancé?" he asked.

Alba spun the emerald on her fourth finger. It slipped against clammy skin.

Of all the men in Zacatecas, Carlos Monterrubio did not want to own her.

That was why she shuffled through her father's papers that night, looking for hard evidence of the Monterrubios' debt. She knew Carlos did not want to marry, but she was a daughter of Zacatecas: She knew the power of silver hinged not on hearsay, but figures.

She found what she sought in a letter dated 1740.

Twenty-five years ago, a man called Victoriano Monterrubio had approached Papá seeking a loan to buy a flooded mine south of Zacatecas.

Monterrubio.

And after that, there it was: cold, hard figures. Enormous figures. The Monterrubios had required a loan that was as much as the mine itself.

But the letter went on:

He says the infant was given a wet nurse to be cared for and grows stronger with each passing day. No one has claimed her, though she is as fair as ivory.

Her heart stuttered in her chest. She stared at the letter—no, she stared *through* the letter, mouth dry. Papá's handwriting related how when he went to Mina San Gabriel to inspect the property, Victoriano Monterrubio told him that an abandoned infant had been discovered. If Papá and Mamá wanted the baby, he would swear an oath to never tell.

Apparently he never had.

No *one* had.

Mamá had a collection of fables about Alba's origins and chose from them as if picking a playing card at random. Alba was a foundling nursed back to health by the Carmelite sisters; Alba was the niece, or granddaughter, of Mamá's favorite housekeeper (dearly departed, may God rest her soul, and therefore conveniently unable to be questioned on the matter); Alba was a wicked fairy child sent to torment Mamá with questions.

Why did they never tell her the truth?

Though she is as fair as ivory. Was it because she was of an unknown casta, but pale enough that they could pretend she was criolla? All in the pursuit of claiming her, shaping her, making her something she was not, owning her, lifting her up on marionette strings . . .

They had never wanted a daughter. They wanted another possession to add to their collection of beautiful, valuable objects.

A hollow had opened in Alba's gut as she read; a hot sweep of anger filled it like water flooding the Monterrubio mine.

She replaced the papers with shaking hands.

By marrying Carlos, she could get away from her parents. She would be free of anyone else trying to make her their own. Free of the sweaty handed, the groping, the ones who told one another they found her ugly but lusted for her father's silver.

And so, the following day, she pulled Carlos aside at a society gathering to speak to him about financial realities. About facts: Papá's impatience, the numbers that tied a sword hanging over the Monterrubios' head on an ever-fraying thread, the truth that Papá would never call in the debts of a family into which his daughter had married.

I don't want a husband, she had said, *only a married name and my own space*. They could continue as they were, as friends. Together, they could hide behind the curtains from a world that would push them in directions they did not want.

Carlos had not looked at her like she was a monster, like she deserved. He rubbed a hand along his jaw. He gave her proposal, such as it was, the weight and consideration that such a decision entailed.

He said: *That sounds mutually beneficial.*

The emerald was on her left hand the next day.

"That is a sin," the priest said.

His voice shattered the spell.

Alba was in a stuffy confessional, still thick with incense and her mother's perfume, on the opposite side of a grate from a stranger.

She should stand and leave the confessional at once. Would Mamá know what she had done and send her right back in?

"You disobeyed your parents by becoming betrothed to someone they did not want you to marry. To disobey one's parents contravenes the fifth commandment," the priest said sternly. "Do you know which that is, mi hija?"

Heat flushed her neck and crept up to her face. Condescension never failed to make annoyance rise like bile in her breast.

"'Honor thy father and thy mother,'" she muttered.

A hum of assent from the other side of the grate. "In Proverbs, it is written that 'the eye that mocks a father and scorns to obey a mother will be plucked out by the ravens of the valley and eaten by the vultures,'" the priest said. "You deliberately disobeyed your parents. I hope you will be more obedient to your future husband."

This struck like a physical blow. She flinched. "Yes, Padre."

"Do you wish to confess anything else?"

She seized the handles of every door that led to her heart and yanked them shut. "That is all I can remember."

Another lie. Forgive her, Padre, for she had sinned.

"Then recite the Act of Contrition," the priest said.

Alba inhaled, leaning her weight on her elbows.

"Oh my God, I am heartily sorry for having offended Thee." She knew the prayer backward, forward, upside down, in her sleep. "I detest all my sins, because I dread the loss of Heaven and the pains of Hell, but most of all because they offend Thee."

She did not detest what she had done, though she sat at the center of a silvery web of deceit, each of the threads firmly wrapped around her hands, a spider spinning herself one step ahead of the snapping jaws of fate.

She had outmaneuvered Mamá and Papá and driven herself forward. For the first time, she decided where to step. If she gave up her plan, she would die, and her body would become an empty shell, a wooden puppet, for as long as it then saw fit to walk the earth.

"I firmly resolve, with the help of Thy grace, to do penance and to amend my life."

The priest's voice on the other side of the grate replied in a low murmur. A suggestion for penance; a novena, or two, or eleven, Alba did not care.

The rite of confession continued, and Alba plotted to sin again.

IV

Alba

THE BEST THING about entering a ballroom with Carlos Monterrubio was how he moved: He was a creature wholly at ease in the candlelight and the music that echoed off gilded walls. He had told Alba that when his parents brought him to Nueva España, they had booked the passage on loans and mad faith in a flooded mine, hanging on to a noble name and reputation by shredded fingernails. He used to hide from the cruel children of the other mineros, ashamed of his family's reputation and how they criticized his clothes, his accent, his home.

And now?

It was as if he were born to walk into wedding receptions like this, filled with bejeweled dukes and the wealthiest merchants in Zacatecas. He shook the hands of the bride's and groom's fathers and joked alongside the bride's brothers, his laughter as golden as the sparkling wine from France and the rings on the men's fingers.

The worst thing about entering a ballroom with Carlos Monterrubio was that he *wanted* to be there. He was not born to hide in the dusty dark. He shone. He was *meant* to be there. And as his fiancée, Alba had to be at his side.

With him, there was no commiserating about how the evening was stretching too long or how her shoes pinched her toes, nor about how late the other mineros might be out drinking. He was kindling aflame with life in a room full of people. The questions he asked strangers and acquaintances stemmed from genuine curiosity; the laughter that followed was rich and warm. He roamed the room like a mountain cat, never resting, the faces and names of the people he spoke with blurring together.

If Carlos was a candle, Alba was the shadow it cast. Always a half step behind, flickering with unease at his every move.

"Shall I get you another glass of Champagne?" He bent his head down to her. His whisper was a shade conspiratorial; his eyes danced as gaily as the couples in the center of the ballroom. "I just heard that the bride's father had it shipped from France at great expense. It would be rude to let it go to waste."

His was a boyish sort of ebullience. He had not outgrown it in their lifetime of acquaintance; he probably never would. It never failed to soften the bristling edges of any annoyance that built in her chest.

Marriage to him was a victory. Any discomfort she experienced now—or at any other social function at his side—was immaterial compared to the freedom that awaited her past the altar. A parlor of her own, cavernous and silent. A bright window by which she would embroider for hours, uninterrupted, content with the hum of silken floss through her fingertips and its vivid gleam in the sunlight. No one telling her what to do or how to dress or where to go. No parents. No children.

She flipped her fan open and batted it gently before her face, as if she were warm. A coquettish gesture, another piece of a game they played.

"It would be rude," she agreed.

But as he walked away, he took her smile with him. Her cheeks slackened.

This was the way it was: warm words, the practiced dance of flirtation. Enough to make any onlooker in Zacatecas believe that they were such lucky young things, to be marrying for love instead of money.

She watched him cross the crowded room back to her, a slim flute of Champagne in each hand, nodding at greetings and returning smiles with a flash of white teeth. He wore the appreciation of women young and old in the room like it was tailored to his shoulders: carelessly, effortlessly. Their fingertips brushed as he handed her the glass with practiced grace.

Alba knew she was envied. But it was envy for the wrong things: Her real conquest was not a golden Monterrubio, heir to a mine that was slowly stepping into its promise.

Victory, to her, was what she had avoided by making this deal with Carlos. She toasted that: She was untouchable now. She had gambled and she had won.

Carlos touched the rim of his glass to hers with a satisfying chime.

"We're celebrating," he said. "Don't ask me why."

He could have flung a door wide open, gesturing with aplomb to a room within, and that would have been more subtle. She could not help the amusement that tugged at the corner of her mouth.

"I never ask," she said. "I demand to know."

"At least demand in a lower voice." As a rule, she hated it when men winked; Carlos was the only exception. "Drink, and I'll tell you."

The bubbles raked the roof of her mouth. Between the collar of pearls at her throat and how tightly the seamstress had sewn her into this heavy dress, she had scarcely eaten. The alcohol would go straight to her head. It didn't matter. The room was already lively, echoing with shouts and laughter. Surely she was not the only one.

Carlos lowered his voice, bending his head to her again. "We've received a large amount of mercury from Spain," he said.

Alba hoped no one noticed how high her brows rose. "But the merchants from the capital—"

Carlos raised a finger to his lips with a twinkle in his eye that was more than Champagne. "They've come and gone, yes," he said. "This was acquired by other means, shall we say."

"Do tell," Alba said, lifting her glass to her lips.

"I will not," Carlos said. "It's a family secret. You'll just have to wait."

Alba's heartbeat stuttered. If the Monterrubios could buy their way out of Papá's debt, she would have no more leverage. Would Carlos leave her before the altar?

"A toast," Alba said. "To family secrets."

Carlos lifted his glass to hers. "To family secrets."

This time, when they sipped, his eyes did not stay locked on hers. They skipped over her shoulder to the crowded room beyond. Something beneath his face shifted, resettled.

"Come with me," he said, extending an arm to her. It was somewhat stiff—with anticipation? Nerves? "There's someone I want to introduce you to."

People parted like waters before them, the golden couple of Zacatecas new money. The candle and its shadow. They moved as one to the far side of the room, where a small group of men in dark clothing talked in a circle.

"He's newly arrived from Spain," Carlos said. "Will you make him feel welcome?"

Alba's mouth parted in surprise. That was why Carlos was suddenly nervous.

"Your old friend!" she said. "The one from your letters. The soldier."

At this, a figure in the circle turned, moving with the confidence of a man who knew he was being talked about and knew it only ever meant good things.

His hair caught candlelight as if it were made to, softly, as the finest silk might. It was tawny brown; so, too, was his skin, as if he had spent a long journey under the sun instead of in the dark interior of a carriage. The effect this had on his eyes spurred Alba's heart to her throat in surprise: They were pale, and piercingly so, like a blinding January sky.

"No longer a soldier," said Carlos.

"Or perhaps still a soldier," the man said. He had stepped toward Alba, but it seemed as if he had barely moved. It was as if the heavens and earth had conspired to resettle the ground beneath his feet. He took Alba's hand and bowed gallantly over it. "Albeit in the army of Christ."

As he rose, his clothing made clear what she had been too distracted by his face to tell: He was a priest.

"This is Bartolomé Verástegui Robles," said Carlos.

"Señorita Alba, I presume," he said. A swift appraisal of her features; this was over almost before it began. Nothing was worthy of note. But he lingered on her clothes: There was wealth blatant in every piece Mamá had chosen for her, from the pearls in her upswept hair to the fabric imported from France and its expensive, ostentatious beading. She had to walk slowly or risk fainting from the dress's weight.

Bartolomé shot Carlos a look. A look she often saw exchanged among men, one that they thought women could not parse: *Well done*, it said. It never left a good taste in her mouth.

"It is a pleasure to meet you at last," he said.

Something made her feel as if she were off the music, a beat behind the other dancers, jostled and heavy-footed and trying to figure out where she had misstepped. Why the melody struck a flat note in her skull. It was something in Bartolomé's pale eyes, in the way he stood. No—she could not help feeling ill at ease around the childhood friend whose arrival Carlos had so eagerly anticipated.

"And what brought you from Spain?" she asked. *Make him feel welcome*, Carlos had said, but instead she was scrambling for purchase. "Surely silver does not tempt men of God."

Her question was forward. She knew it from the arch look she could feel more than see Carlos slide sideways at her. But she needed something, anything, to fill the space between them.

"Indeed, no," Bartolomé said. His smile was a smooth thing, slipping over broad white teeth like fingertips over silk. "The temptation that drew me to the Indies is of a different sort. There are souls to be won here, señorita. Souls to bring into God's embrace."

The way the words fell from his lips, in his accent, sent Alba hurtling back three days to the airless confines of the confessional.

That is a sin.

Her stomach twisted, at once queasy with certainty.

She recognized his voice, but surely he could not recognize hers. There had been a long line of people to give confession that afternoon, from the daughters of dukes to well-dressed solareto landowners who had come in for Mass from outside the city. No one could pick a single voice out from a crowd like that. Not even with the details she had included in her confession.

Or could they?

Especially if they were intimate with the Monterrubios, perhaps with their financial situation... how much had Carlos told his old friend about the state of the mine? Or, for that matter, the mutually beneficial nature of his relationship with Alba?

She kept her smile broad. Her face felt pinned and starched. Her mind spiraled down paths that grew narrower and narrower, and that robbed her of breath. She said something in reply, something empty and pleasant. Carlos agreed; more pleasant nothings.

Her heart was beating too quickly. Sweat pooled in the low of her back, sticking to the too-tight laces of her undergarments. She gave her half-finished glass of Champagne to a passing servant. Its taste had soured in her mouth.

"Are you well, señorita?"

Bartolomé was watching her. Could he see past the mask she wore? She prayed not. She almost laughed at the absurdity of the thought—*Please, God, let me hide from your faithful servant.* As if such a prayer would be answered.

"I could use some air," she said. Her voice struck an affected note. What she said was true—the drum of dancers' feet and the ring of violins and glasses clinking and laughter rattled against her skull. There were too many people moving and breathing in the same room; too many bodies filling it with heat and the tangy aroma of sweat wrestling to be free from the perfume that smothered it.

She unwound her arm from Carlos's. "I'll be back in a minute," she said. "If you see my mother, tell her..." The last thing she wanted was for Mamá to find her and fuss over her and dab her forehead with a heavily scented handkerchief. "Distract her, won't you?"

The understanding that crossed Carlos's face was warm.

"I'll buy you all the time I can," he said. "Shall I find you water as well?"

It was a safe thing, the friendship that bound them. She could almost hate herself for using him so brazenly.

"I'll be fine," she said. "All I need is air."

She had been to gatherings at this mansion before; if she recalled correctly, there was a courtyard off the ballroom. She set her sights on the door at the back of the room and pressed forward, slipping past people, answering greetings with a wan smile or pretending she hadn't heard them at all.

Are you well? Bartolomé had asked. He read her quickly and easily. Anxiety took this information and spun it around her mind like a top. There was no hiding from him forever. Eventually, he would match her name and face to her sins, and then what?

Loyalty to Carlos would not break the vow of the confessional, but could it bend it?

Bartolomé could pretend to be ignorant of his conversation with Alba and still dissuade Carlos from marrying her. He could convince Carlos that she was manipulative. Disrespectful. Untrustworthy. And therefore harmful to the Monterrubio family name and to the reputation that Carlos burnished so carefully—so desperately—among mineros, merchants, and nobles at every social gathering.

Bartolomé could shatter her future. Her freedom.

She inhaled sharply to calm herself. The confessional was a sacred place. Even if he were able to miraculously match her voice to one of the hundreds he had heard that day, vows would prevent him from breathing a word of it.

And she would never confess to him again, that was for certain.

She shook off these thoughts with a stiff shudder as she passed through the doorway at the back of the ballroom and into a dark hall. A draft from her right indicated the direction of the courtyard; she followed it. She had no shawl, and January past sunset was piercingly cold, but she wanted to feel cold. It would clear her head.

She stepped into the courtyard.

A shadow to her left moved sharply away from her. A yelp in the dark; her breath caught in her throat, crisp and sharp.

"You frightened me," a male voice said, tripping over the words as if in surprise.

"You frightened *me*." Alba's hand had flown to her chest; her heart raced beneath her palm. Gooseflesh rose over the backs of her arms; from the shock or the cold, she could not tell. Her breath clouded the air, barely visible in the dark. It felt like being submerged in a freezing bath. It felt biting and good.

"I needed some air," the man said. "I thought no one else would be out here."

"So did I," Alba said. "On both counts."

Being alone in the dark with a strange man was not a position that she wanted to be found in as a newly betrothed young woman. She sucked in the icy air, aiming to clear her head quickly. In a moment, she would be shivering too much to speak; she would return indoors and face the rest of the evening. Perhaps Mamá would have had her fill of seeing and being seen by now—a wan, optimistic wish, but a wish all the same.

"It's packed in there," the man said. "Aren't zacatecanos supposed to be the richest men in the world? You'd think they could build bigger rooms with all that plata."

That was an outsider's observation. But yes, now that she thought of it, you'd think that they would.

"Did you recently arrive from Spain?" she asked, trying to make the man out in the dark. Not a single torch was lit in the courtyard. There was no moon, only a smattering of sharp, faraway stars, and it was difficult to discern his features. He was tall, that she could deduce, but his clothes . . . she could not make out their color or style, only that there was more white than would appear in a priest's dark clothing. So he was no companion of Bartolomé's. Good. Her shoulders released tension that she had not realized they were holding.

"Is it that obvious?" he asked.

She shrugged. Perhaps it was the accent—he struck syllables at a clip that caught her ear, that felt *other*. But it was also the nature of Zacatecas: It drew men from afar like flies to a deer's carcass in the sun. Whether the mines were producing silver or not, there was always someone new to pick over the bones and see if what was left still had ore to give.

"There seem to be a lot of new arrivals these days," she said, thinking of the one she had fled in the ballroom.

"Here to make their fortune?" the man asked.

Bartolomé was a priest, but the paleness of his eyes had hidden little. Hunger brought him to Nueva España—that much she knew from Carlos and the years of letters. Bartolomé was the third or fourth son of some rich family, the only one who had yet to make his mark on the world. The military, it was thought, would bring glory; when that failed him, he sought out the cloth. He sought souls to convert, he said. Was that so different from seeking notoriety from wealth?

"So it seems," she said.

"Then I am far from extraordinary," the man said. "Here to get rich quick and run away as fast as I can."

He was wrong. The thought of running away *was* unusual for a recent arrival. "Run away? From what?"

Her eyes were beginning to adjust to the darkness; she caught his sardonic gesture toward the doorway that led back inside. "Family, you know."

She did. Oh, she did. And because he was, perhaps, the first to ever mirror such a feeling back to her, she found herself intrigued. Who was he? "I know the feeling well."

"Greedy and rotten to the core." His laugh was half a sigh, both relieved by her reply and colored by exasperation—it inspired a swell of camaraderie in her breast. She was no longer eager to flee. She found herself fighting against the chill, rubbing her forearms fruitlessly against winter's bite, so that she could linger in this conversation.

"The sooner I can afford to get to Acapulco, the sooner I'm getting on the first ship that will take me," he said.

"Headed where?" Alba asked.

"The Philippines, China, I don't care," the man said. "Anywhere, as long as it's far, far away."

The dark of the courtyard was what the dark of the confessional should feel like: weightless. Open. Night's chill had wicked away her sweat and left her feeling clearheaded and relaxed. Perhaps the man felt the same. Perhaps as he looked at her—which she could feel he was doing, if not see it, and for once, she was not disgusted by it—he saw past the pearls and starched facade and the tight dress as heavy as battle armor.

Perhaps he saw a person.

His voice, when he spoke again, sounded as if he were sharing a secret, uncurling fingertips around a closed fist to reveal the treasure hidden inside. "Do you want to dance?"

Her laugh was like a sudden clap of hands, bright and startled. Was he flirting with her? Impossible. Men did not flirt with her. She was the only daughter of a wildly successful merchant, and that made her the sum of a financial calculation, the handshake at the end of a bargain.

"I don't even know your name," she said.

"And I don't know yours. But you've already won my greatest secret," he said. "Surely that's worth more than a name."

That was a lie. When people gave away secrets, they peddled in surface metals, never reaching for the deepest ore. Not unless their hand was forced. Even then, some things would always remain buried. Some things should never see the light of day.

But it was a pretty thing to say.

Perhaps it was the Champagne. The cold air making her feel bolder than she was. Perhaps it was her curiosity about this unusual person that provoked her to extend her hand to him.

She gave him a little lift of the chin. She could be flirtatious right back, could she not?

"Fair enough," she said. "Shall we?"

His palm was calloused and warm.

When they stepped into the light of the ballroom, the first thing she noticed was the back of his hand. It was sunbrowned, dappled with small white scars and burn marks—the hands of someone who worked.

His clothes were dark, and—as she had judged in the courtyard—were not those of a priest. They were not the clothes of a particularly wealthy man either—the lines were clean and well tailored, but without the ruffles and extravagances she was accustomed to. None of the nobleman's frills that surrounded them as they walked onto the dance floor.

The violins struck the opening notes of the contradanza. She was rusty—she and Carlos had not danced in weeks. This would be interesting.

She turned, and they faced each other.

The noise of the ballroom fell away behind her.

If she had seen him before speaking to him, she might have been afraid. His face was sharp, windblown; his mouth was broad and did not look as if it smiled easily. His hair was dark, long and straight and pulled away from his face, accentuating high, blunt cheekbones and a gold ring in one earlobe. Perhaps he was nearly thirty. But perhaps he was younger, and it was the squint lines at the corners of his eyes that gave the impression of someone who had seen much of the world and was wary of it.

But his eyes were dark, doe-like. Expressive. Even soulful. They remained fixed on her face as the dance progressed with a softness that soothed the unease she had been carrying in her shoulders. There was something in the way he caught her hand every time she extended it as the dance required that slowed her heartbeat. Slowed time.

Comfort in the presence of men was not something she had much experience with. She doubted that it could be achieved through a single dance. But something had passed between them in the dark courtyard that might be a distant relative of comfort. Of ease. Or trust. That might resemble it, in shape and feel.

She meant to ask for his name. She opened her mouth, but was overcome with a wave of shyness. It had been much easier to speak to him in the dark.

A shriek shattered the ballroom.

The violins screeched. Dancers halted and collided; a glass smashed shrilly, then another.

The man took Alba's hands in his and halted their dance, his eyes searching the crowd for the cause of the disturbance. He had subtly placed his body in between the sounds of a scuffle and Alba.

"She fainted!" a voice cried.

"Ah, it was the bride," the man said, eyes fixed on the disturbance on the far side of the room. "Fainting at your own wedding. That's not a sign of bad luck, is it?"

It didn't seem to be a sign of good luck.

Voices slithered around the ballroom, passing words from ear to ear. *She fainted, they say she has a fever.* By dawn, the news would pass far beyond the direct witnesses of the event and be served as gossip with the next morning's sweetbreads and coffee across Zacatecas.

"Alba!"

Carlos had appeared, pushing through the crowds, Bartolomé at his side.

Carlos thrust out a hand to her. *Come*, it said.

It was an entitled gesture. It was unlike him. She hesitated, but the man had already released her hands and bowed to end the dance. He vanished into the crowd and was gone.

She didn't even know his name.

"I see you've met the convict," Bartolomé said.

Alba whirled her head toward Bartolomé and Carlos in surprise. "Who?"

"My cousin," Carlos said, a darkness settling on his brow. "Elías."

V

Alba

ALBA WOKE TO the rumble of male voices in the parlor downstairs. She lifted her head from her pillow and cocked it to the side, straining to make out whose voices they were.

The pitch and fall of one voice struck her as familiar. Carlos? It was barely light outside.

She thrust off the blankets. Snatched her dressing gown from where the servants had laid it out the night before. Long, skeletal fingers of frost stretched over the window; her breath clouded on the glass as she peered into the courtyard below.

As she suspected. The Monterrubio carriage.

The wooden staircase was cold against her bare feet as she took the stairs two at a time, not caring if the hair worked loose from her plait flowed over her shoulders like the wool rebozo she now wrapped around them.

The city was restive. Four days of mounting anxiety and four nights of ill sleep had passed since the bride fainted at her wedding reception. Some shops shuttered. Solareros vanished from the city, retreating to the countryside; plague did not strike each casta with equal blows. But even most peninsulares and criollos canceled social engagements, retreating into their silk- and brocade-lined shells.

Others still went calling on one another, even as some fainted in the streets, fine skirts collapsing into the dust around limp bodies. And, without fail, a red trail of fever led from house to house, following in the shadow of those brazen enough to flaunt the specter of the matlazahuatl.

The fainting bride had died yesterday afternoon. Coffins began to appear soon thereafter, carried on slumped shoulders through the winding streets of the city.

The hall to Papá's office was empty. Mamá did not allow any servants into the house from outside; only those who resided in the Díaz household were present, and at this hour, were likely preoccupied in the kitchen.

Alba leaned to press her ear against the door of Papá's study. She felt more than heard the click of the door handle.

She hurtled back, steading herself just as Heraclio Monterrubio, Carlos's father, stepped into the hall.

His hair was snowy white—naturally so, not powdered, like some of the wealthy mineros'. His shoulders were bulky enough to cast Alba in shadow as he turned—loomed, really—and registered that someone was there. His face was not a place where one often found kind expressions. Today was no exception.

If he was here, at this hour, did that mean that Carlos was ill?

"Alba!" Papá was just behind Heraclio.

"I heard voices," she said. "Is everything all right?"

"We must go," Heraclio declared. "Good day, Emilio." Over his shoulder, he called: "Carlos. Come."

The tightness in Alba's breast loosened as Carlos stepped

around Papá. He cast Alba a brief, soft smile. It was not enough to dispel the tension that hung thick in the air like smoke, but it did clear it somewhat.

"Will you . . . ?" he said to Papá.

"I'll explain," Papá said.

Carlos reached out one hand toward Alba, then retracted it. Again, apology crossed his face.

"We do have to go," he said. "There is much to be done before tomorrow."

Earthquakes were not infrequent visitors to Zacatecas; this felt like one. A brief but violent tremor. The shatter of china. Sudden, and then just as abruptly slack; the snapping of a chicken's neck. A reminder that her world was not as stable as she once thought.

With the Monterrubios gone, Papá gestured for her to follow him back upstairs. He still wore his embroidered dressing gown—a sign that Heraclio and Carlos's visit had surprised him as well.

"What was that about?" Alba asked.

He held up a hand—*wait*. They traversed the vacant, gaping house, wooden floorboards creaking beneath Papá's slippers and Alba's bare feet the only sounds. From outside, a rooster crowed—only once, the sound anemic and frail.

Mamá's breakfast room was flooded with pale light and the crackle of the hearth behind her. She sat by a steaming pot of chocolate, spectacles perched on the edge of her nose as she scanned a letter. At Papá and Alba's entrance, she lifted her head.

"I saw the carriage leave," she said, lifting the spectacles from her face. "What on earth did Heraclio want?"

"They're leaving the city first thing tomorrow morning," Papá said. He gestured for Alba to take a chair at Mamá's table; he did the same and sat with a long exhale. "To go to Mina San Gabriel."

Hearing the name of the mine from Papá's lips arrested Alba. It yanked what she had read in the letter rudely into the present. It made it *real*.

"Oh?" she said, prodding Papá to continue.

"And," Papá said, meeting Alba's eyes with a nod, "they've invited us to join them. It is a plain house, but spacious, and comfortable. The air will be so much cleaner there, Lucero," he added, perhaps noting—as Alba had—a shift in her mother. Mamá's brows had raised and she leaned back in her chair. "I stayed there once, a long time ago. It was quite agreeable, if rustic."

Alba fought to keep her own face schooled into stillness. Was that *long time ago* precisely twenty-five years ago? When he had returned with a child?

"*Rustic* is not the word I would choose for an hacienda de minas in the mountains," Mamá said. She took a silver spoon and stirred her chocolate. Thin ribbons of steam rose from the cup. "Remote, perhaps. Isolated. Does Heraclio mean to keep Alba prisoner?"

"He must have guessed you have misgivings," Papá said. Gently, almost apologetically, he added: "We are not subtle people."

Mamá gave a mighty roll of the eyes.

"Misgivings? Is this about Carlos?" Alba asked. Mamá's expression settled into exasperation, firmly directed at Papá. The look she gave him said *Why would you say that in front of Alba?* as clearly as if she had spoken it.

"It is nothing, mi amor," she said.

A prick of annoyance flared in Alba's chest. She was not a child, no matter how much her mother treated her like one.

"Mamá," she said sharply. "It's never nothing when you look like that."

"You can't take her by surprise if you decide otherwise," Papá said to Mamá.

It was so blatant, the way they expected her to simply accept their decisions. The way it seemed so obvious that they could end her engagement—the most important decision a young woman could make about her life—whenever they wished.

Mamá loosed a sigh, then turned to Alba. She reached past her chocolate and took Alba's hands in hers. Her rings were cold and hard.

"I look at you and at Carlos and I wonder," she said. "A mother can't help but wonder. All I want is for you to be happy. If we can find someone who makes you happier—"

But it was not about happiness. It had never been about happiness. Every man they had ever introduced her to was a stranger, was rich, owned a mine, owned an hacienda in the south . . .

Family, you know. The voice of the man from the courtyard rose unbidden to Alba's mind: *Greedy and rotten to the core.*

If this were about her happiness, they would not be discussing her marriage at all. They would leave her alone to embroider, not lie to her or to themselves about what marriage meant.

"And whose family can pay their debts," Papá interrupted in a low voice.

And *that* was what this conversation was about: Papá was disgruntled that Alba's engagement had intervened in his ability to call in the Monterrubios' debts.

Mamá shot him a stern look. "This is about Alba's happiness," she said. "Not your investments."

This conversation was becoming a mockery of Alba's intelligence. She had to end it, or she would lose her temper.

To Alba, Mamá said: "Engagements are not binding, mi niña. Youthful passions come and fade. If you worry that you were too rash in deciding, it is not the end. My sister," she added, tapping the letter before her, "knows of a merchant's son in Puebla who is looking for a wife. Emilio," she said, drawing the syllables long and dolloping her voice with sweetness. Her lower lip drew down into a pleading expression. "Let's go to Puebla. Let's escape this."

Mamá squeezed her hands. Alba looked up from their clasped hands to Mamá's face. To her light eyes. To the way her hair barely contrasted with her cheeks, it was so fair.

Mina San Gabriel was where she had been discovered as an infant. The invitation beckoned her with a seductive finger. It called to her, as crisp as if someone had whispered in her ear. There would be people who had spent many years in the mountains, who knew the gossip, who might have heard the story of a foundling long ago. Who might see Alba and recognize someone else's face in her features.

Her heart raced against her ribs. Becoming betrothed to Carlos had bought her some ownership over her life, but perhaps it could mean even more. A plan was slowly assembling itself in her mind as she picked up her cards and assessed the suits in her hand.

"Doesn't disease spread in cities?" Her pulse pounded in her ears. "The matlazahuatl began here, but could it not be carried to and spread in another city? Isn't that what happened the last time it struck?"

Alba could tell Mamá shot Papá a look over her shoulder, but without being able to see Papá's face behind her, she could not parse what it meant.

"Would it not be wiser to remain outside of cities until it passes?" Alba said.

"People carry disease from place to place, yes," Papá said. "That matlazahuatl affected Puebla as well. It is the truth," he added defensively to Mamá's deepening sternness.

"Alba, won't you consider—" Mamá began.

"If you don't want me to marry Carlos, then don't play games with me. Just say it," Alba said.

Her parents both looked at her, shocked at her sharpness. It had come out harsher than Alba intended. A shadow of hurt flickered across Mamá's face; guilt bloomed in Alba's throat, poisoning her words. But she said them anyway.

"I want to be with Carlos," she said. "I'm going, with or without you."

PART OF ALBA expected that Bartolomé would also be extended an invitation to the Monterrubio hacienda de minas. Part of her also expected him to turn it down—perhaps he had responsibilities to the parish in Zacatecas, perhaps he would tend to the sick or something equally Christlike. She did not know, nor did she much care.

All she knew is that she certainly did not expect him to be sitting opposite her in the carriage from Zacatecas the next morning, her knees slamming uncomfortably into his as they ascended rocky foothills and winding passes into the mountains. Her teeth jarred each time the carriage's wheels hit a rock or unexpected divot. She could avoid this if she unclenched her jaw and relaxed, or unfolded her arms and dropped her shoulders.

She did not.

Papá was certainly at ease in the priest's presence. He snored as if he were at home in his chair by the fireplace in his and Mamá's favorite parlor, the west-facing one with a view of the cathedral. His jowls shook gently with the sharp rocking of the carriage, his head lolling gently to one side.

And Mamá? Mamá leaned forward to laugh at Bartolomé's jokes about pagan practices common in these more desolate parts of the colony.

"Perhaps you will find some at Mina San Gabriel," Mamá joked in return.

"I should hope not," the priest replied. "But if I do, I know what my mission is."

"And what is that, Padre?"

"Saving souls, señora," was the reply. It was directed at Mamá, but he met Alba's eyes squarely as he spoke.

A chill ran down her arms. The more she spoke to him, the more she risked discovery. She tightened her arms over her chest. Turned her face to the side and looked out the dirty window.

Mamá toyed with her rosary in her lap, rapt as Bartolomé went on about the importance of conversions in this wild, uncivilized part of Nueva España.

Mamá had been icy toward her ever since yesterday morning's conversation. Yes, Alba had snapped at her. Yes, it was unkind. Yes, Alba had played the moment over and over in her mind like a musician who simply could not master a portion of a song, wondering why she had not bit her tongue. It had not been fair to Mamá to speak so sharply. Mamá's feelings were like perfectly ripe fruit: easy to bruise, easy to spoil. They had to be treated with care. Alba did, for she knew that leaving them to rot had consequences for everyone in the house. Normally, she was happy to placate Mamá.

But was Mamá ever happy to placate Alba?

Each rock of the carriage, each precarious swell of nausea—they led her closer to a life of freedom. She could stomach this journey. She *would*.

Bartolomé said something to draw Alba into the conversation; she ignored it. She focused on the clop of shod hooves on stone. Watched the gray line of the mountains. The road was wide; here, halfway into the mountains, it followed the path carved by an anemic stream. The mountains had seemed to loom over them when they took a short midmorning break to stretch their legs, but now, amid the rocks and silhouettes, they seemed endless. Mazelike. As if the ascent were both barely begun and almost finished.

Mamá giggled at something Bartolomé said, her laugh fawningly girlish and shrill against Alba's skull.

Alba fluttered her eyes closed. Let that keep her from rolling them in annoyance. She certainly felt as if she were in Purgatory in this airless box, smothered by Mamá's perfume and the knock of Bartolomé's knees on hers.

A shout from outside; Alba opened her eyes and craned her neck to peer up ahead of the horses, where Heraclio and Carlos rode.

They turned a bend and passed first one mule, then another, then a whole line of them, each as heavily laden as the first.

A handful of men walked alongside and among the mules.

As the carriage passed, so, too, did their faces pass before Alba: some were indios, but others criollo, weathered and squinting against the sharp, white winter sun. In the middle of the mule train, one face caught her eye and held it.

The man she had danced with.

Elías.

His hair was tied back at his neck; some fell into his face anyway, clinging to temples gleaming with sweat. He had one hand on the neck of a mule and one on a walking stick.

He looked to the carriage, and their eyes met.

The convict.

He faltered slightly as he walked but did not drop his gaze. He lifted his hand from the mule's neck, then did nothing with it—perhaps he meant to greet her, but the carriage was already moving, and he was falling back. Alba turned her head to watch him grow smaller and smaller behind them, a dark silhouette among the mountains, until the carriage turned a bend.

She had not expected to see him ever again. Carlos had many cousins back in Spain; he had never spoken of one called Elías. Perhaps because he was a convict. But if he was—surely he was, there was no world in which Carlos, so preoccupied with the Monterrubio reputation, would allow that term to be used if it were not the truth—then why had he seemed so gentle? Why had she felt such comfort in his presence?

What kind of man was he, really?

For a moment, when they were dancing, she had idly thought she was comfortable with him. It was a silly, girlish thing to think. The Champagne had certainly gone to her head. She did not know him at all, and likely never would.

As the road grew level and the afternoon long, she drifted somewhere on the borders of sleep despite Mamá and Bartolomé's conversation, despite Papá's snoring.

In the murky ripples of half dreams, she thought she heard his voice. Thought she felt a calloused hand take hers in the dark and lead her into the golden warmth of music and clinking glasses and candlelight.

Then the carriage's wheel hit another rock; she jolted from sleep. Her mouth was sour and dry and her neck ached.

They had stopped.

Bartolomé peered out the window, then opened the door.

Cold, dry air rushed into the carriage, clearing any cobwebs of sleep from Alba's mind with a swift strike.

She did not accept Bartolomé's hand to help her down the carriage steps; she clung to the frame of the door as she lowered herself to rocky earth.

The sun had dipped low and reddened the horizon. A distant ring of pickaxes; a whistle of wind through barren peaks.

Mountains rose in a crown of thorns around a long stucco

house. It might have been white once, but now appeared earthen in color. Soot stained one wall, visible even in the long, blue shadows cast by the mountains. Chickens milled by an outdoor kitchen, chittering to one another and to an errant goat as they pecked the hard earth.

A cold breeze bit her cheeks and tugged at her hair. Alba tightened her shawl around her shoulders.

"Rustic," Mamá murmured archly behind her. She followed this with a low, judgmental noise. "Not a glass window in sight. Are we to be imprisoned in the dark all winter? They might as well put us in a coffin."

"Lucero," Papá chastised gently.

"Thank goodness our things are following," Mamá said. She took Papá's hand as he helped her out of the carriage, an arch, critical expression crossing her features as she took in the house. "It looks practically abandoned. Alba, where are you going?"

Gravel crunched beneath Alba's shoes as she walked away from the carriage, away from the house, to slightly higher ground, where the mountains' shadows had not yet eclipsed the last late slant of sunlight. The breeze turned to wind; it tugged more persistently at her hair and at the shawl that was perfect for winter in the city but was already proving far too flimsy for this place. Her ears ached from the cold.

She closed her eyes and stood still as sunlight slipped featherlight over her skin. A brush of weak warmth.

It was fleeting. The sun moved; the warmth vanished. Alba was alone, suspended in the cold, the sole subject of the mountains' long gaze.

Deep in her breast, nestled somewhere against the back of her ribs, something *turned*.

It had a physical weight to it. It was like an organ shifting, lifting and resettling into the wrong spot, crowding somewhere too tight under her lungs.

Her breath caught; she tightened her arms.

Liquid cold filled the cavity of her chest, pouring and splashing and splattering against everything in its path like an overturned bottle of ink.

Leave this place.

A susurration flitted around her awareness like the cold in the wind; it settled somewhere behind one ear, pressing like ice, like a dagger, against the tender skin there. Its edge cradled a threat.

Get out.

"Alba!" Mamá called.

She jumped; her heart hit the back of her throat with a meaty strike. Voices rose in cacophony from the figures moving between the carriage and the house below—Heraclio ordered cedar chests to be brought this way and that; Papá wondered aloud if all soldiers-turned-clergy traveled with Bartolomé's unpriestlike number of weapons in his luggage.

"Come down here before you get hurt!" Mamá cried.

Alba gathered her skirts, fingers half frozen and fumbling, and obeyed. Rocks tripped and scattered down the path before her; they gained speed as they rolled and bounced down the hill, down the mountain, down, down, down—

It was too easy to imagine following them, tripping and tumbling heels over head, smashing the fine bones of neck and skull on the dark rocks below—

Leave.

"Come."

She jumped. Carlos was at her side. She had no memory of reaching even ground, but she was among the bustle again, among

THE POSSESSION OF ALBA DÍAZ

the braying of irritable mules and greetings and men groaning as they staggered beneath the weight of Mamá's luggage chests.

Carlos took her hand. His flesh burned against her icy knuckles.

"Let me show you the house," he said. "You seem exhausted from the journey."

He led her through the narrow doorway of Casa Calavera. Mamá's voice echoed from down a hall that smelled vaguely of mildew, complaining again about the dark and the lack of glass panes in the windows. It felt as if it were coming from far away. Alba felt as if she were no longer in her body, not even as Carlos shifted her hand to the crook of his bent arm and guided her through the house.

For she could not shake the feeling that there was something that did not want her here.

VI

Elías

ELÍAS LOATHED NUEVA ESPAÑA.

Sun beat down on his back as he walked with mules laden with mercury and items from the Monterrubio household into the mountains. It was near noon; he sweat from the effort. Perspiration chilled on his skin, sending gooseflesh racing over his arms and back as a stiff, dry wind snaked through the peaks and down to the mule train. He ran hot and ripped off the wool cloak called a sarape that one of the workers had offered him. Then he was freezing, down to the bone.

It was like having a fever. He would know. He had sweat one out in the days since the ill-fated wedding ball where the bride had fainted and lit the fire of plague at the bejeweled heels of all of Zacatecas. In the ostentatious Monterrubio mansion dripping with all the New World signifiers of new money—plush Eastern rugs, silver candelabras, porcelain imported from the Philippines—he dripped with sweat all night, ripping blankets off the bed and then reaching over to drag them up off the floor half an hour later, hands shaking violently.

The servants of the house cut him as wide a berth as they could. Matlazahuatl, they hissed, which Elías quickly learned meant a certain kind of fatal pestilence. Carlos and Heraclio seemed to scarcely care if he lived or died.

A thump at his door before dawn was all the courtesy he received from Carlos, who he had hoped might be an ally, if not a friend. Not a chance, not anymore. His cousin's cautious *how are yous* and polite conversation had evaporated with a hiss after the wedding reception.

"You coming or staying here to rot?" Carlos had shouted, pounding on the door once more.

When Elías crawled into the courtyard, ready to depart to Mina San Gabriel with the rest of the household, Carlos gave him a cold once-over, from sweat-tangled hair to shaking legs.

"If it were matlazahuatl, you'd be dead already." Was that a shadow of disappointment in his voice? "It was probably just the water. Everyone gets sick from the water when they first come here." He mounted a fine-boned white mare. "The Díaz carriage will be following us to Casa Calavera. Try not to shit yourself in front of them."

Elías hated Nueva España.

As he walked alongside the mules, the Monterrubios' only other azoguero—Nicandro Romero Gallástegui, a burly, short, wheat-colored man whose pockmarks strung his mouth at a leering angle and whose hands shook from years of working with mercury—shouted out the names of wilting cacti and dry wild herbs to Elías as they walked. He remembered none of them. He tried to keep his eyes on the peaks of the mountains, one hand on the shoulder of the mule that bore his books for balance. If he ignored the vegetation, the rocky outcrops and angle of the mountains could be Andalucía. If he forced out echoes of the voices of the dead, there was enough peace to be found in that fantasy to make the time pass quickly, if not pleasantly.

Then Romero tried to make conversation, and it all shattered.

"Señor Carlos says you were a forzado convict in the Almadén mines," he said. "What were you in for?" When Elías did not reply, he pressed on: "Señor Carlos also said you're dark because your mother was a Moor. So is your casta español or morisco?"

Elías clicked his tongue and forced the mule to walk faster over a rocky patch of the road, extending his own stride to leave Romero slightly behind.

Señor Carlos could go lay his golden ass in a grave and rot there, as far as Elías was concerned.

The sharp clop of horses' hooves on stone echoed up the hill from behind him; the mules instinctively moved slightly off the road into loose rocks. He followed. And as he glanced over his shoulder at the passing carriage, he regretted not keeping his eye on the horizon and his mind firmly elsewhere.

The woman from the wedding reception gazed out the window. In moments, she was gone, and Elías coughed on the gray, dry dust kicked up in the carriage's wake.

Just his luck that the only person he had actually enjoyed speaking to since arriving in Nueva España would be none other than Alba Díaz de Bolaños, Carlos's fiancée.

Just his luck that she would look like that: refined, striking, her lines as graceful as a confident hand on parchment. She had a way of looking past someone with those ink-spill eyes that made him think she walked another plane of existence, as if all the silver and opulence of Zacatecas were so beneath her as to be barely worth her notice.

Just his luck that the sensation of dancing with her had branded itself on his daydreams. She was like a palmful of mercury: achingly lustrous in light or gloom, slipping cool through his fingers. Gone before he could catch his fist closed.

She was none of his business.

Good luck to her with Carlos Monterrubio. With Heraclio, with the debt Victoriano had amassed, with the mine—all of it. She needed it.

And all he needed to do was earn enough silver to book his passage on the next fleet leaving Acapulco.

The sooner they got to the hacienda de minas, the sooner he could begin. The sooner he could put the whole godforsaken land of Nueva España at his back and leave.

THE HACIENDA DE MINAS was a white tooth in a shadowed maw between peaks.

"It's called Casa Calavera," Romero said as they left the mules laden with china and food at the back kitchens of the hacienda de minas. "That's where you'll be staying."

Elías snorted. He pulled his heavily laden mule onward with Romero, leaving *Skull House* in their wake. "How perfectly ominous."

This earned him a glimmer of amusement from Romero. His hair and skin were dry as wheat chaff, but something about him made Elías think of oiliness. He was of two minds about the azoguero. Allies were scarce in this cursed place, yes, but what kind of ally was Romero?

"Old Izquierdo named it, not your uncle," Romero said. "Apparently, *calavera* was the closest approximation for whatever gibberish the workers called it." He cast a wary look at the house over his shoulder. "Get Don Heraclio to rename it, won't you?"

As if Heraclio would listen to anything that came out of Elías's mouth.

"Izquierdo?" he asked. It was not a name he had heard before.

"The bastard we all used to work for before your old man suggested that Heraclio buy the mine," Romero said. He stopped abruptly; the mule he led had tucked her ears flat against her skull. She would walk not a step farther. "Come on, you piece of shit," Romero grumbled, yanking the lead.

The mule dug her heels in. Elías could hardly blame her. Romero had pointed out the mouth of the mine in the mountainside ahead of them. In the gloom, it yawned like a bad dream in the back of one's mind, luring the sleeper to fall off the path.

It felt as if it were watching them.

"It was Old Izquierdo's son who died in the cave-in," Romero said. "That's why Victoriano was able to get such a good price. Here, let me show you his workshop. You can put your books there, I suppose."

Elías stumbled. It was not the mule he led, or the uneven ground. Hearing his father's name from the azoguero's mouth was like stepping on a rug already in motion from a prankster's hands.

This was where his father had lived. These were the people with whom he had worked. This was his life.

This.

The gray cacti, the gray dust. The skull house. The ramshackle workshop that Romero pointed him toward before seizing a whip and resuming his battle with the mule who would not walk farther.

An anemic clutch of goats braying in the distance. The ragged peaks. The mouth of the mine watching over everything like the eye of an enormous corpse.

This was what Victoriano had preferred to ever coming home.

This was what he preferred to Elías.

Heat welled like molten metal up his sternum as he walked the path to the workshop. Rage? Tears? Either could come, for all he cared. He was alone as he approached a small, soot-stained stucco building, probably no more than one room; a roof in need of repairs.

Two figures appeared around the corner of the building and hovered near the door.

Not alone, after all.

He swallowed hard, squinting through the shadows. They were women. One older, dressed in local garb that contrasted sharply with the younger's upper-class dress. Upon drawing closer, it became clear that these clothes were threadbare; for all their fine lines and lace, the skirt and sleeves were too short for the girl who inhabited them.

"Elías Monterrubio?" she asked.

Elías stopped in surprise. His heart followed half a beat behind. "Can I help you?"

The girl met Elías's eyes, forward and blunt, even as the older woman turned her face away with something that could have been a sharp sob, or a hissing intake of breath.

It *was* a sob, dry and raspy, for another followed in its wake.

The girl stepped forward, hands curling into fists.

"We wanted to meet you," she said. "Papá always said you would come one day, and here you are."

A chill swept over Elías, an echo of the fever of the last week. Even his bones felt hollow.

"I don't follow," he said, though with each passing second, as the girl looked him up and down with an expression that struck him as eerily familiar, he feared that he did.

"This is my mother, Carolina Hernández," she said, gesturing at the sobbing woman. "And I am María Victoriana."

He was falling, as he had fallen through the floor of Abuelo Arcadio's parlor. His only son. It had had weight to it. Had Abuelo Arcadio known? He must have known.

Elías could hear the old man laughing from here, here in this cursed, hateful land, as the girl finished declaring her name like the terms of war:

"María Victoriana Monterrubio."

VII

Alba

THE BREAKFAST ROOM was cold the next morning. This was thanks in part to the frost on the ground outside, but primarily to Mamá.

She answered all questions with clipped monosyllables and pulled exaggerated expressions of suffering when Carlos asked how she had slept the night before. Her back could not endure the spartan furniture of Casa Calavera, you see. Her knees were not accustomed to stone steps and the chill. She would have to send for her mattress from the city, and blankets as well, for the wool irritated her skin and caused her to wake in the night.

Alba moved her spoon around her plate. She had also slept poorly. She woke by the door in the gray predawn with a start and a heart thrashing against her ribs, as if it were still trapped in a nightmare. A few deep breaths and she had soothed herself. She always sleepwalked in new spaces. This was normal.

Nonetheless, it left her drained. She had not yet summoned the will to counterbalance Mamá's mood. Even the fire felt pummeled into submission—its crackles in the hearth were meek, almost apologetic for how it broke the silence.

It mirrored how Carlos had been since they arrived yesterday evening. The curl of his shoulders struck Alba as sheepish as he showed them around Casa Calavera, apologizing for the fact that the lone housekeeper and cook, Socorro, was busy in the kitchen.

"We keep a lean staff here," he said. To his credit, Alba was impressed that he did not shrink away from Mamá's look of horror that they were still waiting on more servants to join them from the city. "It is usually my father and me and few others. It seemed wasteful to employ a full staff."

"That, or they couldn't afford it," Papá had muttered under his breath.

Alba cringed on Carlos's behalf.

Money problems or not, it made sense that they would keep such a spare staff at the hacienda de minas. It was a working home, not one for entertaining, and it looked it. Most rooms were devoid of decoration; they contained unvarnished chests as storage for tools and instruments, thin woven rugs to ward off the chill, and simple wood furniture. None of the windows had glass; the wooden shutters were kept closed to keep the cold out, and it gave rooms a sepulchral gloom.

Unable to sleep, Alba had risen and opened the window of her room, bracing herself against the chill. It faced directly east. Dawn light poured into the room, breathing color onto the bed and the simple furniture. The mountains were dyed a dark, gemlike blue; as the sun rose, they paled, and finally, as the white sun broke over their peaks and flooded the valley and Alba's room with light, she felt ignited from within. As if someone had set a spark to her kindling.

They were beautiful, in their own stark, unforgiving fashion. She wanted to admire them.

But instead, she had felt a tug at her rib cage. *Away.* She felt it more than heard it, long, dragging nails against the inside of her skull. *Away.*

Breakfast stretched long. A headache left her with little appetite; she left most of her food on her plate. She longed to be outside, away from the gloom and Mamá.

"Carlos, mi amor," she said. Her voice broke the silence like shattering china. "Could I have a tour of the property?"

Mamá shot her a stern look.

Alba caught it. Held it. Mamá would not be embarrassed by this rebellion; Heraclio had eaten before dawn, and Elías was nowhere to be seen. Alba had not caught a glimpse of him since the road up to the hacienda de minas the day before.

Not that she was looking.

"Mamá," she said, "that is not an inappropriate request. I have never seen a mine. For someone whose world is built on silver, it would be edifying to see where it came from, would it not?" She turned to Carlos. Gave him a smile, a small one, one that she hoped was not too warm, but warm enough. "Besides, I want to be educated about my husband's work."

Carlos's face softened; it had been held artificially stiff in a serene mask. Mamá was getting to him. That was not generally something Alba wished on people, and certainly not Carlos, who had done nothing to call such punishment upon himself, but it would mean he would be eager to leave the breakfast room and show her around the property. Exploring on her own was a part of her larger plan to uncover any decades-old rumors about a foundling, but in order to do so, she had to first learn where things were.

"I would be delighted to," Carlos said.

Her smile grew, its warmth genuine this time.

Mamá ensured she was wrapped in a heavy rebozo against January's chill, but she shrugged it off her shoulders as soon as they were out of sight of Casa Calavera. Chickens scattered before her swishing skirts as Carlos led her around the perimeter of the house.

Casa Calavera was situated in a high valley, the palm of a cupped hand. Carlos told her the nicknames of the peaks that rose around it like fingertips: el Águila and el Cerro del Lobo to the north. In the east were las Tres Hermanas; in the west, Nevado de Hueso and la Señora del Sol. Depending on the position of the sun, they traded shifts casting long shadows over the valley. The one exception was an area of flat, high ground to the south of Casa Calavera, which was given over to the task of amalgamation. As a result, Carlos explained, it was difficult to grow anything except in the very center of the valley, where Casa Calavera and its anemic kitchen garden lay.

Which was why the Díaz family was so important to the Monterrubio enterprise. Without food, the mine could not operate. Merchants like Papá were the ones who brought foodstuffs from estates in Michoacán up into the north of Nueva Galicia. Without good relationships with the merchants, the mineros could not prosper.

"Is your mother ... have I done something to offend her?" Carlos asked. His hands were clasped behind his back as they walked. He was dressed in simple attire, muted browns and grays, his sleeves clean but patched, his shining shoes replaced with workmanlike boots. Were all mineros like this? One side of the coin was silks and powder and jewels, shining for all of Zacatecas society to see, and the other side more practical. It suited Carlos. His shoulders were often lost under jackets and vests and layers of lace.

"I don't believe so," she said slowly. It was the truth—Carlos hadn't done anything to offend Mamá. Perhaps Heraclio had done something to offend Papá, though. Papá's grumbling about debts unpaid was deeply unsubtle. Carlos was an unfortunate bystander; the fact that he existed, and that he was bound by promise to Alba, was what offended her parents.

The memory of the long line of mules struggling up the mountain trailed through her mind. Judging from what Carlos had hinted at, they were laden with mercury. So much mercury. Alba knew next to nothing about amalgamation, but every child in Zacatecas knew that quicksilver begot silver, and silver begot everything.

Perhaps her parents learning about this mercury would change their opinions on the Monterrubios and their financial situation. Perhaps that would work in her favor—it might not fully placate Mamá, but the promise of debts repaid would certainly help Papá—and they would allow her to remain engaged to Carlos. Her one task, now, was to maintain peace between Carlos and Mamá as much as she could.

"I don't know why you would ask that," she said, batting her eyelashes as she might a fan in a ballroom. She hoped the effect it gave was one of innocence, not blatant manipulation. "Mamá is never well in the mornings. It's her joints." She gave him an apologetic cringe. "They plague her so."

Gravel crunched under her boots as she followed Carlos up the path, past a rickety workshop, toward the entrance to the mine.

"I should not bring you up here, as it will be crowded with workers, but it truly has the best views of the valley," Carlos said.

Perspiration shone on his brow. It gave him a healthy, attractive look, especially when they climbed high enough to step into buttery morning sunlight. When he reached down to her, to take her hand and help her over the crest of the final rise, he resembled a painting of an angel on some chapel ceiling. San Miguel Arcángel, reaching down to rescue her, a sinner, from temptations that would lead to her damnation.

She turned, and as she beheld the entrance to the mine, these thoughts melted like frost in the sunlight.

Workers shuttled back and forth from the mouth of the mine, looking as if they had settled into a rhythm already though the hour was still early. The metallic percussion of pickaxes against stone rang sharp against her eardrums as she and Carlos wove through a motley fray composed of indios, mestizos, and españoles alike. The faces that beheld her were indifferent, suspicious, hard. None were kind. None welcoming. Perhaps she should not have expected that—she was an outsider, an exotic bird in expensive feathers alighting among the crows.

She could not envision herself approaching any one of these men to ask after an abandoned baby found twenty-five years ago. None of them looked as if they would so much as speak to her beyond a gruff *buenos días*. None of them, especially the ones old enough to have been here a quarter of a century ago, looked willing to divulge any long-dead gossip. To her, or anyone for that matter.

She chewed the inside of her cheek as the entrance to the mine yawned before them. She could not ignore the fact that she had been found here. Not when the truth danced just out of reach of her fingertips, a figure cloaked in shadow, moving beyond the lace of a church mantilla.

She would find a way.

Carlos stopped them right at the mine's entrance, where he introduced an azoguero—one of the two amalgamation foremen—called Romero and began to speak with him. Alba caught none of their conversation. She felt as if her skin were sheathed in ice; she itched beneath its weight. She shuddered from its cold. Carlos and

THE POSSESSION OF ALBA DÍAZ

Romero's pleasantries skittered past her unheard; instead, she looked up, gaze drawn high by the arching entry of the mine. It was oval and seemed as tall as the doors of the cathedral in Zacatecas.

"Romero wants to show me a line of ore that was recently discovered," Carlos said. She jumped at the sound of his voice. "I shall find someone to take you back to the house. Or you could wait here—Romero, you could stay with her while I go have a look."

Romero's oily look skimmed her as Carlos spoke; this told her all she wanted or needed to know about him. He was the type to see little merit in women, to whom women were fixtures of kitchens and nurseries and were not to be seen or heard outside of those realms. She was struck by a powerful bolt of loathing.

"Could I come with you?" she asked Carlos. "I don't wish to be apart."

Coolness radiated out toward her. It was not a breeze, but a reaching. As if the darkness made to embrace her, to bring her back down with it. She wanted to recoil. She wanted to run.

Flee. She felt it more than heard it, a vibration through the fragile bones of her ears into her skull.

But the cool fingertips that emanated from within the mine were coy, playful. Almost flirtatious. Candles were lit, hanging from rough iron sconces in the rocky walls. They gave the space a warm, welcoming glow, like that of an empty chapel. There were still sounds of digging and conversations flung back and forth over shoulders echoing off the walls of the tunnel, but it seemed quieter inside. More peaceful.

"Of course," Carlos said. "Whatever you wish. But for safety's sake, you must stay close."

He took her hand; his grip was tight as he led her inside. Her body followed, even as the vibrating voice strengthened within her.

Out, out. Flee.

Candlelight flickered over the rough-hewn walls, catching on moisture and Carlos's hair as they walked into the mine. The creak of wood; the regular clop of shod hooves. Something like the smell of stables melted through the air. Alba's eyes adjusted and found a team of mules hitched to a great wooden structure, walking in a circle.

"Those power the pulleys," Carlos said, "to bring ore up from below."

They passed the mules. Carlos and Romero began examining one passageway that led off to the right. Alba hesitated, hovering at Carlos's side. The air tasted different than outside, cold and metallic. It tasted like drinking from a tin cup.

She did not remember taking her hand from Carlos's, nor did she realize how her steps had drawn her away from his side until she heard him laugh at something Romero said and the sound came from behind her. She glanced over her shoulder. Carlos was a silhouette against the white mouth of the mine, smaller than she expected. So long as she could still see the entrance and the shadow of the mules moving in a circle against the bright light, there was no harm in exploring, was there? Being inside the mountain felt intimate, as if she were crawling into someone's embrace.

Get out.

Keep going.

Out.

Down.

Two impulses warred in her chest; her feet kept moving. Voices grew distant. The sound of pickaxes distorted them; the echoing made it impossible to know where sounds came from anymore.

A panicked squeaking; a rush of wings. Something brushed past Alba. She gasped. Dropped the rebozo as she ducked, flinging her arms over her head. With a volley of high-pitched keening, a flock of bats soared past her. Wings and claws brushed her forearms and hair; she shuddered, her breathing coming sharp and swift.

All at once, they were gone.

She grabbed her rebozo and stood abruptly, shaking, and whirled around, expecting to see the silhouette of Carlos and other men moving back and forth like shadow puppets.

There were only the walls of the passage she was in, curving around a corner. Some candles had been snuffed out—by the bats, by the rush of wings or the breeze they created. The remaining ones flickered weakly, wax dripping heavily down their sides and pooling in their sconces.

"Carlos?" she called.

Her voice echoed, echoed, and died. The sound of pickaxes was faint. The sound of men's voices even fainter.

Her heart gathered its skirts and began to race. Suddenly, the embrace of the mountain had no more romance to it—the ceilings swung low and dripped and seemed to be reaching lower with each quickening beat of her heart. Soon they would be grazing her hair. Soon, pressing on her skull, on her shoulders, and she would have to hunch to run out of the mine, then crawl—

Get out.

She gave in to the feeling. She had to get out of here. She sucked in a steadying breath. Curled her hands into hard fists, digging her nails into the heels of her hands. The pain felt sharp. The pain felt good. Enough nonsense. All she had to do was retrace her steps and she would know precisely where she was. She would be able to see Carlos and then they would step into the light. She would breathe deeply. And they would continue their tour of the property.

Her steps echoed as she placed one determined foot in front of the other. The passage curved to the right; the ground seemed to rise, but so, too, did the ceiling. The grip of the mine was loosening around her. It rose up to relinquish her to the light. One more turn, and the tightness that held her body in a viselike grip loosened.

There was light. Carlos, Romero, voices. She shook out her shoulders, released her fists, and began to retrace her steps. She would not tell Mamá about this misadventure at the midday meal. She doubted she would tell Carlos either.

She passed a slim passageway opening to her left. It was narrow enough for only one man to pass at a time. Ore gleamed black as crow feathers in candlelight. She paused, admiring the veinlike streaks through stone. It was as variegated as the flesh of a living creature, graceful as the fracturing of a stream over stones.

A wail lifted from down the passageway.

The hair on Alba's arms rose on end.

Another wail, and another—that was not the sound of an injured man. That was not the sound of an injured woman either.

It was a child.

The wail caught; began again. The sound of fingernails on glass, or silverware scraping china.

It was an infant. Howling as if it were hungry, as if it were in pain.

Alba turned and stepped into the passageway.

The crying grew sharper, pitched and excruciating.

"I'm coming!" She walked faster down the passageway, one hand lifting her skirts so as not to trip, the other running against the cool wall to keep her balance as the path sloped down. A fork in the path opened before her; she paused, listening.

The right. That was where the crying was coming from.

Or was it the left?

One side was lit, the other dark. She stepped down the lit path—no, that was wrong. The crying was too faint here.

"Where are you?" she called. "Don't worry, I'm coming!"

The weeping was coming from behind her. Sharp, panicked gasps of it, hitching and drawing out. She could picture the infant's face: red, twisted, their mouth pink and mewing, their arms flailing for someone to latch on to.

"I'm coming!" she cried and turned around to retrace her steps.

But when she did, it was as if she had never gone down the fork. To the left, darkness. To the right, light. If she had turned right, then by turning around ... that meant that the darkness should be ahead of her, or to her right. Not the left.

She would not get lost. She was certainly not lost.

The crying was coming from the darkest passage.

"I'm coming!"

Cold enveloped her as if she were sinking into a pool of water, so sharp it stole her breath. She slowed. Stopped.

The weeping had ceased.

"Where are you?" She meant to call the words, but they came out fainter than she expected. As if the pressure of the darkness strangled them as soon as they left her mouth. "I'm right here. I'll find you."

She bent and began feeling the path before her with her hands for a blanket that the infant might be wrapped in. It was almost too dark to see. Her fingertips brushed over stone and dirt and gravel, searching for something soft, searching for something warm, or cloth—

Instead, they found wet.

Wet that was *warm* to the touch.

She drew her hand back. In the gloom, she could not make out what her fingertips were wet with.

"Hello?" she called.

The mine swallowed the word whole.

She stood sharply. Roughed her shoulder against the side of the passage. Took one shuddering step back, then another.

She was lost. There was nothing down here.

Gravel shifted behind her, stone crunching against stone. She froze. Her heart thrummed in the hollow of her throat. She could not go forward. She dared not step back.

There were walls on either side of her, so close that she could not even extend her arms out to the sides.

She was trapped.

Panic rose like a wave inside her chest.

It was only when something seized her by the shoulders that she began to scream.

VIII

Elías

ELÍAS WOKE IN Casa Calavera with his back and legs aching from the journey from Zacatecas, immediately resentful of how he could see his breath on the air as he yanked layers of clothing onto his stiff body.

The kitchen was outdoors, as kitchens were in his grandmother's village—the familiarity struck him like a blow, leaving him dizzy. The line of workers' houses beyond Casa Calavera caught his eye like a vision from a half-remembered dream. Yes, those things were familiar, but the slant of light from the east? It was all wrong. It was sharper here, cutting and white and glass-like. The breads were different. Everything was made from a grain called maíz and had an unfamiliar texture. The water smelled foreign. Even the woodsmoke had a different edge. This he did not mind—it was spiced and rich, as if it were reaching toward him from a bazaar many seas away.

He remained mired in thought as he walked toward Victoriano's workshop to assess it in the light of day. There was much to be done: Not only did he need to introduce himself to the other workers, he needed to become acquainted with the work of an azoguero, and fast. His mind had thrown out old papers on alchemy and rewritten itself full to bursting with knowledge on mercury refinement methods and diagrams of amalgamation patios over the course of the long voyage. But theory was only theory until he mixed the powdered ore with the sun beating on his back, until mercury slipped through his fingers. And what theory he did have was decades out of date. Surely the azogueros of the Indies had improved their techniques since the publication of *Problemas y secretos maravillosos de las Indias*. Surely the Peruvian methods and terms referenced in that text could not be perfectly applicable in Nueva España...

He was so distracted that he did not notice a figure scrabbling from shadow to shadow behind him until she—for the figure was she, the exact she he never wanted to speak to again—had fallen into step with him.

"The earthquake ruined the roof after the rainy season," María Victoriana said. "Same as some of the buildings on the amalgamation patio, but those got fixed right away."

He lengthened his stride to pull ahead of her; she broke into a jog to keep up. She was neither tall nor as small framed as some—Alba came to mind, as fragile and as fine as crystal beneath his hands as they danced, but he shoved this thought away.

María Victoriana's dark brown hair was plaited and wound around her head like a crown; her bright red-and-brown rebozo gave her the look of a winter bird hopping over stones to keep up with him. Her face was broad-paned, her nose a brief, pert accent above a mouth that moved in an eerie echo of his father's. Strange, that he should see his father's features for the first time in twenty years on a stranger's face.

It wasn't *strange*. It was fucked up, that's what it was.

"I maintained it as best I could, but Mamá didn't want me visiting. It upset her," she said.

She was an older adolescent, maybe fifteen or sixteen. He had been about the same age when he gave up on his father ever returning. The tempests and lashing out had passed, and he had accepted that it was him and Mamá. They were in Sevilla then. They had to rely on Abuelo Arcadio and the Monterrubio family, for Victoriano had stopped sending money for them from the Indies.

Elías worked, first at the river docks, helping cargo from the port disembark, then keeping books for a merchant. He saved. He worked into the night until his eyes burned. Each coin earned was another coin toward leaving the Monterrubios behind.

He was practically a child. He *had* been a child, when Victoriano left him and Mamá.

And what had the man been doing, as Elías burned in the sun overseeing chests coming off ships, as he filled every sunlit hour and others besides with work so that he and Mamá did not have to rely on sneering relatives?

Taking care of someone else.

Elías kept walking. Bit his tongue until it hurt.

"Papá said that when you were in prison you learned about mercury. Because the prison was a mine."

That stung like a foreman's whip. How lovely, that Abuelo Arcadio had kept Victoriano apprised of Elías's failures over the years while keeping Elías in the dark about Victoriano's. May Abuelo Arcadio rot where he stood.

"He said that you learned magic with metals," María Victoriana continued as Elías approached the workshop. "That you were trying to turn lead into gold. Are you a sorcerer? The priests say that sorcery is the Devil's work. Did you make a deal with the Devil?"

Perhaps she was younger than sixteen. Fourteen? He never spent time with young people and had no ability to discern their age.

"My father said a lot of things," Elías said flatly. "He didn't always mean them."

"Are you calling Papá a liar?" María Victoriana's voice turned stony and defensive.

Elías tried the door of the workshop. The handle fell off in his hand. He tilted his head back at the blinding sky and shut his eyes. Sighed deeply, then gave the door a sharp kick.

It swung inward.

The room was dark and smelled of mildew and the same kind of spicy woodsmoke from the kitchen.

"I guess this is yours now."

He turned, surprised by the maturity of the bitterness in María Victoriana's voice. She stood in the doorway, sentry-like, hunched shoulders silhouetted against the bright white light from outside.

"But that's fine," she added. Harsh, cold. It was clearly not fine, as far as she was concerned. "Papá said that when he was gone, I would inherit the mine."

This startled a bark of dry laughter from Elías's throat.

"Is that so?" he said. "Have you chatted with Heraclio about that?"

María Victoriana's face firmed into a haughty expression. "Mamá is worried you'll want Papá's share of the mine. That you'll take it from me. And that you could, because you're a man and a peninsular. But you're different from Heraclio and Carlos. You're peninsular, but you're not like them."

Elías's hackles lifted. "And what is *that* supposed to mean?"

Her stance had grown defiant. "You're new here, so I'll explain it nice and slowly. Nueva España has castas. The closer you are to peninsular, the more you get out of the world. I'm mestiza, and you're... different. So we're on even footing, you and I. If you try to take *my* mine, *my* inheritance, I'll sue you in court. And you'll lose."

Elías had no time for this. He was meant to meet Romero at the entrance of the mine, and then supervise the collection of ore to be taken to the amalgamation patio.

María Victoriana stepped back abruptly, but the defiance in her stance did not retreat.

"Oh, would I?" he snapped.

"Yes," María Victoriana said. "Because I have Papá's will, and you're not in it."

It was a slap across the face—swift enough to snatch the breath, leaving a stinging, hot flush in its wake.

"Look," Elías said. "I don't want this damn mine. I don't want these fucking rocks. The only reason I am here is because my father—"

"Our father," María Victoriana interrupted.

"He left *us*"—Elías matched her stress with his own, exaggerated and with no small amount of mockery—"in a staggering amount of debt, both to the family and to the merchant who is currently staying in Casa Calavera. As his only son, that is *my* inheritance. Will or no will." His breathing hurt. Perhaps because his chest hurt. Because everything hurt. "So unless you plan to embrace this newfound familial loyalty wholeheartedly and help me with *that*, then leave me alone."

Her mouth, once level, had dipped into a crescent, its ends pointed down. Her lips trembled.

What better way to begin his time at the hacienda de minas than making a child cry?

The right thing to do would be to apologize. She was his sister, wasn't she?

He had danced around the word in his mind since he arrived, avoiding it all night. *Sister.* How bitter it tasted.

"María Victoriana!"

Her head snapped toward the sound of her name. It came from the direction of the mine entrance—and judging from the sudden alertness in María Victoriana's expression, it had to be her mother.

She gave him one last harsh look. "If Papá was a liar, then he lied about one thing," she said, eyes fiery. "You're awful."

Then she turned on her heel and raced away.

CLIMBING UP TO the entrance of the mine meant that Elías roughly followed María Victoriana and her mother away from the workshop, up the footpath to the ugly maw in the side of the mountain. When they peeled off the path and nipped around a corner, enough workers also headed in that direction that Elías followed thoughtlessly. Romero's instructions the night before had been vague, primarily consisting of *up* and *you won't miss it.* If people were moving that way, then it had to lead to the mine.

He turned a corner around a large rock and stopped.

A small grotto opened before him. Its opening—a doorway of sorts—was as perfect as if it had been hewn by human hands; high enough, he wagered, for him to slip in without brushing the crown of his head against stone.

This was obviously not the mine. Yet a curious sensation curled through him, moving him forward, as if his veins themselves had lifted and tugged against bone and sinew to follow ... follow what? A beckoning. An invitation. *Come*, it whispered. *Come.*

Inside, the ceiling swept high, higher than he had expected from so narrow an opening; he would think it carved if not for the roughness of the rock overhead and the faint glistening of liquid, which accentuated needle-thin stalactites.

A soft glow brought his gaze down and forward. The ground at his feet sloped down, gently, almost imperceptibly, a coy finger coaxing him inside. The grotto was deep enough to be shielded from the noise and bustle of outside, but not so deep that the air tasted metallic or foul. In fact, the air had a different taste to it: incense. The taste of which—though unfamiliar—immediately brought the word *church* to his lips, though this wasn't one.

Candles lined the back of the grotto, thick and satisfied, their short stature and long drips of wax attesting to frequent use. A small carved effigy stood in the middle of the glow, its face cast in flickering shadow, its shoulders swathed not in the deep, virginal blue he had become used to seeing in Nueva España but in white.

The strike of his boots on stone echoed through the empty grotto, off the walls and ceiling, curling around him like shadows. The effigy was thin and tall and lean as a skeleton—or *was* it a skeleton? It was too cloaked in bone-white cloth and layered with silver jewelry to tell. He drew closer, then a reflective glint caught his eye.

He knew the luster of quicksilver like he knew his mother's face: No matter how long it had been since her death, he would still whirl in a crowd if he accidentally caught the right angle of crow's feet or set of her chin in a passerby's face. No matter how long it had been since Almadén, that reflective glint stopped him like the sting of a whip.

Before the effigy's feet, just as one might find scattered roses or angels before la Virgen, was a small silver bowl filled with mercury.

"'El azogue, por la ya dicha amistad, se abraza con la plata,'" he whispered, the recitation as reverent as prayer. A line from *Problemas y secretos maravillosos de las Indias*.

One must understand that silver and mercury love each other, Juan de Cárdenas went on. They embrace and unite, the one with the other.

Mercury embraced the silver of the bowl, reflecting candlelight with a soft glow. The surface caught the flames and the shadows of the grotto alike, refining light and dark, blending the two into an intoxicating alloy.

It drew at him. Like called to like. After years in Almadén, there was mercury in his blood, in his bones, in his lungs, stiffening the empty caverns of his heart, and as he reached forward, his mind blank but for the allure of the gleam, his hand shook. He observed this with a detached curiosity—it had been months since his hands had shaken so badly. More months still since he had last breathed the metallic fumes of Almadén, since he endured the foul dark and the heat of the bowels of the earth, closer to Hell than any living man above. It was as if his body remembered the poison and trembled in its presence. It cowered before its venom, its power.

A presence at his side. Before he could register who it was or how it had gotten there, so quickly and so silently—or perhaps they had needed neither swiftness nor quiet, for he had been so ensorcelled by the gleam—a hand slapped his away.

The sting brought his senses crashing back into him.

Carolina, María Victoriana's mother, shouldered her way between him and the effigy, candlelight burning a corona around her silhouette.

"Back," she snapped, and so stunned was he by her appearance that he obeyed, allowing himself to be all but shoved to the entrance and out into the light. Sun seared his vision; he stumbled back a step or three, blinking to adjust. She blocked the entrance to the grotto, sentinel-like, arms folded over her chest and every stitch of her stance bleeding bellicosity.

Elías sputtered the beginning of a surprised I'm sorry, scrambling for further apologetic words. He faltered—what was he apologizing for?

What *was* that effigy?

"You're just like him," Carolina spat. "Never knowing when to keep your nose out of business that doesn't concern you. It'll be the death of you."

THE MINE SMELLED different from Almadén. It *was* different—and not simply because he was not shoulder to shoulder with other forzado laborers, shirtless and pouring sour sweat in the heat of the furnace, choking on its thick fumes. Here, the ceiling was higher. Air flowed into the grand entryway, crisp with the bite of winter morning. It swept away sweat and the earthy aroma of mules. Sconces lined the walls with thick tallow candles, filling the space with light almost all the way up to the hewn ceiling.

It was beautiful.

Romero must have caught him looking up, for he pointed heavenward with an annoyed edge to his voice.

"Your old man wanted more space," he said. "Dug up instead of down for years." He then rubbed the fingertips and thumb of one hand together, a wordless, universal gesture for *tanta plata*. "Better conditions cost a few reales, I tell you. So enjoy it." The sound he made was part scoff, part laugh. "Your family's paying dearly for it."

Elías did not reply. He was not a recluse by nature; he could make himself comfortable among others wherever in the world he lay—or was forced to lay—his head. Between his encounter with María Victoriana and his experience in the grotto, he was ill at ease. He did not feel like being friendly with Romero or any of the foremen and miners he had met that morning. He was grateful when Romero asked him to descend into the mine to examine a newly discovered vein of ore, accompanied by a silent older man with another candle for light.

He followed the man's directions into the dark passages and allowed the chill to embrace him. He breathed deep of the cold, metallic air. Almadén was thick with forzados serving their sentences and slaves captured from Barbary galley raids, swarming like an anthill kicked for sport. The population of this mine was spread thin through cavernous chambers. Its passages spread from the entrance like a dozen plaits, curling and twisting over one another as they followed veins of ore, as shafts dove deep into the mountain. Sound carried through the narrow tunnels on reeling, drunken wings, echoes leaping from wall to wall. Digging, sharp as the strike of stone on stone. Voices from the entrance, calls to one another, songs to pass the time and keep rhythm. No clank of chains nor snap of whips as in Almadén.

Then they turned a final corner, and it all faded.

The friends he made among the other forzados had laughed bitterly when he once said that he found being in a mine peaceful. In the darkness, in the chill, in the silence, he felt as if he were walking through his own mind. Time ceased to pass here. He ceased to have a name. He was simply existing, moving, at peace. Running his fingertips along cool stone, examining the black veins of ore.

As he did so, a voice, so soft it almost felt distant, curled up against the side of his neck.

Where are you?

He straightened abruptly, gooseflesh racing over his forearms.

I'm coming.

He exchanged a look with the other worker. "Did you hear that?"

It was a woman's voice. Calling out, and calling out again, the echoes folding over one another.

To his relief, the whites of the other man's eyes glinted in the candlelight. "What the fuck was that?" he said.

Elías was not mad. He was not hearing things. His heart still raced, but that knowledge alone helped him steady himself.

"Are we the only ones down here?" he asked.

"We're the only ones who should be," the worker replied.

I'll find you.

It echoed coyly toward them from a deeper passage.

"Someone must be lost down there," Elías said.

"None of our women are that reckless," the worker replied. He avoided Elías's eyes. "We must be hearing things, señor."

"Really?" Elías said, staring at the man's face until he lifted his gaze again, looking almost sheepish. "Both of us, at the same time, heard a woman's voice calling out . . . in our heads?" He raised his brows toward his hairline. "Next you're going to tell me this mine is haunted. Should I have brought my rosary?"

"No, señor," the man said.

"Then we'll take a look," Elías said. "Both of us."

For that was the foremost rule at Almadén, a law he could never forget, even if it felt as though a lifetime had passed since he had been in a mine: When you descended into the dark, you never went alone.

IX

Alba

HER SCREAM TORE out of her, shredding her throat. Its echo ricocheted off the walls of the passage, over and over and over...

"Alba?" a man cried. "Joder." He cursed once, hoarsely, as a peninsular would.

It shocked her into silence. Finally, she could gasp for air. One breath begot another; her chest heaved with them.

"You shouldn't be down here," he said, pulling her to her feet. "Are you hurt?"

A candle flickered beyond the man, carried by a second figure. She could see long hair falling into the first man's face, severe features, the wink of a gold earring.

Elías.

It was his hands on her shoulders, firm but gentle. He would listen. He could help.

"There's a baby!" she cried. "Somewhere down here. It's crying, can't you hear it?"

A glint as his eyes flicked past her, into the darkness beyond. She could not read his expression, not in this much shadow.

"It's so close, I swear it is." Her voice cracked over a sob. "It needs help."

She tried to turn to point down the passage, but met resistance from Elías. He moved his hands from her shoulders to tighten on her upper arms. Over his shoulder, he called: "We need to shut this passage down. The air is bad."

"Then let's get the hell out of here," the second man—the one who held the candle—said. He turned and began walking up the narrow passageway, his quick steps sending loose stones scraping against one another.

The crying lifted again, tugging on her loose threads, unraveling her. He had to let her go so that she could find the baby. Wrap it in her arms and spirit it away from this terrible place.

"Can't you hear it?" she cried.

If he could not, did that mean she was going mad? Had she imagined it all? It was not possible. It simply was *not*. She could still hear the crying ringing in her ears, as if it were a room away—

"You need fresh air," Elías said.

His hands were on her shoulders again, this time with firm pressure to force her to follow. She stumbled, wrestled against him. She craned her head over her shoulder. The baby's breathing pulled ragged; it whimpered. Her heart wanted to reach for it. Wanted to find it and find it *now*. The damn candle was ruining her ability to see in the dark, but she swore that if they snuffed it out, she would be able to see the baby *right there*.

"We can't leave it!" she said. Her breath came in short, panicked gasps. "It'll die down here. It's hurt, it needs help."

"Stop." His hands slid down her arms to catch her fingers and, holding them tightly, he drew her close to him and dipped his face down to hers. She avoided meeting his gaze, still trying to look back into the dark, to search the ground for a bundle of rags, for flailing arms. "Look at me."

She obeyed. The man with the candle had moved far enough away that she could not make out Elías's features at all. A memory of a dark courtyard flitted through her mind. This voice in the dark, woven with Champagne and the crisp, good cold. It was a week ago. It was a lifetime away.

"Focus on my voice. Don't listen to anything else," he said. "Don't think about anything else."

He began to sing. Low and rough, in a language she did not know. Something lilting, sad and heart-twistingly sweet, repetitive as a lullaby.

They were moving up the passage. The candle bobbed beyond Elías, leading them out of the dark. Rocks shifted beneath her feet; when she stumbled, he steadied her. Never released her hands. Every few meters he cast a look over his shoulder to check where he was going, but he kept singing. Soft enough that it did not carry, did not echo, that even in this mine with a thousand ears and eyes, it was only for her. His voice cracked once, maybe twice; he hit flat notes. But he kept singing. Kept her close. Kept her steady.

When the passage was wide enough, he turned. He did not release her hands.

Then, with a blast of brilliant white light, she could see the entrance of the mine.

It was a bucket of icy water to the face. Fresh air; the sound of pickaxes. A mule's disgruntled whinny; the clop of hooves. Voices.

A heaviness spread through her breast, seizing the beat of her heart. It wanted her down, it wanted her in stone, it wanted to consume her. It was as if a cloak of iron had been placed over her body, squeezing her ribs, causing her to stumble.

She swayed and collided with Elías, then regained her footing.

"Get your hands off her!"

She lifted her head at the sound of Carlos's voice. He swooped in and snatched her from Elías, squeezing her hands in his as he tugged her away from the entrance of the mine and into the bright light of morning.

"Did you bring her here?" Elías snapped. His gentleness vanished; in an instant, he and Carlos were all raised hackles and bared teeth. "And let her wander off, like a fucking idiot?"

"How dare you speak to me that way," Carlos snarled. His grip tightened on Alba's hands. His rings pressed against her bones.

"Do you know how dangerous it is in there?" Elías said. "Bad gasses, abandoned shafts, falling rocks—people have *died*. She could have been hurt."

"I don't need to be lectured like a child about my own damn mine," Carlos snapped. "Keep your hands off my fiancée."

"Then keep your fiancée out of harm's way," Elías said archly. He turned his back on them and retraced his steps into the mine.

"My father will hear about this," Carlos shot at his retreating back.

Without so much as looking over his shoulder, Elías raised one hand and flipped Carlos an obscene gesture. He kept walking.

To Alba, Carlos said: "I'm sorry, cariño. I let him get to me." But then he raised his voice, his eyes sliding back toward his cousin, and it was obvious that he was not speaking to her at all. "He's an embarrassment to everyone in this family."

But Alba was not listening. When Elías raised his hand, it had been smeared with something dark. Something that glinted in the sunlight. Something wet.

Her gaze strayed down to her own hands, and what she found caused bile to rise hot at the back of her throat.

Her hands were covered in thick, darkening blood.

X

Alba

SHE WOKE WITH a start.

A moment passed before she breathed; when she remembered how, she sucked in desperate, cold drafts. It felt like ice water splashed in her face. No—when she threw off the blankets, placed her feet on the handwoven rug and stepped to the washbowl, that splash of water stung like a slap. She gasped, then straightened, bracing her hands on either side of the bowl.

The sight of Elías's hands covered in blood, then looking down and seeing blood on her own hands—it was a dream. Looking up from her hands and seeing Carlos with his face slick with blood, dripping with it, his blond hair clumped and wet and red. Flies buzzed around his head, corona-like. When he drew close, a clot of blood slipped from his hair and splat on his cheek, fat and shining and—

She splashed her face again.

It was a nightmare.

Yesterday, Elías had led her out of the mine and handed her to Carlos. The men had snapped at each other, yes, hungry dogs measuring each other's bared teeth. But when Elías had saluted Carlos with his longest finger, there was no blood. No blood on her own hands.

And the wetness on the ground deep in the mine?

That, too, had to be a part of the dream. There was no other explanation for how *warm* it felt.

A shudder coursed through her shoulders.

Dawn slipped long, pale fingers through the cracks in the wooden window shutters, a scant glow of light from outside. There was a distant cluck of chickens, but no rooster crowing; whatever the hour, it was early enough that no one had fed the birds, early enough that there were no sounds from Mamá and Papá's room. But it was late enough that she had no desire to fall back asleep.

Especially not if it meant falling back into such a dream.

She reached for the chest at the foot of her bed, for the rebozo that lay folded atop it.

As she shifted her weight, sharpness pressed into the sole of one bare foot. "Ow."

She dropped herself onto the bed and lifted her foot to examine it. Low light left little to see, but when she brushed fingertips over her sole, she heard small rocks rain onto the floor.

Gravel. It must have slipped into her shoes the previous day, worked its way through her stockings, and remained there as she slipped into bed.

Her stockings must be in need of mending. How odd.

THE DAY ITSELF looked as if it would be nothing but tedium. Mamá would hear nothing of Alba further exploring the grounds of the hacienda de minas after the previous day's misadventure.

This she resented: It kept her plans to uncover the truth of her origins on a tight leash. This, when paired with yesterday's findings, dampened her hopes of discovering the truth of her past with ease. Asking Papá about Victoriano Monterrubio—the man mentioned in Papá's letter, who turned out to be Heraclio's younger brother—as casually as she could turned up the news that he had been dead for nearly a year. Mamá had sharply cautioned her not to speak of the man to his relatives, and that was that.

Mamá held tightly to Alba's elbow as they walked from Casa Calavera to the small adobe chapel that was set slightly apart from the house.

Alba lingered in the doorway of the chapel, even as Mamá stepped inside. It was box-shaped and windowless but for a few keyhole slits near the roofline. Inside was dark; she could already taste how choked the single room was with incense and the closeness of other people's bodies. The roughly hewn pews were filled with dark heads; figures stood shoulder to shoulder at the back of the room, hands clasped penitently before them.

It was airless as a coffin, dark as a crypt.

Reluctance flushed her like an instinct. Perhaps she could be ill—her monthly blood and its usual pain and fainting was a faultless excuse.

But it was too late. Mamá clawed her arm like a bird careless with its talons; she was surprised the fabric of her sleeve had not ripped. With her other hand, Mamá dipped her fingertips into a small stone basin of holy water at the door and crossed herself.

Alba reached for the basin. Cold bit her fingertips, lacing through her bones like a shock of ice to the nape of the neck.

So many bodies in the chapel, and yet her reflexive hiss echoed.

It came back to her after bouncing off the wall of the chapel. It sounded as if a wild animal had been struck.

Mamá shot her a stern look.

"It's cold," Alba said as she crossed herself.

When they sat in the spaces reserved for them in the first pew, she folded her hands over each other, rubbing them together in a vain attempt to create warmth. Thin red scratches over the backs of her knuckles stung when touched. She must have grazed them against something—a wall, or the splinter-prone, unfinished wooden bed frame—without noticing.

Bartolomé—*Padre* Bartolomé, though it was hard to remember to add this honorific when he seemed to be no older than she—descended on the chapel like a vision. He gleamed. It was as if he drew every sliver of light to himself and reflected it back out on his gathered flock. He was benevolence, he was holy grace. His smile was easy and soft, saintly, as he began to chant in Latin.

She hated him.

It flashed through her chest, the only thing with heat for miles and miles, so hot that she wanted to hold her aching fingertips to her breast to warm them.

Shame dropped her eyes to her shoes as she rose alongside everyone else in the chapel. There was no reason to hate Bartolomé. That was a childish impulse, born of exhaustion and an empty, gnawing stomach. The cold made her churlish. It made Mass interminable. It made her mind wander, reaching for something, anything to toy with as Latin droned on.

Whispers wove delicate lace behind her. She shot a glance over her shoulder as she sat. Through the lace of her mantilla, faces bled together: peninsulares and criollos, predominantly men. The women who lived here in the mountains were mestizas and indias and were seated farther back in the chapel. Were they gossiping about her? It seemed that there were no faces turned to whisper, no exchanged, knowing looks; if anything, the occupants of the chapel were focused on Bartolomé or turned heavenward as if in silent prayer.

Alba turned her head forward and lowered it as Bartolomé read from the Scripture, his words a perfectly holy, level buzz against her skull.

Whispers drew cold fingertips at her hair, at her ears.

It couldn't be a breeze. The windows were too high; she felt no draft, despite the cold that was slowly turning the delicate bones of her hands to ice. The sound was louder than the shift of clothing; softer than a speaking voice. Judging from the prickle at the back of her neck, it had to be about her.

She rolled her shoulders to release the agitation that curled snakelike there. Let the people whisper. She was the city-born fiancée of Carlos Monterrubio, visiting the mine for the first time. She was bound to be the subject of curiosity, whether she liked it or not. Besides, she was visiting during a time of pestilence and unrest in the city below the hacienda de minas, when it was said that dozens, if not hundreds, were succumbing to fever by the day. The price of coffins, Papá had reported at dinner the night before, had shot through the roof. Demand for good wood was high, and merchants like him were profiting from it.

She settled against the back of the pew. Bartolomé, it seemed, loved the sound of his voice; she wagered that they would not be released to breakfast until he had stretched his wings with a good, fat homily.

She wagered wrong. In the end, the homily—which had centered around Bartolomé's impassioned retelling of the story of Moses destroying the golden calf—was surprisingly short. Bartolomé was a zealous orator, but a concise one. Alba stood when Mamá did and genuflected when she reached the end of the pew. Her arm was stiff as she made the sign of the cross; it felt heavy and bloodless, as if she had fallen asleep on it bent in an unusual position. She shook it out as she rose, willing blood to flow back into the limb. It didn't. Her arm hung numb as Carlos came and took it to lead her down the aisle to the doors of the chapel. They opened. A bright light; a sudden, biting draft that sent mantillas fluttering and arms folding across chests. She blinked as her eyes adjusted to the light. Stepping into the fresh air outside the chapel brought a measure of relief, but not much. Her body ached, and lightheadedness rose into her skull like fumes. Perhaps she had fallen ill. No—announcing that she felt ill would send Mamá into a frantic mood, for she would insist it was the matlazahuatl and they were all going to die. She was not ill. It had to be her monthly blood. She always felt faint during those weeks.

Carlos had taken Mass as an opportunity to introduce and re-introduce her to a number of strange faces. These blurred: Romero, the pale, oily azoguero, flashed yellow teeth in what looked like it was meant to be a smile; the faces and names of different foremen bled together.

Elías's face was not among them. He was meant to be the other azoguero, was he not? And yet he was nowhere to be seen. Had he come to the chapel at all?

Why was she bothering to look for him? Carlos had made very clear how negatively he felt about his cousin, and she should respect that.

"And this is Señora Carolina Hernández. She is a figure of importance to the townspeople." This name caught Alba's ear and drew her attention: Carlos's voice had shifted—it now had an edge that was not kind and that sounded unlike him.

This was a middle-aged woman, though younger than Mamá,

shielded from the January cold by a bright red patterned rebozo that brought color to her cheeks and highlighted how her black hair was reddened by the sun. Her assessment, when it fell on Alba, felt uncommonly sharp—this was what it was like to be analyzed as the future wife of the owner of the mine. She felt she was beneath one of the expensive magnifying glasses Mamá used for her own embroidery, each and every one of her imperfections enlarged for this woman to see.

Alba straightened beneath the weight of her regard. She ignored the darkness that began to thicken at the corners of her vision. Her monthly blood was very early, it seemed.

"It is very nice to meet you, Señora Hernández," she said. She meant it to be warm, but each syllable chipped her teeth like ice.

Carolina's eyes widened. Her nostrils flared. She took a step back from Alba, then spat at her feet.

Alba gasped—in surprise, in shock.

"You have no place here," Carolina said.

"I beg your pardon?" Carlos snapped.

But no one heard him. Carolina had given a pronouncement. One that had the threat of a roll of thunder, that moved through all those gathered around Alba at the door of the chapel. Whispers took flight like a flock of sparrows, leaping thick and all at once, clouding the air with dark wings.

Carolina lifted her right hand as if she were going to make the sign of the cross. She touched two fingers to her forehead, above where her brows met. Then she lowered them to her left hand and touched them to the veins on the inside of her wrist.

The shadows at the edges of Alba's vision grew thicker. One hand rose to her breast, then to her throat—she could not breathe, *she could not breathe.*

Blackness shuttered around her in a swift, deafening blow.

THE POSSESSION OF ALBA DÍAZ

AS THEY SAT before a rustic meal of fried eggs and tortillas made from roughly ground maíz, Mamá reported that Carlos caught her when she swooned.

"Socorro says that woman has a reputation for acting strangely," Mamá added after speaking to the cook to ask for a cold compress for Alba's head. "We will waste no more breath on her."

It did not shock Alba when Mamá declared to the silent breakfast room that she would be returning to her room to rest her nerves after the events of the morning, and that Alba would do the same.

Alba obeyed resentfully. Curiosity curled thirsty at the back of her throat; she longed to slip unseen through the townspeople and listen to what they had to say about what had passed between her and Carolina. But these were a close people, wary of outsiders. She would learn nothing from them, not now, anyway. Not after Carolina had marked her as wholly unwelcome.

Why had Carolina reacted so strongly to her presence? What manner of sign had she made with her hands? She would have to wait until Carlos reappeared—he and Heraclio had been conspicuously absent at breakfast—to ask such questions.

She kicked her thoughts impatiently around her room, pacing like a caged hound, until she could abide its four walls no longer. She gathered some embroidery and left.

She flexed her hands as she walked. They ached from the cold. Zacatecas grew chilly over the winters, but she felt a deep ache in her bones, as if she had been bitten by something with ice for venom and could only be cured by being dunked in a bucket of sunlight. There were no such buckets of sunlight to be had, not on a slate-gray morning like this. But there was an abandoned patio that overlooked the chapel and what once might have been a garden. It faced south, or southeast enough that it received light. She dragged a chair out, wrapped herself in a thick, stiff rebozo, and began to work on a piece of embroidery with cold-stiffened fingers. She waited in vain for any scant drip of sun. Here among the fragile, blackened skeletons of plants frozen to hard ground, it was almost comfortable. It was quiet.

Until the drag of wooden chair legs on stone announced that someone was joining her.

It was hard to look at Carlos's face without picturing how it had appeared in her dream that morning: a slick of slaughter, the whites of his eyes bright as bone against viscera.

She forced herself to keep looking at him as he pulled the chair next to her and sat.

"You found my favorite spot."

"Just waiting for the sun," she said.

"Don't hold your breath. It could be days."

His humor was a translucent thing. It hid nothing. The laugh lines at the corners of his eyes and mouth were slack and deep, giving his face years it had not earned.

She extended a hand and touched his arm. The warmth of another body soothed the ache in her bones. Her fingers were stiff from needlework.

"I apologize on behalf of Señora Hernández," he said. His words were stiff, staccato and crisp as the fall of a pickaxe on stone. "Of course you are welcome here."

His eyes caught on something behind her; a frown deepened the lines of his face. When Alba turned, she caught a glimpse of dark hair and blue skirts before they vanished.

Someone had been eavesdropping on them.

THE POSSESSION OF ALBA DÍAZ

Carlos leaned back, his expression settling into something resentful. "They simply won't leave me alone," he muttered.

"Who?"

"My uncle's mistakes," he said darkly.

Alba raised her brows, seeking explanation.

"Victoriano had a second family out here. He and Señora Hernández had a daughter to whom he gave the Monterrubio name," Carlos supplied, still watching the place where the skirts had disappeared.

Perhaps Alba's brows lifted higher without her intent, for he added quickly, "I don't plan on mentioning it to your parents, trust me."

"Mamá would certainly be scandalized," Alba said.

"She won't hear a thing. The workers have strict orders to say nothing about it."

How long did she have before Mamá learned the truth of Carlos's family and their mess and reached for her smelling salts? Two weeks? A matter of days? She would prevent it as best she could—she *had* to, for she could already imagine Mamá wanting to put an end to the engagement even more than she already did.

She let her eyes linger on where the skirts and dark hair had disappeared. That eavesdropper often haunted the house: She was a girl dressed in fine skirts with tattered, too-short hems; her knuckles were gauntlets of tarnished rings.

Was she spying on Alba? Was she curious about her? Did she know something about why her mother was so opposed to Alba's presence?

Or perhaps... perhaps they knew something about the foundling that Victoriano had given to her father twenty-five years ago.

They were Victoriano's family, after all.

It was unlikely the girl knew anything directly. She was younger than Alba, perhaps by nine or ten years.

But Carolina?

She would know. And she was the *least* likely person to tolerate Alba asking her questions.

But the girl . . . she was someone who had been raised in this place. She would know its secrets and rumors. She could ask questions and pry where it was too conspicuous for Alba to do so . . . perhaps even ask her mother. And if she was attached enough to finery to wear rings on every finger and keep the elegant skirts she had outgrown . . . well, Alba was not attached to finery. She would easily part with a trinket or three to buy the girl's help and discretion.

Carlos had carried on speaking. He sounded a bit exasperated; she caught the name Victoriano and the words *shameful* and *reputation*. He turned his gaze on the chapel; his features settled into a brooding expression that she did not often see.

"He never came into town, did he?" she asked. Anything she could find out about Victoriano could be useful, especially if she planned to approach the daughter. "I don't remember meeting him."

Carlos shook his head. "He preferred it up here, if you can believe it." A delicate sniff; he obviously could not.

But as sunlight began to seep through the low clouds, as the gray began to dissipate and become the piercing white blue of late morning, Alba thought she could believe it. She had an uncanny sense when she put her foot to the earth that first day. She felt as if a sickness had settled in her breast, an apprehension so powerful it seemed close to dread. The mountains rose dizzyingly around her, threatening, dark, as if they had an awareness, as if they *knew* her. As if they could track her movement back and forth across their central basin. Their presence could strike either terror or awe; they gave an austere beauty to Mina San Gabriel, an asceticism to the days that was the opposite of life in Zacatecas.

"And his son is no less of a wreck," Carlos said. "If you really want to keep your mother from things that might scandalize her, I'd start with avoiding him."

There was a serrated edge to his voice that caught Alba by surprise; she had no choice but to add Carlos's blatant dislike of his cousin to the list of things that made her curious about Elías.

Everything she heard from Carlos was at odds with what she had experienced: the rush of comfort she felt with Elías at the wedding ball in Zacatecas, the gentleness of his hands and lullaby as he led her out of the mines.

And yet that had vanished, evaporating like a dream interrupted, when he snarled like a cur at Carlos. Elías evidently had two sides at least, if not more. A knot of threads that she had no business untangling.

She stroked the embroidery silk in her lap thoughtfully. The first problem here was that Alba was villainously skilled at untangling knots in her needlework, and she knew it. Nothing could resist her obstinance, and this pleased her.

The second problem was that she had been raised being denied little.

Her curiosity would win, in the end. There was no point in resisting it.

She tugged at a thread, testing its give.

"The convict?" she asked, voice innocent.

Carlos cast a look around them, over his shoulder, to make sure no one was listening. Or perhaps to ensure that her mother was not leering over their shoulders, waiting to be scandalized, waiting to snatch Alba away from this marriage and Mina San Gabriel both.

He leaned toward her.

"He was condemned to Almadén for murder. Four years of forced labor. Should have died there," he said in a lowered voice, its husk barely above a whisper. "Abuelo Arcadio wrote that it almost ruined the family name, whatever it's still worth back in Spain. It would certainly ruin our reputation here."

Alba's brows would grow stiff with the effort of reaching for her hairline if Carlos kept talking.

"I shall not cross him," she said firmly.

Her mind drew back to the mine, to Elías's hands covered in blood. To her own hands, drenched in blood.

"You really shouldn't," Carlos said, ignorant of how her mood had dipped dark. "He's nothing but trouble."

XI

Alba

THE NEXT DAY, Padre Bartolomé was hearing confessions in the chapel after breakfast. Alba opened the wooden shutters of her room and watched as Mamá picked her way up the dusty path to the chapel. Her bright silks and black lace mantilla gave her the aspect of a jungle bird, deliriously out of place in the midst of gray rock and gray dust.

There was no confessional in the chapel. No grate between sinner and confessor. She shuddered to rid herself of the swell of revulsion at the thought of confessing to Padre Bartolomé's face. Imagine having him watch her with those pale, piercing eyes as she picked out the darkest parts of her soul and hung them on the line to dry. Loathing prickled over her skin like the needles of a sleeping limb.

"I would rather swallow a knife," she murmured, then paused. Her voice struck her own ears as hoarse. It caught on a dissonant, unfamiliar note, and sounded deeper than it normally did.

She cleared her throat and closed the shutters with a firm snap. She snatched her rebozo from where she had abandoned it at the foot of her bed after Mass and slipped out of the house as quickly as she could.

SUN BROKE THROUGH the clouds in long, pale shafts, bright enough to make her shade her eyes and bring sweat to her brow and underarms as she ascended the wide path to the incorporadero. Carlos had pointed the amalgamation patio out when they had first arrived; the need for sunlight in the refinement process meant that this was one of the few places at the hacienda de minas that did not seem perpetually cast in shadow. She welcomed the warmth as she climbed, letting the shawl slip from her shoulders, letting light sink into her bones.

After Mamá left for the chapel, Alba had slipped into the kitchen to pepper Socorro with questions. The cook seemed startled at first, for one of her hands flashed in quick motion: fingertips to forehead, then to the opposite wrist. The same gesture Carolina had made.

Nausea burgeoned in Alba's throat. Perhaps Mamá was right—perhaps she was unwell and should stay in bed.

But once Socorro warmed up to Alba, she began to talk at an energetic clip as she washed dishes. Evidently, the greatest effect the lean household staffing had on her was the scarcity of willing ears in her general vicinity. Alba lent her own pair out of gratitude for the information poured into them.

Victoriano and Carolina's illegitimate daughter was called María Victoriana. She lived in the village of San Gabriel, the adobe hamlet beyond the chapel, where the workers lived. That was where Victoriano had stayed when he was alive instead of in Casa Calavera. Apparently, he had only shared Heraclio's company when merchants visited the mine, or when the brothers rode to the capital alongside mules laden with silver ingots to be minted.

No love lost, it seemed.

Socorro mentioned that María Victoriana was most likely found in the azoguería every morning after Mass.

La azoguería. The mercury room. Was that near the incorporadero?

"Where is that?" Alba asked.

Socorro had shot her a look, its dubious slant enhanced by the low set of her dark brows.

"No fine señorita such as yourself should be bothered with incorporo work," she said, and moved seamlessly back into a story about her niece's upcoming wedding to a wealthy solarero who lived in Tonalá Chepinque, south of Zacatecas.

But to the incorporadero Alba went regardless, sweating and out of breath as she took the final switchback of the path and stepped onto flat ground again.

Before her was tumult.

Fine dust, perfumed with mule manure and a sharp, chemical tang, rose to choke her; she pulled a corner of the rebozo to cover her nose and coughed into it as she squinted into the sunlight.

When Carlos had said *patio*, she expected something the size of the patio they sat on together outside of Casa Calavera. The expanse of the incorporadero mocked her. This was a vast, open space, larger than the land taken up by Casa Calavera. It had to be for the scale of work occurring. Teams of mules pulled an enormous millstone in a circle; below them, on a flat, broad expanse, men and mules walked back and forth through what appeared to be thick, metallic mud, deep enough that it came up to the men's knees. Dozens of people moved ground black powder from the mill into large piles and poured water into the mud where the men and mules trudged.

A girl should stand out like a bright flower among the gray, the dust, the mud—and yet there was no sign of her. Where was the azoguería?

And why was María Victoriana there?

A line of low buildings stretched along the northeastern side of the chaos. Dark smoke rose in a thin, sinuous cloud from one. She would start there.

She kept the rebozo close to her face as she cut a broad path around the dusty mill.

A small group of three women were gathered near the low buildings, chatting and laughing with one another. Two held baskets of food on hips and head; the other had a jug of water.

This was what her birth mother must have looked like at one point in her life, gossiping with friends. The realization flashed through her, hot and painful, leaving an aching sense of absence in its wake.

What had happened to her birth mother that drove her to abandon an infant? Where *was* she now?

These women looked about Alba's own age, far too young to know anything. She *had* to find María Victoriana, and through her, gain access to the memories of the deceased Victoriano.

"Excuse me," Alba said, lowering the rebozo from her face. "Which is the azoguería?"

It was as if a priest had descended among sinners. One woman elbowed another; their conversation cut off abruptly. They pulled back from her as one, retreating a few steps each, the motion swift as a reflex. Three sets of coolly judgmental eyes swept over her, assessing her skirts—embroidered silk, covered with dust—to her throat, where her customary pearls sat against drops of perspiration.

Embarrassment flushed through her cheeks. Hadn't she been thinking how Mamá looked like a tropical bird? She was just as ridiculous. Perhaps even more so, for she had alighted and shaken out her fine feathers in the midst of the dust and the work.

"Over there, señorita," one said, pointing to an open door.

"Thank you." The sooner she left them, the better.

She turned, but as she did, she caught motion from the corner of her eye—in unison, two of the women had touched fingertips to their foreheads, and then to left wrists. The third made the sign of the cross.

Darkness swamped the corners of her vision; her breath caught, cold and sharp, somewhere between her ribs.

She coughed, heaving and straining against her dress, and reached for the doorway to the azoguería. A few deep breaths and the darkness cleared. She was not unwell. She was *fine*. She had merely overexerted herself walking all the way over here.

As she entered the azoguería she had expected to find María Victoriana immediately, or at least alone—and she was wrong. The room bustled like the inside of a hive. She would have stepped back to reassess her plan, but a lustrous glimmer caught her eye: A large table was laden with pine boxes and glass jars of a silvery, viscous substance.

Her whole world was built on the ingots it refined, but she had never seen mercury before. Even in the cloudy, workmanlike jars, it had a celestial quality, as if the full moon had wept and men collected the tears for their greedy, worldly affairs. She wanted to take one of the jars with her. To stare at it. To see if it emitted its own light after the sun set.

"I know what your stupid book says," a girl's voice snapped. "I read it when I was ten, and I'm telling you, this ore is good enough that we can use less."

Alba stepped into the room, tracking the source of the voice. A wooden scale large enough to weigh three chickens at a time hung from the ceiling. Two figures stood before it, one tall, one shorter... and in skirts.

Her quarry.

She began to weave her way through the bustle toward the girl, then stopped mid-step.

Elías—for of course it was Elías who stood next to María Victoriana, setting small metal weights onto the scale—lifted his face toward her.

Pieces of his dark hair had been pulled loose from the horsetail at his nape and fell into his face. He pushed them back quickly, leaving a line of powdered black ore smeared across one cheekbone like Ash Wednesday soot. His shirtsleeves were rolled up to his elbows, baring lean, muscled forearms and a dark inked mark on the inside of one wrist.

The mercury room. Of course the two azogueros would be there. She should have expected to see him, she should not be so caught off guard by his presence—

"Señorita Alba," a voice oozed toward her. "We weren't expecting you. Buenos días."

She whirled and found Romero grinning at her. He stood before a full white sack that swung heavy from the ceiling. It appeared he had been striking it with a wooden paddle; mercury dripped from it, which he collected in a glass jar.

Somehow, when he said *buenos días*, it felt as if he were saying *get out*. Which was what she should do. She should find another way to speak to María Victoriana, another time, another place.

The activity in the room had stilled; it felt as if everyone was staring at her. Her mouth went dry.

"Here to steal some mercury? We punish thieves at this mine, you know," Romero said, his smile slipping wide. "Some hands will be cut off for what went missing last night. Or did you simply get lost again?"

A low chuckle rippled through the room.

Suddenly, she was a child, alone and burdened by too many silks and jewels, trapped in a dark hallway. A figure looming over her with lascivious arms reaching, reaching, reaching—

A hot streak of humiliation; a vision, vivid and sharp as a fever dream, of Romero being pushed into the mud outside. Of him being swallowed whole. Of her walking over his body, relishing the pull of the mud, the silty glimmer of the ore mixed with water—

"No," she said sharply. She adjusted her rebozo primly around her shoulders. "As I will soon be mistress of this hacienda de minas, I want to see its workings." She hoped that this flaunting of her soon-to-be status would remind Romero that she was untouchable. That he should speak to her with respect. Even if her voice wobbled a touch. "I will have someone explain your work to me. Señorita," she said, pointing at María Victoriana, who had now turned toward the commotion and gaped at the sight of her. "Will you speak with me? Show me a place where I may observe unobtrusively."

"Of course," María Victoriana said. "This way."

Alba followed the girl's gesture to the scale, holding her head high as people moved out of her way.

"Ignore Romero," María Victoriana muttered as Alba drew near. "That theft will get him in trouble with the patrón, and he knows it, so he's drunk. I mean, he usually is, but not this early."

"That is . . . an unfortunate circumstance," Alba said. "If it is disruptive to your work, I can speak to Carlos or Heraclio about it."

María Victoriana made a rude sound—half laugh, half darkly amused snort.

"I'd like to see them care, for a change. Oye, tonto," she barked at Elías, "I said less mercury, didn't I?"

She turned to face the bustling azoguería before her, as stiff-backed and imperious as if she were its general. To Alba, she said: "Outside is where the harina—the crushed ore—gets mixed with salt and then mercury into a slurry. Here is where we measure the mercury. First, you must know how high-quality the ore is." She pointed at the small piles of black powder on the central table, replicas of the larger ones outside. "Then, you measure the amount of mercury needed to refine it. That is what our new azoguero is struggling with. He apparently knows *everything* about mercury," she added with a healthy dose of youthful sarcasm, "but can't seem to figure out how much to use."

Elías's cheeks colored at María Victoriana's comment. If he felt Alba sneaking glances at him, he did not acknowledge this—he kept his own gaze demurely downcast.

Nothing but trouble. A murderer. A convict condemned to the infamous mines of Almadén, who would never have survived its conditions if he had not been both unyielding and dangerous.

And yet.

Not only did he defer to the refining expertise of a young girl but, as Alba passed, the curl of his shoulders spoke of nothing but shyness.

She tugged at the tangled threads of this paradox, scraps of a lilting lullaby winding through her mind, as María Victoriana spoke. The girl leaned over the table and ran her finger through glittering powdered ore, explaining to Alba how to identify quality by its color.

THE POSSESSION OF ALBA DÍAZ

"My father was chief azoguero," she said as she straightened. "He taught me everything he knew. If it weren't for me," she added, lowering her voice with a surreptitious glance at Romero, "I don't know if we would be talking about this mine becoming profitable at all."

Romero continued to take the wooden paddle to the white sack. Mercury dripped sluggishly through the cloth. It looked as if he were beating a corpse that bled quicksilver.

"It's lucky that we have you," Alba said solemnly.

"Oh," María Victoriana gasped, then snatched Alba's left hand. She lifted it into a shaft of light that cut into the room from a high window and admired the cut of the emerald on Alba's fourth finger. "That used to belong to Señora Monterrubio."

She used such formal language to refer to her own aunt—truly, there must be no friendly ties between these relatives. If there were, this sharp girl would have been formally educated, raised in Zacatecas, forced into tight dresses and starched crinoline and heavy jewels just as Alba had been.

But she had not been. Perhaps that was for the best.

Alba kept a firm stone wall between her and strangers. This stranger, however, had somehow found a crack in the mortar.

What is your place in this world? she wanted to ask her. *And can you help me find mine?*

"Never thought Carlos would ever get married. Especially not to someone sensible," María Victoriana said, releasing Alba's hand. "Señora Monterrubio almost never came up here. It's good to know how the mine runs."

She stepped back from the table and motioned for Alba to follow her to the scales. "Over here, by that burro, is where we weigh the mercury," she said, jerking her chin at Elías. He had a jar of mercury in his hand and was pouring it into a small jícara container to set on the scale. "Papá always said that you can tell the quality of ore by sight, but you weigh the mercury with your heart."

"I was sorry to hear of his passing," Alba said, lowering her voice. "That must have been difficult for you both."

"It is. For me." María Victoriana's voice thinned, as if it were struggling to navigate a thickness in her throat.

Elías said nothing. He lowered the jícara container onto its side of the scale, but his hand shook. Quicksilver spilled, speckling the base of his thumb with drops of moonlight.

Alba leaned forward to see how much had spilled, to see how it moved—

"Stand back," Elías said. Alba obeyed the gruff command as swiftly as if she had been burned. "It's poison. Never touch it."

"But you are," she said.

He placed the mercury on the scale and did not reply.

"It's less now," he said to María Victoriana. "Tell me what you think."

The girl squinted at the scale. "It's fine. You can put that aside for mixing. Now do it again."

Alba watched as Elías followed the girl's orders. María Victoriana was not a cruel overseer, but she was sharp with her brother.

It was difficult to remember that they were siblings. Each must take after their own mother, for beyond the difference in height, María Victoriana was all rounded edges and quick, confident movements. There was a softness to the set of her expressions that blunted her sharp tongue.

"See, his shakes are why Mamá won't let me touch mercury," María Victoriana said, pointing at Elías's hands. "By the end, Papá couldn't even write. It gets your hands first. Then you lose your mind."

"I would prefer not to hear that, thank you," Elías murmured as he weighed out more mercury, measured and deliberate. This time, it did not spill.

"I bet this one is really doomed, because he worked in a mercury mine too," María Victoriana said. "For years."

Elías sketched a sideways look at Alba. To gauge her reaction? To see whether she knew? She kept her face carefully impassive—she discovered, with a small lilt of surprise, that she did not want him to know that she and Carlos had been speaking about him. It felt invasive. Inappropriate. It would mean admitting that she thought about him when she left his presence.

"I prefer not to discuss that," he said. A slight edge to this—perhaps María Victoriana was prodding a wound that should be left alone.

"Yes, but then Papá said you went to China to study alchemy," María Victoriana said. "That's what Abuelo Arcadio wrote."

China? Convict, murderer—and he had been to China? The tangle of knots tightened.

"Constantinople is not in China," Elías said as he measured out more mercury.

"Constantinople!" Alba repeated, too taken aback to conceal her wonder. A city so distant that it seemed it could be populated by fairy tales.

Was it her imagination, or did the corner of his mouth twitch? Was he resisting a smile?

"Pay attention," María Victoriana interrupted. "This montón of ore is less good."

Elías adjusted the pour of mercury. Another worker called for María Victoriana; she turned and shouted back at him, then, with an impatient huff, crossed the room to answer whatever question he had.

The men here listened to the girl. They respected her knowledge. A twinge of envy tightened in Alba's breast. Who would ever listen to her that way? Never her parents, likely not Carlos. In what matter of expertise could she ever claim such authority? What had she *done* in her life?

Vanishingly little.

She needed *more*. Marrying Carlos was the first step. Maybe once they were wed she could travel. Go to Europe. Go beyond Europe.

"What is it like?" she wondered aloud, leaning back against the wall behind her. "Constantinople, I mean."

Something in her chest longed for him to speak as she might for a drink of something cool on a hot day. Shyness danced over her skin. Since when had she ever thought that about a man's voice? She wasn't a girl infatuated with some acquaintance's unobtainable older brother. She was a grown woman. An engaged one at that, even if it was an engagement born from *mutually beneficial*—as Carlos had phrased it—prospects and not romance.

She was merely curious about this paradox of a man—convict, alchemist, maligned yet gentle. He was a knot to untangle. That was why she wanted to hear him keep speaking.

Elías did not answer for a long moment. He focused on changing the weights on the other side of the scale.

"It's hard to know where to begin." The gruffness in his voice eased. "It's larger than your capital here. Built on seven hills, like Rome, and cloven in two by a great passage of water, one of the deepest and swiftest in the world, which they call *the throat*." He gazed past the weights on the scale, into the wall and through it, as if he were seeing clean to the other side of the world. "You will never feel smaller than when you take a boat across it. You feel suspended between two worlds. It feels . . . I felt I have never been more apart from the world and at once as if I am at its very heart."

Alba felt her heartbeat in her ears. What convict could spin spells like that with his words? It was as if the whole azoguería fell away from them and they were embraced in the crisp, cold quiet of that courtyard back in Zacatecas.

The more she tugged at this knot, the more impossible it became.

"Will you go back there?" she said, keeping her voice low. "When you get rich quick and run away as fast as you can?"

There—that was a smile, though a reluctant one, tugging at his otherwise stoic expression.

He shrugged. "I should." He paused as if changing course. "I borrowed money to make my way here. I need to repay it. But after that, I'm not sure."

The whole world was at his fingertips. This was an envy unlike any she had felt before: a bright, immense yearning, swelling in her like a bird with cramped wings longing to take flight.

"You already have such riches," she said, "being able to even dream of such a life. Unbound to anything. Free."

A soft exhale—it was almost a laugh, but it was too dry to be amused.

"You, of all people, know what riches truly are," he said. "Silver and jewels, bought and paid for."

"You know that's not what I mean," she said. "Some of us are shackled to the world we are born in. We cannot change. We cannot leave." The bitterness of her own voice tasted like ash. "We can only dream of bigger cages."

"Looking forward to the wedding, I take it?" Elías said.

That stung. Was he mocking her? It didn't matter—the spell was shattered. The floodgates opened, and the noise of the azoguería rushed in.

Alba straightened sharply.

María Victoriana was returning; she gave the girl a clipped excuse for her departure.

"I'll see you at Mass," she said. "Hasta luego, señorita."

She turned her back on Elías. She did not bid him farewell.

XII

Elías

"WE ARE PUTTING on a show of family unity," Heraclio said that night, casting a disapproving look at Elías's clothes. "We need Emilio Díaz to respect us."

Elías had not brought clothing for dining with merchants; at Heraclio's summons, he had dutifully washed his hair in freezing water and put on the cleanest things he had, and that was it. There was nothing else to be done about his appearance. If it offended Heraclio so, then perhaps he would allow Elías to return to the kitchen of Casa Calavera in silence, where he had dined since arriving at Mina San Gabriel. There, he gingerly avoided the cook and scant servants recently arrived from Zacatecas and was avoided in return. They all seemed to whisper about him; he had caught his father's name and María Victoriana too many times, but this he could bear and ignore.

Heraclio's commands, on the other hand...

"Do not talk about your father," Heraclio said. "Or your mother. Or Almadén."

That was fair. None of these things would impress the family's silk-clad creditors and Carlos's future in-laws. Barring his father—who seemed to lurk in every shadow of this place ready to trip him and land a strike where Elías's underbelly was softest—they were easy enough topics to avoid.

Heraclio made to enter the dining room, then paused. He turned back to Elías. "Don't pick any fights with Carlos."

A childish flash of indignation in his breast. "So long as he picks none with me."

Heraclio scrutinized him, perhaps to gauge whether or not he spoke in jest. Good luck figuring it out. Elías hardly knew himself.

"On second thought," Heraclio said with a measure of consideration, "it would be better if you did not speak at all."

"A show of family loyalty indeed," Elías said, half under his breath.

"Do you want your silver or not?" Heraclio thundered.

Heraclio had always turned like the flip of a page, from silence to anger and back again. Cobwebbed memories floated through Elías, a guiding instinct. *Do not bait.* Only Abuelo Arcadio ever got away with that, and Abuelo Arcadio best loved a bullfight when blood was drawn.

Elías said nothing.

"That's what I thought," Heraclio said. "Show up, shut up, then take the money and leave. It's what you want, it's what I want. Don't fuck it up."

"Understood," Elías said. He did: Emilio Díaz could call in their debt whenever he wanted to, and according to the law, they would have to pay immediately. This would ruin the Monterrubios, regardless of Elías's mercury. And if they were ruined, he would never escape this godforsaken place.

And Emilio, Elías thought as he sat opposite the merchant at the table, seemed like a flighty fellow. He and his wife filled the cold, stucco room with incessant chatter over dishes of steaming food; their touches of hands and exchanged, secretive looks read to him like an affection long lived in. This did not endear them to him. They were high-strung, fussy rich people, the kind of family that would not hesitate to ruin another if they so much as smelled fear in the wind.

Alba sat at her father's side. Thin, red scratches marred the skin of her forearms, just barely revealing themselves from under the sleeves of her dress. It looked as if she had been scratched by a small animal or by splintered wood. She pushed food around her plate and did not acknowledge her wine. Likewise, she studiously ignored Elías's presence, turning her face toward an impassioned conversation occurring down the table between the priest Bartolomé and Romero, who had also been invited to dinner.

"If the reports I have heard are correct, mercury constitutes a vital part of idolatrous practices happening here," Bartolomé said, turning to Heraclio. "I'd wager that's where your stolen mercury has gone. If we could discuss this, perhaps in private—"

"Enough business talk, Padre Bartolomé." Heraclio dismissed this with a wave of his fork. "Let us enjoy this meal together first."

Elías might have been interested in this conversation if he were not staring at the dark wine in his glass, wishing he could drink away his shame at having mocked Alba in the azoguería. Bright points of furious color had appeared in her wan cheeks; her shoulders had pulled back as if drawing away from something offensive. Him. He was that offensive thing. She had been polite, more than polite, even friendly, which was more than he deserved, more than he could have ever dreamed of... and he might as well have spat in her face. He should have held his tongue about Carlos. He was an idiot.

He ducked his head and obeyed Heraclio. He ate and did not speak.

Carlos was asking about Emilio's estates in a place called Michoacán, which seemed obviously more fertile than here. Perhaps more tolerable too. Should Emilio choose to ruin the mine, perhaps it could be a distant and pleasant enough place to escape to.

"Where is Michoacán?" he asked.

Emilio and his wife both turned to look at him. To stare at him, in fact, and suddenly he felt as if he were an ogre, a hideous creature too large and brutish to fit even in this rough-hewn room.

Alba turned to Carlos; when she put a light hand on his forearm, he inclined his golden head to her. For a moment, as she whispered something inaudible in his ear, they looked as at ease with each other as a couple who had been married for years. Elías was weak for noting this. Weaker still for how his heart smarted with something akin to jealousy. No, he was not jealous. Jealousy was for men who stood a chance.

"I take it you've recently arrived from Spain," Emilio said. His tone was pleasant and conversational; his eyes shone from wine.

Elías's fork clattered against his plate as he set it down. He could feel Heraclio watching him. Three words, and he had already spoken too much. But he had to reply. It would be rude not to.

"Yes," he said.

Silence stretched, long and awkward. He should have answered with more detail, or at least with a pleasantry or two. Comment on the crossing. But now too many moments had passed; now it would be even more awkward to add to what he had said. He was trapped. He hated dinners like this. He would never accept Heraclio's invitation again. Well, it hadn't been an invitation, it was more of an arm-twist, wasn't it?

"Same crossing as me, I imagine, though on different ships in the fleet." A smooth interjection from Bartolomé. "Which were you on? I made the journey with *Nuestra Señora de Regla*."

The flagship. Naturally the bronze priest would travel to the Indies in the beating heart of the treasure fleet.

"*América*," said Elías. It was a bit too flat to be considered polite.

Elías went to Mass because Heraclio told him to, because it would be conspicuous if he were not there. Mass did not interest him. He had prayed in cathedrals and Friday mosques and the darkness of a prison alike and had never once felt it did any good, so he no longer did. But the way the priest had looked at him when he did not stand to receive Communion lingered under his skin. It felt like looking directly at a surface that he knew should have been reflective and catching no glimpse of his mirrored self.

He had met men who were frank and men who were opaque. Bartolomé was neither, too much of *neither*, and this—even more than the way he turned the conversation like a cat with a toy—was why he struck Elías as uncanny.

"Michoacán," the priest said to Emilio, layering unnecessarily exotic stress over the syllables. "I have read that it is greener than El Dorado. Tell me more, señor."

Talk turned to travel and where Bartolomé had been when he was in His Majesty's army. Elías watched the plates like he would an hourglass. When they were empty and the bellies below were full, he could escape this room. He could escape the glint of jewelry from Alba's throat and the way it drew the eye.

"I hear from Heraclio that you're a well-traveled man."

Elías looked up, taking two moments too long to shake off his thoughts. "I beg pardon?"

Everyone was looking at him. Emilio in particular peered at him across the table. He mused: "An alchemist who came all the way to the New World... from Constantinople."

It was not a question, but Emilio landed on the final word of the sentence with a musician's flourish. Elías could practically hear brass cymbals rattle his teeth.

A monosyllabic answer would not suffice.

He glanced at Heraclio; a low tilt of his uncle's chin indicated that he should speak, and he should get on with it.

But then Alba lifted her attention to him. She met his eyes—a lustrous flash of ink spilled in the candlelight. Just as quickly, she refocused her attention on her plate.

He was filled with a powerful desire to be something other than an ogre. He wanted to be suave and urbane and interesting. It was an unnerving wish, root deep, almost adolescent in fervor.

"Yes." He placed his fork down. Without the metal in his palm, perhaps his hands would feel less clammy. "I live—I mean, I lived there for almost three years."

"Fascinating, I say!" Emilio cried, his delight a childlike, untainted thing. "This family is interesting after all."

Carlos sliced a murderous look down the table at Elías.

"Did you ever see a Janissary?" Emilio continued, ignorant of Carlos's simmering displeasure.

"I... yes, actually." Neither Carlos nor Heraclio had ever asked about his life in Constantinople, nor expressed any interest in learning more about him; the shift in the attention of the room toward him felt like a sudden, bracing draft. "We frequented Janissary coffee shops. My fellow students and I, that is. It is where one goes to hear everything that is happening in the city."

In his mind, gulls rose and obscured his friends on the docks as they turned, not knowing that would be the last time they saw him. The last time they saw their money.

He hoped they assumed he had perished at sea. Drowning—or even capture by Barbary slavers—would be mourned. Forgiven. Eventually, forgotten.

All you ever do is leave.

Drawing up memories fed them, and they grew fat and muscled, visceral with color and voices. They lumbered into the room and hung behind those who sat at the table like overfed, ghostly wallflowers. Reminders of his past lives intent on filling his belly with dark shame.

But he was here. The past was gone. It was *now*.

No matter how strange it felt to talk about what was once daily life, what was so common and easy, haunts so comfortable he had assumed he would spend the rest of his life there—he was here. Yes, it felt like talking about a dream to a roomful of strangers—and worse, family—but Emilio was looking at him like he had just declared that he had succeeded at transmuting lead into gold.

Gold. Silver. Cold, hard metal would be stamped at the treasury and pressed into his palms, weighing the lining of his coat once more as he boarded a galleon bound for the Philippines.

Unless Emilio decided to call in the Monterrubios' debts.

He was no good at faking smiles, so he did not try, but he could lean forward, mirroring Emilio's eager posture.

"I once overheard a group of them plotting to rebel against the Grand Turk," he said. "To overthrow him, like they did his father. We often went to the same coffee shop, but after that, I never saw them again." He let his brows lift in a way he hoped was suggestive of the truth: Those men had been executed, and the sultan ruled on.

"Did you ever see the Grand Turk?" Emilio asked.

"I'm afraid not," Elías said, shifting his weight back in his chair. "The Grand Turk doesn't meet with foreigners, especially not with so lowly a scholar as myself."

Alba straightened in her chair. She was luminous with curiosity, a silvery light drowning all the ghosts in the room until there was no one but her, no one he heard as she parted her lips to speak.

"Did you—" she began, then was cut off.

"But were you a foreigner, really?"

Romero sat next to Elías. His wineglass was empty, its sides smudged from the oily fingertips of frequent use. "If your mother was a Moor, then does that make you a foreigner to those people or not?"

A chill seeped into the room.

Elías stood, letting his napkin fall to the floor, filling the room like the ogre he was. No, he did not want this man as an ally. He would live friendless in this godforsaken land. He was alone.

And that was fine with him.

He looked Romero dead in the eye. Solemnly—priestlike, even—he lifted his own wineglass.

He dashed it in Romero's face.

Then he turned away from the table. Chaos erupted behind him as he walked out the door.

XIII

Elías

ELÍAS FUMBLED KINDLING with frozen hands. Within a few minutes, he had coaxed an anemic fire to life in the hearth of the workshop. He had stalked directly here through the cold, not bothering to find where he had put his sarape. No need, not when anger flushed his neck and chest with heat.

"Candles," he muttered, stepping back from the fire and rolling his sleeves up his forearms.

He lit them around the room. Their glow, though homey and inviting, did little to warm the space.

He had not been here since that morning with María Victoriana; it was as if the mess and ruin conspired together to force him out. The earthquake she mentioned must have been what had left the small spill of rubble on one side of the simple building; adobe bricks had closed most of the wall up, but not entirely. The night could still glimpse him within, still whisper a cold greeting whenever he passed by that corner of the room.

The room itself was square, with the hearth on one side, a worktable in the center, and a bookshelf of unsanded, unpainted wood against the wall on the far side. Three chairs cowered from his presence in different corners of the room; the worktable had a stool. This was stacked with books and covered in dust.

It would take hours to clean. Perhaps days.

He began.

Movement kept thought at bay; at bay was where thoughts belonged. Rags were found and thrown in a bucket. The presence of a bucket necessitated a plunge into the icy darkness and walk to the well. The stars were tired. Their winks were weak, faraway things. Only the moon kept him company as his boots crunched up the path to the well.

The mouth of the mine loomed far above him, somehow darker than the night sky. That mine and all that lived in its foul belly was the source of everything that had plagued him since his father first left for the Indies so many years ago. Elías had run far away, and then farther, and farther still; and yet the forces at the heart of the world had conspired to play a divine prank and bring him back to the rock where all his troubles began. There, they bound him to it with silver chains. How uproariously funny.

He made an obscene gesture at the mine.

He took water back to the workshop. He scrubbed.

The soap smelled foreign and stung his hands, but repeatedly plunging his arms in cold water up to his elbows was medicinal.

Stop dawdling, ya Elías, there's work to be done, Mamá would say, pointing to the corners of the room, the highest shelves and corners of the windows. Even when they were relegated to the smallest, darkest rooms near the cellar in the Monterrubio mansion in Sevilla, she had insisted on keeping the space spotless. To her, cleanliness was second only to the nobility of holding one's chin high in the face of humiliation.

After his father left, she neither dried Elías's tears nor coddled him. Perhaps she knew even then that Victoriano would never return. Perhaps she had intuited that one day Elías would be alone in the world and gentleness would not prepare him for that. She was hard, but she was good. She loved him. She was noble. And she never, *ever* deserved to be treated the way she had been by the Monterrubios.

Hot stones hissed as soapy water scalded soot away from the hearth.

Years ago, Abuelo Arcadio had no patience when Victoriano returned from his work selling goods to the overseers of the North African presidios with a half-Spanish, half-Arab wife and their infant son in tow. His attitude rippled through Elías's cold, narrow-faced aunts, who made it abundantly clear that they looked after him and his mother as a matter of charity, not familial loyalty.

He and his mother swallowed every insult. For where else would they go? Mamá's family was across the sea in villages outside of Ceuta. In Sevilla, she had no one but the Monterrubios. She had to wait, first for a long time and then even longer, for the money that Victoriano promised from the Indies.

Elías had forced himself to grow. The sooner he worked, the sooner he saved, the sooner he would amass enough to sweep his mother away from the sneers and sideways glances of the Monterrubios.

Work, take the money, leave. Never look back.

He had done it once. He would do it again.

Victoriano's books slowed his fevered cleaning. He had pushed a pile to the side; one fell off the top of the stack and opened on the worktable.

Equations and diagrams caught his eye; the handwriting stopped his heart in its tracks.

It was his father's.

It was like hearing an echo of Victoriano's voice through a tunnel, layered and dissonant from the distance and the passage of time. He hadn't seen that hand since Victoriano had stopped writing.

Or at least since Victoriano had stopped writing to *him*. Apparently, he had kept writing to Abuelo Arcadio.

Summon Elías. Elías knows mercury.

How little shame the man showed in summoning his son when he was of use. Never mind when his son needed *him*.

Victoriano's grave lay just beyond the chapel, outside the town of San Gabriel. Elías had noted its location when told by Heraclio and refused to visit it.

He should throw the book in the fire. Watch Victoriano's handwriting shrivel and melt in the flames and turn to dust like his body beneath the cursed earth of Nueva España.

He was about to do so. He walked to the fire and tilted the book at an angle that would give it satisfying heft when he cast it into the hearth.

Then, a leaf of paper slipped from between its pages and drifted to the floor.

He paused. Picked it up before the drafts could nudge it toward embers. Victoriano's messy scrawl slanted in an uncanny echo of Elías's own; after a moment, he found it easy to skim.

It was a map of Mina San Gabriel.

There were descriptions of cave-ins, notes about where certain lines of ore led and how to follow them deeper into the mountains, comments on where the air was bad . . .

This was actually useful. Would have been even more useful to know a few days ago, in fact, before Alba had gotten lost in the dark.

He flipped through notes on refining silver by mercury. There were diagrams and measurements, instructions followed by second-guessing and corrections in brighter, fresher ink. The margins were thick with comments on how Romero was a mediocre azoguero and a drunk whom he suspected of skimming silver for his own profit.

Perhaps he should not burn this notebook after all.

Elías laid it flat on the worktable. He pulled a candle close, ignoring the burn of hot wax against his fingertips, and read by its flickering light.

... a figure swathed in a white shroud, before which they leave mercury on the altar as an offering. She is skeletal and, to me, sinister; Carolina scoffed at my foreigner's eye when I said this to her, for she claims that this so-called goddess is a neutral, if not benevolent, force. I am not so certain. The shrine casts fear into my heart whenever I draw near; I am not brave enough to enter it, not when so many go there and pray for Young Izquierdo's demise. I fear that this force—be it goddess, spirit, angel, or monster—may grant their prayers... I can only hope that they do not pray for mine.

A draft slipped over Elías's back, so close as to be intimate; his shoulders seized with a violent shiver.

He looked up. The candles had burned low. The fire was embers. Darkness thickened in the corners of the room; wind groaned through the valley and slipped through every crack in the mud brick, lacing the room with ice.

He had been dozing; he should head back. Though he had no idea what time it was, the current inhabitants of Casa Calavera tended to turn in early. If it were just Carlos and Heraclio in the parlor, it would be easy to sneak past them and deal with whatever they had to say about dinner in the morning.

He shut the notebook and left it on the worktable. Turned to the door, dreading the long walk back to Casa Calavera exposed to the wind and without a sarape.

He braced for cold. He was not braced for what he saw when he opened the door and stepped into the night.

A ghost.

No, of course not. There were no such things as phantoms. He was a man of reason; he would not permit such thoughts to cross his mind.

It was a woman.

A woman walked to the mine dressed in nothing but a white nightgown.

That was not the only ghostly thing about her appearance. She moved as if animated by an invisible puppeteer, and a bully at that—she jerked slowly, inch by torturous inch, her weight slinging with each awkward step.

Something like the aftertaste of fear hung metallic in his mouth.

Black hair, unplaited and long, swung with each drunken movement of the puppeteer. Its luster gleamed familiar in moonlight.

It couldn't be.

"Señorita Díaz?" he called.

The woman walked on.

He followed. First hesitantly, then with more confidence when the woman did not reply—when Alba did not reply, he corrected himself. For indeed, it was Alba. It *had* to be. There was so little he trusted in this godforsaken place except this: For better or for worse, he could pick her figure from a crowd out of the corner of his eye.

"Señorita Díaz! You'll catch your death of a cold. Where are you going?"

The mine.

The place where, when he had found her, she shook as hard as someone dying of fever, her eyes glassy with panic. She swore she had heard voices.

Mines were not safe places, but mines were something known. Her panic that day was not.

This was not.

This felt like a scene from a strange dream, but he knew he was not dreaming. The air was piercingly clear and cold; there was enough light from the moon to see the mine ahead, to feel as if it were watching them.

Something was not right.

He picked up his pace. "¡Señorita!"

He caught a glimpse of her face through her hair as he drew alongside her. It was contorted; she was in pain.

Her eyelids were shut.

His heart stuttered as it caught itself; he loosened a breathy half laugh.

Sleepwalking he understood. He was always careful to take Mamá's elbow gently during her episodes; the trick was to guide her back to bed still sleeping, for if she were to wake and find herself standing in a strange place, she would burst into breathless weeping.

He could not guide Alba back to the house without waking her. It was too far; there was not enough time. The longer she stayed out here, the more certain he was that she would fall ill from the cold.

"You need to wake up, señorita," he said. "I am sorry."

Bracing himself for the shock and the weeping, he touched a hand to her shoulder.

She whirled to face him.

His hand was ripped from her shoulder with a force that her slender frailty belied; before he could cry out in surprise, before he could so much as draw breath, she was facing him, she was upon him with anger in her stance, and she was hissing, hissing like a cat, and—

She had no eyes.

Dark holes gaped in her face like a corpse's, like a skeleton's, black and deep and endless and growing and gorging themselves on darkness.

He recoiled.

He was not seeing things. The moonlight on her hair and skin was real, so, too, were the shadows cast by her cheekbones. He could see the lines of taut skin at the edges of those massive sockets, waxen and tight. Her lips pulled back from teeth in a snarl. The glint of spittle on her teeth was *real*.

Invisible hands yanked her shoulders back, one at a time; she jerked and shuddered. A delicate foam seeped through her teeth, gathering at the drawn corners of her mouth.

She jerked again, her chin lifting, her arms flying to her chest and twitching there, her wrists limp. The cords of her neck jumped and tightened.

She released a wail like a bat's cry, high, piercing. Enough to send Elías's hands clapping over his ears with a gasp of pain.

Then, it was as if a rope snapped: Her body dropped.

She collapsed on the rocky path, catching herself on her forearms. Hair poured over her back. It shimmered like mercury with each of her heaving, ragged breaths.

He stood mute. He did not bend down. His heart hammered as if he had been running.

Her hair slipped over her shoulders and obscured her face from him. He could not bring himself to face that lack of eyes, but he could not look away, could not tear his frozen body from the earth to run—

She lifted her head.

Her eyes were soft, glistening with tears that rolled down her face. Her arms trembled violently; her elbows smeared dark blood on the front of her nightdress. Her chest rose and fell with sharp, shallow breaths that shook her whole body.

He was going mad. Losing his mind to mercury poisoning already. He had to be. It was the only explanation.

He fell to a crouch before her, scanning her for further injury.

"Señorita," he said, ignoring how his voice cracked over the word.

She lifted her head to him. He hated how he braced, how his whole body wanted to flinch away.

He used to dread the moment when Mamá woke in the midst of sleepwalking. When he saw himself reflected in her eyes as a stranger, something to fear, a long-clawed monster ready to seize her soul at the fragile crossroads of dreaming and waking. Alba might shriek and push away from him—and who could blame her? He was a stranger, and she was in a strange place far from home, far from even the meager comforts offered by Casa Calavera.

Calavera, calavera. The eyes gaped hungry and black, endless, famished, coming for him—

"Are you all right?" he asked.

She was not. She was still sobbing, but as she held his gaze, she caught her breath. She inhaled, first shallowly, then again, and deeper, as if she were steadying herself.

As if seeing him made the night less frightening.

"Elías," she said, and it sounded like relief.

His heart turned over.

Oh. Somewhere in the back of his head rang a detached, concerned voice; it was thin and distant. *That's probably not good.*

It was easy to bat away.

He took her hands in his. "They're like ice," he cried.

She looked past him, at where they were: on a rocky path halfway between the house and the mouth of the mine, nothing around them but biting wind and sallow starlight. Her breathing quickened; soon it would be racing out of control again. "I ... where ... ?"

"You were sleepwalking."

She tugged at her hands; he released them. They shook as they rose to her face, as tears slicked her pale cheeks afresh.

The wind cut at his shirt and bit his skin. She needed to warm up, to be protected from the wind, and immediately. She was barefoot, for the love of God.

The workshop was not the coziest place, but it was protected from the wind. There were embers. There was more firewood.

"Come inside," he said. "Can you stand?"

She shook like a leaf barely attached to a dead, wintry branch. She could scarcely keep her hands covering her face; they knocked clumsily against each other.

Without waiting another moment, he slipped his arms under Alba's legs and around her back. Her skin was so cold it burned where it met his arms and chest. With a grunt, he lifted her, and, holding her tightly to him, retraced his path to the workshop.

The valley went quiet. A sensation slipped over his arms like a ghostly brush of fingertips, raising hairs and gooseflesh in its wake. His boots slipped on stones in his haste; he set his teeth hard and walked as solidly and as quickly as he could.

They were too exposed. Each breath he drew tasted like danger, though he could not say why, nor what caused this. The valley was deserted; there was nothing but them and the night.

The night had never frightened him like this before.

But he had never before experienced a night like this.

XIV

Alba

TWO NIGHTS HAD passed since Alba heard the weeping in the mine. Nights could no longer be counted by the hours she slept but instead the number of times she woke. And *where*.

She woke standing by the bolted window.

She woke halfway down the hall.

She woke with her sheets drenched in blood. No—she woke *again*, and it was sweat, just sweat, clammy and clinging.

She fought sleep. She burned a candle long into the night, swearing she would not waver until dawn broke.

She failed.

She prayed at her bedside to San Miguel Arcángel, the woven rug cutting roughly into her knees. Mamá had seen this and had approved. She never once asked what might cause this sudden religiosity, this desperate fervor; Mamá only thought of herself, after all, didn't she?

The harder she avoided sleep, the worse the dreams became.

She never remembered her eyes fluttering shut. But when she opened them and she was in the cold, in the dark, her feet stiff and aching—

Elías was there. Speaking, saying something; his voice came as if from a distant room. Far behind him was the smudge of Casa Calavera against the black. Then, there were mountains. Black peaks watching, curling over her, breathing down her neck in biting gusts.

Cold stone fell away beneath her. She had not been carried since she was a child and did not at first realize what was happening—perhaps she was still dreaming.

Then she was in a small room, perched in a hard, creaking chair. Its discomfort was enough to confirm that no, she was not dreaming. She looked around: whitewashed adobe walls, dark corners. Stacks of books and metal tools that glinted dully in the red light of burning embers.

Elías crouched before her, focused on stoking the fire. It jumped and curled upward at his command; shadows licked his face and the strands of hair that fell into it.

There was no sound but the crackle of the fire, the dull howl of the wind beyond the walls.

"I'm sorry I don't have any blankets," he muttered, half to himself. "Or sarapes. Or anything. I'm so sorry."

He turned to her. Did not look up to meet her eyes. He put the back of one hand to her foot, as if to test its temperature.

His hand was hot.

She shuddered.

"That is like ice," he declared.

Without further ceremony, he took her foot and rubbed it roughly between his hands. It stiffened with a flush of blood and heat, needles pricking over her skin. Her toes were red and swollen, her heels blackened with gravel. But his hands were large and warm, their movements firm and rough; what if he were to rub her calf as well? She was cold, so cold—

Shame was a slap to the face, ice water against blazing cheeks.

She was in her nightdress. She was barely dressed. She was alone in a room with a man she scarcely knew, and he was rubbing her feet, and there was nothing on earth, no explanation from anyone's mouth that could make this scene appropriate in Mamá's eyes. Or in Carlos's, for that matter. They were not marrying for love, but they were marrying, and that meant that her behavior reflected on his reputation. After a childhood of being ridiculed for belonging to a struggling immigrant family, he obsessed over his family's reputation in Zacatecas.

And he hated Elías so much.

She drew her foot back.

He released it immediately.

Both her feet were dirty, their bottoms sore from walking on rocks. The hemline of her nightgown was gray with dirt and shredded from dragging on the ground.

She folded her arms over her chest, as if that could conceal her state of undress.

"Why am I out here?" she asked, flattening her voice to build a defensive wall around herself.

"I don't know," he said. "I was here. I saw a figure, and when I went outside, it was you. You . . ." Here he trailed off; a distant expression drew his gaze somewhere over her shoulder. "You did not seem like yourself."

He did not speak in anger, or in fear, yet something in his tone struck a dissonant note behind her sternum.

She felt ill. She had since she first stepped out of the carriage. Her face prickled and flushed; to her shame, tears wet her cheeks before she was even fully aware she was weeping, before she could stop herself.

A warm weight on her knee—his hand was there, then taken back again, as if he had realized the impropriety of such a gesture.

A wet laugh muscled its way through her tears. There was nothing appropriate about this situation. Carlos would be apoplectic if he saw this, if he knew. He was going to find out, he was going to snarl at Elías and transform into someone she did not know.

Or would the snarls turn on her?

Lips curling back, exposing white teeth through the gore and gristle.

Flee this place. Put the mine behind you. Flee, begone, be rid of them all—

But she couldn't. People were choking to death on their own blood in Zacatecas. Matlazahuatl was still thick on the air. She wouldn't: Carlos was her great gamble, and she could not back down now, not when she had everything she wanted in her grasp.

Everything, it seemed, but her sanity.

Her breath hitched at the thought.

"Tranquila." It was firm more than comforting, the kind of voice that would be used to soothe a panicking horse. That weight was on her knee again. It was steadying. It was good.

He knelt before her, his chin tilted up to her. Firelight caught the golden ring in his earlobe. Much of his hair had pulled free of its horsetail at the nape of his neck and hung around his face, casting shadows. He was much more disheveled than at dinner, when she caught herself musing that he resembled what she imagined a pirate might look like.

He looked younger than he had then. Softer.

"Are you all right?"

Shyness bloomed in her chest.

"I haven't been sleeping well."

As if those words could possibly encapsulate this: dirty-hemmed night wandering, dreams of Carlos slick with blood clots caught in his golden hair, dreams of falling, falling, falling...

"Sometimes, I wake on my feet. In the hall. I—" She caught her sob in her throat. She would not weep again, even if her voice dragged its heels wet and husky over every word, begging to collapse.

"It happens," he said, calm and even, as if she were a child blubbering over a bellyache in the middle of the night. "It's nothing to be afraid of."

"It is!" she burst out. She gestured widely at the workshop. "Am I not here?" So far from her bed, wandering through the night. She could have fallen, she could have encountered one of the sharp ravines near the mine, she could have—

No, she had not been wandering. Moonlight guided her bones. Somehow, in sleep, she had known precisely where she was going.

Dread pooled leaden in her belly.

"Good point," Elías said slowly. "Perhaps you should lock your door before you go to sleep."

"I don't know if my door locks."

A soft, dry laugh. "If it's Heraclio's house, it will have a lock." He made no effort to hide the derision in his voice.

Greedy, he had said of his family. *Rotten to the core.*

The silence between her and Elías stretched long. He was watching her carefully, his eyes grazing over her cheeks. It was not an idle look, nor one that was simply concerned after her well-being.

It was more than that.

This knowledge drew up warmth in her; she pushed it back.

She looked down at the man who knelt before her like a supplicant with a hand on her knee, whose weathered face was softened by the innocence of newfound devotion.

Carlos did not know how right he was.

Elías Monterrubio was nothing but trouble.

"I need to go back to the house," she said.

"I will take you."

She was a fool to trust him. But when he offered her his hand, she took it.

It was warm.

She slipped into the house through a side door, with Elías at her back. He cast looks over his shoulder with increasing frequency as the door creaked shut behind them. Without the wind shrieking past her, the house seemed to gape its dark mouth wide and swallow the sound whole.

A swell of laughter rose in its wake.

She froze. Elías, too, stopped in his tracks, a step behind her—waiting to be discovered? By Mamá, or Carlos, or worse?

But the laughter came from down the hall, where the parlor was, next to the dining room. Was that Carlos? Other voices joined in: Heraclio, and a less familiar bark of male speech—perhaps from Romero?

It would be best to get to her room and out of sight.

She turned down the hall and walked quickly toward the bend in the house's spine that led to her bedroom; when she heard no footsteps following her, she cast a questioning look over her shoulder.

Elías gestured in the opposite direction.

"I'll be going that way." Then he added, as if to clarify: "My room is with the servants'."

"Oh."

A lift of the shoulders. If it was meant to communicate indifference, it failed. "Family, you know."

"Yes," she replied, though she did not know, though her mind wandered with him down the hall toward that room. Watched as he laid his head on the pillow. When he slept did he look softer and younger, as he had in the firelight, in the workshop? Now, with his face cast in shadow, he seemed a stranger to that man. He looked more like the trouble he was.

"Thank you," she added, "for this."

"It was nothing."

There would have been silence between them, a dark, solemn eclipse, if it were not for the lift of Romero's voice from the parlor, bawdy and unwelcome.

Finding nothing else to say, she whispered, "Good night."

The silence behind her meant that he lingered there. It meant that he waited, watching her, until she turned the corner and disappeared from sight.

XV

Alba

ALBA HEARD MAMÁ rise early. She lay silent in her bed beneath blankets, waiting for the shuffle of footsteps throughout the house that indicated that Mass would begin shortly.

She waited. Then, she stepped out of bed. Dirt smudged her toenails; her scouring of her soles with the freezing water must have been an imperfect rite, performed as it was in the dark.

She deliberately made herself late to Mass, for this was how she would find herself—as planned—falling in step with María Victoriana.

Establishing a rapport with María Victoriana at the azoguería had allowed Alba to confide in the girl before dinner yesterday about her search for a story about a foundling some twenty-odd years ago. She did not provide many details, only that the manner was sensitive, and—for good measure—adding that she was asking on behalf of a friend in Zacatecas.

"My mother seemed to know something," María Victoriana

whispered. Alba had learned that she was fifteen, both old enough to appreciate the weight—and monetary value—of what Alba offered and young enough to be delighted by the idea of espionage. "When I brought up an abandoned baby in the mine."

Alba kept her face schooled into impassivity. Let it be a pane of glass: translucent, unmarked. "What did she say?"

María Victoriana gave an exaggerated roll of the eyes. "That it was none of my concern. And refused to say more when I pestered. I did not want to pester too much, for the secrecy."

"I understand." Alba said, casting a quick glance around to ensure that Carolina was nowhere nearby. María Victoriana had told her she had been forbidden from speaking with Alba, and if anyone observed them together, she could be punished.

But their conversation went unheard, thank God—searching the path from the house to the chapel revealed no one in their vicinity but Elías, who walked some ways ahead of them.

She did not admire how his workmanlike clothes drew tight around his legs and waist, how obvious it was that, in addition to being tall, he had a powerful build. She did not linger—nor had she as she sleeplessly watched the ceiling of her room grow paler with each step of gray dawn—on how effortlessly he had lifted and carried her. How weightless she had felt. How safe.

"What do you know of him?" Alba said, nodding at Elías ahead of them. She kept her voice low and conspiratorial. "I hear conflicting things."

"Little. My father said I would like him." María Victoriana snorted, the sound at once delicate and gruff. But then, when she spoke again, her tone turned thoughtful: "I'm not sure what I think yet. He says he wants to leave, but men never do when there's this much silver."

Elías ducked into the darkness of the chapel. Here to get rich *quick and run away as fast as I can,* he had said in the holy darkness of a courtyard in Zacatecas.

A swell of emotion caught her in an unexpected gust. She wanted to draw her rebozo tighter around her shoulders, but it had already struck. It sank deep into her chest.

Her time at Casa Calavera would end with her taking the Monterrubio name in a glittering cathedral, surrounded by flowers and laden with silver. That was the price she had decided to pay for her freedom. She was a merchant's daughter; she knew a good deal when she saw one. A lifetime with Carlos over a stranger who wanted nothing but to rule her life and possess her body? It was a bargain.

Elías was an obstacle, a distraction, but one that she could easily step around and pay little heed.

"He will. He loathes the others and wants to leave as fast as he can," she said briskly to María Victoriana. "Best not to get attached."

"When did you two talk?"

That was a shade of accusation if she ever heard one.

"Thank you so much for your help," Alba said, slipping a golden chain out of a pocket hidden in her skirts. María Victoriana snatched it away quickly and without any indication on her face that something had passed between them. They drew perilously close to the chapel and Padre Bartolomé as he greeted the last of the latecoming parishioners. They should separate, lest someone mark their acquaintance and report back to Carolina.

"Do you think your mother would ever speak to me?" Alba wondered aloud. "She seemed . . . she reacted strongly to my presence."

"I don't know. She's stubborn," María Victoriana said out of the side of her mouth as she stepped away. "But if you want to try, she'll be in the kitchen this afternoon. She doesn't usually help out in the house, but with all this company, Socorro could use the help."

THE POSSESSION OF ALBA DÍAZ

"Thank—"

Alba's words were cut off as cries erupted from those gathered at the door of the chapel.

A young man had come at a run and dived through the people, shouting señor, señor, sweat flying from his brow and pumping arms dark with it. Frantic gestures, accusatory pointing.

Heraclio appeared, his face as white as his hair. Padre Bartolomé was now stiff as a wooden effigy, his face carved deep with shock.

A shift of gravel: Ahead of Alba, María Victoriana faltered. Then she turned and swept past Alba, retracing her steps toward the house. First briskly, then, when she reached the house and passed it, she broke into a run.

Something unnatural swam beneath Alba's skin: both a feeling that something was terribly, terribly wrong, and a sense, at once distant and quivering beneath her fingertips, that all was well.

And yet.

A flock of crows alighted from the roof of the chapel, smudges of soot against the gray sky. The chapel heaved gently, a breath of stillness, then it vomited its inhabitants out onto the path, their noise and movements both fevered and enraged.

"¡Mija! Thank God you're safe." Mamá struck her with an iron-armed embrace. She held her bag of smelling salts in one hand; this thumped against Alba's back and tripped her breath. "Emilio!" Mamá called out so close to her ear that Alba flinched. "We must leave at once. I cannot endure this awful place, I *cannot*."

"What is going on?" Alba sputtered through Mamá's mantilla.

Mamá stepped back but kept a tight grip on her arm, as if worried that the slightest breeze would carry her away.

Papá was there; his eyes were not on Alba but on the chapel and the writhing mass of people before it.

"The azoguero is dead," he said, grim and level. "That brute at dinner. They just found the body at the incorporadero." He suppressed a shudder. "Drowned in slurry."

"And *he* did it!" Mamá cried, as shrill and accusatory as the gesture of her finger pointing at the chapel.

Elías staggered into the light, shoved from the maw of the chapel. His shoe caught on a rock; he fell.

Alba's heart flung itself to her throat.

"But—that's impossible," she breathed. "That's not true."

No one heard her. No one was listening. Carlos, hair mussed as if from a scuffle, leaped on his cousin and began to drag him by one arm. Others came to his assistance when he cried for it, when he needed it to subdue Elías; three men piled on Elías and began to drag him through the dirt toward the stables.

Mamá's grip was hard on her arm. "This is all too upsetting. Come, mija. I must sit and take my smelling salts."

It could not be true. Yes, Elías was upset at the other azoguero last night. Who could blame him? The insult to his mother, and to himself, was nothing short of shocking. But it was *impossible*. She had *heard* Romero when they returned. Elías went to his room. Or . . . well, he had said that he was going to his room. Alba had believed him. Still believed him. Unless they had found the body inside Casa Calavera—which they had not—then Elías could not have done it. And she had *heard* Romero leave, for he was loud, and she had been sleepless all night, moving between turning over restless in bed and lingering at the window until dawn broke. Elías had never followed. Elías had never left the house.

This she knew, for she was certain she had not slept. Or if she had, it had only been for a few moments. Dreamless snatches near dawn, perhaps.

But she would have seen anyone leaving the house to go toward the incorporadero and the mine. The path was in full view of her window, and unobstructed.

She had been walking toward the mine when Elías woke her. What if whoever had killed Romero had seen her instead?

"I hope Padre Bartolomé will say Mass later today," Mamá was saying.

How could Mamá be so concerned about that, when an innocent man had been accused of an atrocity? When his own family was treating him so coarsely?

Rotten to the core. Elías's voice floated back to her from that cold courtyard.

The mysterious shipment of mercury and Elías had arrived from Spain at the same time. Alba was no idiot. It had something to do with Elías.

Perhaps Heraclio and Carlos *wanted* him to take the blame for Romero's death, even if they knew he had not done it. Perhaps, with Elías gone, there was more money to be had for Heraclio.

And Carlos.

But Carlos was not capable of such greed, not at the expense of a family member. Even one he raised his hackles and snarled at— that was protective. He knew Elías's history and wanted to safeguard Alba from a perceived threat. That was not cruelty.

As Mamá strong-armed Alba toward the house, she cast a look over her shoulder at the many-limbed monster dragging Elías in the direction of the stables. At the blond hair that led the way.

That wash of horror had swept through her chest and limbs and pooled somewhere in her belly, where it began to sour, where it began to taste something like doubt.

Carlos had not listened to her at the mine when she said that Elías had helped her. Would he believe her now? Or would it take someone else's voice to speak on her behalf before he paid attention?

"Perhaps Padre Bartolomé will hear confessions in the interim," Mamá said to Papá. "You will speak to him, won't you?"

"Confessing to someone young enough to be my own child?" Papá's scoff communicated he had no intention of doing so.

"I haven't said confession since we arrived," Alba blurted out.

She felt as if she were racing up a staircase and building it at the same time; if she was not careful, she could run off the edge. And she did not feel careful. She felt desperation rising in her like a swell of locusts.

Mamá gave a sharp intake of breath—not because she was breathless from their swift walk back to the house; no, indeed, if anything, she was haler in constitution than Alba was, a healthy color rising to flush her cheeks.

"It's not as if I am not in a state of grace, Mamá," Alba said.

"You mean to say you haven't committed a mortal sin in the last three days?" Papá wondered dryly. "How else do you keep yourself entertained out here?"

"This is not a joking matter," Mamá snapped. "Emilio"—she slipped into a plaintive, childish tone—"can't we leave?"

Yes, can't we leave? The thought curled into her like a burr, sinking into her skin and pushing deep, deep, deep. *Flee the mine.*

But if she did and gave up Carlos, she might as well be signing away her body to the highest bidder.

They had to stay. She *would* stay, even though her cold, cold bones felt ready to turn against her own will and begin walking down from the mountains of their own accord.

"You saw my letters," Papá said to Mamá. "The coffin makers cannot keep up with demand."

"I have heard that people hemorrhage from their eyes as they succumb," Alba lied breathily, with perhaps a bit more color than was necessary. "They choke on their own blood. I won't have you exposed to it. Your constitution is too delicate."

"Indeed, indeed," Mamá agreed. She dabbed at her face with her kerchief, her bag of smelling salts swinging with the motion.

Alba deposited her with Papá in the one drawing room that had good light and air, giving only a wan excuse about going to her room to find her embroidery as she left.

Instead, once she was out of sight, she gathered her skirts in cold palms. She set off down the narrow halls at a quick pace, at a prowl, on the hunt for the one person who could help. Her heart thrummed against her chest as she turned this corner and that; the sense of hunt infused her with energy, as if someone had poured hot light through her veins to wake her from a long, cold sleep. Where was he? She would find him, she would find him, and when she did—

"¡Señorita!"

She had turned a corner and nearly walked directly into him.

Padre Bartolomé fell back a step, then two, a reflexive recoil. His nostrils flared; his eyes went wide. A faint pallor swept over his cheeks.

"Are you well?" It was close to a gasp.

"I need to say confession, Padre," she said, ignoring the question, even as he appeared to scan her face for signs of illness.

"Not now, surely?"

That lilt of uncertainty was unlike him. He stumbled half a step behind their interaction.

"Now, yes," Alba said. "I fear that time is of essence. Please," she added, tardily, almost as plaintively as Mamá. "I need your help."

Bartolomé shifted his weight as he considered this—in a fluid gesture, he moved from the stance that suggested *retreat* into a more confident posture. As if he had caught up with himself, caught himself, and slipped himself back into his own body with a relieved, short exhale.

"Well." For a moment, that was all he said. "I would never deny anyone the sacraments. Come, let us find a place to sit. After you, señorita."

That place ended up being the same terrace where she had spoken with Carlos.

"We could find somewhere more private, if you prefer," Bartolomé said, setting his hands on his hips as he assessed their surroundings. "But if you say that time is of essence, then . . ."

"I will speak quietly," Alba said. She settled into one chair; Bartolomé followed suit and began to recite.

His voice fell to a distant hum. Her breath seemed to drain out of her, rushing down like rain through a steep arroyo. She would not faint.

A stray thought curled around her mind protectively. *Something is not right*, it said, observing the disarray, the spinning. This was not an ordinary plague of sleeplessness. Her skull felt desert dry, laced with dull pain. She leaned back in her chair; when the tightness of her dress pinched her and shining sparks of color smarted in her vision, she straightened.

She could not faint. What good would she be to Elías then? He had saved her; she *must* help him.

"Padre," she interrupted, "if I confess, will you promise not to tell, but will you intervene?"

Bartolomé's brows drew close together. For the first time, she caught a glimpse of bruised shadows beneath his eyes, a fragile sliver of humanity beneath a hard shield. Perhaps he was exhausted from speaking to so many people in the hamlet of San Gabriel—or so said Socorro.

He's looking for something, the cook had said dismissively. *Good luck to him.*

"We say vows to protect everything that is said in confession." This was somber, yes, but underscored with a waver of concern. "You may put your heart at peace, señorita."

"Yes, but will you *say* something?" The sharpness in her voice caught on her own ears; if it were a blade, it would have drawn blood.

For a moment, he did not reply.

He watched her. Perhaps he was tired, but if there was a hint of exhaustion in the delicate skin beneath his eyes, there was none to be found in his gaze itself—this scrutinized her. It made her want to peel her skin off and flee.

No, she had to stay. She could tell him what had happened; she was safe within the sacred space of confession. Describing what had happened aloud might sound damning, especially to the wrong ears—Carlos's—but she had done nothing wrong.

How *dare* he look at her that way, when she had done nothing wrong. He was ready to condemn her with fire and brimstone, all priests were like that, ready to attack whenever they smelled that she was weakest—

"I don't understand what you mean," Bartolomé said gently.

Alba sucked in a sharp breath. Shut her eyes. Forced the tumult in her mind to still.

She thought of Elías taking her hands in the mine. The lilt of his sad, sweet lullaby.

"Forgive me, Padre, for I have sinned. It has been two weeks since my last confession. I think," she added. "Perhaps slightly less." The onset of the matlazahuatl in Zacatecas had paused even Mamá's usual daily confessions; then they had traveled to Mina

San Gabriel, where the only confessor was Bartolomé. "But never mind: I sleepwalk."

She opened her eyes. He sat leaning slightly forward, one hand on his knee, which gave him a look of studied attentiveness. Or it would have, had it not been for the perplexity spelled across his features.

"You sleepwalk," he repeated, voice falling flat on the words.

"You can ask my parents, they will confirm it," she said. "I have done so since I was a child, but I have not suffered from it in years. Perhaps it is this new place, or the distress of matlazahuatl back home, but lately I wake in strange places. In the hallway. By the window. It is not my fault," she added, throwing up a shield. "Ask Mamá. She will tell you it is the truth."

She spoke quickly, ready to plow through any interruption or accusation, or any demand to know why on earth she had hunted him down and insisted on confessing only to talk about sleepwalking.

He did not.

He did not prompt her to continue; he did not grow impatient or fidget. He simply studied her and waited as she searched for words.

You cannot trust him. He will hurt you.

It felt like a whisper against the back of her skull, a brush of dust-dry wings.

But this was the only way.

"Last night, I woke and I was outside." It broke like a thunderclap; then the torrent followed: "I was far from the house. Halfway to the mine. It was so cold. I could have been harmed, if it were not—"

There was no turning back. She did not have much faith in God, but she felt faith in Bartolomé's adherence to the dicta of his vocation. Each of his choreographed moments in Mass sang his love of order. He was polished. He was Squared-off edges and wet ink that would not smudge. He was a row of perfect stitches.

"If it were not for Elías," she finished.

To his credit, if Bartolomé was surprised, he did not allow his face to betray it.

"He was in that hut, halfway between here and the mine," Alba said, gesturing toward the house, as if she could point his gaze through the building in that direction. "I think it's some kind of workshop. He said he saw me sleepwalking. He came and woke me. He prevented me from going farther. He made sure I was warm and then escorted me safely back to the house." Her voice rushed quickly; if she lost her way now, she did not have faith that she would find her courage again. "When we returned, we heard Romero with Heraclio and Carlos. They were talking and drinking. I returned to my room, but I could not sleep after that. I was too afraid of it happening again. The sleepwalking. So I stayed by my window. I did not see anyone leave the house apart from Romero. And I stayed awake until *dawn*, Padre."

Or she could have sworn that she had. Perhaps there had been a wink of drowsing here and there, but admitting that would besmirch everything she had said with doubt, and there could be no doubt. Elías had helped her. She had to help him. If something happened to him... she would never forgive herself for inaction.

Bartolomé's face shifted, resettled. He straightened and leaned back in the chair. "I see," he said, rubbing the line of his jaw with one hand. "Why do you think this is a sin, señorita?"

Alba opened her mouth; for a long moment, her mind was a buzzing flush of white. The way she had told it, it was not a sin, no—but that was not the whole story.

She did not *want* to tell him the whole story.

"I was unaccompanied in the presence of a man who is not my fiancé," she said. Her tone was a shield: She spoke as if this were the most obvious thing in the world. As if she were Mamá lecturing her younger self.

And you had sinful thoughts.

Yes, she had.

She was in confession. If she was to keep the pretense of the fact that she was in confession and not simply begging him to intervene on her behalf, she had to pay for it.

"And I . . ." She inhaled sharply, shut her eyes. She thrust the words out as hard as she could. "I had sinful thoughts. But don't tell Carlos that part, please," she added, opening her eyes.

Bartolomé's face was studied, impassive. She could read no indication in the lines of his mouth or the set of his jaw or even the shade of his eyes that what she had said caused any emotion. Did he look that way behind a confessional grate? Was he always this infuriatingly patient, or, in the dark of the confessional, would he react with the judgment he *must* feel?

"I don't want him to be angry," she said. "Elías could not have hurt Romero. He was with me. And then he was back at the house. You *cannot* tell Carlos how you know."

Bartolomé's eyes dropped. She followed to where his gaze sketched over her wrists and the backs of her hands.

Thin red marks stretched over her skin, peeking from under the sleeve of her dress.

She had noticed them when washing in the morning and paid them no heed. Winter in Zacatecas habitually dried her skin and made it itch; the mountain air was even more arid. She should keep her nails shorter, perhaps wear gloves to bed, as Mamá made her do when she was a child.

Bartolomé looked away, chewing his lip as his gaze settled on the chapel, then traced the line of the mountains beyond. In thought, he looked more human than he ever had: fragile, breakable. Skin and bone, like any other man.

"Señorita Díaz." When he spoke at last, his voice was soft. "You do not strike me as someone who gives their trust over easily to strangers. That is fine and fair. Everyone has their reasons for being the way they are."

She had heard him smooth his tone while speaking to the people of the mine, and to Mamá; she had thought it studied and superficial. She dismissed it as manipulation. But now? She could not help the scrap of hope that fluttered in her chest, the last sail of a sinking ship reaching for the sky.

"Our histories write who we are, and it is not my place to question or challenge that or demand change. I will not demand that you trust me. But I promise"—and this he swore with a blaze of barely reined passion, so fierce that she wanted to lean back from its heat—"I will defend the innocent from evil."

XVI

Elías

THE STABLES WERE predominantly empty; the mules were already at work in the mines. Unlike the stables of the Monterrubio residence in Zacatecas, they were neither large nor ostentatiously decorated. Like most buildings in this hellhole, it was white stucco, with stains that smeared across Elías's vision. Adobe brick. Dirt floor. His knees dragged against the ground until he was unceremoniously thrown onto it.

He caught himself before he skidded far; pushed himself up and whirled—

The door of the room slammed shut. The scrape of a rusty bolt; a clang of finality.

"That'll keep him," Carlos said. "Stand guard. I need to speak to my father."

Elías's mouth lifted into a snarl. How *dare* he.

Good thing he was already accused of murder. It might make what he did to Carlos less shocking. He rushed the door, raising his fists. It was wood, it had cracks, it would give beneath the force of his rage, nothing could stand before him—

If Heraclio didn't have to pay Elías, as Abuelo Arcadio had promised he would, that meant more money for him and Carlos.

Elías stopped. Fists high, head drumming. Mouth gone dry as hay.

It was true, wasn't it? If they took his mercury but didn't pay their end of the deal, there would be more silver to line their pockets and fill their ugly, rotten mansion in Zacatecas.

Shame rose in him like a sun, like a blazing, lidless eye, to stare at him until he took the words back, swallowing them whole.

It was not his mercury. It was mercury he had stolen. From people who trusted him.

A madman's laugh soared in his chest. He dropped his hands and let it ring, throwing his head back, filling the storeroom with irony. Indeed, how dare they steal what he had rightfully stolen. How dare their avarice outstrip his.

They didn't really believe he killed Romero. Did they? Or did it even matter?

They were trying to get rid of him, as they always had when he was a child—from the moment Victoriano had first brought him to meet them, it felt like.

"Fuck this family," he declared at the locked door.

He turned and faced his prison: horse feed, tack, buckets. A hay bale would be his throne. He resigned himself to it and brooded over his kingdom. Perhaps they'd send him to another prison. Perhaps another condemnation to hard labor in penal mines awaited him.

The idea seized him like the nightmare that recurred every time he put down his head. Chains and lashes and going down, down into the dark, with no way to reach Fátima, to tell his wife—the one person left in the world who cared for him, in her own complicated way—where he was, or beg forgiveness for what had happened. Even thinking her name was a blow to a deep, yellowed bruise. He had been condemned to Almadén when he was *needed*. And when he at last emerged, years later—

A scuffle outside the door.

Carlos's voice, surprised and exclaiming. Then another, accusing. Self-righteous.

"Where is Heraclio? I demand to speak with him. With both of you, at once."

The priest? How odd.

It shouldn't have struck him as odd that Carlos, much less Heraclio, would actually listen to the man, but that was what he thought when the three entered the storeroom. Well, Carlos crept, braced as if for an attack; Heraclio strode, his face red with anger, and perhaps shame. Bartolomé swept in with the righteous fury of a storm, demanding that the men at the door shut it and let no one else in.

His pale eyes alighted on Elías; they were not warm when they found Elías's crossed arms and sullen lean against the storeroom wall. It was as if Bartolomé had swanned into the room to save, for saving was his duty, and had found that which the Lord enlisted him to save lacking.

"What is the meaning of this, Padre?" Heraclio began.

At the same time, Bartolomé spoke over him. He barely raised his voice, and yet it filled the room, devouring everything in its path: "He didn't do it."

Heraclio's face transformed in surprise.

Carlos whirled on the priest. "How could you know that?"

"What proof do you have?" Heraclio wondered.

"He didn't do it," Bartolomé said. Flat, plain. But from his lips, it was a commandment.

Carlos sputtered. "You were at dinner last night, you saw how angry he was. He's killed a man before, another crime of passion is—"

"He didn't do it."

Elías straightened. This was getting interesting. He did not kill Romero, no—but he had been prepared to take the fall. He was already falling. And he had not even bothered to grab for purchase or for any hand extended to him.

For who would speak for him, who would believe him? Who would reach out? His life was one of falling and striking the ground and rising on shaking limbs when he had gathered his strength and breath, and not a moment before. No one had ever helped him.

"Padre, how do you know this?" Heraclio asked, shooting Carlos a meaningful look. *Calm down,* it said. *Keep it together.*

Carlos looked as if he had no intention of keeping anything together, especially when Bartolomé spoke again.

"Señor, I cannot tell you," he said.

Betrayal transformed Carlos's features; he sputtered, his fury an indignant thing, as if the priest had taken a dagger and stabbed him. "Did someone tell you in confession?"

Bartolomé's posture went rigid, his voice like ice as he turned on Carlos. "He did not do this."

"Why would you side with him?" Carlos demanded, his voice cracking. "You're *my* friend, not his. This isn't fair."

"Stop being childish," Heraclio snapped. "This isn't about fairness."

"That's exactly what this is about. Justice." The righteousness in Bartolomé's voice seemed to cause him to grow several inches. His virtue loomed over man and son.

It occurred to Elías that he would lay a fine amount of silver on the table to see this moment immortalized in a painting. If he ever made it out of here with what he was due, perhaps he would commission one.

"I will not allow the innocent to be condemned when there is no proof of wrongdoing, only evil suspicion. Not when I have the power to stop it."

"You dare call me *evil*?" Carlos's shirt was damp with sweat, his face flushed and taut with anger. "Is that what this is coming to?"

Bartolomé remained level. This was not a fight to be won by bringing himself to Carlos's level, and he seemed to know it. A lesson that perhaps Elías could study.

"There are judgments being drawn from this man's past to his present," Bartolomé said. "It is un-Christlike to throw the first stone."

Carlos threw it anyway.

"He is a murderer," he spat.

"He did not harm Romero," Bartolomé said.

"Then who did?" Heraclio thundered.

Bartolomé was a blade as he turned on Heraclio, gleaming with an archangel's white rage.

"You," he said, pointing at Heraclio. "If you were not so blinded by prejudice, by arrogance, both of you"—and here he pointed at Carlos as well—"would see that there is a sickness among the people here. An evil spreads among your workers, your flock, beneath your very noses."

So the priest had found the shrine, had he? Carolina had more to worry about than Elías poking his nose where it didn't belong.

"Idolatry," Bartolomé spat. "Worship of the Devil."

Carlos took a step back. It was only when he did that Elías felt pressure against his shoulder blades and realized that he, too, was leaning away from the heat of Bartolomé's anger.

For he was *angry*.

"I let the natives keep their customs as a privilege," Heraclio said. "So long as they come to Mass as well. They have more energy to work when they're not fighting us and are more likely to obey when they have things that can be taken away."

As if the shrine were a toy given to a child.

"There is a line that surrounds the village, carved into the earth and filled with mercury. I have been told it has magical properties and is meant to ward off an unnamed evil that has been brought here. The people are frightened. And so they turn to sin," Bartolomé thundered. "They are your responsibility, and you turn a blind eye as they stray off the path toward darkness."

So that was where the stolen mercury had gone. Romero had harangued Elías for its disappearance for nothing.

Carlos scoffed. "Enough melodrama."

Bartolomé turned his thunder on Carlos.

"Would you say that if this evil were to touch the very people you care about? Your family? Your guests?"

Alba.

Elías's mouth dropped open.

That was what this was about.

He had told himself it was a trick of the light, last night. It was his eyes struggling to adjust to the dark. He was seeing things. He was surprised. That was all.

But he had barely slept; whenever he drifted off, he slipped into the same nightmare, one where those eyes—no, that lack, that darkness, those pits—found him, and he was running, running, running, but no matter how hard he pumped his leaden legs, they were at his back, breathing down his neck . . .

Something was wrong with Alba. Wrong in the way that a dream could be wrong: Its appearance could be bright, quotidian, unremarkable, or even beautiful, but if the dreamer looked upon it and tasted visceral fear sinking into his skull, then it was no dream at all, but a nightmare. Looking at Alba last night . . .

She needed help. Bartolomé must have sensed it too.

Carlos had shut up at last. His jaw was clenched and a muscle twitched below his ear. His eyes glistened. Did they smart with shame? Elías's would, if he had been so roundly scolded by a friend.

And that friend was not finished yet.

"I have been in communication with the Inquisition in the capital," Bartolomé said. "I came to Nueva España at their recommendation but have not yet taken up the position they offered me. I convinced them that rumors of idolatry in remote towns were worth investigating because I wanted to spend time with old friends." He did not so much as look at Carlos when he said this, but Elías did and marked the flush that rose beneath Carlos's collar. "But perhaps the Lord saw me tempted to take my leisure, for He has brought my work to me."

Elías could not help his brows from lifting. Pallor crept beneath Heraclio's weathered cheeks. To have the Inquisition brought down around one's head would be a death blow to his business.

Part of Elías wanted to see it happen. He wanted to sit in a box at the theater and watch the morbid opera unfurl, his heart swelling with selfish rapture as the singers died and the curtain fell on the whole Monterrubio mining undertaking. Never mind that he would be brought down with it—part of him would gladly sink to the bottom of the sea if it meant bringing Carlos and Heraclio down along with him. He and the greed of the Monterrubios would strike the silt and settle and rot there for eternity; his ghost would cackle forever at the bottom of the deep.

But if the Inquisition came to the hacienda de minas, they would find Alba.

"That shrine is the Devil's work," Bartolomé said. "So was

Romero's death. I do not have the information to link the two more than that, not yet, but I am on the hunt. I know one thing for certain." Righteous fire blazed in him as he declared: "The shrine must be destroyed. Immediately. You must destroy it, and forbid your workers from worshiping idols and demons, or I shall summon the Inquisition."

Heraclio was not a man to sputter. His way of being in the world struck the same prideful chord as Abuelo Arcadio's; he had neither the charm nor the patience nor the curiosity that Elías remembered, albeit reluctantly, in Victoriano.

And yet: He sputtered.

"I swear it, Padre," he said with an emphatic sweep of one hand. "There is no need to write to the Inquisitors. It will be gone before nightfall."

"Good," Bartolomé said. "Now release this innocent man."

Heraclio turned to Elías, almost surprised, as if he had forgotten he was there. He gestured at him to stand.

No apology, no excuse. It was stupid of Elías to anticipate groveling; Heraclio and Carlos did not grovel, and certainly not to him, but the priest's presence and what had transpired had given rise to a brief, curious flicker. Would they?

Of course not.

They watched in stony silence as Elías rose, dusted the dirt and hay from his trousers, and followed Bartolomé out the door.

There were workers lingering in the central aisle of the stable; they parted like the proverbial sea before the priest, their curiosity lingering on Elías's shoulders and back as he stepped into the sun.

Mere minutes had passed since he was dragged away from the chapel, but it felt as if the sun were higher in the sky. As if it were burning brighter behind that low veil of clouds. He expected Bartolomé to be drenched in its holy glow, but when he drew abreast of the priest, he found instead a man who looked tired. Profoundly tired.

They walked in silence.

For a few steps, Elías did not know where he was going, only that he was walking free and shaking off the sensation of clenched hands on his arms and shirt. Then the chapel loomed in his vision.

He slowed his stride; Bartolomé matched his step and gave him a look that was half question, half invitation. Join him in the chapel?

"I'll be going," Elías said and belatedly jerked a thumb toward the workshop. The other option was to return to the house for breakfast, but . . . walking into a room of people who still considered him a murderer was not how he wished to resume his morning. He would first let Bartolomé spread the good word that Romero's murderer was still on the loose. "Thank you. I owe you."

Bartolomé brushed this away with a gentle gesture—again, all Elías could read in it was tired.

"You owe me nothing," Bartolomé said. "But you do owe it to yourself to receive the sacraments. If you are not in a state of grace, I am always here to speak with." He slowed his walk further and paused, as if reexamining what he had just said. "I can't imagine that is appealing to you. I know you don't like me—whether by nature of my friendship with Carlos or your feelings about the Church. You lived under the rule of the Grand Turk. I can't imagine that experience endears you to a strange priest in a foreign land."

"Indeed," Elías said, so taken aback that frankness stole his tongue, "no."

A weak smile. A glint of amusement in those pale eyes; a shade of gratitude, perhaps, for the honesty. "Nevertheless," Bartolomé said, "I am here."

And when he walked to the chapel, it was Elías's turn to pause, and watch.

He had been raised to distrust golden veneers and holier-than-thou comportment; this had never led him astray.

He wondered, for the first time, if he was wrong.

HIS HANDS SHOOK as he stacked books. Gripping the broom helped; when there was no more floor to sweep, when the dirt had been scoured away near to bedrock, he sat on the chair Alba had sat in last night and wiped the sweat from his brow with his forearm. Still, his arm trembled.

He should get food, but even going to the kitchen... His mind ran six steps ahead of him and flung open the doors to men gasping and pointing, to Socorro grimly rolling up her sleeves and coming at him with her tools for grinding maíz.

It was a stupid fear. Romero had not been loved. Most cut him a broad berth. His temper was foul and his sense of humor fouler; young women walked more quickly in his presence, their eyes trained on the ground. That was indicator enough of bone-deep rot in a man. It was difficult to imagine more than a superficial show of grief for his sudden absence.

But who had disliked him enough to kill him?

Rather: Who disliked him enough to risk Heraclio's wrath?

The door of the workshop swung open.

"You're all right," María Victoriana said. Her silhouette entered, holding a clay bowl with one hand and a basket in the other. It wasn't a question, but he answered anyway.

"I am."

María Victoriana stalked to the table and moved stacks of books to one side with her elbow. Then, she emptied her arms. The bowl was filled with scrambled eggs that still steamed in the pale light from the door, that smelled of that vibrant red sauce he had come to love the burn of. The basket was filled with . . . cloth? Or so he thought. Then she unfolded it, and the scent of tortillas, hot and perfectly spotted with char from the stove, rose like the coming of a new prophet.

"You never came to the house for breakfast," she said by way of explanation.

He was already at the table and reaching for a tortilla.

She plopped herself onto a stool.

He ignored her and ate. Dinner was so many hours ago; it was only now that he realized how much the nerves of being in the formal dining room had prevented him from eating his fill.

"I don't know if I like you, but I don't want you to die," María Victoriana said.

This surprised him enough to tear his attention from the food. The answer that tripped to his tongue: Well, how funny that she should say that, because he also did not like himself and also did not want to die. They had a great deal in common after all.

He swallowed. Reached for another tortilla and tore it in two.

"I won't," he said instead.

"You look too much like him to die. It wouldn't be fair."

She did not look at him as she spoke. Her eyes were fixed on the empty hearth, and though her expression was stony, the words wavered. As if they struggled to carry the weight of what they hid.

Elías set his hands down. More softly, this time, he repeated: "I won't."

"Promise?"

Being dragged to the stables had cast his world on its side; those moments had tasted of a liminality that he was still familiar with, many years later. The cruel wrench of fate that had him thrown into the mud of Almadén to fight or rot crept in like a sly twist of the breeze: it was never there, until it was, and then his life would never be the same.

He hadn't thought that death would come for him. Prison, absolutely, because that was what had awaited him before.

Perhaps that assumption was naive. He did not know the laws of this land. He did not know what Heraclio and Carlos were capable of, not until the latter had laid hands on him.

Perhaps he still did not know.

"The priest doesn't think it's me," he said to assure her. To assure himself. "Heraclio and Carlos listen to him."

"Fine, then."

She folded her arms over her chest and watched as he spooned water from the well bucket into a cup for himself. He hesitated before he drank. He held it out to her instead.

"You want . . . ?"

She shook her head.

He drank. Cleared his throat. Another peace offering, then: "Did Victoriano have any books on better ways to reserve and reuse mercury? Other than beating that sackcloth with a paddle, I mean. Feels like that would fall to me, now that . . ."

"Of course he did," María Victoriana said. The arms folded across her chest loosened. She made as if to stand, then paused. She eyed the stacks of books on the table but made no move toward them.

Was she waiting for his permission? Were they his, as this crumbling shack was? No matter—they wouldn't be his forever. When he left this awful place, she could take all the spoils she wanted.

He waved her toward the table.

She required no more invitation. He had barely finished the gesture before she was on her feet and had her hands on the books, lovingly sorting through them and reorganizing them. Dust from thick, moisture-wrinkled pages rose into the air as she opened them and inhaled deeply of their smell, her eyes fluttering shut with delight.

In earnest, this time: Perhaps they did have something in common after all.

"I bet he journaled about it," she said. "He wrote all the time. He never thought a full sentence without having me write it down somewhere."

And yet he never wrote to Elías.

"Wait," he said. "Without having *you* write it down?"

María Victoriana did not look up as she pawed through the books. She lifted one hand and mimed a tremble.

Elías tightened his grip on the tortilla. Salsa dripped down his hand—he was aware, more than usual, of how it fluttered, no matter how much he focused on keeping it still.

"I talked about his shakes the other day. They got so severe that he couldn't write," she said. "He taught me when I was five and dictated everything to me. Until his mind started to go, too, that is."

She set a stack of books aside with a satisfying thump. The movement of this pile had revealed a leather-bound tome, slender and dark.

She frowned.

"This isn't his." She cracked it open. "Oh. Oh . . . my."

She laid the book open on the table and snatched her hands back as if she had been burned.

A page of pentagrams gleamed luridly up at them, their lines as thick and black and lustrous as if they had been inked that morning.

"What on *earth* is that?" María Victoriana cried.

Elías tilted his head to the side, wondering the same. Then it occurred to him: a swoop of gulls; the crowds of the book bazaar behind the Sultan Ahmet Mosque. He wiped his hands on his trousers and abandoned his breakfast to investigate.

"Ah! El Libro de San Cipriano," he said. "It's a historical artifact. See the stamp here, inside the front cover? It once belonged to the library of a prince in Granada, someone who ruled before los Reyes Católicos retook the south." María Victoriana stared blankly at him. "I bought it because it's written in aljamía."

"Al . . . jamón?" María Victoriana said. "These glyphs are about food?"

"No. Aljamía," he repeated. "The letters are Arabic, but the words are castellano. Listen—"

He pointed to the ligatures and began to read aloud. At first he was slow, stumbling as he grasped where the author had chosen to represent vowels or drop them entirely, assuming the reader's familiarity with his meaning. Then, his pace quickened.

"'And I call upon thee, and thy power, and thy strength, to carry out my will—'" Here he paused. "See, castellano this old sounds somewhat like Portuguese, and then the author uses Arabic verbal nouns when discussing *summoning*. Why *summoning* in this context, though . . . ? It doesn't make grammatical sense."

But María Victoriana was not listening. She was looking around the workshop, wide-eyed. The air had shifted around them; there was a breeze in the room that did not come from the door. That was not wintry cold. That could have smelled, faintly, of sulfur.

But he had to be imagining that.

María Victoriana reached over and shut the book. It closed with a hearty *snap*.

"I wouldn't let the priest know that you have this," she said, and there was no scolding in her voice, no harshness, only a frankness that sent a wave of fear rolling through his gut. "He might not defend you after all."

XVII

Alba

BIRDS CHIRPED. SHE flinched from the morning light; waking with a start was never comfortable, not in this place. Her nightdress clung to her stomach and thighs—she had sweat in the night and become trapped in it. As she sat up, strange dreams still littered the back of her skull like the aftertaste of metal, as if she had chewed the inside of her cheek in sleep and woken with the taste of old blood on her tongue.

She shook her hair out; snarls caught on her fingers. The pillows here, too, had minds of their own—her plaits had never disobeyed her before sleeping in this bed. But so it was. She would untangle the knots and confront the day with a splash of cold water to the face.

And it would be a good day: She felt well rested for the first time in days. Locking the door before extinguishing her candle had allowed her to slip past her tangle of anxious thoughts into a deep sleep.

Then she set her feet on the floor.

It was as if the ground beneath her shifted. As if someone had taken her world and flipped it as neatly as a tortilla on the stove.

She felt gravel beneath her soles.

After she had scrubbed her feet and dressed to go downstairs, she set her hand on the door. Belatedly, as she turned the knob, she remembered that she had locked it behind her when she came to bed. How silly of her to forget, she would have to get the key from her bedside—

But with a gentle give beneath her palm, the door swung open.

SHE PACED THE drawing room until Mamá summoned her for lunch; she moved her food around her plate with practiced interest. Neither Carlos nor Heraclio had joined them.

"It's the workers, unfortunately," Bartolomé explained. Mamá nodded sagely as if she knew precisely what he was talking about before he even continued. "Heraclio and Carlos finally enacted discipline for idolatry and destroyed the mercury barrier they put around the town." Here, Mamá's eyes widened—like Alba, she appeared not to have known about this worship of false idols. "Their mood is quite foul today," Bartolomé continued, sounding absolutely delighted by this fact. "Carlos asked me to pass along his regrets and apologies."

"Apology accepted," Mamá said, adding, with an exaggerated shudder, "I, too, would be in a foul mood if I knew there was a murderer in our midst."

Visions flashed through the back of Alba's mind like memories, as if they had happened already and were unchangeable past: Bartolomé gasping and straining, clawing at hands gripping his throat; Bartolomé's hair weightless, almost playful, in the breeze of free fall; Bartolomé's body striking stone, far, far below her, and cracking with a sound like dried chicken bones. Bartolomé splayed like a bright dancer against the dark rock of a ravine.

Alba's fork shuddered against her plate. The sound put her teeth on edge; from the ripple of movement that went around the table, it was clear it had affected Mamá, Papá, and the priest similarly.

Mamá shot her a reprimanding look.

"Mija, are you unwell?" Her lips pursed as she took in Alba's appearance. She had not done her hair as tidily as she had earlier in their stay at Casa Calavera, nor had she dressed with as much precision and care. What was the point? Carlos scarcely saw her; even then, what use was there in impressing him?

"Thank you, Mamá, I am perfectly fine," Alba said.

She was going mad. The sight of meat on her plate made her want to vomit. She wanted to fling it against the walls of the room. Watch the tough pork slide down whitewashed stucco, trailing thin juice in its wake like blood.

A vicious hiss broke this reverie: *the priest.*

It was as if she were hearing it in her ear and not in her mind; she could *feel* the sibilance against her ear and the tender flesh behind it.

"And I, for one, am glad the murderer is not Señor Elías," Papá declared, ignoring the interaction between Mamá and Alba. "It's not every day one finds oneself in the company of an alchemist. I have so many questions."

Bartolomé made an agreeable sound into his soup. His brows were raised . . . were they? Alba could not be caught studying his face, and the glance she stole did not settle her curiosity.

"What is an alchemist, anyway?" Mamá asked dismissively. "Some kind of pharmacist? I wouldn't expect a tradesman in the family of my daughter's betrothed. Nor"—she added, with a sip of her drink—"would I desire it. But the heart wants what the heart wants, doesn't it, mi niña?"

Alba chewed at the sawdust food as deliberately and thoughtfully as was required to hide the madman's smile that threatened to play at her mouth. If only Mamá knew precisely how undesirable Elías was. Convict, murderer.

"No, not at all," Papá cried, incredulous. "An alchemist is a mystic! He is versed in arcana and science and—"

Mamá's sigh was long-suffering. "You read too much."

"And you read not enough if you cannot appreciate how interesting that is!" Papá said, jabbing at Mamá across the table with his fork. "This is someone who has studied the *transmutation of metals*. And they have him doing incorporo work like a common minero. Bah! He is too interesting for them by half."

Mamá turned to Bartolomé with a scoff. "That sounds like the work of charlatans, Padre. Don't alchemists make deals with devils?"

So subtle had been Bartolomé's lack of attention that it had escaped Alba's notice: how a soft glaze had come over his eyes, veiling a wandering mind. Then, at once, he sharpened, a sun breaking through a heavy layer of gray clouds to blaze down on one's brow.

He was next.

Next.

She knew this with a profane certainty. Knew that *next* meant someone racing to the chapel looking for Heraclio, their pallid brow beaded with sweat and hands shaking from shock.

She set her fork down. Her own hand trembled.

Images from a nightmare abruptly remembered did not a death sentence make. She could tell herself it had been a dream. A terrible dream, yes, but just a dream. She could tell herself that she was a fool to give the intruding thought any credence. She could ask herself if she felt ill and tell herself to go back to bed. She should leave Casa Calavera altogether, flee the mine, back to Zacatecas, to the ends of the earth, anywhere but here, *anywhere but near that mine* . . .

She brushed at her ear, miming tucking a loose lock of hair behind it. That voice felt *apart* from her mind, outside of her skull, and she felt as if she could bat it away as she would a fly. She was not going to leave the mine. Not when Carolina was here, dangling the secrets of her past a hair's breadth out of her reach. Not when leaving the mine meant leaving Carlos. Meant surrendering herself, her spirit, and her body to a stranger, and nothing would make her do that. Nothing. She stabbed her food with her fork—though she had no intention of eating it—and ignored Mamá's sideways look at her lack of manners.

"There are superstitions, of course," Bartolomé was saying.

"But the real alchemists are scientists, first and foremost," Papá said. "I wonder if Heraclio would permit me to watch the amalgamation process," he added, half to himself. "Mercury is the source of so many mysteries. It's almost supernatural."

"I shan't allow it," Mamá said, setting her napkin down on the table with an emphatic slap. "You won't go near that poison. Didn't you see how his hands shook?" she asked. "These azogueros all die an early death. And for what? Money?"

She and Papá slipped into another of their shrill dances, an argumentative mode that displayed their worst qualities: shrewishness and nagging, poor listening and interruption. At home, Alba would watch the clock. Within two minutes, without fail, they would be joking and teasing each other.

Here, she had no clock to watch, and no patience to spare.

She stood abruptly. A sweep of nausea hit her behind the throat. "I will lie down early, I think."

All eyes turned on her, including those of Bartolomé. She felt herself shrinking away beneath her skin at the sensation.

"I slept poorly," she said. A weak excuse.

"Don't we all, in this place," Mamá agreed. "I shall retire as well."

It was not what Alba had wanted to hear. It meant that her plan had to wait until full siesta instead of beginning directly after lunch, for Mamá was not, in fact, all that tired, and Alba could hear her shuffling about her room and calling for Papá. She even came into Alba's room to check on her twice.

The afternoon grew long. Alba waited.

When at last the house was drowsing in the little warmth that afternoon afforded, she rose from her bed.

She was not meant to notice that Elías stayed in the workshop during mealtimes and siesta. She only noticed his absence because it would be impossible not to, with such a limited host of faces at the table and so few bodies coming and going from the house. It was not because she yearned for his presence.

It was because—if Papá were to be believed—as an alchemist, he was someone who rubbed elbows with the supernatural. He might be the only person who listened to her with an open mind.

Her path took a loping route, one that brought her out of sight of the house and around the back of the workshop. Then, without knocking, without so much as a hello, she pushed open the door.

It swung inward with a lusty creak.

Elías sat at the table. His body was positioned so that if he lifted his head, he would be looking directly at the door, but he bent over a book. His elbows were on the table. One hand was curled into a loose fist on which he rested his cheek; the other was blackened with ink as he took notes in the margins of the book.

The door hit the wall. Alba flinched at the sound. She hadn't meant to open it with such force; the hinges must be weak.

Elías startled. Lifted his head. Jumped again, this time back from the table and to his feet, the stool on which he sat clattering to the ground.

"I . . . I didn't see you there." He stuttered slightly; his hair had fallen into his face, for it was not bound back as it usually was.

Shame flickered over her skin, hot and prickling, when she realized that she had, after all, barged into his space without invitation. As if she were entitled to it. As if she were calling on a friend.

"I didn't mean to surprise you," she said. "Or interrupt. I'm sorry."

They were not, in fact, friends. She barely knew him. She thought about him enough that perhaps she had deluded herself into believing that they had spent more time together, that they would become friends, that they were already more than acquaintances, more than starched, distant in-laws-to-be, but that was not true.

"Thank you." She could have flinched at how awkward she sounded. "For the other night, I mean."

His stance had softened. He was no longer a deer braced for flight, but a man with both feet on the ground, watching her attentively.

This realization brought still more heat to her skin. She should leave.

"You helped me back, didn't you?" he said. She had never liked peninsular speech. It was too slippery, too lispy. But his way of speaking was neither. It was without ornament. Direct. It had a grit to it that she liked. "With the priest."

Perhaps she had been too obvious. Carlos had not exactly been warm toward her over the last day; whether this was preoccupation or prejudice for having assisted in clearing Elías's name, she did not know.

"Thank you," he said. "Whatever you did, it was clever. Everyone trusts Bartolomé."

Not everyone. María Victoriana and the cook, Socorro, were dismissive of him at best; the townspeople, she deduced, had no love for his presence or his zeal.

And as for Alba? She did not know. He slipped through her judgment, evasive as a thin fish. The repulsion she felt at their first meeting was a taste that would not leave her mouth. But then, she sought him out to save Elías.

And Bartolomé had. Moreover, it seemed he had veiled her own part in the matter in secrecy, as she had requested. That made him worthy of at least some trust, did it not?

At least enough to not want him to die.

"But you didn't come here just to say that," Elías said. "Are you all right? Something is troubling you."

She loved Mamá and Papá, she did, but the fact that Elías and Bartolomé—two near strangers—had been the only ones to notice this brought a stinging to her eyes. They noticed. That fact should make her feel less alone.

It had the opposite effect.

She could not stop the sharp intake of breath. She could only try and control the damage in its wake: bite the lip that threatened to tremble, stiffen the shoulders to prevent them from lifting.

Elías moved toward her like a reflex. He reached for her, stopped before her, and stayed there, his hands upturned, impotent. As if he had realized he had no way to comfort her.

"Would you like to come in?" he asked.

She nodded, sharp and jerky. It was foolish to linger in the doorway, in full sight of anyone who happened to pass by.

The workshop was warm and smelled of mesquite smoke from the fire that crackled in the hearth.

When he shut the door, she blurted out what she had to say before she lost the nerve.

"I fear Bartolomé is next," she said.

He did not gasp in shock. He did not call her mad. Far from it. Instead, he found a stool—they seemed to grow around the workshop like wildflowers—and sat.

"What makes you say that?" he asked.

"I have been having horrible dreams," she began, "since we arrived. I have often had bad dreams, since I was a child. The dreams and the sleepwalking... if they occur, they tend to come as a pair."

It was easier to pace. If her feet were moving, she could be focused on the path before her and not how he was watching her. How he was waiting for her to speak. How he was listening.

He nodded slowly, his chin resting thoughtfully on one hand. A hint of his earring glinted through his dark hair.

"What happened in your dream?" Dryly, as if attempting thin humor, he added: "I think I should be prepared if I am going to be accused of the priest's murder next."

The floor was hard, packed dirt. The room was so small, even compared to Casa Calavera, and there wasn't much room to pace. What if she were found here? She should leave at once and forget this ever happened.

"It doesn't matter." The words came out sharper than she intended. "I just know it's him. He's in danger. That's all I came to say. I should leave."

She made for the door.

His hand brushed her elbow—it was not enough to stop her; she could have pushed right past it.

She hesitated.

"Alba."

Looking at him twisted time. At once, it was night, and they were in firelight. Her limbs were stiff with cold; his hands were warm.

He had been refuge from that nightmare. Why couldn't he be again?

You don't know him, you can't trust him. You told him enough. Leave. Flee.

"Warn the priest," she said.

"And what exactly will I tell him?"

His hand was still on her elbow—only fingertips, barely a weight. She could walk away, she could flee. Nothing was stopping her.

But Bartolomé was in danger. It felt as real as the dirt and gravel on the soles of her feet.

Remembering that sent a shudder down her spine. Her flesh went cold, as if a hand of ice had run its claws across her shoulders.

Elías dropped his hand.

She immediately wished he hadn't. She was untethered, unmoored. A madwoman in a desolate place.

"I . . . I know you do not know me, and that perhaps you do not trust me, but I will listen, if you wish me to," he said. "I *want* to listen. If you are troubled, I want to help."

But what could be done to help? She covered her face with her hands. She spoke into her palms—it was so much easier if she was not looking at him, if she could pretend that she was speaking into an empty room.

"When I woke . . ." Her voice cracked. It came out as a whisper: "My feet were dirty."

She peeked through her fingers to gauge his reaction. Realization, then horror, swept across his face. "Your door—"

"I locked it. But it had been unlocked."

His shoulders stiffened. "That is not good."

"You think I don't know that?" Her voice pitched dangerously close to shrill again. "Why do you think I am here?"

A breath of silence.

"Desperation," he said, drawing the syllables out. She resisted the urge to flinch away from the dryness in his voice. "That is the only reason you would risk dear Carlos's wrath."

But Carlos was not alone among her worries. "Think of my mother," she said. "I am endangering my reputation."

"That's it," Elías said, snapping his fingers. "Danger. You are in danger, not the priest. Well, perhaps the priest as well," he revised quickly, "but foremost, you."

It was passionate and sudden, a turn that made her want to step away from him.

Danger, the voice at her ear purred. *Flee this place, never look back.*

"When I found you outside, the other night," he continued, "you were not yourself."

His tone sent a trill of fear up her spine. She dismissed it.

"I was sleepwalking. Of course I was not myself," she said.

He looked away from her. A muscle twitched in his jaw. "You did not look like yourself," he said. "You were angry that I stopped you. So angry that I was afraid of you." He paused, as if searching for words. When he spoke again, the tone of his voice was careful, as if he were taking trembling steps along the edge of a precipice. "But—it wasn't you."

Claws of cold dug into the column of her neck, so forceful she was surprised they did not lift her as if she were a pup seized by the nape. When she had caught her breath, she said: "That does not make sense."

"You were angry that I stopped you. I thought you were headed toward the mine, but that path also leads to the incorporadero. Where was the body found?"

Alba inhaled sharply through her nose.

"You were walking toward danger," Elías continued. "What if you had come upon the murderer and Romero? What if you witnessed it, what would happen to you then? What if they hurt you instead?"

"I hadn't thought of that," Alba said.

"I never thought I would say this, but I agree with the priest. Something is wrong," he said fervently. "Your dream troubles me, yes. But the facts trouble me more."

He turned to the table, where the book he had been reading lay open. He began paging through it, eyes flicking across words as if he were searching for something.

The words themselves were alien to Alba—a language she could not place, crowded black letters ornamented with sharp gestures in red and blue ink.

"You walked as if led by something," he said. "Animated by a will not your own."

"That is the nature of sleepwalking," Alba said, "is it not?"

"My mother would sleepwalk," Elías said without looking up. "This was *different*."

Bitter cold drove into Alba's bones. She had a sensation that she was apart from herself, that she was watching the scene between them unfold from some high perch instead of through her own eyes.

"I don't understand," she said.

"And I am trying to," he said. "I am trying to make sense of the facts and approach this logically, examining what evidence we have and drawing reasonable conclusions, but all I think is . . ."

His feverish turning through the book stilled; the pages settled and were silent.

A large block of glyphs graced the top of the page he looked down at. He took it in, the set of his mouth grim.

"Would you look at that," he said softly, as if half to himself. "How helpful."

"What is it?" Alba asked.

His finger fell to the page. "'An assessment,'" he read aloud.

"Of?"

His eyes flicked up at her, wary. His shoulders were tight, his voice strained, as if afraid of how she might react to what he said next.

"'Of possession,'" he finished.

Alba fell a step away from him. He thought she was mad. No, worse.

"You think I am possessed?" she cried.

"I . . ." He did not move from where he lingered over the book; his face shifted, as if he were searching for words and failing to find them. "I think it is worth considering. I once knew a man who suffered from—"

"'Worth considering?'" she snapped, incredulous. "I came here to ask for help because I am worried about Padre Bartolomé, not to be accused of making deals with demons."

Whispering gestures reached through her mind, weaving bridges through once-disparate moments. The thoughts that felt not her own. The feeling, in sleep, that something guided her.

Fear swept over her, encasing her in ice.

Elías was wrong.

"I should never have come here," she said. "I will warn the priest myself."

"By telling him what?" Elías wondered.

THE POSSESSION OF ALBA DÍAZ

She shot him a hard look. Curled her hands into fists. Set her jaw.

He was right. What could she say that would not sound like a madwoman's ravings?

She was unmoored, alone. She would find no help here.

Yessss, the voice at her ear hissed. *Away from him. Away. Leave.*

She turned on her heel and left the workshop.

XVIII

Elías

THAT NIGHT, ELÍAS curled on his side in bed, staring into darkness. El Libro de San Cipriano lay at his bedside, a small strip of leather marking the page he had read to before his candle burned low and drowsiness made his vision swim. Yet somehow, sleep evaded him.

Another afternoon of skirting the house had been eased by María Victoriana bringing food from the kitchen to the workshop. It seemed she considered this the tax she paid for spending hours burrowing in Victoriano's books there. When asked if she was meant to be anywhere else, or if her mother was missing her, María Victoriana had given a dismissive wave, as effortlessly haughty as a duchess.

"She's busy, she won't miss me," she said, not even bothering to lift her head from the journal she combed through as she added, in a deceptively light voice: "By the way, don't go out at night. It's not safe right now."

Unease had swept through him upon hearing this. Alba's fevered words from earlier wound through his mind, looping like a nightmare he could not escape.

What was Carolina busy with? He was not sure he believed in coincidences, not anymore. Not when whatever was plaguing Alba was... well, *was*. He was not sure of much, but he knew it was there and it was *wrong*, no matter how much that offended her.

"What do you mean?" he pressed.

He received another haughty wave of the hand. "Thank me later."

All day, the mine had buzzed like a smoked wasp's nest. It was no secret that Bartolomé's wishes had been carried out: Heraclio saw the shrine destroyed. He bragged that he and Bartolomé had been shoulder to shoulder, armed with hammers, as they brought down the shrine together. A crusade against idolatry and the Devil's work.

Was Bartolomé right? An evil spreads among your workers, your flock...

"That's not at all ominous," Elías said.

María Victoriana set her book down. She had produced slices of a root vegetable called jícama and was steadily snacking through them. When he tried one, it had crunched with the satisfying give of a tart apple. Not all things in Nueva España were as awful as they had seemed from the start.

She narrowed her eyes at him, chewing thoughtfully. If she was going to explain what she meant, she decided against it.

"You have enough on your mind," she said. "Refining enough silver to leave, being accused of murder, mooning over Señorita Alba every time she walks by..."

"Excuse you." He was both too surprised and too offended to question the wisdom of defending himself. "Grown men do not moon."

It turned out that defending himself was not wise. María Victoriana did not laugh at him, but amusement rippled across her face like a flock of birds alighting. She returned to her book with a smirk.

"It must be so depressing to be in love with Carlos's fiancée," she said.

"I would hardly call it *that*."

María Victoriana shot him a look with brows raised high—how eerily she resembled Abuelo Arcadio in that moment. And, like Abuelo Arcadio, she had prodded him right where he was softest. He hadn't even known that spot existed, and oh, it was tender to the touch.

He could see everything plainly now, as if they were players on a stage, the lights throwing their silhouettes into sharp relief. Let the folktale unfold: the prince, the princess, and an ogre, lumbering, enormous, horrifying. A monster devouring the stage.

Pathetic. He should have concealed his feelings better. But how could he have? Alba . . . she was a sickness that had not plagued him since boyhood; his defenses had grown weak. They were atrophied muscles that collapsed at the slightest breeze.

The feeling had caught him unawares, in that cold courtyard, and in that golden ballroom. Before he could draw steel to defend himself, it had already drawn blood. The wound wept all the way from Zacatecas to this purgatory, here in the mountains—and apparently, the gleaming trail it left was apparent for even this girl to see.

"You're young, so I'll explain it nice and slowly," he said, echoing her own words from when he had first arrived. It was too easy to mock himself. So much easier than the alternative. "Infatuations come and go. So long as you don't make any rash decisions, they're harmless."

Upon reflection, hours later, lying awake with the conversation looping through his skull on a bat's drunken wings: what a rational thing to have said. He should take his own advice.

Not even when Alba sought him out, luminous in the doorway of the workshop, an apparition of loveliness as stark as this desolate place.

Alba was none of his business.

Bartolomé already sensed that something was wrong with her. Bartolomé had threatened Heraclio with the Inquisition. That priest was armed to the teeth. If his suspicions mirrored Elías's in any way, then he would deal with the problem swiftly and as he saw fit.

Physical revulsion coursed through Elías at the thought.

He rolled over and stared at the ceiling, a vain effort to shake off the dread blackening in his chest.

If he shut his eyes, he knew what he would see: black pits, bared teeth. Staring into the darkness now, all he could see was how agitated her face had been as she paced the workshop. How it twitched, as if she were rehearsing an argument in her mind and could not keep the aggression from bubbling to the surface.

The other forzados at Almadén had called the man El Loco. Elías had never learned what his conviction was nor how long he had been in the mines—no one grew close enough to speak to him, and El Loco only spoke to himself. Long, spirited conversations, his eyes rolling with agitation, his laughter filling the dark, airless tunnels and sending Elías's hair standing on end despite the heat of the furnaces.

Possessed, the guards explained to newcomers among their ranks. *Do not engage.*

He had not seen El Loco in many years, not since leaving Almadén. He had not thought of the man in just as long.

And yet.

When Alba had come into the workshop, the name rang through him like a bell. El Loco's face—and how it moved—were as fresh in his mind's eye as if he had seen him yesterday.

It was not comforting, looking at Alba and being powerfully reminded of a man possessed. To say the least.

A long, thin creak splintered the darkness.

Elías sat up. Squinted through the gloom. Had the latch of the door come loose somehow? Had he not shut it? He could ignore it, but he was already awake, so he rose—might as well shut the door properly.

It swung open.

A woman in white stood in the doorway.

He fell back a step, heart thick in his throat, as the woman swept into the room. A glint of metal at her side—in one hand, she held a long knife.

He registered this in a quick glance; then his eyes were drawn back to her face and he could not look away. Even in the dark, he knew what he was seeing: pits where there should be eyes, lips peeled back from teeth as she charged forward.

He turned to flee, but tripped.

His back hit the hard mattress. Breath cracked from his lungs; he gasped, and she was on him, straddling his chest, a black curtain of hair pouring down as she curled over him.

Cold metal pressed against his throat.

He was going to die.

He did not want to die.

Almadén had given him reflexes; he had to fight or would rot in the mine forever, his body tossed down an abandoned shaft like so much refuse. He gritted his teeth and seized her forearms. Forced the blade away from his neck.

She forced back.

They remained locked like that, his hands gripping her arms, her weight pinning him down, a strength that belied her slim arms forcing the blade toward his throat—

And those eyes. Gazing down at him, blacker than mines, blacker than coal—

Ask for the demon's name. This was what El Libro de San Cipriano had instructed. *Ask it questions. The more you know, the more deliberately you can proceed with harnessing or banishing it.*

"Are . . . you," he forced through gritted teeth, "the Devil?"

To his horror, she replied.

"The Devil," she repeated. Her voice raked like stone on stone, a metal pickaxe deep into his teeth. Her red tongue moved behind canines that were too long, as if the mouth were gumless, fleshless, the maw of a skull. "As if there were only one!"

A trill of laughter—it was silver castanets, it was water falling on coins, it jerked at his heart with how lovely it was.

"Is your master the Devil, then?" he asked. Sweat slicked his brow and palms; she was still pressing down hard, fighting to bring the knife to his throat, and she was stronger than anyone he had ever fought off, impossibly strong. "Why are you here?"

"Men want kings!" she trilled. "Order, tidy, clean. No luck for you, ya Elías, ya Elías, *ya Elíasssssssssssss.*"

That red tongue flicked out and caught the tip of his nose. He flinched in disgust; his grip slipped.

The knife stuttered down.

He caught her wrists and shoved back. His hair was wet with sweat, sticking to his clammy nape.

"Whom do you serve?" he forced out.

"There were gods here, once." Her breath was metallic. It washed over him like being submerged in fouled mine water.

"When we arrived. Don't know where they are now. Maybe we ate them. Maybe we became them."

Another trill of impossible laughter, punctuated with a toss of the head, revealing white throat.

A second of distraction. Elías seized it: He inhaled sharply and wrenched his weight to the left. The crack of a skull against the wall.

A soft cry of pain, like a cat's mew.

Alba.

He faltered. It was a mistake.

She sprang on him, jaw wide, so wide, as if she were going to devour him whole—

He flung her off him and ducked out of the way.

A strangled cry; the knife flashed. It soared and fell to the floor, striking it with a sharp clatter.

He lunged. Now he pinned her down, keeping his weight on her waist no matter how she kicked and bucked, wrestling her writhing arms and pinning them beneath his knees.

"We are what there is now," she said. "I serve me. Me me me me."

Red tongue, white teeth. Black eyes boring into him.

But it was Alba's hair that splayed across his blankets, shining like mercury. Alba's body beneath him, positioned as if they were locked in an amorous embrace, nothing but thin nightclothes separating flesh.

It was a fatal lapse of concentration. His distraction turned the tables: Her arms escaped from under his knees; her hands flew to his throat. Nails dug into skin; thumbs pressed hard against his windpipe.

He gasped. He could not breathe. He clawed at her hands. The pain was crushing, crushing, crushing—

Darkness curled around his vision. Strength would not save him. The only advantage he had was weight.

He threw himself to the side. Wrenched them over the side of the bed.

They tumbled and struck the ground.

Her hands fell away from his neck; he gasped. Air flew down his throat, so cold it felt wet. He choked on it and coughed and sucked in air as he pushed himself up on his feet—

Metal at his throat.

He lurched backward. The back of his skull found the wall; he gasped in pain.

She pressed against him. Every curve of Alba's body was flush with his, legs and hips and breasts, but—

One hard hand gripped his neck. The other held the knife inches from his throat.

"You see too much," she hissed. Her tongue flicked serpentlike through her teeth. "You are in the way. Die, you rat, die."

He needed El Libro de San Cipriano. It was too far—it had fallen from his bedside and lay open, face down, on the ground. Out of reach. What tools did it have? How could he defend himself? He needed to fight back. She was going to slit his throat.

"Leave Alba," he said, gagging as the hold on his throat tightened. "Leave her be."

Bared teeth. This hiss was angrier. Predatory. He wondered if she was going to devour him whole.

"You only care because you're guilty about Fátima," she said.

Elías's heart stuttered. He had not heard her name aloud in years. He could not even choke through shame and speak it himself.

The demon grinned wide, so wide that lips could split at the seams. "She bled bled bled and hacked and hurt, and then the doctor hurt her more, didn't he? She screamed, oh she *screamed*, but you weren't there, you were rotting, all because you wanted to be an animal." A rumble of laughter, this time deep, dissonant; he could feel it more than hear it as it emanated through Alba's chest and vibrated against his. "Being an animal thrown in a cage is easy, isn't it? Poor, powerless Elías in the mine. He couldn't possibly look after the people who needed him."

"You don't know what you're talking about." The words stuttered and caught but he forced them out, even though speaking moved his Adam's apple against the blade of the knife. A pit had opened beneath his feet, and he was falling, falling, falling, strangled by Fátima's weeping and slicks of blood so wet they were like rain.

Wider went the smile. A wash of wet, metallic breath. "Don't I, ya Elías?"

This she hissed in derija, and it was then that he realized she had been speaking derija since she had pushed him against the wall, and that he hadn't noticed how habit tripped his tongue into the same dialect.

"This isn't possible." He forced himself to speak castellano. Derija was the past, dead and gone; castellano tasted like now, and he needed it to be *now*. "Alba!" he said. "Alba, this isn't you. Alba, can you hear me?"

"Alba, Alba, Alba. But what about Fátima?" crooned the demon, tongue caressing clipped derija syllables. "Fátima needed you and you left her to die. She died alone, choking on her own blood, with no one to help her, no one to hear her weep. Shall I send you to her to say sorry? To explain how all you did was *leave*?"

Derija cracked open memories from long slumber, and they

roared to life, bearing a blazing verse to his lips: "Bismillah al-Rahman al-Raheem."

In the name of God, the Most Compassionate, the Most Merciful.

He continued with what he remembered from the Fatiha, hoarse and accented and unsteady. "Al hamdu-lillah Rabb al-'alameen..."

The knife lifted from his throat; weight off his chest. Spittle flecked his face. She was sputtering and hissing, black pits burning at him, and that red tongue lolling out of her mouth. The knife swung high—

There were gods here, once. Maybe we ate them.

Then why was this working? Why, when he reached the frayed end of his memory of the Arabic verses, did he reach for more prayers?

"Our Father, who art in Heaven, hallowed be Thy name..."

And why did it keep working?

The knife swayed. She stumbled back, chest heaving, gasping. A hand flew to her neck and began clawing there, as if she could not draw breath.

It bought him time. He lunged for *El Libro de San Cipriano*, still reciting the prayer as he flipped pages, searching for what he had read earlier that evening. Reading and reciting different things sent his mind skittering sideways. His tongue tripped, and when he faltered, she was laughing again. Bright and rich, like the ringing of bells.

But still she clutched her throat.

"Weak little magician," the demon spat. But it was gasping. *It*, Elías distinctly thought, for there was a difference between *it* and Alba. It staggered, seeking balance, and leaned against the bed. "You are weak."

There it was: a long list, titled Incantations for Dismissing Demons of Various Orders.

Elías dove down the page, searching for the strongest antidote. He began to read aloud.

A guttural growl built in the woman before him. The demon was curled over where it stood, as if nursing a wound; as the growl built, as it began to rumble through the floor and travel into his bones, it rose, unfurling, teeth bared in a snarl.

Elías's breath caught; his words grew faint. But even whispering, he would not stop, he could not stop. When he reached the end of the incantation he began again, more confident this time, faster, even as the hairs rose up his arms and fear scuttled down his spine with a thousand insectile legs.

The growl transformed into words, but barely—they were thickened and distorted by vibrations, by rage.

"You draw on nothing but yourself." The demon inhaled sharply through its nose and flung the knife to the ground. "You will need stronger allies if you want her."

Its chin shot up, pointed to the ceiling; convulsions seized shoulders and arms, twitching wrists and yanking elbows in uncanny directions.

At once, the air left the room.

Elías gasped, felt there was nothing to breathe, gasped again, and it was like he was drowning, then—release.

The air was still. His pulse throbbed in his ears. He was still desperate to flee, limbs still a twitch away from seizing the knife and fighting.

She gasped. She was Alba: tear-streaked cheeks, closed eyes, soft lashes. Shaking as if she were standing in the freezing mountain air outside.

"Alba?" Elías whispered.

THE POSSESSION OF ALBA DÍAZ

From her lips—for they were *her* lips now, soft and natural and parting as they should—came a soft cry, a single faint keening.

His heart splintered at the sound. He dropped the book on the bed.

She collapsed.

And when she did, he dove to catch her.

XIX

Alba

ALBA OPENED HER eyes to darkness. To cold ground beneath her thighs. To the yank of her breath lifting her chest sharp and hard. She had fallen out of bed. How odd.

Someone was holding her. Lifting her.

She twisted away, a cry rising in her throat. The arms released, and she slipped sideways. Struck something soft. Blankets; hard mattress. Bed. Her throat felt ragged. She must have been crying in her sleep.

A figure moved away from the bed. She raised her head.

Elías stood over her, chest heaving, a white sleep shirt clinging to sweat on his skin.

Her mouth dropped open. She was in her nightdress; it wasn't the first time he had seen her in so little clothing, yes, but in her room? She felt naked. Exposed.

"What are you doing here?"

His brows flew toward his hairline. "Really?" The word was

breathless and cracked; his breathing had not slowed. It was as if he had been running. "Really?"

"Keep your voice down," she said, a scold in her whisper as she reached for blankets to cover herself. Fear lifted at the back of her neck, deep beneath the skin. Something was not right. She should remember being with him in a dark room. Had she invited him? "And get out of here before someone sees."

"You are in *my* room," he said, as flatly as his breath allowed. "You were sleepwalking. And you brought *that*."

He pointed at the ground.

She lifted her chin to see past the side of the bed. Metal glinted dull in the gloom.

A kitchen knife, big enough for butchery.

That was not possible. She had locked the door and heaved the chest in front of it. This was a dream. She—

She looked around her, loose hair falling over her shoulders.

The window was not in the right wall. The nightstand—wrong side of the bed.

Her fingertips were at her lips and shaking; her hands had risen to her mouth in horror.

"I . . . I . . . I don't understand." She jumped from one word to the next in staccato leaps, barely making the connections. She should go back to her room. If she fell asleep again, this would melt into her memory alongside every other nightmare. It might rear its foul head through the murk of waking once or twice, but it would be banished, and it would be gone. She wanted to be gone. She wanted dark oblivion to soothe her aching head. Oh, it hurt. Her monthly blood gave her headaches, but never this bad, not before.

"Who told you about my wife?" Elías demanded.

The word was a bucket of cold water over the head.

"You're *married*?" she cried.

"Shh." It was severe. "It couldn't have been Carlos," he continued, low and urgent. "Was it Heraclio? How did he know?"

Elías wore no ring, and the way he looked at her . . . if he was married, that was sinful. She felt a flash of hatred—and found, to her shock, that it was directed at Carlos, because he had been right. She had never wanted Carlos to be right about Elías, perhaps because she was young and stupid and Elías's rough-hewn beauty caught her, his mystery pure temptation, but now she knew better.

"I didn't know that you're married," Alba said. The acidity with which she spoke was clarifying. She was awake, and she ached. Blood throbbed in her skull and, oddly, her forearms.

Seize the knife and end this.

"She died when I was in Almadén," he said. "But you knew that part already, didn't you?"

Dead. For years. So Elías was a widower.

"Carlos mentioned Almadén," she said slowly, absorbing this information. "I didn't want to bring it up—"

"You know why I was there?"

It was impossible to parse his expression in the gloom, but the line of his silhouette vibrated with tension. He gripped a book hard, held at an angle that made it seem like a weapon. He would not relax. To him, this was urgent. This was important. This needed to be discussed *now*.

Alba worried her lower lip. It tasted of blood.

"He said that you killed someone," she said. "That you were a danger to the family's reputation. He said I should stay away from you, because you were . . ." She trailed off.

"A convict," Elías spat. "A murderer."

She let him say it. The anger in his voice was stark, though strained; mentioning that Carlos had also called him *trouble* would help nothing.

"I did kill a man," he declared. "I was young, I was drunk, I was acting out because my mother had died and my wife had tuberculosis, and for that—for a stupid, shameful accident—I was sent to prison. It was the most selfish thing I have ever done. One moment of rashness, one fight that got out of control, and I lost everything. I left Fátima. That was the worst part of it. She was alone and sick and she needed me, and I left her."

His voice pitched toward cracking, then broke off; the silence that fell in its wake had the weight of a confession.

"So . . . Fátima was the name of your wife?" Alba asked.

"Really?" Elías cried. Alba flinched—his anguish and anger cut like twin knives.

Now it was her turn to hush him. She kicked her legs over the side of the bed and stood, swaying from the rush of blood to her throbbing head.

"You were *mocking* me about her," Elías said.

The rush subsided; slowly, the bright specks faded toward the edges of her vision and disappeared. "I'm leaving. Something is wrong with you."

"Yes, she was my wife. My mother arranged the marriage when I was eighteen, and I let her because it made her happy." He saw that she was turning to leave; in two steps, he cut her off, standing between her and the door. "She was convinced that it would keep me from running off like my father had. I barely knew Fátima and felt I never did, but that was because I didn't listen to her, not even at the end, not until it was too fucking late. It was all my fault. And somehow, *you knew that. You said that.*"

She shook her head. Her eyes stung.

"I swear," she whispered, "I don't know what you're talking about."

"You don't remember what you just said," Elías said. "But you knew my past. You knew things that I have never told a living soul. You recoiled at prayers. You spoke to me in my mother's tongue, and I swear, that was worse than you attacking me with a knife."

"A knife?" she repeated, horror rising in her throat. "I would never."

You say that now, a voice curled in the back of her head, *but what if he hurts you? He stands between you and safety. He wants to hurt you. You must defend yourself. Seize the knife.*

It was not her own voice.

"You are possessed, Alba," Elías said, low and fervent. "And I no longer think you were in danger of being harmed by whoever killed Romero. I think you killed him."

XX

Alba

ALBA SAT WITH her head in her hands on the ground, her knees pulled up to her chest. Elías stood over her; every muscle in his body was tense. As if he were ready to fight.

Or to defend himself.

From her.

From what coursed through her, what spurred her anger and curled cold at the back of her mind, rattling its tail in warning.

He is wrong.

She pressed her hands to her head. If only she could thrust her hands into her skull and sink them into the darkness to untangle these knots. Loosen the snarled threads. Make things make sense.

If Elías was wrong and she was not possessed, then *why was she here?* Sleepwalking alone could not explain why she had attacked him with a knife, if what he said was true. Sweat still darkened his sleeping shirt. A wild fear lingered behind his eyes. These did not strike her as rehearsed.

Therefore: Was it true?

"I should go back to my room," she whispered, curling her fingers against her scalp. She wanted to sleep. She wanted to sink into dark oblivion and never wake. If only she could float forever on the silver river of sleep, tenderly rocked like a baby in a cradle. If only.

"I don't think you should," Elías said.

She peered up at him, taken aback by his refusal. "It would be very bad if we were discovered like this." In his room, in the middle of the night. Carlos would have no choice but to break their engagement to save face, and then not only would she and her parents be forced to leave the hacienda de minas behind but her mother would also arrange for her to be wed to someone else.

Her mind was water circling the belly of an hourglass, spiraling, spiraling, spiraling...

"We won't be discovered," he said firmly, as if determination alone could make it true.

He crossed the space between himself and the knife and picked it up. He grasped it gingerly, as if it were a serpent about to strike him.

"I fear," he began, "that if you return to your room and fall asleep, it will happen again."

It. Said with the kind of emphasis that she would reserve for a plague, or a nightmare.

A shudder coursed through her. She rested her forehead against her knees, letting her arms fall to the floor. A helpless gesture, yes, for what else could she do? She felt like a slaughtered pig drained of blood, her mouth dry, her shoulders weak. She was aching and exhausted, in a room in the house she had never been to before but that she had found in her sleep. Alone with the one man—the only man—whose presence made her feel as clumsy-footed as a fawn.

And she was alone with him because she had tried to kill him.

She should rise and leave, disregarding Elías's fears—for the reality of Mamá discovering her in this room was more tangible than the threat of possession.

But she could not. Even lowering her legs so that her thighs rested on the floor, even leaning back against the bed, sapped her of energy. She sighed and shut her eyes.

"Don't fall asleep," Elías warned.

"I won't," she mumbled, but she could already feel it slipping into her face like morning mist into a valley: slowly creeping, one tendril at a time, and she welcomed it, she wanted the gray unconsciousness to fall over her with cool comfort and—

Cold against the side of her face.

She opened her eyes to see Elías pulling a hand away from her. He had put the back of his hand against her cheek.

He had placed the knife somewhere she hadn't seen. Intentionally? Ha. No doubt in case—God forbid—whatever infected her attacked him again.

"It will come back if you fall asleep," he said.

His intonation moved through her swift and cold, like a bolt of lightning in the dark, lifting the hairs on her arms and leaving gooseflesh in its wake.

It.

"You must stay awake," he said. A shuffle of clothing and the scuff of feet on the floor; he sat on the ground next to her with a thump, his back leaning against the bed.

He had that book from the workshop in his lap.

"What is that?" she asked, reaching for it.

He snatched it away and rested his palm on the cover protectively.

"Constantinople," he murmured. "There is a book bazaar, a famous one, where you can find anything you have ever dreamed of.

I barely remember picking it up, but it was a curiosity. So I did." He ran a thumb down its spine—a gesture that was almost sensual in nature. "I wasn't familiar with its contents, not even as I packed for the Indies. What luck," he said, darkly, for luck had nothing to do with the situation they found themselves in, sitting on the floor in a strange place, isolated, alone, danger humming at their backs.

Or, in Alba's case, in her back—a heavy sensation, a pressure, almost like the tenderness of her belly during her cycle—weighed at the top of her spine and in the base of her skull. A headache, she had told herself.

It had never occurred to her that it might be something foreign.

"If you hate your family so much, why did you come here?" she asked.

"If you dislike Carlos so much, why did you?" he countered softly.

"I never said that I disliked him," she said.

"Your body speaks otherwise," he said. "Every time I see you together you look like you have a plank of wood shoved up—"

"I beg your pardon!"

If his intention was to keep her awake with sheer force of indignation, he was succeeding.

"—up the back of your dress," he finished, a note of slyness in his voice.

She sputtered as she fought for words. Settled on some, though as she spoke them, she could hear how stupid they sounded: "I like him."

His laughter was like mesquite in woodsmoke. A hint of coarseness, an unexpected texture. A sense that she would find any smoke without that bite forever lacking.

"A powerful declaration of love," he said. "Isn't the wedding in May?"

"April." She hoped that the grumble in her voice conveyed the glare she gave him, even if he could not see it in the dark. "If at all."

"If at all!" he crowed. "Now that's something to talk about. Getting cold feet now that you've seen the state of this place?"

If she was being honest, it was the state of this place that gave her parents cold feet. She would have to fight tooth and nail to get to the altar.

"I don't want to talk about him," she said.

"My apologies, of course. Let us return to the subject of my dead wife," Elías said dryly. "Let us excavate every wound I have to offer in the interest of keeping you from sleeping and *attacking me again*. That seems perfectly fair."

Guilt struck with a sour pang. She pulled her knees back up toward her chest and set her forehead against them. The fabric of her dress pressed against her eyelashes; she shut her eyes. She must resist the heavy invitation of sleep.

"I met him when we were children. He was kind to me." Her mind flitted back to dusty curtains, her rear growing numb from sitting on the floor for hours. The safety of the dark. The security of knowing that, despite everything, she was not alone.

They were allies then, and they would remain so now. She would not reveal her true reasons for wanting to marry him to anyone, even someone she trusted . . . not least because Carlos clearly disliked that particular person so much. "He knows me, or knows me well enough, and it's comfortable."

"You *like* him. He's *comfortable*," Elías repeated. Lifting her head, she caught a glimpse of a gesture in the dark. Was he miming . . . fanning himself? "I am overcome by the heat of your passion."

Mockery was a veil, a disguise she wore with skill to conceal other emotions: anger, fear, loathing. She was well acquainted with its use. And here? She could taste jealousy behind the words.

He was jealous of Carlos. Envy was a sin. She should not relish it. She should not rejoice at its presence.

She should not.

She flattened her mouth to a straight line, fighting the pleasure that threatened to lift its corners.

"I challenge you to find someone in Nueva España who would both please my parents and not disgust me," she said. "If not him, Mamá would have me marry some duke three times my age. Someone who has no respect for me and only cares about filling his wife with heirs."

"And six times as wealthy, no doubt," Elías said. "Can't say I don't see the wisdom in that."

"You would marry for money?"

"If it got me out of this mess." Elías gestured expansively into the dark: at Casa Calavera, at the mine beyond its walls. "Marital bliss is not something I am accustomed to anyway. Why not get some financial stability out of the union, if not love?"

"Yet you mock that I find Carlos comfortable," Alba said.

"I'm not mocking. I simply don't believe you," Elías countered. "Do you even like being out here with them?"

Them, he said. As if they were not his own family. She exhaled, long and slow. She wanted to be here. She fought to stay, even when every voice in her head urged her to flee. The reasons why were none of Elías's business.

"No," she said. "Though I wonder if our days here are numbered." Silence, but she could almost hear him saying *go on*. "I am trying my best to prevent it. I don't want to talk about it."

"Señorita, I must beg you to explain. I want very little else in this world," Elías said.

She let herself smile this time—but grimly.

"I have been trying to keep my parents in check, but they have been on edge," she said. "Heraclio has done little to endear himself to Mamá, and not enough to assuage Papá's concerns about his finances. I think Papá . . . he wants to call in the debt. Sooner rather than later. No matter what I say to them."

"And no wedding," Elías said, his low whistle expressing how he appreciated the enormity of what Papá might do to his family. "For you will leave us ruined in the mud."

A shift of blankets to Alba's left. Elías leaned his head back to rest it on the mattress. As if he were staring up at the ceiling in despair, or resignation.

"Thank you for nothing, Victoriano," he said at the ceiling. "You've done it again."

A glimmer of a question in the back of her mind, all her own. Would he know why Victoriano had told Papá about a foundling infant? Did he know anything about that? Perhaps his father had written about it, perhaps there had been some hint . . .

But Elías had arrived at Mina San Gabriel at the same time as her. He was as much a stranger to this place and its history as she was.

"If Papá plans to let the axe fall, I'll let you know. It would be best to get on that ship to the Philippines," she said.

No reply from Elías.

"When does the fleet leave from Acapulco?" she asked.

"Middle of April," he said. Another long pause. "I had assumed I would find a place on a ship next year."

"I am doing all I can to hold them off," Alba said. "For if they do, I will have to wed someone else. Or go to a convent." She worried her lip again. It was beginning to throb, the pain dull and persistent. "Perhaps I should give up and be sent to a convent."

"You don't have to control them, you know," Elías said. "If they want to go, let them. Let them ruin Heraclio. Let them return to

Zacatecas and bleed out from matlazahuatl. Let them bear the burden of their own mistakes."

"Easy for a man to say," she said, sharper than she intended. "I don't have a choice but to try and control them. It's my life in the balance." It was her autonomy. Her happiness. Her body.

"We always have choices," Elías said, then trailed off, as if he had wandered into a thought and gotten lost there. "It's hard to make the right ones, though."

When Alba sighed, it loosened something in her shoulders; they sagged.

"No sleeping," Elías said. "Please," he added, with a gentleness so tender it made her teeth ache pleasantly. "I don't want to hurt you."

"And I don't want to hurt you," she said, letting the back of her skull rest on the mattress. It was heavy, so heavy.

Sleep, it whispered. *Sleeeeeep.*

She lifted her head.

The words walked up the back of her skull like fingertips across a waxed tabletop, coaxing and smooth—yet undeniably foreign.

Something was wrong. She knew this. Every time she put her feet to the ground in the morning and felt the unmistakable sensation of gravel pushing into her bare feet, she felt wrongness ring metallic and cold in her bones. Denial had not helped at all.

And now that Elías had put it into words, she could not avoid it.

"Perhaps I should speak to Padre Bartolomé," she said.

"No."

The fervor in his voice surprised her. "Excuse me?" fell from her mouth before she could stop it.

"He is a direct line to the Inquisition," Elías said. "He threatened Heraclio with them, when he told him to destroy the shrine."

"Calling them would ruin this family as badly as my father

could. He wouldn't hurt Carlos like that," she dismissed. "All I need is a confession and blessing, perhaps some holy water..."

"He will call the Inquisition."

"But I am innocent," Alba said. "If I have an affliction, it was not my fault—"

"Alba," Elías said, softly this time. "A man is dead."

She stopped speaking.

"That... that wasn't me," she said. Her throat felt thick. "I didn't do it."

Or had she?

"Just as you didn't come in here?" he said. "With a knife, and attack me?"

"It *wasn't me*," Alba said, a panic rising in her voice. Wetness—from frustration, from fear, from how powerless she felt—stung her eyes. "I would *never* hurt you."

"I know," he said. "I don't know you well, but I do know that."

He loosed a sigh of his own—exhausted, at a loss. "Everyone here is a stranger to me, even my own kin, but somehow, not you. Ever since that night we met. God help me," he added, a soft, sad *ha* punctuating the thought. Warmth rushed up her cheeks. "I don't believe in fate or destiny. But I have learned the hard way that I must listen to my gut. And in my gut, I fear... I don't want you to be harmed, and I fear going to the priest will harm you."

Her eyes had adjusted to the dark. It was still full night, but she could see marks around his neck. Long, scored marks, as if someone had scratched him. Discoloration that in the light might be redness, might already be bruising.

It was easy to be bold in the dark. She reached and ran her fingertips over the marks, feeling how his skin rose into low welts over his neck and down his collarbone, to the hollow of his throat. There thrummed his pulse; it picked up pace, beginning to race hers. Or perhaps that was her imagination.

She dropped her hand.

"I'm so sorry," she whispered.

"It wasn't you. Not exactly," he said, low and rough. Again, she thought of woodsmoke. Of bite and spice. Of what that voice might taste like against her mouth. "Don't be sorry."

Had any man ever spoken to her with such gentleness? Another brush of softness and her composure would shatter. She had never met anyone like him before. Apart from Carlos, he was the one man whose presence did not inspire fear for her own well-being. Fear for her freedom.

No, in fact. He wanted to preserve that freedom. He wanted to safeguard it from a force far more threatening than another man.

She shuddered.

"I want this thing gone," she said.

"Then we fight it," he said.

Had anyone stood by her side and fought for her?

"How?"

Elías patted the book in his lap, a single gesture, firm and determined: "We fight dirty, that's how."

XXI

Alba

ANY OTHER DAY, siesta's thick, harsh slants of light would send Alba collapsing into bed, her leaden eyelids falling shut at last. Her every bone ached for it. Instead, she crept out of the house, tripping over the toes of her lace boots with exhaustion and scuffing their polished points.

She entered Elías's workshop without announcing herself and found him crouched on the ground, his book open before him. One hand tracing a line, the other following it with charcoal.

His shirtsleeves were pushed up his forearms. These were muscled and tanned by the sun; the sight of them sent a flush of heat down her throat. She hastened to remind herself that they were arms, nothing worth noting. Arms smudged with dirt and charcoal, for what he drew on the ground arced around him in a circle.

"What is this?"

He looked up with a start. "An experiment." Hair fell into his face; he brushed it away quickly, leaving a smudge of charcoal along one cheekbone. "How are you feeling?"

She had not eaten enough. She spent the morning numb, nauseous, Padre Bartolomé's sermon a dull buzz as she sat in Mass next to Mamá. As if a pickaxe were breaking a new tunnel through the side of her skull, above one temple. As if sand filled the hollows beneath her eyes, weighing them down with itchy grit. Mercury undulated through her mind, formless, heavy, reflecting light at deceitful angles.

Elías wiped his hands on his trousers and stood, his brows drawing together as he studied her.

Her heart raced as if she had run here from Casa Calavera; she could break out in cold sweat any moment now, and sweating was not a comely state. And, despite everything, she was shocked to realize that she *cared* about appearing comely before him. Had she not checked her face in the silver hand mirror before leaving her room? She found it wan, yes, but she cared enough to pinch the skin above her cheekbones and adjust her hair.

If someone had asked her weeks ago which would be more shocking to her, the fact that her sleepwalking was driven by demonic forces or that she would be sent into a girlish fluster by a rough-hewn peninsular with a sordid history...

Well.

Naturally she would have been more shocked by the notion of demonic possession.

That did not make the warmth that rose in her cheeks as Elías studied her less unsettling. She did not blush before men. She never had. As a child, at twelve or thirteen, she entertained vivid fantasies of gilded strangers on horseback, riding into the courtyard of their house to spirit her away to some castle. But then she was forced to speak to men, and the fantasies dissolved like sugar in hot water, leaving a fading sweetness that quickly turned stale between teeth.

He was waiting for an answer to his question. What on earth was she supposed to say? *Oh, feeling awful, but much better now that I'm in your presence. Still exhausted, but don't worry, I won't give in. Wouldn't want to murder you in my sleep.*

She shrugged, feigning nonchalance.

"It is what it is." She approached the circle and walked its perimeter, studying the black glyphs.

They studied her back.

Or perhaps she imagined it.

"We're going to do this," she said. She meant for it to sound determined, but when she heard her own voice, it warbled with doubt.

"If you want," he said. "If you're ready."

She nodded, once and curtly.

"All right," he said, and resumed his work on the floor.

She clasped her hands as she watched in silence. They were clammy.

An experiment, he had said.

She would never be ready for what lay before her: marks that seemed blacker than the charcoal they were sketched in, their foreignness sending alarms ringing through her. Would the Devil himself appear in the circle when it was completed? Perhaps he would give a cordial bow and ask for her hand in marriage or perhaps for some of her blood to sign the bottom of a contract like in the plays from Spain she had read.

Perhaps the Devil was already inside her.

A shudder unspooled up her back. She crossed her arms over her chest and hugged herself as Elías muttered at the floor.

She did not want to do this. It was wrong, yes, but worse, it frightened her.

At the other end of the scale: A knife glinted in the dark of her memory. The scratch marks on Elías's neck had reddened since last night. Her wrists ached; bruises had bloomed across them over the course of the last few hours, causing her to tug at the wrists of her sleeves to ensure they were covered. There would be no explaining such marks to Mamá.

She could have killed him. He was strong and had fought back, but what if... what if she had tried to harm someone else? Romero was gone. The thought of him filled her with loathing, but what if it had been someone she cared about?

Her parents?

Someone innocent, like María Victoriana?

Or perhaps Padre Bartolomé?

A shift in the back of her skull, like a cat stretching and resettling on a sunny windowsill. An image, bright as the memory of the knife, of Bartolomé splayed at the bottom of a ravine: arms akimbo, the cross around his neck shattered. His skull broken like an egg, his hair wet with blood and pale pink splatter—

She shook her head sharply to clear it.

Elías leaned back on his heels to inspect his work, cross-referencing the pages of the book with the markings on the floor.

"In the study of alchemy, we follow the laws of science," he said. "If you and I don't know what matter of force we are dealing with, then we cannot pick our tools appropriately."

He flipped the pages of the book back; then he rose and stepped over to Alba to show her, taking care to avoid any of the markings he had made.

"Here, there is a list of different classes of demons," he said, pointing to a line of writing in red—a heading, perhaps, luridly set apart from the rest of the black on the page and the slanting handwriting in the margins. "According to San Cipriano, each class has a different method of eradication. Say, for example . . ."

His finger moved down the page; his eyes skipped back and forth over the words, as if he were reading and translating at the same time.

He bit his lip as he did so, then released it slowly.

Elías was worried about the Inquisition if she spoke to Padre Bartolomé. What concerned her the most: the prospect of saying the phrase *sinful thoughts* aloud in confession for a second time. She wanted to cringe with her whole body at the thought.

"Imagine a weed with roots that go deep into the ground," Elías said. She steered her imagination away from his mouth and in the direction he suggested. "If you try to eradicate the weed by simply chopping off the blossoms, or even cutting it down to the earth, it will grow back."

"Because the roots are still there," she said.

"Exactly."

The thought of roots spreading through her bones, pushing through soil, curling around her joints and pulling tight, tight, tight . . . it made her want to yank her skin off and rip the roots out with her bare hands.

"So we need to try and determine what kind of . . . *thing* we are dealing with?" she asked.

"Yes," Elías said. "I'm going to translate precisely what the book says as we do so. You must know and understand everything that is happening."

"That will take too much time," she said with a dismissive wave of the hand. "Just get it over with."

"Alba." He lowered the book and turned so that he stood directly before her. Her eyes came to the level of his chest; she kept her gaze there, shyness preventing them from rising.

"Look at me," he said. "Please."

She lifted her eyes slowly, tracing the buttons of his work shirt, skipping over stray threads from buttonholes that needed mending. The rise of his chest and the opening of his shirt; the suggestion, faintly, of dark hair beneath. His throat. The scratches she had left there last night. The stubble on his chin, the faint scar on his upper lip.

Meeting his gaze was not a sin. It should not feel like one.

"If we do this, when we do this, I want you to understand every single step," he said softly. "I will not do anything without knowing that you are ready, you are willing, and you understand what is about to happen."

"As you wish," she said. She could taste the indifference in the words. Perhaps he could hear it, for he continued.

"If you ever feel uncomfortable, or if you do not understand what is happening and do not want it, tell me to stop. I will stop. Immediately. I swear it," he added, low and passionate. "This is your life. Your fate. You are in control."

A frisson passed through her shoulders—not a shudder, but a pleasant sensation. Control made her feel safe, and he had sensed that. He was giving her a gift.

She accepted it. "I will."

"Do you promise?" he said, and when she nodded, he put the book down on the worktable next to her. "Do you want to practice saying no?"

She tilted her head to the side, considering what he meant.

"I was never taught how to say no," he said. "I simply did what I knew people expected of me, sometimes before they asked. To please them. To be less of a burden. I ended up in regrettable situations. You don't strike me as someone who was taught to say no either."

He took her hand. Her heart leaped to her throat as he held it up against his, palm to palm. Then, he pushed gently against her.

"Tell me to stop," he said.

"Stop."

He did.

Then he pressed again, harder this time, a gentle force that could bring him closer to Alba if she let him, close enough that they might breathe the same air, close enough that she might feel the warmth of his body.

"Don't stop," she said.

This surprised him enough that the weight of his hand lifted.

The air between them shifted. Her heart had resumed its place in her chest, but now it was racing, terrified by her own brazenness.

Elías pressed his palm against hers again. She had been watching their hands; now, she looked up at him, tilting her chin to do so. His eyes were so dark she could barely distinguish pupil from iris.

"Tell me to stop."

She felt the rasp of his voice more than heard it. He had shifted closer to her; if she wanted to, if she were bold enough, she could lift herself onto her toes and place her cheek against his. Feel the roughness of his stubble. Compare it to his voice.

"But I don't want you to," she whispered.

His breathing hitched. He did not stop pressing against her hand. He was woodsmoke and the bite of mesquite and the warmth of skin. He inclined his head; hair that had been tucked behind his ear fell forward and tickled her cheek.

"Tell me to stop."

The throb of her pulse in her ears, the warmth that coursed from their joined hands through her body, the flutter of anticipation of *more* that perched on her lips, ready to take flight—it was all sinful. She wanted to sink her teeth into it. To know what it tasted like. To know how it gave.

"Don't stop," she whispered.

His eyes fell to her mouth. Dark lashes, lowered and bashful. A grown man, bashful before her? A ripple of something like victory; it vanished in a swift, desperate pang as his lips brushed hers. A kiss, yes, but one that was almost timid in its softness. Chaste.

She stood on the edge of a precipice. She could step back, or she could leap forward.

She caught his kiss between her teeth and returned it stripped of chastity.

And this was what sin tasted like: lips that were soft, a mouth that gave with an unutterable tenderness. It was walls melting away. It was a blazing road tearing through her toward an unknown horizon, hot and white as the center of a star. It was their hands breaking apart to explore the profane geographies of bodies: his to her waist, to her back, her breath catching as he pulled her close and held her fast. It was his chest against hers, the hardness of his back muscles under her palms. His calloused hands running up her body and leaving burning embers in their wake, brushing against the soft flesh of her neck, cradling her jaw as if she were delicate glass. She wanted to be held as if she were delicate, she wanted to be broken. Through headiness thicker than wine, she thought: *I want you to shatter me.*

"Don't stop," she begged.

What a feeling it was, to *want*, to crave, to bend toward someone's touch, so desperate for it that it was exquisite, that it felt akin to pain. To be bruised by a reverent mouth, to gasp when teeth found the soft fruit of lips and bit, to drink his moan as if it were the one oath binding her to this world. To scarcely breathe, for what was the work of breathing when mouths could do this?

"Alba," he prayed, for it was a prayer, anguished in its desire. If—

The creak of the door opening.

The spell shattered with a gasp, with a clumsy shuffle of feet, with the swirl of skirts and the abrupt placement of bodies on opposite sides of the table. With thundering hearts. With faces swiftly rearranged into studied curiosity—not at each other but facing the door.

María Victoriana stood crowned by afternoon sun, a single brow raised. Even the set of her weight, balanced to hold the basket of food before her, had a sardonic cast to it.

"Didn't expect to see you here, señorita," she said, the words lengthening into a drawl. "I hope I am not interrupting."

Their chorus of *no, not at all, come in* could not have been more stilted. Alba fought against her heaving chest, fought the urge to lower her burning face and hide it in her hands, fought the urge to cringe at the false ring of their voices. She wished she could vanish into the ground, not because she was ashamed of what she had done—for she knew without a doubt that she would do it again, if given the chance, a thousand times—but at the fact that they had been discovered.

Her heart raced out of time with itself, fighting and failing to find its footing even as Elías had smoothly resumed studying the circle with charcoal in one hand and the book in the other. She could barely arrange her thoughts into sentences. He might hide his feelings well, but she would wager that despite his coolness, despite the undisturbed calm in his face, the book was open to the wrong page.

"Thank you, María Victoriana," he said. Affecting an unperturbed air, he turned the page of the book. "I appreciate not having to go to the house."

His hand trembled.

"I wouldn't want to deal with them either," María Victoriana said. "Did you know that Heraclio . . ."

Her voice trailed off as she stepped into the workshop and her eyes fell on the circle that Elías stood over.

She set the basket on the table with a decisive thump. Steam and the aroma of warm tortillas rose from within.

"That," she declared, "looks rash."

"Rash?" Alba repeated.

Elías flipped a page of the book, eyelashes lowered as he scanned for something. Turned another. He *had* been on the wrong page.

"I'm not sure what you mean," he said.

"Black magic. Are you insane?" María Victoriana said, gesturing at the marks on the floor. "That priest is ready to put people to death for drawing lines of mercury around the town and putting candles in a cave. You're the one who said you weren't supposed to do anything rash when you're infatuated with someone."

A dark flush rose to Elías's cheeks. "I didn't mean—"

"Why don't you throw yourself off a cliff to save them all the trouble of killing you?" María Victoriana snapped, a sudden wet brightness flashing in her eyes.

Her voice had lurched high and ragged, propelled by a surge of emotion that took Alba aback. Perhaps Elías thought his kin were all strangers, but here, he might be wrong. María Victoriana cared for him.

"This is me trying to not get killed, believe it or not," Elías shot back, but his words chased the girl's turned back. "Wait—"

She had spun on her heel and fled the workshop. The scattered cluck of chickens from beyond the adobe walls announced that she had run in the direction of the house.

Silence hung heavy in the workshop. What had burned between Alba and Elías was now rudely doused with a cold, metallic hiss.

Elías chewed his lip again. He, too, was still breathing hard. "I really hope she doesn't tell anyone that we are in here alone," he muttered.

Somehow, this had slipped down the list of Alba's concerns. Yes, it was inappropriate that they were in here unaccompanied—and discovered in such a position—but María Victoriana was right. Of all the crimes that had occurred in this room, the presence of the dark glyphs on the ground was undeniably the worst.

"And what if she tells someone about that?" she said, pointing at the ground.

"I think she fears Bartolomé too much," he said. "I get the sense that they all do, with this idolatry business."

Alba leaned forward and rested her forehead on the table before her. Her racing heart was beginning to slow. But with the panic of being discovered draining away, she felt as if the marrow had been sucked from her bones. Before she had entered the workshop, she was a husk, dry and wilting; kissing Elías had set her aflame, and now she was an extinguished candle. A single curl of smoke rising and dissipating.

"I don't want this to be real," she said into the table.

"Neither do I," Elías said softly. "Well," he amended, "not all of it."

She lifted her head. There was color in his cheeks again; he was focused on the book very studiously.

He meant her. He meant *them*.

Alas. How desperately she wished that they had not been interrupted. But perhaps it was for the best—María Victoriana said the glyphs on the floor were rash, but what of their behavior? If Elías was right, and Alba was possessed by something that had attacked him with a knife . . . the truth was, she did not know the laws of when she would be taken over. For all they knew, the distraction of each other might be a perfect opportunity for it to emerge. To seize her and put Elías in harm's way.

She took in a shaking, unsteady breath.

She yearned to retreat in time, to step back into his arms. But cruel Time had shoved them out of that moment, lustrous and perfect in its headiness, and locked the gates behind them. She could only move forward.

"If this possession is real," she began, and then hesitated, choosing her words carefully, "do you think it will be difficult to eradicate? Do you think it has . . . deep roots?"

A moment of silence as Elías considered this.

"I fucking hope not," he said at last.

To someone raised in a gilded cage as she had been, his profanity should have been shocking. From him, it had always been bracing. Now, it was a shock of cold water. A harsh reminder of the severity of the situation.

"Only one way to find out," he added.

He inhaled and exhaled swift and hard, as if steadying himself. He gestured at the circle.

Alba swallowed. There was only forward.

She stepped into it.

XXII

Elías

THE MOMENT THAT Alba stepped into the circle, the air in the workshop changed.

When she turned to face him, it was as though she moved through water: with a slowness that seemed caught in time, where light did not strike her the way it ought to. There was never much light in the workshop, not with the shutters closed against the cold. There was only one open now, to the south where there was no wind, and it allowed a shaft of white to slice the shadows between Elías and Alba.

She had been wan when she first came to the workshop, but now her cheeks burned with high points of feverish color. Her lips were reddened by his own mouth. Her hair was in a simple plait, as if she had indeed been about to sleep for the siesta. It fell low between her shoulder blades and had swung as she turned. He wanted to wrap it around his hand like a rope. To admire its luster and strength. To lift it to his lips and inhale deeply of its smell. To pull her toward him and feel that sinfully eager gasp against his throat—

He held a book of the occult in his hands. He was about to step right over the boundary between the licit and not, to follow a dead sorcerer's instructions and address the demonic.

And at a time like this, *that* was what he thought about?

Her *hair*?

He was a ship lost at sea. Sextant overboard, no wind in his sails, and only her star, her brilliant star, guiding him through the dark.

It felt like falling. It felt like knowing precisely where he was, for the first time in many, many long weeks.

"Fuck this," he breathed.

Of course it was here, in these barren mountains, in this cursed corner of the world, that he rediscovered the softest parts of his guts. This was where he found someone who made his heart beat out of time.

Good things had brushed past his life; he had even had the opportunity to grab some of them. The world offered him learning; he seized it like a dying man clawing for the light. Learning made him proud of himself. It gave him worth. He found a place to live that instilled peace, where the sun rose and set over hills and swift currents. He found companions that he did not deserve, from whom he had stolen the moment he was given the chance.

To come here.

He had shattered enough fragile things to know that he must treat them with care. To pay attention, when something caught the light and held his attention fast. When something made him want to be good.

Or, in this case: very, very bad.

"I'm ready," she said. That lift of the chin, that same determination with which she had said Don't stop.

Those words were carved so deeply into his chest that merely thinking them made him want to groan. He might never sleep again.

He set the book on the table next to him, open to the questioning incantations. He had notes transliterating aljamía into plain castellano with its Roman characters. He had taken a spare page out of one of his father's journals to write out the Latin that occurred mid-page that the scribe had rendered, as phonetically as he could, in Arabic letters.

He left the index finger of his right hand on the first incantation and looked up at Alba one last time before he began.

She was not fragile. The bruises around his neck were proof of that. She was a woman of flesh and blood. She would not break.

"Be strong," he said. "Tell me to stop whenever you need to rest. Whenever—"

"Stop stalling." The syllables were edged in flint.

He had been. He was afraid of what lurked under her skin, burrowed like a worm, like a parasite. The infection that he was about to willingly call forth.

If she had the courage to face it head-on, then so must he.

"We begin," he said, and at last, he did.

IN THE STUDY of alchemy, there were practitioners who pursued it as if it were a science—this was the correct path, for science was what it was, was it not? Weights and measures, chemical reactions. Stoked embers and beaded sweat.

But some students approached alchemy with gold glinting in their eyes. Some had traveled far, and would travel farther still, in search of the philosopher's stone. These belonged to a school of alchemy that Elías had not touched, one where skill was not built with one's own aching muscles but bought and bartered for. Men who would not dirty their hands with real work reached into darkness and signed contracts in blood. By promising the Devil their souls, they received the tools they needed to seek eternal life.

Or so the stories went.

It was said that the world had but a finite amount of power. There were men who were born with it—who were often burned for their witchcraft—and there were men who had to buy power. The reason these men made deals with the Devil was because they could not otherwise harness the power for the acts they wished to undertake, and so they bargained with the only immortal thing they might ever possess: their souls.

They were lazy.

Every time Elías had taken a caique across the Bosporus to Üsküdar, power shuddered beneath the boat. Every time he stepped into the darkness of Mina San Gabriel, here, on the far side of the world, in the exile his greed had doomed him to, he could feel that power wash over him like cold water.

This was what Almadén had taught him: Fight or rot, yes, but in its foul caverns, in the dark, among the screams and the soot, he had grown a sense of wonder. A sense that the deep places of the world were *other*. That alongside ore ran mystery—mystery that no man who lived life on the surface could understand.

Now, in this workshop, with a grimoire beneath his fingertips and a rare good thing encircled by the marks of black sorcery before him, he turned to that mystery.

Incantations rolled from tongue and tooth; he paused to explain their meaning to Alba, then continued. He could repeat with confidence now, with rhythm—albeit imperfect—and guide his starving mind as it reached for sustenance, as it grasped for energy, for air to feed the black flame that burned in his breast.

He could reach around him. As he recited, he became acutely aware that the room was crowded. That bodies—beings?—shifted behind him and jostled for purchase within the adobe walls. That if he took his eyes off Alba and allowed himself to investigate what forked things flickered in the corners of his vision . . .

He would not. He would not reach out around him.

Instead, he shut his eyes.

He had made no bargains for power, nor had he been born with it. He was unextraordinary. He was no one.

He envisioned his hand gripping a pickaxe: knuckles pale, teeth gritted. As he had been in Almadén, where he faced the power in the depth of stone with straining muscles and sweat.

In his mind, he swung the pickaxe and drove it deep into blackness.

Something surged forth in return.

It was a spring with rocks cleared from its mouth; a cloud that could no longer bear the weight of rain. Gleaming lustrous as mercury. Flush with it, chest and throat and cheeks hot, his eyes flew open.

Alba looked at him expectantly.

"Is that it?" she wondered.

The room was empty of demons or illusions of power; silence buzzed in his ears. It stretched long.

"No," he muttered. "Uh . . ." Had he read the incantation incorrectly? He dropped his gaze back to his notes, shuffled papers with hands that shook, squinted to see where he had gone awry.

From the circle where Alba stood, a low, guttural growl rose—at first it was no louder than that of a cat, but it built in depth and filled the room. It vibrated through his ribs, lifting every hair on his body in terror.

He turned to Alba.

She was gone.

A skull stared back at him, its bare teeth gnashing. Its jaw was held together by gristle and sinew but little else. A red tongue flicked behind teeth.

He met its gaze directly. Ignored how dry his mouth was, how his gut had turned to liquid with fear.

"What do you want with her?" he asked.

Given the circumstances, he should not have been shocked when it answered.

And yet.

"She is mine."

It was not Alba's voice. It had a strange timbre, a raspiness. It had the taste of old smoke, neither stale nor fading. It left a tang on the roof of his mouth, a sulfuric bite in his nose.

"She is her own," he replied. "Leave her be."

This was not in the script. It sprang to his lips in passion. Perhaps in error.

For the demon grinned.

Demon.

He named it and now he could see it.

Alba's dress was nothing but shredded rags. Beneath, there was white bone, only occasionally bound together by dried leathery skin. A mist slinked through the bones, gray as smoke and just as intangible: It slipped over and under ribs, caressing the cavity where heart and lungs should be, hanging around the gristle of her throat like a garland.

"Jealous, are you?" With no flesh, every grin from the demon was the same—too wide, with luridly red flashes of tongue. This one, however, left a clinging sensation of mockery on his. "Such greed." Somehow the mouth went wider, so wide. "Such *hunger*. Eat her flesh, lick fat and gristle. Suck the marrow from her bones. Do it. Take it. Go on."

Disgust tasted like bile; it swept up his gullet and lingered there as the demon went on.

"Take take, eat eat, pick the bones and drink deep," the demon sang, and Elías distinctly thought the word *sang*, for it was musical, it was rhythmic, and that oily mockery stained his clothes, his skin, was rank in his hair.

He flicked his eyes down at the book.

"I give you no power over myself," Elías announced, as instructed. He forced himself to look back up at the dry skin peeling off cheekbones, and those pits, the darkness that devoured all they stared at. "I reject your offer. Now tell me: What do you want?"

"I want you *dead*. Meddling busybody."

If only the demon would tell him something he didn't know.

"What do you want?" he repeated.

"The priesssssssst."

A glee, a hunger, a fey crackle in the air. The demon lurched forward. Feet scarcely touched the ground; Alba's ankles turned at angles they should not have, popping and cracking as the demon lifted its arms and reached for Elías.

The demon struck the boundary of the circle and wrenched back as if burnt. It hissed—not in pain, but long and low, with an anger so palpable, so searing, Elías was certain his hair might catch flame.

Then it laughed at him.

"You are *weak*," it said. "You will ebb and run dry. Patience is all I need," it added, hissing: "*Patience*."

A ring of dread, echoing like a gong. It was right. He would run dry. Already he felt as if he clung to consciousness by fingernails that were shredded and bled; the abyss beneath him yawned ravenous and closer, ever closer.

He did not have much time. Could he ask one more question, before he turned the page and began to close this ritual?

"Where does your power come from?" he rasped. His throat was so dry, he felt as if he spoke through a mouthful of ash. "I demand that you tell me."

Sinews flinched and twitched; its head snapped to the side, then rolled. Did resisting his question pain the demon? Good. He asked again: "Where does it come from?"

Its head lolled back; its arms lifted from its sides like a dancer's, languid.

Then a cry burst forth: wet and weak, almost a sob, almost a mew, almost... human. It sliced through him, a hot knife meeting tender flesh.

"Alba?" Was she fighting to be free?

The demon's neck snapped upright and it sprang forward, arms outstretched for him.

Coming for his throat.

Elías lifted his hand from El Libro de San Cipriano. His arms shook as if he had been pushing a boulder up a hill for hours; his shirt, soaked with sweat, clung to the low of his back.

He would not run dry. He would not allow Alba to suffer any longer. He held both hands before him, as if that alone could stop the demon.

It gave a strangled cry and fell back from the walls of the circle. Elías shuddered as if it had flung itself bodily against him. His teeth clashed together, crystalline sparks breaking wild across his vision. He gasped for air—his lungs were empty, so empty, as if he had been flung to the ground from a height, and every one of his bones shook from the impact.

He breathed. And he braced.

"I will take you!" it howled. "I will punish you."

He would not let it break through. Black dread was all he knew, all he felt, and that alone gave him the strength to be a wall to the demon's battering ram. He did not know anything except this: He could not let it through.

Burning flesh seared his nostrils; bile swept up rotten from his gut, threatening to choke him.

He braced. He reached down, into the stone beneath his feet.

Rivers of mercury rose in reply. They flooded his veins as if through a cracked dam.

"Begone," he roared. His throat was shredded flesh. His cheeks were slick with wet—tears, or blood, or the demon's spittle, he did not know. It was brinier than sweat, hotter than his fear. It lined his lips with tin and sulfur, stinging as if his mouth were an open wound. "I have had enough of you. *Begone.*"

A crack of a whip. A snap at the back of his skull, like the crack of bone, a muscular tweak that left his face throbbing with pain.

It had killed him. This was death.

He fell to his knees, a husk, bleeding from every orifice.

He lifted his head—blood slipped from his nostrils, pouring over his lips, dripping from his chin to his trousers. One circle of darkness appeared in his vision, then another, then another.

The taste of blood was warm and ironlike, salt and red.

"Elías."

Sunlight streamed into the workshop. A blast of cold air from behind him—the door had swung open; the window shutters had fallen from their hinges and struck the ground.

Bright, clean, fresh.

Alba stood illuminated before him, bright as a saint. Her face: her own. Lashes and lips and cheeks flush with blood. Her chest was whole—her ribs were hidden beneath flesh, her clothing draped over breasts and waist. No mist. No gristle. No clacking teeth and lolling tongue.

Dark eyes, wet with tears. Lashes that caught them and held them like the jewels they were, glistening and shattering the light into a thousand colors.

Something dripped from his chin. Absently, he reached up—his fingers found wet. Warmth. When he drew the hand back, it was slick with blood.

Oh.

His hands flew to his face, searching for the source of the blood. His eyes? His ears? No—only his nose. Streaming as if it had been broken, but already the flow had slowed.

He was not dead. But the blood was real.

Also real: Alba stepping forward, out of the circle, on uncertain feet. Falling to her knees before him. The workshop filled with the soft exhale of skirts. With her breathing, and with his, hoarse and unsteady. She reached forward for his hands. Hers were ice, his fire, and she dropped them as if scalded. They fell, too heavy—then rested, palms up, on his thighs.

His fingertips were black. As if he had dipped them in ink or run them through soot. Smoke rose from his fingertips, leaving a hint of sulfur on the air.

"Are you all right?" he asked.

She was whole, but like him, her clothes were dark with perspiration. She shook. Her lips were dry; they had split in places, the seams bright with delicate lines of blood.

She shook her head. "We need help."

Her voice cracked. He sensed what she was going to say before the words came. He was not surprised. He was relieved. He could have killed them both in his hubris, and she was right.

"We need Padre Bartolomé," she said.

XXIII

Alba

THIS POSSESSION, SHE remembered.

She remembered feeling as if her voice had been wrenched from her clenched fists, no matter how hard she fought to keep it. She felt as if every one of her fingers had been shattered. She felt her jaw working but heard no sound coming out; she felt a mist rising in her, filling her lungs, choking her, moving from her chest into her face, up her nose and stinging as if it were water rushing back into her skull.

She heard it.

She heard Elías, too—a voice rippling as if through a deep underground cavern, resonant with echo and movement.

But it was *it* that filled her skull and jerked her around as if she were a puppet on strings.

This was what happened when she woke with her bare feet aching and dirty from having walked over gravel. Her limbs animated by a spirit that was not her own. Seized, stolen, wrenched from her.

That's what it was: theft.

A need for justice burned in her. It wasn't fair. This was her body.

Was this what the demon had done to kill Romero? Seized Alba as she slept and spilled blood with her hands?

It filled her with revulsion. With a sense of helplessness and despair. Elías and the demon carried on, out there, in the realm of bodies and voices, but in here, behind her eyes, trapped in the fog of the demon's captivity, it was all Alba could do to stay aware. Time moved sluggishly.

Was this how defeat happened? With the desire to rest? Was this how her soul would be damned to eternity in Hell—her giving up to a demon because she was *tired*?

She forced herself to look, to listen, and when the entrapment broke, with a booming *begone*, Alba flooded through her own body with a flush of ecstasy.

Air was sharp and cool against her skin; every inch of her tingled as if it were a limb woken from bloodless sleep. She could levitate, if she wanted to. She could burst into flame.

Elías knelt on the ground before her, spent, bright blood streaming from his nose. When he took her handkerchief, it was with a wariness that bruised her.

He was afraid of her.

But he took her offered hand and allowed her to help him to his feet. He dabbed at his nose and winced. It had stopped bleeding, but his upper lip was streaked with blood; the handkerchief was a lurid masterpiece. He folded it up, but not before she caught hints of dark clots.

"We should speak to him now," Elías said. His voice trembled with exertion. "The priest."

This took her by surprise; it must have shown on her face, for he continued: "When siesta is over and the others wake, there will be no getting him alone to speak privately until after nightfall. And I do not want to wait until it is dark."

Sleep had fled her mind. She was restless. She could run to the mouth of the mine and back without her breath hitching, without breaking a sweat. Her body thrummed with life, and it was hers.

"But shouldn't you rest?" she wondered. She gestured to a chair by the hearth. "Sit with me," she said. "Catch your breath."

His eyes flitted to where she pointed, and a flash of yearning swept under his expression.

"No," he said slowly. "We ought to go now."

Did he not trust her? Did he worry that it was the demon who wanted him to stay, to prevent him from seeing Bartolomé?

It was a wise fear. This she had no choice but to admit.

THE EUPHORIA OF autonomy over her limbs faded as they walked back to the house and exhaustion set in, gray and itchy and heavy as a penitent's hair shirt. It seemed as if miles stretched between them and the house; with the siesta ensuring that the Monterrubios and Alba's parents alike were resting, they did not bother to hide.

It was as if each step sapped the flare of energy that had animated her in the workshop; she had burned bright and burned out, and she was again a husk. Dry, bloodless, parched.

She followed Elías down the hall, for he had murmured that he knew the way to the priest's room—he had seen Carlos disappear there in the evenings.

Elías stopped them before a door and raised his hand to knock.

She put a hand on his arm to stop him—for fear coursed through her, sour and swift as nausea.

He looked down at her in surprise; she loosened her grip so that her knuckles were no longer pale but held his arm down all the same.

"What is it?"

"We should go back," she whispered. "This is a mistake."

He frowned, searching her eyes—for the demon?

Was it the demon that was causing her to act this way? She did not think so—it felt like her own force that animated her; the taste of her fear was familiar. The sudden sense of *no* in her gut—that was not the demon. Or was it?

She wanted to trust herself, but she could not.

The priesssssssst.

Her breath caught. The demon had shown its cards. She released Elías's arm as if it had burned her.

"It doesn't want us to see him." She could feel the waver in her voice before she heard it; it sounded childish to her ears. Weak. Hot tears burned the corners of her eyes; she batted them away. This thing within her had stolen her confidence. She felt adrift without it. She felt unlike herself.

"I am afraid too," Elías whispered. "But I am here. You are not alone."

A tear rolled from the corner of her eye; she swept it away with a fierce, proud gesture. "Knock."

Elías did, twice and softly.

A shuffle from within; some movement toward the door. The door opened a crack.

From where she stood off to the side, she could not see Bartolomé's expression. She regretted this slightly—Elías, with his bloodied nose and hair falling out of its leather tie, was a sight. She wagered she looked no better: exhausted, shaking, her own hair pulling itself loose from its plait.

THE POSSESSION OF ALBA DÍAZ

"Padre," Elías said. "I'm sorry to disturb you. We wish to speak with you, and . . . it is urgent."

The door opened more, and Bartolomé peered out into the hall, looking for the *we* to whom Elías had referred.

He saw Alba.

He leaped back from the doorway in fright. A solid thunk; a hiss of pain. A mangled *joder*. When he opened the door and nodded for them to step inside, he held a hand to the side of his head.

A flush of mist shot through her skull like steam escaping the lid of a boiling pot.

Again, it hissed. Harder. Smash. Bleeeeeeed.

Her face stung behind her nose and eyes, as if she had inhaled water, but it relented and cleared.

"Please, come in," Bartolomé said through his grimace.

He ushered them inside without another word and shut the door softly behind them. His room had kept the austere look of the hacienda de minas before Mamá had descended with half of Zacatecas' interior adornments in tow: simple wooden furniture, plain white walls stained, near the fireplace, with years of soot. A single rug over the swept stone floor. A solitary chair by the hearth, which he gestured to for Alba. Elías lingered behind her right shoulder, a handsbreadth away.

Bartolomé produced a stool from near his bed and pulled it beneath him. He sat and faced Alba, leaning forward and watching her face carefully.

She wanted to split her skin and flee, to rush out of this room and get out of his presence. She stood suddenly, hands twitching at her sides.

"Never mind, Padre," she said, words jumbled and barreling over one another to get through her teeth. "It's not important. I'm sorry to have disturbed you."

A hand on her shoulder.

"Let's talk for a moment," Elías said. His tone was soft, even, as if he were calming a spooked animal.

She could feel Bartolomé watching this interaction, eyes moving from her face to the hand on her shoulder—so familiar, as if it belonged there—to Elías and back again.

Years ago, Papá had owned a white dog, one with pale eyes that were both shifty and watchful—they were as empty as the sky at noon, clear as a mirror. They were not eyes that inspired trust. The dog was already old and impatient when she was a child; it nipped her when it perceived her as being underfoot, which was often. Sometimes it drew blood.

"Will you sit?" Elías asked.

She did not want to sit. She wanted to wrench her head to the side and bite off his fingers, hear the crunch of bone between her teeth and—

The mist was in her face again, stinging her nose, clouding her eyesight. Her throat felt as if it were closing, as if it were turning to stone and twisting tight, tight, tight.

"Alba?" Elías's voice came from far away.

This was her body. Hers. She would be the master of it.

"I am not well, Padre," she said. Her voice vibrated with an undercurrent not her own, something dark, something that tasted of below, that was tinny on her palate. She swallowed.

"Physically or spiritually?" Bartolomé asked.

"Both, all of it," she said. "I need help."

It sounded like babble to her ears, but she said it all the same, and it felt freeing to do so. Her throat had loosened; it felt easy to swallow again.

But she had let down her guard too early.

For when Bartolomé asked her to describe what the matter was and Alba opened her mouth to reply, she was seized with a violent shaking.

Elías lifted his hand from her shoulder, mouth parted in shock, and looked at Bartolomé as if to say *this isn't me.*

The walls bent. The room was distorted, a kaleidoscope of color and rattling. She was a bag of dry bones, shaking and shaking. Clatter and smash and—

Firm hands on her shoulders.

"Alba," the tall man said. "Alba, can you hear me?"

She wanted everything to go dark. The priest had a rosary in his hand and the tall man was holding her too tightly, as if he would wrench her toward the priest. She had to get away, she had to get to the darkness, to stone and water, for there she could lick her wounds and recover, there she could plot—

"In nomine Patris, et Filii, et Spiritus Sancti. Amen," the priest murmured. First quietly, then again, and again, with more force, a muscle in his jaw flexing.

She would sink her teeth into that muscle. Ligament and gristle, wet and rubber against her teeth, rrrrrrrip from bone—

Water struck her face, so cold that it burned. Her flesh was seared, it would melt away.

Alba gasped.

She could have sworn that the water was a torrent, but it was not—when her eyes focused on Bartolomé, when she steadied, chest heaving, she saw his hand outstretched, water dripping from his fingertips. It was only a dew-like sprinkle from the small bottle he held with the rosary in his other hand.

Color flushed his cheeks; his eyes burned with an emotion that made her want to shrink back. When she did, her spine curling away from him as if she were a trapped animal, she was stopped by a solid body.

Elías stood behind her, his hands on her shoulders. A glance down showed his fingers gripping her so hard that they would doubtless leave marks. His knuckles were pale.

The tips of his fingers were black.

Not as black as they had been in the workshop—the color had faded somewhat—but the evidence was there all the same.

"I see," Bartolomé said. His voice shook, close to cracking. He cleared his throat. "I see."

"And that's not the worst of it, Padre," Elías said, voice hoarse as if he had been shouting.

"I thought I had seen something," Bartolomé said. "I thought I was wrong."

He lowered his outstretched hand. The motion was tentative, a test—could he, without her launching at him with a snarl?

He could, for she was spent. She slumped against Elías; her legs folded beneath her like playing cards.

Elías caught her beneath the armpits. A shift of his weight, a soft grunt, and he placed her in the chair opposite Bartolomé.

"Would you like water, señorita?" Bartolomé asked, and before she could reply that yes, her mouth was so dry, he was pouring her a cup from the pitcher at his nightstand. He was already back before her, crouching so that he was at her eye level.

An instinct pulled her away like hands on her shoulders. Her heart, weary though it was, lifted its exhausted head and panted.

But whose instinct was that—hers, or someone else's? *Something else's?*

This was *her* body and she would do with it what she wanted. She would speak to whom she wanted and not fantasize about mauling them. She would maintain control. It was her right.

She took the water from Bartolomé and drank. Her throat felt as if it were lined with inflamed welts; the water slaked her thirst, but swallowing pained her.

"I hoped it was the light playing tricks on me," Bartolomé said, softly, as if half to himself. "Or my own superstition, my fallibility. An overzealous imagination..."

"I thought the same," Elías said, "but I have seen too much, and in broad daylight, to be in any doubt that something is very wrong."

"Señorita," Bartolomé said softly.

She met his pale eyes. Flinched, then settled. Every muscle in her back tensed. Her shoulders ached with the desire to fling back, to get away.

"Does this have to do with the sleepwalking?" he asked.

She forced herself to nod.

"I wake with dirty feet," she murmured. "Almost every morning. And no memory of where I went. Where I was taken. No memory of anything."

"How long has this been happening?" he asked.

Alba let the silence stretch long.

"I saw her the night Romero died," Elías offered. "Sleepwalking toward the mine."

Bartolomé nodded; he knew this much from her confession and seemed to be piecing the shattered vase back together. Picking up each shard and examining it in the light, then putting it down with care.

"I fear it began before that," Alba said. "I fear..."

An infant's wail rose in the back of her mind, hungry, desperate, gratingly pitched.

It moved out of her skull and into the room, and *it was there*, it was so close and so loud and so *insistent* that she was certain that if she only turned around in her chair, she would see a red-faced infant on the floor by the door, screaming to be helped.

But there was nothing. There was only silence, silence that rang white and clear with anticipation as Bartolomé waited for her to speak.

"I fear it began in the mine," she whispered. "It began here."

Bartolomé leaned back on his heels. Was the exhaustion that marked his face a mirror of her own? Were the hollows beneath her eyes shadowed with that same bruised shade? Did her skin look thin and parched, sucked dry by the mountain air? She felt she would collapse to dust if anyone so much as put a hand on her.

Bartolomé sighed deeply.

"I need . . . I need time to pray," he said. "And you need to rest. You look as if you were dragged here from the gates of Hell."

Her laugh, when it came, was dry and cracked, and unexpectedly high. Such humor from the priest was startling. Not unwelcome. But painfully apt.

Rest. It was as seductive a word as she had ever heard. Sleep. Her whole body ached for it.

"Padre," Elías began, "there is a problem with that."

Bartolomé lifted his head to Elías, his expression a question.

"It . . ." Elías trailed off, then tried anew: "Everything bad happens when she falls asleep. Perhaps her defenses are down. It is a clear pattern."

"He's right," Alba said.

"She cannot stay awake forever," Bartolomé said. He stared at her in silence for a long moment. "That will only weaken her further."

She felt pinned to the chair, as if lances were stuck through each of her shoulders and a knife were held to her throat. Her heart was racing again, and it ached, oh, it ached from the effort.

Bartolomé stood. His back was straight as a rod; energy lifted through him to the ceiling as if he, too, were animated by a force beyond their understanding.

"Elías," he said, and it had the weight of a command. "I will tell the others she has signs of matlazahuatl and must be kept in isolation. I will tend to her and keep watch. But I cannot do it alone."

"Whatever you need, Padre," Elías said. "I will help."

Bartolomé's piercing gaze was on him now, weighing his willingness, examining it in the light like a jeweler searching for flaws in a stone.

A new hum of unease ran over Alba's bones.

Elías had brought her here at a time when everyone ought to be resting. Elías had brought her here *alone*. What would Bartolomé suspect?

If any of those thoughts were moving through Bartolomé's mind, he was mercifully focused on logistical matters.

"I need a fellow watchman," he said. "Starting tonight."

"Done." Elías spoke without hesitation, before Bartolomé could even draw breath at the end of the sentence.

"Good," Bartolomé said. "And in the meantime," he added, looking down at Alba, "we must confine you."

XXIV

Elías

WHETHER BY LUCK or by the grace of God favoring Padre Bartolomé, the house was still silent as Elías and the priest escorted Alba to her room in a funereal line. Elías waited in the sitting room that was connected to Alba's bedroom, listening to the murmured prayers that Bartolomé made over Alba. His feet itched to move; he could not be still.

They needed Bartolomé. They could not do this alone. Elías's very bones still shook with what he had done in the workshop, and yet it had not been enough. He was not strong enough. He was not smart enough, not even if he memorized *El Libro de San Cipriano* from cover to cover. They were outmatched. Coming to the priest made sense.

And still he paced. Still his agitation hummed as Bartolomé left Alba's bedroom and sprinkled holy water over the doorway.

The priest stepped back from the doorway with a soft sigh. "I need incense. More holy water. Candles, yes. Another crucifix." He cast a look around the room. "There should be one in here . . . unless, perhaps, she destroyed it." He laughed to himself; it was thin, humorless. "Dear God," he said. "What are we doing?"

Each moment Elías spent with Bartolomé made the priest seem more human. He would have preferred to hold him at a distance, a faraway painted saint in a gilded chapel. But here they were: two men facing each other, empty-handed, at a loss.

"I was hoping you'd know," he said.

Bartolomé ran a hand over his face and rested it on his cheek.

"So was I." The tilt of his mouth could have been either amusement or despair. Elías felt strung between the two sentiments himself. "We don't have much time to talk now," Bartolomé said, "before people begin to wake. I plan to get tools from the chapel. If you stay here and keep watch, I will return as fast as I can. But first—"

He turned and searched the room, then moved to a small table that appeared to have been used as a writing desk—papers and ink lay scattered haphazardly across its surface. He took the chair before the table, gesturing for Elías to sit near him.

"I need to know more before I write to my superiors," Bartolomé said in a low voice, casting a nervous look over his shoulder at Alba's bedroom as he took a pen and filled it with ink.

A cold bolt of fear shot through Elías's gut.

"You're writing to the Inquisitors?" What a stupid question. Of course Bartolomé would. This was a case of demonic possession. To whom else would he write?

Bartolomé gave him a level look. "Is there a problem?"

"In my family, there are stories of great suffering. Unjust treatment." His heel began to tap rapidly; his knee bounced, jittery with nerves. "I will not stand by and allow harm to come to her."

Bartolomé tapped the tip of the pen against parchment. A drop of ink pooled; he was thinking, and he ignored Elías.

"She is in harm's way now," he said.

Elías cursed softly. "I know."

"The Inquisition in Spain has a history," Bartolomé said slowly, as if choosing his words with care. "Some would say it has been overzealous. Legends abound. I do not mean to invalidate your ancestors' suffering," he added, seeing that Elías's expression had shifted to one of offense and that he had opened his mouth to combat the term *legend*. His mother would never have lied about what had happened to her great-uncles and cousins. "I wish to point out that the Inquisition in Nueva España is different. I know you heard me threaten Heraclio with them, but it is a methodical body. A lumbering bureaucracy, if you will," he added, with a touch of dryness. "I can only pray that it moves quickly enough to help us. Which it might, if I can provide enough detail about Señorita Díaz's condition."

"Do you swear no harm will come to her?" Elías said. "Do you swear that you will tell no one else?"

His voice resonated with more passion than he intended. Perhaps too much, for Bartolomé's reply—though quiet and measured—had a precision of diction that felt pointed.

"She is the fiancée of my oldest friend," the priest said. "No harm will come to her under my watch."

Elías chewed the inside of his lip. He and Alba had made the choice to trust Bartolomé; he must face the consequences of that decision.

"Now," Bartolomé said, noticing the growing pool of ink on the paper and moving the pen. It smeared, marring the top of the page where he had written the date. "How did you come to understand that Señorita Díaz needed the Church's help?"

Elías's shoulders corded tight; he let out his breath in a firm, determined huff.

Pen scratched across paper as he described the last few days: Alba sleepwalking; his shock when Romero turned up dead. But when Elías described Alba's fear that Bartolomé was in danger, color began to drain from the priest's cheeks.

"But instead of you, I was attacked next," Elías said.

"Attacked? By whom?"

Elías jerked a thumb at Alba's bedroom door.

"Last night," he said. "Sometime after midnight. She came to my room with a knife and attacked me."

The lift of Bartolomé's brows cut creases in his forehead.

Elías sped through the details, remembering mid-breath to omit anything to do with El Libro de San Cipriano.

"She knew things," Elías said. "Things that I have never told *anyone*."

Bartolomé raised a finger to his lips before returning to writing. Elías lowered his voice; his throat felt rough, as if he had spent the whole day shouting.

"She spoke in a different language, Padre."

Bartolomé looked up, startled.

"Before Victoriano came here, he was a merchant who sold goods to the North African presidios," Elías said. "He met my mother there, and I was born in Ceuta. After we moved to Sevilla, she still spoke Arabic to me. But our dialect is very specific, Padre," he added, searching for a way to emphasize how wrong it had felt to hear it from Alba's lips. "It is as different from other dialects as galego is from castellano. She . . . *taunted* me with it."

"Elías . . ." Bartolomé trailed off and turned his body so that he was staring at the door to Alba's bedroom. No sound came from the room except, faintly, the deep breathing of sleep. "These are classic signs of possession by a powerful force."

A cackle of chickens came from the courtyard outside; distantly,

Elías heard the echo of voices and the clang of pots from the direction of the outdoor kitchen.

Something about the sounds—so quotidian, so blissfully unaware of the gravity of the conversation taking place in this shadowed room—shattered his chest like glass.

He was so far from anything he knew. He was alone in a room with a stranger, someone who had the power to either harm or heal the one person he cared about on this whole godforsaken continent, and he was powerless.

He had come to the Indies for silver. A means to an end. Zacatecas was a door through which he would pass to another life.

And this was what had happened.

Despair was a wave, but it did not drown him. He was still aware of the scratch of Bartolomé's pen, of Alba's calm breathing, of the chickens, the fucking chickens, clucking and fussing over their feed outside without a care in the world.

"You said she came to you in the night," Bartolomé said, pen scratching as he spoke. "Had she done that before?"

Elías's back stiffened. There was no sacred oath of the confessional to defend what he said. One misstep, and what thin ground he had beneath him would crumble and fall away, taking him with it.

"No, Padre," he said, channeling every bit of earnestness he had in him. "I swear on my mother's grave. Never."

The pen scratched on. "You said she attacked you? She is a small woman."

"With a knife," Elías said. "With strength that caught me off guard."

"What manner of knife? One for opening letters, or ... ?"

"It looked like it was for butchering hogs," Elías said flatly. "I have it in my room still, if you want to see."

The pen stopped.

"Right," Bartolomé said. If possible, he had grown paler. "A butchering knife. Uncommon strength." He set his pen down and rubbed his temples. "So Señorita Díaz, or rather, an unknown, malevolent force animating her"—here he lowered his voice—"tried to kill you. You said her strength surprised you. Do you think she is actually capable of doing so?"

"I fought for my life." Elías's heel was tapping again. "It was a close thing. It made me fear . . . Padre, is there any evidence of who killed Romero?"

A moment of silence passed as Bartolomé considered this.

"Poor Carlos," he murmured at last, leaning back in his chair. He set his hands palm to palm, index fingers resting against his lips, and stared into space. "This does not bode well."

A sound from Alba's room made them both jump; it was only Alba turning in bed, sighing in her sleep.

If Elías listened closely enough, he wagered he could hear the priest's heart racing as fast as his own was.

"Romero did not try to make himself well-liked," Bartolomé said, "as you know." He tapped his fingers against his lips. "He worked here before Heraclio bought the mine. Carlos said he was much hated by the workers both before and after the purchase. My working hypothesis . . . is revenge," he said after a pause. "Someone wished to remove a person who had treated them ill."

"So there is no proof implicating Alba," Elías said.

"Only fear," Bartolomé said. "My fear, frankly. And that is not an easy thing to inspire. Sometimes, when I look at her . . ."

Elías straightened. "Do you see it?"

Bartolomé looked up at him suddenly, his lips pale, they were pressed together so hard.

"Do you see it?" he hissed.

"The—" Instead of searching for the right words, Elías gestured at his own eyes.

"Yes. That," Bartolomé gasped. A shudder took his shoulders; his eyes fluttered shut as he crossed himself. "My God." Then, sharply, he asked: "Why you?"

"What?"

Bartolomé had stopped writing, but this was the most pointed question yet. The first that made Elías realize that perhaps he had been the subject of an interrogation this entire time.

A swish of seasickness; the tilt of the deck on steep waves.

"Why you?" Bartolomé repeated. "I am a priest. A logical adversary. But you . . . you are *involved*." He scanned Elías from head to toe. If his gaze caught on Elías's fingers, perhaps all he saw was soot and ink, and not whatever lingered, still warm, beneath his skin. "Why not confide in someone close to her, like her mother or father? Or Carlos?"

Elías had reflexive answers: Carlos was a self-centered brat; Alba's parents were no better. He had stupid answers: the rich crackle of potential between him and Alba; the way a simple brush of hands in a ballroom in Zacatecas had lifted the world out of his grasp and shattered it like a glass of Champagne on the floor.

Instead, he said: "Perhaps it was easier to confide in a stranger." He gestured at the priest. "Isn't that the way of things, sometimes?"

This answer seemed to soften Bartolomé.

"Indeed," he said. Then, with a sigh, as if it wearied him to ask, but he had come across the question at the bottom of a mental list and could not proceed without it: "Did you ever come into contact with the occult in the East? Did you ever attempt to communicate with spirits of any kind in pursuit of arcane knowledge?"

"No, Padre." Not in the East, no. "I was aware of a man—a fellow prisoner, that is—in Almadén. People said he was possessed. But I did not know him."

Bartolomé thumbed his chin. "I worry that your studies might have created an openness in you. Demonic forces find the thinnest cracks in our defenses, even those as slender as the eye of a needle. They will force their way in by any means necessary. It is possible that this being . . . sensed something in you," he finished, "and drew Alba to you."

Perhaps.

Or perhaps Alba had simply found herself surrounded by idiots and had decided that Elías was a slightly more compassionate idiot than her narcissist in-laws-to-be and parents.

He bit his tongue.

Bartolomé pushed himself to standing, weariness settling around him like a cloak.

"I must pray about this. It would be best if you stayed out of sight," he said. There was a shade of apology in his voice. "I suspect that the news of Señorita Díaz's illness will make members of our party agitated. For her sake, we must not risk trouble."

"I understand, Padre," Elías said.

"I will deliver news of the 'plague,'" Bartolomé said. He reached for his belt and unwound the rosary that he kept hooked there. He held it out to Elías. "Keep this with you."

The beads and crucifix were wooden and rustic. There was no gold, no mother-of-pearl, no scent of roses or expensive wood. It was the rosary of a simple man. Perhaps of a trustworthy one.

He took it.

"There is holy water in the bottle on the table," Bartolomé said. "And prayers in your heart. May I?" he added, holding out a hand toward the crown of Elías's head to bless him.

Any other day, Elías would flinch away. Give a dry *no, thank you* and move on.

Though the incantations of San Cipriano still burned under the calloused pads of his fingertips, he inclined his head toward Bartolomé and closed his eyes with unfeigned gratitude when the priest rested his hand on his hair. Latin washed over him, soft as a magic charm.

Perhaps that was what it was, in the end: a magic charm. The Lord's Prayer, this blessing—was it any different from an incantation from *El Libro de San Cipriano*?

"I will return as soon as I can," Bartolomé said and walked to the door.

Elías wrapped the rosary around his left hand.

"Vaya con Dios," he said, and for once, he meant it.

Bartolomé paused, hand on the door.

"You did well, to come to me," he said. "You might have saved her life."

Elías's mouth was dry from speaking, from exhaustion, from thirst.

"I hope so," he said, and his voice cracked.

It was not until Bartolomé had shut the door behind him and voices lifted in the hall that Elías set his head in his hands—which shook hard, harder than they ever had before—and wept.

XXV

Elías

WHILE BARTOLOMÉ WENT to inform the rest of the household that Alba had fallen victim to matlazahuatl, Elías sat. He ran his fingers over the rosary. He did not pray. Or perhaps he did: He gazed at Alba's cracked door as one might at stained-glass windows in a cathedral. His mind wandered back to the workshop, back to the circle scored on the packed dirt floor with charcoal.

There, he hit a vat of dread, thicker and heavier than quicksilver.

What if someone went to the workshop and saw what he had done?

María Victoriana was right.

He was on his feet, pacing the fine rug that covered the stone floor of Alba's sitting room. Half his mind noted, distantly, that it was Eastern made; wasn't that pattern Isfahani? It would have been brought to Nueva España at enormous cost via the Philippine fleet. Would be a shame to wear it thin.

The other half of his mind flung itself against the walls of his skull in panic, desperate to run to the workshop and scrub the floor until his hands bled.

But a demon was in the next room, latent beneath Alba's skin, a predator lying in wait for its quivering prey.

So he paced.

When the rumble of his stomach and the shift of light outside told him that twilight was near, Bartolomé returned.

"Has she stirred?" he asked, thinly veiled anxiety lifting the pitch of his voice.

When Elías shook his head, the priest murmured, "Thanks be to God. Now you go rest."

THE WORKSHOP WAS as Elías and Alba had left it.

Stools were thrown on their sides, mineros felled by a blast deep in some underground cavern. The hearth was cold and black. The charcoal lines he had scored on the ground mere hours ago, when he had been buoyant with mad optimism, with a convert's arrogant belief, seemed deeper. As if some great dragon had taken an idle claw and traced each curve of the circle, each demonic letter.

At the center of it all lay El Libro de San Cipriano. Its pages were splayed open, shameless as a nude on brothel sheets. Its diagrams of circles—annotated with Elías's hand—gazed brazenly up at the world.

He lurched forward and snapped the book shut.

It had been lying on cold ground for hours, but its cover was warm.

He was imagining it. Imagining the bite of sulfur on the delicate insides of his nostrils. He was weak, exhausted, his stomach so empty that it brought to mind his first days on the Atlantic crossing, when he had ached for food but even a sip of water made him retch acid into a leaky bucket.

He set the book down on the table. On second thought, he stacked several other books atop it. To keep it from discovery, or to keep it from opening of its own volition? He was not quite sure.

Discovery would spell his doom. Had he not watched Bartolomé write a letter to the Inquisitors? He had practically dictated half of it himself.

"Joder," he said to himself. And again: "Joder."

He fell to his knees and began scrubbing the circle.

It was only by bringing dirt from outside that the circle could be properly covered. He filled in the gouge marks—for they were gouge marks, though he had traced the glyphs with charcoal, a material much softer than the hard-packed earth—and walked back and forth over the circle, tamping the fresh earth down and spreading it to blend with the rest of the room.

The circle laughed at him. It was as if it had tossed a blanket over its head to play, as with an infant, and winked coyly at Elías as it did so, for it was also in on the joke that it could not be seen.

Elías stamped the dirt harder.

If the mercury was taking his mind at last, he was not letting it go without a fight.

"Elías?"

His heel caught on nothing; he stumbled backward into the hearth.

María Victoriana stood in the doorway, shadowed by a second figure, one whom Elías had not seen since he first saw the shrine.

Her mother.

"To what do I owe the pleasure of your company?" he sputtered.

Neither looked fooled by this haphazard attempt at normalcy. He had been caught hiding something, and it was evident from their expressions that they both knew it.

"You need to come with us," María Victoriana said.

His heart skid to a stop. "I beg your pardon?"

"Have dinner with us," Carolina said, casting María Victoriana a look he could not parse. Her request was carefully casual, unlike María Victoriana's accusing tone. "I wish to get to know Victoriano's son better."

"Now?" Food was appealing—this he could not deny—but the timing?

"Now," Carolina said, with a measure of forcefulness that seemed to have a power of its own. He straightened. The workshop was still in a state of disarray, yes, but perhaps something closer to its quotidian disorder. Nothing occult had occurred here. Nothing at all.

"Let me..." He grabbed a small leather satchel from its hook on the wall. This he normally used to take small pouches of mercury to and from the incorporadero, keeping his own supply under tight control; he moved the pile of books and stuffed *El Libro de San Cipriano* inside.

He could almost feel it humming with pleasure. It did not want to be parted from him.

"Books do not *want* anything," he muttered as he swung the satchel so that the book was at his back.

His face flushed hot when he realized that he had spoken aloud.

María Victoriana raised a brow. "If you say so," she said, and, as she turned to lead the way, she added under her breath: "Loco."

ELÍAS HAD SEEN the mud brick structures that formed the small town of mine workers and their families on his way to the entrance of the mine, but he had never come close to them. They crossed a thin line etched in the dirt and lined with a faint gleam—

mercury, perhaps? It was difficult to tell as twilight lengthened dark, purple fingers of shadow across the valley. The workers' huts fell into their clutches first, and the farther he walked from the workshop and Casa Calavera, the more he felt as if he were walking into the night itself, descending into an unknowable darkness.

They entered a grander home among the other adobe structures. It boasted more than one room; in addition to the half-outdoor kitchen where a fire crackled merrily beneath an earthenware pot, there were living quarters, and a wooden door separating the bedroom from the rest of the house.

He sat when and where Carolina insisted, never taking the satchel off. A clay bowl was put before him, steam carrying the aromas of comino and rice. Tortillas served as cutlery, which was good, because he was so famished he would have eaten with his hands anyway. His teeth sank into chicken so tender it fell off the bone.

Perhaps the Inquisition should come speak to Carolina. How one made the anemic, half-naked birds that pecked the earth outside Casa Calavera into this had to be nothing short of witchcraft.

Presently he was aware of María Victoriana eating next to him; across the wooden table from them sat Carolina, who had no food before her. For a moment, she traced the whorls of the wood in the top of the table, then she cut him a sharp look.

"There are some things you need to understand because you've used that," she said, pointing at his satchel.

Elías choked; cleared his throat. He pasted a look of what he hoped was utter innocence on his features. "I don't know what you're talking about."

María Victoriana kicked his shin under the table.

"Don't play stupid with Mamá," she muttered out of the side of her mouth.

His second interrogation of the day, but this one had an enforcer.

"I'm sorry," he said, lifting his eyes to Carolina. A lesser man than he might have withered under the intensity of her look; perhaps he was that lesser man, for he felt a profound urge to shrink away. "There... there are things that are dangerous to speak of."

"And things that are dangerous to do," Carolina said. She gestured expansively at him, then seized one of his hands. Before he could protest, she flipped it, palm facing up, and examined his fingertips.

They were still black.

"Before Victoriano died," she began, one eyebrow arching gracefully as she released his hand, "he made me swear an oath." She wore a mask of careful, studied indifference, but beneath it, her voice trembled. "He was not sure if you would come. But if you did... he said that when he first came to México, he felt lost. Alone. He did not wish for you to feel the same. He asked me to look out for you." Her eyelashes—which were long and straight and black enough that her eyes appeared lined by kohl—batted forcefully. She took a sharp breath, as if to fortify herself. "I have not. Not yet," she added.

Elías did not want to feel kinship with Victoriano. He did not want to think of his father as a man, simply a man, alone in a friendless land just as he was. No. He did not need his father's favors nor to be looked after as if he were a child playing with dangerous toys. He did not *want* any of it.

"I don't need—"

"First of all: We don't use books like *that*." Carolina cut him off brusquely. "I don't know what exactly you're doing or how to prevent you from killing yourself, but for Victoriano, I must try." She leaned forward. "You must know what it is you face."

Elías's heart beat in his ears.

"I'm listening," he said.

"It was more than twenty years ago. Perhaps twenty-five. Victoriano was new here, and therefore foolish, because he did not yet know the Izquierdos as well as we did.

"By us I mean us who live here, of course—it has always been us and them, el pueblo and la casa. My mother's mother was brought here by force from Texcoco, along with many others, not long after the opening of the mines in Fresnillo. There were people who had lived here before, but by the time my grandmother arrived, they were dry bones, done in by matlazahuatl or pox or the musket when they rebelled."

Carolina stood and began to pace as she spoke. "My grandmother said coming here was like walking into a crypt: no trees, no beasts, no life, only stone and ghosts in the shadows of the mountains. But then the Izquierdos opened the mountain. And they found what was within."

The air around them grew chill.

"My grandmother swore it was something that was as foreign to this place as the peninsulares. It was said that it first arrived with the ships generations ago, with peninsulares and their iron, with their priests, and like a disease, laid waste to all that it found here."

"A haunting?" Elías asked.

"Ha," Carolina scoffed. "Worse. Long ago, in my grandmother's time, there were rumors that a brujo had bound it to stone to keep it deep in the mountain, watched over by a powerful force, but it endured. It was something that lived, and kept living, deep in the mountain, for decades."

Alba's voice echoed through mine tunnels, rising all around him.

I'm coming. I'll find you.

"Victoriano and I knew each other, but not well. I think I was the only woman of el pueblo he knew at that time, for he came to me with the baby."

Gooseflesh raced over Elías's arms, raising hair in their wake.

"I lived in my mother's house then," Carolina said. "I immediately stepped outside and shut the door behind me so that she would not see a peninsular with a newborn, a baby so weak it could scarcely draw breath, much less cry. But even in the baby's weakened state, I could see it."

It's crying, can't you hear it?

Elías clutched his satchel to his chest, food forgotten.

"It—that evil, that thing—was *inside* the baby. Victoriano said that someone had left her in the mine," Carolina went on. "I knew that. In fact, I knew who had done it, who had been cornered by Young Izquierdo and grew rounder and more miserable in the months since. Who had given birth—to a stillborn, everyone would be told—and fled Mina San Gabriel before dawn broke. She was not my friend, but I had known her all our lives. I knew why she acted as she had. But she had also acted in panic. If she wanted the baby dead, she should have done it herself. Instead, she created a monster. A monster that Victoriano found and brought to me." Carolina shuddered. "Suddenly, I found myself standing before it and the rest of San Gabriel. When I told Victoriano to put the baby back where he found it, he looked at me in horror. He did not listen." She shook her head. "Years later, he told me the truth of what he had done. That night, the Izquierdos had been hosting a merchant from the city. A man who had mentioned, while deep in his cups, how desperately his wife wanted a child. Victoriano gave the baby to the merchant, and it—that evil, that *demon*, the priests would call it—was spirited away to Zacatecas."

Waves rose around him, sheer and thick, tilting the decks, sweeping him overboard.

"At first, I was angry with him, but then I saw that in his ignorance, he had acted in the interest of el pueblo. The evil was gone. It was no longer our problem. Until she arrived."

"She." It was thick on Elías's tongue.

All he saw was long black hair, unbound, as lustrous in the moonlight as mercury.

Carolina stopped pacing and turned on him, silhouetted from behind by the hearth. For a moment, there was no sound but the fire crackling.

"Victoriano had the chance to destroy that thing, and he failed," she said, forceful as a priest warning against the fiery pits of Hell. "And I lacked the courage to tell him how. But you can fix this. You can end this."

"And how," he managed, mouth drier than sand, "would I do such a thing?"

"Kill the host in open air, on a windy peak," Carolina said without hesitation. "Underground is useless. It was chained there before and it escaped. It will escape again. Such things cannot be killed by man, but on a peak, the wind will carry it away, and we will be free of it. You," she said, jabbing a finger at him, "you alone have this chance. Or it will be the doom of us all."

Elías's mouth parted; for a long moment, nothing emerged.

"You want me to kill Alba," he said, hoarse, barely above a whisper.

"I want you to correct your father's mistake," Carolina said.

Elías stood sharply, the feet of the chair scraping harshly against the floor. He had been sent here by Abuelo Arcadio to fix his father's mistakes. He would be dragged down to Hell and burn with his father's mistakes bound around his ankles.

Fuck his father's mistakes.

"You," he began, voice a low warning, marking Carolina with his own accusing finger, "have sorely misjudged me, señora."

"I told you he was too soft."

María Victoriana's interjection seemed to surprise Carolina as much as it surprised him; the girl had been so still while absorbing the details of her mother's story that he had forgotten she was there.

"Now he's going to run and tell her, and it'll be all your fault for not believing me," she continued, folding her arms across her chest. "No one listens to me."

"I would deny everything," Carolina spat at Elías, a dare, a challenge.

"You have all but ordered the death of an innocent woman," Elías said. "That will not go unpunished."

"Punishment? Ha!" Carolina's laugh was caustic. "You know nothing of punishment. You know nothing of how we have suffered. All you peninsulares want is your silver, your women, and you will take them by force, and take—"

"I am not like that," Elías snarled, leaning over the table toward her.

"Then why does your greed smell the same?" Carolina snapped, mirroring his posture so that her sneer filled his vision. "I've heard the stories. You're a convict. A murderer. Taking lives is nothing new to you. So do it again, for the greater good."

Hatred seized his heart in a white-hot vise. How *dare* she.

"He should use the damn book," María Victoriana cut in.

Elías and Carolina whirled toward her.

"I told you. He's in love with her," María Victoriana said. "You're not going to convince him to kill her. And we're not going to kill her because that's a death sentence," she said flatly. "So what do we do? Watch as the demon has its fill, waiting and wondering when it will be our turn?"

She looked up at Elías. "I watched you use sorcery this afternoon..." She trailed off, her voice pinched, her face losing some of its color, even in the warm glow of the fire. "You're mad. You're going to get yourself killed, or worse. But if you know who to ask, you might be able to banish the demon and keep Alba. That's what she wants, you know. It's why she's being so rash."

Elías, as a rule, did not blush. He did not.

"Did I not forbid you from going near that woman?" Carolina thundered. "That is enough."

"There's a goddess who lives in the mountain," María Victoriana carried on, her words building like a rushing stream, as if she were worried her mother would pounce and steal her very voice if she did not speak quickly enough. "That force Mamá talked about, that watched over the thing when it was bound in the mountain? We call her Death. I mean, we think that's what she is—she was here before Bisabuela was brought here, or so Bisabuela said. The shrine is for her. Maybe she will listen. And help."

"Padre Bartolomé ordered the shrine to be destroyed," Elías said. His mind fought to catch up to his words, racing a pace and a half behind the conversation. A goddess. A demon. Reality and unreality swirled in a thick fog as Carolina clicked her tongue dismissively.

"As if we would allow that," she scoffed. "We moved it before they could touch it."

Her tone struck him like a blow. Carolina's stubbornness, her strength, the way she spoke . . . all of it reminded him powerfully of his own mother.

Perhaps that was why, alone in this desolate land, Victoriano had found Carolina and stayed with her. But Elías would never know for certain, because he could never ask Victoriano, because Victoriano was dead.

A well of something that tasted salty and soft and viciously sad surged in his breast.

He crushed it down.

"I will not kill anyone," he said, voice shaking. "The demon must be banished, but I will do it without harming Alba." He took a deep breath, not believing what he was about to say until the words came from his lips. "Will you take me to the new shrine?"

XXVI

Alba

ALBA SLEPT. EVEN as daylight thickened and scratched her eyes, she slept. When she woke in the late afternoon, her mouth so dry it tasted sticky and foul, she sat up.

Bartolomé was there, murmuring to himself. He sat in a chair beneath the window, his legs crossed, his fingers moving over the beads of his rosary. He looked as if he were in a trance.

He was covered in blood.

Each rhythmic movement of his foot, keeping the time of the prayer, dripped dark liquid onto the floor. His hair was slick with it, plastered to his skull; his eyes, when they lifted to meet hers, were heavy with blood-wet lashes. Profane in their paleness against the blood.

The meat was ripped away from the side of his face, exposing the pink bone of his jaw as if he had been mauled by a dog.

He stopped mid-rosary and lifted his right hand. A thick black clot rolled down the side of his palm and fell to his lap with a wet, sickening splat.

"In nomine Patris, et Filii..."

He made the sign of the cross over her. A shudder built in her and extinguished itself with a powerful shake of the shoulders.

"How do you feel?" he asked.

There was no blood on him. Not a drop of red besmirched his clothes, his hair, his shoes.

She could not trust her own eyes. She could not trust her own body. She was trapped, she would die like this, there was no hope—

"Thirsty," she croaked.

She drank. She ate food that had been brought for her into the sitting room. She brushed and plaited her hair as she did first thing in the morning, as if she were alone preparing for the day. She was far from alone. Bartolomé hovered, ever watchful, his hands twitching by his sides, as if they were ready to fly up and make the sign of the cross at the slightest provocation.

The decor of her sitting room and bedroom had been much changed over the course of her sleep-filled day. Her room's sole crucifix had gone missing at some point over the course of her stay in Casa Calavera. It had been replaced—and multiplied. She recognized one silver-embossed cross from one of the parlors, another from the chapel. Candles had appeared, and incense, and at Bartolomé's side was a bottle of water.

Something under her skin flinched at it.

Holy water, no doubt.

In the midst of the crucifixes and incense, Alba sank to her knees when Bartolomé invited her to join him in prayer.

Novena melted into novena. Hail Marys bound themselves into chains. It reminded her of making flower garlands as a child: They were pretty things, yes, but gave at the slightest yank.

How could words change anything?

In Elías's workshop, she could feel the ripple of something other when he spoke. It had the timber of a current, the force of an earthquake. It felt like something was happening.

As the night deepened, her knees ached. Her spine felt stiff, her shoulders wanted to curl over and collapse in on themselves.

Bartolomé's voice grew hoarse. He made no conversation with her. He continued to use holy water with abandon and rarely made eye contact with her as he guided her into the next mystery of the rosary.

It was as if she *did* have the matlazahuatl. That which moved beneath her skin was a sickness, and he was afraid to catch it.

That knowledge made her want to rear up and taunt him. To step close and threaten to breathe on him or pull his hair, to waggle her demon-infected fingers at him and his piety.

As if he had heard these thoughts, he lifted his head and took her in with an intensity that caught her off guard. She swallowed half a Hail Mary by accident.

"It will take will, you know," he said.

"I don't understand."

"Nothing will change unless you want it to," he said. "You must *want* to be rid of this evil. You must commit to being free of it."

"There is nothing I want more." The words were abrupt, bordering on harsh. She did not care. Let Bartolomé feel the harshness. He deserved it, for daring to insinuate that she might feel otherwise.

"Then pray," he thundered.

"I *am*," she snapped.

"You lack focus, señorita," he said, tone honed like a blade. "I know you are weak by nature—womanhood and sangre india breed sloth. But you must overcome these. You must *fight*." This struck like a slap. His sword was drawn—whether because he was irritated by her or feared what was within, it didn't matter. Did he think that she wanted to be hounded by visions of blood? To have her limbs seized and stolen, to have her very body yanked across the mountain valley as if it were a puppet? To look at her own hands and fear that they would not obey her, even as she willed them to clasp in prayer?

She did not ask for this. She did not want this. All she had ever wanted, all she had ever lived for, was the *inverse* of this perverse imprisonment. To command her own life. To command her own body, to decide to whom it was given and when.

"What will you gain when you are free of this?" he said.

Silence from her. So Bartolomé supplied the answer, his voice condescending, as if he had prompted it very obviously and she had failed the test: "Eternal life."

But in the silence, Alba's mind had wandered far. It had found a path and raced down it, faster than a runaway horse, and suddenly, she found herself in the shadowy workshop with Elías, palm to palm, hearts thundering, their very breath suspended in silvery anticipation.

Desire was glass shattering on a stone floor. It rang aching and clear, sharp enough to draw blood.

That, again. That.

The demon wanted Elías dead because Elías had acted to help her. He had thwarted the demon, first by accident, and then with dogged purpose.

For that, the demon had commandeered her flesh and seized a knife. It had nearly succeeded in achieving its goal.

It would try again.

She would not let it.

She had come to Mina San Gabriel to prevent her parents from breaking off her engagement to Carlos. For more than that: for the freedom to govern her own body. To not be forced to bear a stranger's children. To live in a house without fear of the person she shared it with. To walk where she willed and simply be.

Instead, she had lost it all.

Or she would, unless she fought. On that point, at least, Padre Bartolomé was right.

Her limbs were hers to command. She would walk only when and where she wanted to. Her hands were hers. They would rise to her will and her will alone.

She folded them before her.

She closed her eyes. Set her jaw. Latin rolled determined from her tongue, and though it made something in her swill with sickness, though she knew the foul-smelling sweat of fever slicking her palms and underarms was because of it, she would not stop.

Padre Bartolomé's voice droned on. His presence alone was not the panacea she longed for. What good was a priest if he could not cure her with a snap of his fingers? She shoved her annoyance aside. When he began describing the Luminous Mysteries upon which they would be meditating for the next round of the rosary, she meditated on something else entirely.

Palm to palm. The faint aromas of sweat and woodsmoke, of leather and paper, of his skin.

She ran her fingers over the beads, settling on the small silver medal that bound the rosary together.

She no longer lacked focus.

The glint of a golden earring in the gloom. The brush of his hair against her cheekbone. The taste of his mouth and the fire left by his hands.

She could feel a smile draw at her lips, wilder and more full of hope than anything the demon could conjure across her face with its grasping fingertips.

She began.

"In nomine Patris, et Filii..."

XXVII

Elías

A THICK FOG had rolled into the mountain valley of Mina San Gabriel, obscuring the stars and moon, cloaking Elías in a whisper of moisture. He shivered—unlike Carolina and María Victoriana, who were wrapped in rebozos, he had not thought to bring a sarape for warmth. He had left Casa Calavera in a hurry, intending to return to the house straight away.

No longer.

Padre Bartolomé would expect him in a few hours. Until then, he walked through darkness. He could not retrace his steps if he tried. San Gabriel was a cluster of adobe houses haphazardly stacked—some practically atop one another—against one side of the valley in a ferocious competition for sunlight, leaving the alleys that cut through them an impossible snarl. They left the village via a rocky passage narrow enough to thread a needle.

María Victoriana led the way, scrambling like a mountain goat as the path wrenched upward. He did not want to lose her in the gloom; he pushed himself forward as quickly as he dared. The fog was too thick for him to judge how high they climbed, but the burning pull of his breath on thin air and the bite of the cold slicing through his sweaty shirt were enough for him to know that if he were to fall, he would keep falling until he struck the gates of Hell.

Carolina walked behind him—or so he reminded himself, at least twice, for he could not hear her footfalls over María Victoriana's scramble and his own labored breathing. She moved like a ghost. Perhaps she had become one. Perhaps they all were, and this was Purgatory: a mad dash ever higher, higher, with a plummet to doom below and no salvation in sight.

The entrance to a small grotto appeared as a new scene in a dream. First, there was nothing, nothing but Elías's hoarse panting and the hesitant crunch of footsteps on loose stones, and then, there it was, as if it had always been there. A narrow opening in solid stone, slim enough in appearance that he might have mistaken it for a crevice unworthy of attention.

But a soft glow winked from inside.

"Mamá always leaves the candles lit, in case anyone wants to come here," María Victoriana said. "Come on."

She approached the grotto; the top of her head nearly brushed the apex of the natural arch in the stone. Elías would have to crouch to enter the new shrine.

Carolina appeared from the mist and seized María Victoriana by the arm. She yanked her daughter to the side.

"You stay here," she said firmly.

Elías's heart stumbled in his chest. He would have to go in alone? It had not occurred to him that he might be afraid to enter, but he was. A sensation of dread had been building behind his sternum throughout the ascent, and now, it swelled with the overbearing power of a wave. *No*, it said, *not alone*.

"Why?" he asked.

He felt more than saw the cut of Carolina's look.

"What you have been doing—what you plan to do—is dangerous. We"—and this had a weight to it, an emphasis that marked him as other—"do not touch the darkness like that. It is against nature. That is why the priests call it the occult. It is as foreign to us as they are."

"Then why would you bring me here?" he asked.

Her eyes glinted in the gloaming, fierce and determined.

"Darkness," she said, "can only be undone by its like."

She gestured for him to enter the grotto.

She would sacrifice him for the greater good. When this understanding unfurled in his breast, he expected it to be met with anger—a frustration at being used, a feeling of injustice.

Instead, he felt a bright pang of relief.

In a way, this was confirmation of all that had gnawed at him over the years, tunneling like maggots through his very bones. He was evil. He left people. He betrayed them. He was prideful. He lusted. Greed drove him. He had never been an angel, but he had fallen like one, and would keep falling, through flame and smoke and sulfur, down, down, down . . .

And that might actually help Alba.

"We will wait for you," Carolina said, tone indicating that she considered this a great mercy. "The descent would kill you otherwise."

AT FIRST, THE soft embrace of being underground was familiar. It took on an uncanny edge when he remembered that he was dozens of meters, if not a hundred or more, above the village of San Gabriel and Casa Calavera. He focused instead on the metallic drip of moisture striking stone. On the smell of candles grazing against humid air. On the bite of foreign incense, its taste as thick as a tapestry.

The grotto's ceiling rose overhead; cautiously, he uncurled his hunched back and found that he could stand. A quick glance over his shoulder revealed the small mouth of the entrance, its edges gray and shimmering with fog.

The material world lay behind him. He had chosen to cross beyond it. Each step he took forward was into the empty quadrant of the map, uncharted, unmarred, for here, there be monsters.

Forward he went.

The new shrine was similar to the one he had stumbled upon when he first arrived at Mina San Gabriel. At first it appeared humbler, for it was smaller in size, but as he took hesitant steps toward it—searching for purchase with the toe of his boot and only settling his weight when he found flat ground—he realized that he had assumed wrong.

The same thin, white effigy held pride of place in the back of the grotto, placed on a low wooden table that served, in a way, as an altar. She was swathed in white cloth, like a statue of a saint, and before her on the table sat that same silver bowl of mercury.

But as he drew near, the air thickened. Incense coalesced around him like fingers of fog, its weight heavier than air as mercury is heavier than water. No sound from outside could reach through it; he was underwater, he was enveloped. There was nothing but this: the white effigy, the silver bowl. He found his hand hovering over it, drawn as if by the power of a magnet. The silver caught the candlelight and drank it in, consuming it, alchemizing it, transmuting it into a glow that lit the metal from within.

Mercury was like silk, its luster like sin. It was moonlight on

Alba's hair. The burnished gleam of her eyes. The touch of her breath on his lips.

He plunged his fingertips through the surface of the element, relishing its cool sweep over his blackened fingertips. Its give, its resistance, were softer than skin, so soft it could not be metal, so soft it had to be living.

Azoguero.

A voice thrummed through him. He could have sworn it was only in his head, but the surface of the mercury rippled, as if reacting to a forceful sound.

Sorcerer.

He snatched his hand from the bowl—or rather, he meant to, and found with a tumble of panicked heartbeats that he could not. It held him fast. Mercury lifted into him and filled him, burgeoning as if it had broken through a dam, and all he could see was a river of quicksilver, molten and gleaming and thick with life, rushing as if toward a thundering waterfall, down into darkness...

I have been waiting for you.

The hairs on the back of his neck stood on end. When faced with that rush of being, that awareness, that thundering voice, his mind cleaved in two. One half was calcified by terror; the other was alight with awe.

He kept his eyes on the bowl, as if to respectfully avoid meeting the gaze of the effigy, when in truth he studied the surface of the mercury. It trembled; ripples spread across its surface. The force of the voice was able to move something physical.

It was real.

Words from his father's journal echoed through him: *The shrine casts fear into my heart whenever I draw near; I am not brave enough to enter it.*

Given the choice to fear it or worship it, he would fall to his knees in prayer. It almost felt as if he had no choice but to do that.

But there *was* a choice. For him, at least, as someone who had brushed his fingertips over the words of El Libro de San Cipriano and found himself lacking. He had burned like gas: a bright flare, then nothing, extinguished without so much as a sputter.

He was desperate for fuel. Brujos were born with their own; he had none. He was a man, he was mortal, he was flesh and bone that blackened and shook with poison more each passing day.

Charlatan alchemists made deals with the devils.

Was this a devil? It was certainly no saint. This shrine brought to mind the Bosporus, the throat of swift water and deadly cold that cut between ancient hills; this was black veins in solid stone, hundreds of meters inside the earth. This was a sweeping darkness so complete it would burn through his veins, through his skull, and leave him a pile of ash in its wake. This was a power that would send the priest into a righteous fury if he knew. This was worse than idolatry. This was sin of the blackest cloth.

Darkness can only be undone by its like.

"I came to ask for your help," he said. His voice was barely above a whisper. His breath created faint ripples on the surface of the mercury. "A demon plagues a woman here. I have tried to deal with it on my own. We sought the help of a priest. But I am afraid none of it will work." He inhaled sharply through his nose to steady himself. "I am weak," he added. "I seek aid."

I move with quicksilver, the voice said. *I am wherever it runs. Your veins are thick with it. Your lungs are heavy with it. It is the road to me. Walk that road.*

The mercury seared with light. A burning sensation snaked up his arm, moving through his body faster than a lightning strike. It was a bolt of pain, like metal to the tooth, and it was *everywhere*—in his limbs and gut, in his lungs. It shone with a fierce, scorching heat through his skull.

Use quicksilver, the voice said. *Rid my land of the foreign devil.*

"I will," Elías gasped. "I will."

XXVIII

Alba

THE CHANGING OF Alba's guard happened deep in the night. She had lost track of the hours since sunset; one seemed to bleed into the next, novena after novena. It had been long enough that her voice was hoarse, no matter how much water she drank to soothe it.

She rose from her seat on the edge of her bed when Bartolomé went to answer the knock at her door. An exchange of low male voices; retreating footsteps. The door shut. Then it locked.

Her pulse marched against the well of her throat.

She had spent hours thinking about Elías, about everything that had occurred before and during their attempted exorcism in the workshop—mostly before, if she was frank—and now he was *there*, mere steps beyond the doorway.

She peered into the sitting room.

Elías sat in a chair, leaning forward with his elbows resting on his knees, his hands clasped before him. Bartolomé's rosary, small glass bottle of holy water, and Bible were at his side on a small table, but he had not touched them. He worked his hands together—the movement was part fidgeting, part purposeful. As if he were massaging them, preparing them for work.

He stared at the wall; he was far from this room, lost in thought.

His hair was tied back, and was damp, as if it had been recently washed. There were familiar shadows beneath his eyes and a slope to his back that spoke of exhaustion.

"Did you rest?" she asked.

He looked up at her, and when he did, her heart stopped. It was not shyness at his beauty—this she felt regularly, and she had grown accustomed to the sweep of warmth through her chest, the sudden heaviness of her tongue and need for her hair to be touched, to occupy fidgeting hands.

This was not her.

Something—someone?—seized her heart in a clawed fist and squeezed it so hard it had to be bleeding, it had to be crumbling from the anger in the grip.

She gasped; one hand flew to her chest.

Elías was on his feet. "Are you all right?"

There was something in Elías that had seized the demon's attention, and now, Alba tasted it, too: a presence, a vibration on the air, something that was *threat*, and she knew if Elías drew so much as one step closer—

"Stay back." The words came out strained. Airless. The grip on her heart was slowly relenting with deep breathing. "I'm afraid."

Elías did not retreat, but he did not grow closer. "Of what?"

"Of how I respond to you," she said. His cheeks darkened with color—yes, it sounded suggestive, but she did not care. Pain radiated through her chest. It was a magnet, and Elías was metal, and it wanted to yank her close to him.

"Of how *it* responds to you," she clarified.

His hands were outstretched. Ready for any weapon: prayer, embrace, occult practice.

They trembled slightly.

Her mother's voice snaked through the back of her mind. *These azogueros all die an early death. And for what?*

A powerful ache seized her lungs. She did not want him to die. She knew some of his secrets, but she needed to know them all. She wanted to know him. She wanted him.

But when a dull hunger woke within her chest, it was not want. It was something else's bloodlust, its itch for revenge.

"Are you all right?" Elías repeated.

Padre Bartolomé had called her condition a holy war, illustrating a romantic tableau of a battle between good and evil as if with a painter's brush on a chapel ceiling: darkness billowing in sulfurous clouds, fallen angels, and above it all, a bright, cleansing light, scalding away sin and evil from her mortal soul.

But Bartolomé did not live in her skin. Bartolomé, for all his talk of battling to save lost souls, did not know the feeling of true confrontation. This was a war of wills, and her body was the battlefield.

There would be no more casualties. She would make sure of it.

"I want to be close to you," she forced out. "But it wants me to be close to you, because then it can hurt you."

Elías, to his credit, did not retreat. His weight resettled, a shift of feet on the carpet. He was ready to spring into action.

"Do you know why?" he murmured.

She took a deliberate step back toward the doorway of the bedroom. She had not noticed that she had drawn several steps closer to Elías, into the sitting room—that was not good. Pain clawed at her breast with each step; her breathing burned her throat.

"I think"—she gasped for breath—"it sees you as a threat."

Why would he look *satisfied* to be told this?

"I am a threat," Elías said, his voice reaching a lower, menacing register.

Alba's body shuddered against her will. It wanted to lurch out of her grasp, it wanted flesh, it wanted blood, it wanted to consume his blackened soul—

"Don't say that!" she gasped. "At least not so loudly."

Contrition transformed him immediately. "How can I help you?" he asked. He was already reaching for the rosary.

Alba flinched.

"Toss that to me," she forced through gritted teeth.

He obeyed. The beads glided through the air, a strange bird. Alba marked it with her eyes, she told her hands to reach for it as it drew near—

And then watched it strike the floor before her feet. Her hands hung immobile at her sides.

Frustration burned in her throat. She wanted to stamp her feet on the carpet, to throw a tantrum as if she were a child. *She was her own.* Her body was *her own* and it would follow her will.

"Obey me," she spat at her hands, and slowly, as if she were clawing her way through heavy, wet sand, she crouched and picked the rosary up with cautious fingers.

She brought the crucifix to her lips out of habit; it felt like frozen metal, and it burned.

She exhaled forcefully and straightened. The weight of Elías's gaze was on her—she could almost feel him drawing calculations from each of her gestures, evaluating where her movements stopped and began, as if one could possibly pinpoint the moment where *it* seized control.

"Why me?" she said, feeling her voice slip high, close to a spoiled child's whine. It wasn't *fair*.

"I actually think I know the answer to that," Elías said softly.

There was a gentle pull, somewhere under her skull, somewhere behind her ears, that she now knew was not *her*. The demon had become guileless. Sloppy. It did not care if she knew what it wanted or not; it pulled her recklessly toward what it wanted.

"Perhaps ... you might want to sit," he said. "It is a long story."

The demon lifted her feet and padded them over to a chair. She dropped into it. Elías's words unlocked famished curiosity; what he had to say, as he sat opposite her, tracing a fingertip over the cover of Bartolomé's Bible absently, slaked her thirst.

And left her hollow.

The tale tread a familiar opening. She was found here. In the mine, to be specific. She had been left to die there.

But now, she knew by *whom*.

By someone nameless, a woman whom Carolina knew but had not seen in decades, who was no longer a part of this tale. A woman who, like Alba, had been pursued and trapped—perhaps not in a dark hallway at a ball, but trapped all the same. By Young Izquierdo, Carolina said—the man whose father had sold the mine to the Monterrubios.

Then, she left San Gabriel behind and had never returned. Carolina would not even give her name.

She was a woman who had taken her life by the reins and cut away the burdens that threatened to strangle her freedom. In a way, it was an admirable thing to do: to ruthlessly carve a new place for herself in a world that would give her nothing.

But in doing so, she had carved away Alba.

Alba felt no closure, though this was what she had searched for, and she had been right, *she was right*—Carolina knew. Hollowness yawned wide and empty through her: an absence of feeling, of the grief she expected. She would have welcomed grief, for grief meant that she had belonged to someone, and that someone had been robbed of her.

But she hadn't belonged to anyone. She wasn't someone's daughter before Mamá.

She was someone's punishment. A consequence.

A curse.

Her mind cut to blankness. It was filled with a high-pitched buzzing, as if a thousand black flies were trapped between her ears.

The demon was impatient.

It surged; agitation rippled under her skin like a living thing. Elías spoke, but the demon within her knew that he could have spoken more. He was hiding something. Thousands of ants crawled over her sinew, through layers of muscle. She twitched. She scratched at her forearms, roughing the sleeve of her nightdress.

"You're leaving something out," she said through gritted teeth. "It won't leave me alone."

Swift as leaves resettling in a breeze, victory flickered across Elías's face—then he schooled his features into stillness. "There are things I don't want it to know."

Alba flung herself forward with a growl that ripped at her throat and shook her ribs.

She caught herself. Feet on the ground. She would not harm Elías.

"What can I do to help?" Elías asked. He was on his feet again, alert, hands outstretched.

Words failed her; any breath for speaking transformed into a low, menacing rumble in her chest. Her teeth gritted so tightly she could hear them grind against one another. The hinge of her jaw clicked painfully.

She lifted her arm, though its weight was wooden and impossibly heavy, though it was stiff and pained her—and pointed at the holy water.

Elías snatched the bottle from the table next to him; did that shift of his weight mean he was going to come close to her?

She whirled around to the back of the chair, placing it between herself and Elías.

Good thing she did. He was stupid enough to take a step toward her.

"Don't come near me," she gasped. The rasp of her voice felt too deep, too *other*. "Please don't."

He looked from the holy water in his hand to her. "Shall I . . . throw it to you?"

"Yes," she said. "Then back away."

He complied. The bottle struck her palms like ice. She uncorked it. Dabbed some on her fingers, hissing in pain as she did so—it stung, by God it stung, as if she had caught her flesh on the spikes of a cactus and *yanked*. She inhaled deeply and made the sign of the cross.

The water in the pot still boiled, but she had capped it with a heavy lid.

"Why can't I—" Elías began.

"Because it wants to hurt you, and I won't let it," she burst out. "I won't come near you. I won't touch you." A pause. Perhaps it was because her heart was racing, because control was a laughable myth, a folly, or perhaps because her sanity spun wildly in a wind, clinging only by a single, fraying thread, but she said: "Even though I want to."

His eyes widened; his cheeks flushed dark.

"Don't say that," he breathed. "You would only regret it."

"Don't tell me how to feel," she snapped. He flinched at her tone. "Everyone assumes how I feel and makes decisions based on that and *no one* ever asks me."

He said nothing. Perhaps he was waiting for the demon to seize her, to leap at him with hands outstretched. Perhaps he believed the demon already had her.

No. Let him know that this was all *her*, all Alba, and nothing else. No one else.

"I proposed to Carlos and manipulated my parents into coming here because it was the only way I could have control over my life," she said, her voice quavering. "And what have I gained from it? The opposite." She fought to keep her voice low—Mamá's room was next door, and she did not sleep deeply. "Something steals my body. Something wants me to lay waste to this place and is using *me* to do it. It attacked you. Without my knowledge, without my desire, without my choice."

Her voice cracked at last. Elías's face was transformed by pity; she wanted to swat the expression away. She did not want to be pitied. She did not want his sympathy.

"So don't tell me how to feel," she said. "My feelings are the only thing I have left."

"I am sorry," he said. "I . . . I have hurt people in the past. I don't want to hurt you."

Alba clutched the holy water. "I want you to," she said. "Hurt me. Give me something that is *mine*."

He inhaled sharply. Apart from that, neither of them spoke or moved, and yet—it was as if the air between them had tightened. It had grown more difficult to breathe.

Between Bartolomé and Elías, and the tools at their disposal, a shy tendril of hope had begun to take shape in her heart. It was still weak, but it reached for words that would have been unimaginable to her even days ago. When I *am* free, she found herself thinking. When my body is my own.

When. Not if. Not speechless despair.

It went to her head like Champagne on an empty stomach: fizzing and fierce and glittering in her veins, powerful enough to lift her off her feet.

She would be free of the roiling darkness beneath her skin.

And in the meantime: She reached for the rope that Padre Bartolomé had left behind. She set herself down in the chair with purpose and began tying rope around her ankles. It was rough against her palms and difficult to pull tight; she swore at it softly.

"Do you need help?" he asked.

She nodded. "But be careful," she said. "Stand back if I tell you to."

He dropped to one knee before her and retied the knots she had made around her ankles. She tried to ignore the roughness of the rope fibers, focusing instead on the brush of his fingertips against her skin.

Heat rushed up her neck. It made her reckless. Everything about the last few days had made her reckless. The despair of losing her body; the promise of fighting and winning it back. But it was proximity to this person, this man, most of all, that filled her with an awareness—so bright, so keen it was painful—of how much *more* was possible.

She inhaled deeply.

"Bartolomé told me I lacked focus," she said. "I am to think about what I might gain when I am free of this."

Elías brought the rope to where her wrist rested on the arm of the chair and waited for her nod of assent before he began tying it down.

"When I am able to govern myself once again, I want your help," she said. "I want to leave this place. Forever."

"Done," he said. "I never want to see this mine again." He drew breath, as if to speak again, but she interrupted.

"I mean that I want to buy passage on the Acapulco fleet," she said. She bit her lip to keep from hissing at the burn of rope against her wrists. It would leave marks atop the scratches that already marred her skin. "I want to see the world. The places you spoke of. Will you help me?"

He paused and opened his mouth as if to speak, then resumed working on her wrist. Moved to the next.

When at last he spoke, his voice was low and hoarse. "I can promise you that," he said, "but I won't promise to hurt you. I am doing everything in my power to prevent that. I *care*, Alba." The words cracked as he lifted his face to her. There was a desperate glint in his eye, something akin to fear. For her? "I care so much it is like a physical pain, right here"—he tapped his chest with two fingers, hard—"and I don't know how to stop it. I don't think I *want* to stop it." His fingers curled around the rope, gripping it tighter. "But I have never felt so helpless."

Even as he tied her right wrist tight to the chair, it was a profession of ardent devotion. She had been right to trust him. Back in Zacatecas and every moment since then.

Her cheeks prickled with welcome warmth before the words even left her lips. "Then when this is over, and we leave, and we are alone—promise to touch me."

His eyes had not left hers; in them, she read the same sin she desired. A flush of longing raced up her throat.

Reckless. She should be chastising herself for being so bold. She had never once wanted to be forward with a man; she had never been so forthright. But when her body was her own to govern, *that* was what she wanted: palm to palm, the taste of their breath mingling. That weightless, blazing heat and the crush of his chest against hers.

She wanted him. She wanted to look at him as they stood on the prow of a ship bound far from here, sailing toward a new life. A world where she was not possessed, nor the ugly daughter of a wealthy, well-connected family, but her own.

His Adam's apple bobbed as he swallowed.

"I can do that," he breathed.

"Promise."

"I swear it."

He would, then and there, if she had asked him to. She could taste it on the air between them—it was woven thick with the profane knowledge that each wanted what the other craved, each would give and take and give from the moment she whispered her assent.

But not yet. Not here, not now.

"Stand back," she said.

He rose with thick reluctance, as if moving through heavy mercury.

"I fear it will be a long night," she said.

XXIX

Elías

THE NEXT MORNING broke pale and white. It was the day Alba would undergo what Bartolomé called an opening parry: Elías was to report to the chapel at siesta and be present for the priest to first face the demon that plagued Alba.

Elías did not volunteer the information that he had already tried this, nor that he had visited the shrine. Every sinew of his being vibrated with an intoxicating mixture of hope and fear through the night, even after Bartolomé took over watching Alba to allow him a few hours of sleep. He was on edge from the moment he woke, dreading what would happen when afternoon's shadows grew long. He was so lost in thought over breakfast that he did not notice Heraclio come into the kitchen until Socorro had vanished, leaving the place eerily silent but for the crackle of the fire.

Elías looked up from his food, saw his uncle, and said nothing. Would the bull charge? Or would it retreat? It was better to wait and see.

"Come with me," Heraclio said.

He followed Heraclio to a storeroom that had been turned into a study of sorts. The walls were lined with shelves with miscellaneous items: bags of rice, books with hacienda records. Dust that smelled vaguely of horse feed.

Heraclio motioned for him to wait near the door. He rummaged through a chest and then withdrew a purse. He set it atop a nearby shelf; it struck the wood heavily. Another purse. Another.

Elías watched as Heraclio set a small fortune in silver at his eye level, and then turned to face him.

"I want you gone," Heraclio announced.

Of all the things Elías had imagined happening this day, this was not one of them. "I beg your pardon?"

"The misunderstanding with Romero was unfortunate," Heraclio continued. This was not an apology; Elías neither expected nor cared for one. "But it showed me something important." He set his hands on his hips and surveyed Elías from boots to face. "You bring out the worst in Carlos. It's bad for the family. It's bad for his engagement."

He shoved the purses toward Elías. The clink of silver on silver struck pain through his teeth.

"Based on my calculations, on the amount of ore in the mines and the amount of mercury you brought, this is the equivalent of your share," Heraclio said. "Per the agreement you made with my father. Take it and go."

It was a prince's ransom. He could ride to Acapulco. There were still many weeks until the fleet left for the Philippines; he could spirit himself onto one of those boats. Buy his passage. Buy his life.

Without Alba.

"Go back to Spain," Heraclio said. "Or stay in the Indies. I don't care, as long as you're far from here."

Elías put a hand on the first purse. Its weight was a balm that loosened his shoulders. Silver fixed things. It always did. This could be his inheritance: a new ship, a new sea, new soil beneath his feet. A life free of pain.

But a fleeting image appeared of Fátima hovering in the doorway of their home, her dark eyes cast down at the ground, blinking furiously. Silent tears rolled thick down her cheeks.

All you ever do is leave.

His greed went foul in his mouth.

No matter how hard he ran from his life, his past kept pace with his shadow. No matter where he went, how long he lived, this would always be true. His shame was a body long gone to rot, but it would poison everything he touched if he let it. Forever.

Alba was not his penance, his history to repeat, but a miracle. A chance. An opportunity to take his regret and rewrite it.

Not even a prince's ransom could buy that.

In Fátima's memory, he prayed, though he did not know to whom, or to what, only that perhaps it reached down, down through the floor of Casa Calavera, down into the stone of the mountains: *Give me strength.*

He lifted his hand from the bag of silver.

"No, thank you," he said.

Heraclio stilled. "What?"

Elías steeled himself to lie and lie eloquently.

"Being here," he began, "I cannot help but meditate on my father's memory. I feel closer to him here. Closer than I ever felt when he was alive." It tasted honest enough, for it had a seed of truth in it. Reading Victoriano's journals, spending time with María Victoriana, and even with Carolina . . . it had brought him closer to his father. He still refused to grieve, but instead of anger, he now felt an ever-present soreness—akin to a pulled muscle—when he

THE POSSESSION OF ALBA DÍAZ

thought of the man. He did not like it. "I think he would want me to help make the mine profitable, in his name. At least for a time," he said, seeing color rise up Heraclio's neck, the first sign that the bull would be unleashed. "I have no desire to stay forever. But I plan to stay for now."

"Fool," Heraclio spat. "I'm being excessively generous." He took a purse and threw it at Elías, who caught it against his chest. Its force was almost that of a blow. "I made calculations, but there's no guarantee of what's really down there. This could be more than I owe you. Take it and go."

Or there could be twice as much, whispered a voice in Elías's ear, with a smile that felt as jackal-like as Abuelo Arcadio's.

"I'm looking out for you," Heraclio said. "Not even your father gave a shit whether you lived or died, much less if you had something to live on."

This was his inheritance.

He weighed it in his hands and found that he wanted no part of it.

He threw the purse back at Heraclio, whose face contorted in surprise as he caught it.

"We're Monterrubios," Elías snarled. "We don't look after one another. We look after the money, don't we?" And he would not. He had made Alba a promise that he intended to keep. "I'm staying."

NOON CAME AND went. The hive of the hacienda de minas settled into a low, sleepy buzz, and Elías stepped out of the cold of Casa Calavera into a rare break in the clouds. Brilliant sunshine blinded him as he crossed to the chapel.

He heard voices, raised and argumentative.

"What is he doing here?" Alba was saying.

When he stepped inside, heads whirled at the sound of his footsteps.

Three heads.

"What is *he* doing here?" Carlos cried, pointing an accusing finger at Elías.

"What," Elías said, "the fuck."

"Mind your tongue," Carlos snapped.

Alba threw her hands up in frustration. She stood before a chair on the altar with the others, dressed in a simple white gown. She glowed like an angry saint. Santa Alba, patron of those who suffer under the yoke of pig fiancés, hear our prayer.

"Enough. We are all here in the service of helping Señorita Díaz," Bartolomé declared, his voice ringing through the chapel as if the space were made to amplify him and him alone. Did they teach that in seminary? It was an enviable skill.

"Does he even know what's going on?" Alba said, directing her exasperated question at Bartolomé.

"Exactly. No one even talks to him," Carlos said. "Why would he be here?"

When Elías laughed, he let it ring as mockingly as he wished. He let it die a long, natural death, admonishing look from Bartolomé be damned.

"I'm shocked that you broke our confidence, Padre," he said, letting his feelings bleed into the words. They tasted acidic. Good. "You promised that you would not tell—"

"I made no such promise," Bartolomé interrupted crisply.

Indeed.

He hadn't.

Uncertainty cracked the ground beneath Elías; fissures sliced past him, running deep and black, fracturing the floor on which he stood.

Who else had he told? Who else would he tell?

"Confidence?" Carlos's voice pitched in a way that reminded Elías distinctly of Alba's mother in her shriller moments. Though it was abundantly clear that Bartolomé was the arbiter of secrets kept and broken, Carlos whirled on Elías, fangs unsheathed and ready to provoke. Was that not the Monterrubio way? "You *dare* presume to keep secrets from me involving my fiancée?"

Elías counted the secrets he kept, stowing them in a velvet box like so many jewels: the silkiness of Alba's feet as he rubbed warmth back into them; her palm against his; Don't stop; the hungry crush of her mouth; her weight in his arms, mercury held fast at last; the sinful oaths he swore to her in the blackest night. Oaths he would keep if it killed him.

He took a brief moment to admire their luster and, satisfied, held his tongue.

"I swore to you that no harm would come to Alba under my watch," Bartolomé said to Elías, ignoring Carlos's outburst. "I plan to follow this ritual to the letter, and part of that involves trustworthy assistants. It is unwise for the priest to be alone; therefore, the company of one who has been privy to this . . . situation since the beginning." He nodded at Elías. "In the event that Señorita Díaz needs to be restrained, it was necessary to ask for further assistance. For propriety's sake, the ritual suggests female family members."

Alba flinched.

Bartolomé turned to her. "I do not wish to assume, but I wagered that your mother—"

"No, you assumed correctly," Alba said. Her face strained as Carlos took her hands and turned his back to Elías.

"Why didn't you tell me?" he asked, low and passionate. "Is this why you've been so strange?"

Alba took a deliberate step away from him, toward Bartolomé.

"Padre," she said sharply. "Get this over with."

"Yes, Lomé," Carlos said. "I need my fiancée back before we return to Zacatecas. If anyone knew that this happened to our family, our reputation would never recover."

Alba gave a mighty roll of the eyes and turned toward the altar as Bartolomé began to describe the basics of the ritual to Carlos. She placed a hand on the back of the chair and slumped slightly, using it to hold her weight.

Elías ran to reach her side and caught her by the elbow. A delicate green vein lifted prominent on her forehead; sweat beaded along her hairline and temples.

"Sit," he urged. She deflated into the chair. "Is there water?" he asked the others.

There was; he brought it to her. Water sloshed over the sides of the cup when she took it. Splashes darkened the front of her dress as she lifted it to her mouth.

"As I told you, it's not going to be over in one session," Bartolomé said. "I am but one man. Some cases take days. Others, weeks."

"Weeks!" Carlos cried.

Elías glanced down to gauge Alba's reaction. Her plait lay against her back, but beneath it, her neck—

Loose hairs tangled in the exposed bones of her spine.

He could see her bones.

"Padre," Elías said softly. Perhaps his tone conveyed that something was very, very wrong, for both the priest and Carlos fell silent and looked his way immediately. "We're not alone."

XXX

Elías

ALBA FLUNG HER head back, her spine striking the back of the chair as her eyes rolled back in her head. She forced herself to standing, but Elías had her by the upper arm. If he didn't look at her face, it would be fine. He focused on her shoulder, the bend of her spine. The elegant pale curve of one bone stacked on the next.

They were not living bones, wet with blood and sinew. They were sun-bleached and picked clean, by carrion bird or beast.

He swallowed hard.

"May you please sit?" he murmured. "We would like to talk."

A wet, vicious snarl.

"Rope, Carlos!" Bartolomé snapped.

In the periphery of his vision: her cheekbones, the panes of her face. Skin began to peel away, to dry and disintegrate, revealing more white bone.

"You charlatan." The voice was not Alba's. He was becoming accustomed to the demon's hoarse rumble, the sensation that it drew from deep waters. It set his teeth on edge. "You whore. I can taste your filth and sin. I shall feast on it."

She struggled to free herself from his grip. No, it was not Alba—it was the demon. It.

"Quick, Carlos!"

Elías held fast, even as white teeth gnashed and a stale smell washed over him. Dead air in a mine. It smelled of suffocating in Almadén, of men rotting in the shafts, of metallic fumes stinging his throat and making him gag—

Carlos was at her other side, his face colorless and drawn. He was stiff with paralysis as Elías took Alba's arm and slipped rope around it.

The demon whirled, yanking at Elías. Caught off guard, he stumbled; when he found his footing, it was to Carlos's scream.

The demon had buried its teeth in Carlos's shoulder. Carlos's eyes were so wide they looked as if they might pop out of his skull.

Forgive me, Alba, Elías thought and, seizing Alba's shoulders, yanked her away. Hopefully not hard enough that Alba would suffer, but hard enough that the demon was surprised.

A snap of teeth; a flash of red tongue. The demon turned and pounced on Elías, its hands flying to his throat.

The demon's grip crushed his windpipe. He gasped, but he was a fish on land. Sparks pocked his vision. *He had no air.*

"Interfering rat," it growled. Darkness bored into him. No eyes, *no eyes, no eyes*—

A cool spray of droplets caught Elías's cheek. The demon dropped him as suddenly as it had turned on him, flinching and hissing.

Elías pulled in raw, harsh breaths as Bartolomé continued to fling holy water at the demon, then tossed Carlos the rope.

Carlos had not moved. He held one hand to his shoulder, his face slack with horror.

With a frustrated grunt, Elías grabbed the rope instead. The demon was distracted; they might not get another chance to restrain it.

He seized Alba by the waist and flung her down into the chair. Echoes of last night fluttered at the periphery of his vision: the smell of her hair, her skin; how close he had been to the silken well of her throat as his reverent fingertips tied her down.

Promise to touch me.

He would. By God, he swore he would, and it would not be like this. It would be worship. It would be profane.

"I'm sorry, I'm so sorry," he murmured.

He thrust his shoulder against her chest to pinion the demon to the chair as he tied down forearms.

The demon tried to bite his ear. Bartolomé made the sign of the cross over their struggle, and it growled. He could feel the rumble of the sound passing through his body; it left his hair standing on end in its wake.

When Elías flung himself back at last, it was with a throbbing head, scratches along his cheeks, and—fortunately—both ears still intact.

The demon writhed, but the rope held fast.

Elías expected Carlos to snap at him for how inappropriately he had touched Alba; that was the whole reason Carlos was there, wasn't it?

Elías expected a swell of hatred. Carlos was paralyzed, his presence only making this entire undertaking worse.

But Carlos's expression was grief-stricken. He continued to clutch his shoulder as Bartolomé instructed the men to kneel.

Elías did not welcome the sympathy that seeped into his bones. Why was he putting himself in Carlos's shoes, thinking, in an agonizing flash, how it must feel to see Alba like this for the first time?

Perhaps it was because his anger was directed elsewhere, at the priest who began the ritual. He knelt as instructed, lowering his head respectfully... but kept his eyes on the legs of the chair and the bare feet before him.

The Litany of the Saints washed over him. Carlos knew every response—whether to say *Lord, have mercy on us* or *Christ, graciously hear us*; Elías stumbled often.

"All ye holy bishops and confessors—"

"Pray for us," Carlos said, and Elías echoed.

"All ye holy doctors, Saint Anthony, Saint Benedict..."

The sound of struggle against the bonds had lessened. Elías lifted his head as he murmured *Christ, have mercy* slightly out of rhythm.

Alba slumped in the chair. Hair that had worked loose from her plait fell into her face.

This was a charade. There was no demon, there was only an injured young woman, bound in a chair. Her breathing was labored; her breast rose and fell against the rope that bound her, leaving irritated red marks on her skin.

He needed to take her away from this. It would only cause her pain. Only cause her suffering. He wanted to kiss her brow and undo her bonds and—

A hand stretched into his vision and caught his attention. Bartolomé did not touch him nor stay him, but the signal was clear. *Be still. Stay back.*

Elías had not even realized that he had risen to his feet.

He knelt again.

Bartolomé spread his feet in a firm stance that reminded Elías that the priest's past life had been spent on battlefields.

"I command thee, unclean spirit, whosoever thou art," Bartolomé began, his voice ringing like bells, "along with all thine associates who have taken possession of this handmaiden of God—"

"You're all whores." That rough, foreign voice emerged, though Alba's head still hung forward and her body remained limp.

Bartolomé did not waver. "That by the mysteries of the Incarnation, Passion, Resurrection, and Ascension of our Lord Jesus Christ—"

"Shut up, you fat possum."

Out of the corner of his eye, Elías saw Carlos shudder, his face the color of parchment. Evidently, the demon had fully returned in its favored aspect.

"By the descent of the Holy Spirit, by the coming of our Lord unto judgment—"

"You," the demon purred. "Carlosssss. I know you."

Carlos made as if to stand; without stopping his recitation, Bartolomé put a firm hand on his shoulder.

A dark, hoarse laugh.

"How sweet of him to protect you," the demon purred. "How sad that that's the closest you'll ever come to him fucking you. He never will, and you know it, and still you weep in the dark about it. How pathetic."

Carlos's cheeks flushed dark; he inhaled sharply through his nose as if he had been struck.

Everything the demon had flung at Elías hit like a fist to the teeth because it was true. This, too, must be true. He should not be fascinated by this revelation. He should *not*. Nor should the idea of telling Alba cross his mind.

No—she *knew*. Of course she did. That was why she wanted to marry him. They would wed and leave each other in peace—once the pieces fell together, it made perfect sense.

"I command thee to obey me to the letter," Bartolomé snarled at the demon, lifting his hand from Carlos's shoulder. "I, who—though unworthy—am a minister of God." He stepped forward. One, two—that was all. It was a prowl, a predator's dangerously soft approach. "Neither shalt thou be emboldened to harm in any way this handmaiden of God, nor these bystanders, nor any of their possessions."

The demon flailed and spat. Bartolomé traced the sign of the cross over the gaping darkness where eyes ought to be.

"What is thy name?" he thundered. "How many spirits inhabit this handmaiden of God?"

"They call me . . ."

It growled.

"Bartolomé," it said at last. It tilted its head back and loosed a wild cackle that sang up to the rafters.

Bartolomé began the Litany of the Saints again. Carlos murmured replies; Elías tried to. But he had made the mistake of looking up. He was spellbound by the sight of the demon facing down Bartolomé, how the shadows of the chapel seemed to writhe and snarl at the scene unfolding before them.

Another application of holy water; the demon hissed like a rattlesnake, its red tongue flicking through teeth.

"What is thy name?" Bartolomé demanded.

"I have none in your tongue," it rattled.

"When did you enter Alba Díaz de Bolaños, and what is the cause thereof?"

"She is mine," it growled, and repeated it over, and over, and over, the words overlapping and resonating through one another, filling the chapel, filling Elías's skull. Mine, mine, mine.

How dare this foul being lay claim to her?

His hands were meant to be folded before him, ever the image of the faithful Catholic supporting Bartolomé. But the priest had betrayed his confidence. Elías balled his hands into fists at his sides as anger festered in his throat.

The next sound that shattered the chapel: a cry, wretched and broken. A girl's cry.

"Alba!" Carlos lurched forward.

Bartolomé seized him by the arm. The priest's jaw was set; sweat dripped down his temples. He did not take his eyes off the demon as he snarled, "Stay back."

It *was* a snarl. He and the demon were two animals alike in rage, two wolves ready to tear each other's throats out over their prey.

Bartolomé thrust out his right hand. He announced a gospel reading and made crosses over his forehead, lips, and breast, and then did so over the demon.

Another cry—this one was the demon's. Elías flinched away from it, hands flying to his ears. Metal over his teeth, back and forth, back and forth. Blood pounded in his ears; it would be pouring down his jaw any moment now.

"In the beginning was the Word, and the Word was with God, and the Word was God," Bartolomé cried.

A flex—that was how Elías would think of the change later. It was as if the air in the chapel bent around the demon's will and rippled outward, bringing waves of heat. Nausea churned through Elías's head; it was the heat of being close to a fire, but too close, and it increased with each wave.

"Just you wait." The demon's voice cut through the heat, through Bartolomé's droning, like a knife. "I'll tear the flesh from your bones. I'll peel the veins from your face. I'll stay in this wretched place, too close to *her*, if it means I can suck your liver dry."

Her.

Elías saw ripples across mercury. He felt an echo of the terror that had flooded him in a dark shrine in the mountain.

Bartolomé continued reading, making crosses over the demon.

Distantly, Elías registered the sound of retching to his left, where Carlos was kneeling.

Another cry. Alba was in there, in that heat, in that cage.

She had not chosen this. She never wished for this. It was not her fault that she had been left to die in the mine as an infant. She was innocent. It was not her fault that returning to this place had somehow, it seemed, reawakened what lay inside her like a parasite.

He rose. His hands were fists at his sides.

Alba is her own. She is her own. She is her own.

It rolled and unspooled in his mind, humming like an incantation.

"Come, my darling," the demon purred, its voice vibrating through the heat. "You could take me in. Let me lend silver to your tongue." A flash of red through teeth. "You and me. Think of the power. We could conquer this foul land with bullet and blood." The demon spat at Bartolomé. The glob flew through the air and struck him square on the cheek; surprise cut off his voice and let the demon's fill the chapel: "I anoint you with it," the demon added, mocking, and spat again. A blood clot hit his face. Bartolomé swiped it away, but the streak of blood remained.

"In the beginning was the Word!" Bartolomé bellowed.

"Priest of death, priest of pestilence," the demon spat back, its voice reverberating through the chapel. The air rippled with it. "Priest of filth and rape."

Bartolomé struck the demon across the face with the Bible.

Alba cried out.

"Stop!" The word broke on a sob. That was her voice. *That was her.* "Please, stop!"

Bartolomé's eyes burned fey and wild, as if the cry only stoked his fire. He struck her again.

THE POSSESSION OF ALBA DÍAZ

"Enough!" Elías cried. He lurched forward; someone caught his arm.

Carlos. White, sweating, looking as if he was going to be sick again. He shook, his eyes wide.

"He said to stay back," he said hoarsely.

"I cast thee out, thou unclean spirit!" Bartolomé roared, raising his right hand like a prophet.

The demon went limp.

The heat in the room vanished. Sweat went clammy on Elías's back, on his arms.

Carlos relaxed. "Thank God," he whispered, and babbled it over and over again, clinging to Elías's arm to support himself rather than to restrain. "She will be delivered."

Indeed, it appeared so: Bartolomé stood over Alba in the chair, hand outstretched like Moses commanding seas to part, the Bible he had struck her with clutched in his other hand.

Alba's head hung before her. Hair in her face. Her limbs impotent and slack.

Bartolomé was breathing hard, the rasp of his panting filling the chapel. After a moment, he lowered his hand.

But the hairs on Elías's neck still stood on end. Something still crackled in the room: the promise of lightning, or distant thunder.

"In the name of our Lord Jesus Christ," Bartolomé said, more softly this time. He made another sign of the cross over Alba. "Depart and vanish from this creature of God."

Alba lifted her head.

A gasp slipped from Elías's lips.

For it was not Alba—it was the demon, its lack of eyes devouring everything in the room. The ropes that had bound Alba went slack, and in a single, swift motion, they rearranged as if at the demon's command.

Into a noose.

"Stop talking," the demon rasped, "or she dies."

The rope tightened. Its end lifted.

Elías thrust Carlos off his arm.

"For it is He who commands thee," Bartolomé thundered. "He who ordered thee cast down from the heights of Heaven—"

Alba let out a strangled cry. Her body lifted from the chair; though her face was still the demon's, she was clawing at her throat.

This was not enough. It was clear from the first time Elías recited the Fatiha and the Lord's Prayer that religion helped, it did, it had some power against the monster within Alba, but it was not enough.

Another thundering voice joined with Bartolomé's; it overpowered it, it filled his head.

It was his own.

I move with quicksilver.

Years in Almadén drew his life's string taut, awaiting the sharp shears of the Fates. The bowels of the mine were filled with fumes of evaporating mercury. The punishment was not the work but the poison he breathed, the poison he drank, the poison he touched, the poison he still touched every day in the incorporadero, running his fingers through mud-thick slurry.

Quicksilver had always been his psychopomp, omnipresent as a loyal dog, watching and waiting for the moment to bring him into the land of the dead.

Now, it would be his weapon.

It is the road to me.

It was a direct path, a conduit, to the power of the gleaming shrine in the mountain. To the horror within that even the demon seemed to fear.

Incantations from *El Libro de San Cipriano* flowed from him like a spring with the stones cleared away: clear, fluid, without effort, without him even trying to remember them. His skin burned, his lungs burned—all of him burned with a searing, metallic heat, white and untouchable.

Alba lowered.

Elías surged forward, shoving Bartolomé out of the way. Shouting behind him; no one could touch him. He was wholly focused on Alba, on the demon that flickered in and out of her body, on its foul hands clutching the rope.

He seized the rope around Alba's throat and rent it. It snapped in two. Alba fell into the chair, neck and limbs limp. Red marks blistered her throat.

A shadow rose behind her like a plume of smoke. It coalesced, darkened; a skull formed out of the smoke.

It grinned at Elías.

"Stronger than I thought," the demon rumbled. Wisps of smoke reached out and stroked his cheek. Elías shuddered, bile scorching the back of his throat. "Would you like to play? Come, let's bargain. Borrow some of my power. All it takes is a drop of blood and a promise from those pretty lips, and we can both get what we want. You blast that foul priest and his pathetic lackey off the face of the earth. Blacken this mine. Blacken them all. Destroy everything and run away with your woman. Isn't that what you want?"

Elías's heart pounded. It was eerily silent, as if the chapel, the others, everything, had faded away. Even Alba felt distant, though she was slumped in the chair before him.

The demon was weak. It *needed* him.

And he would not play nice.

"I want you gone," Elías growled, and he thrust his hands into the smoke.

Smoke turned to bone beneath his hands, a skull beneath his

fingers. It burned his skin, but he seized it harder, he held it even as its jaw worked and snapped, as a tongue shot through teeth and reached for him.

Foul breath washed over him; still water, rotten mine. Gnashing teeth.

"Leave this woman," he commanded. A swell of a wave beneath his feet, crashing and rushing through his poisoned veins. "Begone and stay gone."

He flung the skull as hard as he could through the smoke.

It struck the floor and shattered.

The ground bucked.

"Earthquake!" Carlos cried, and suddenly, Elías was in the chapel, flung to his knees before Alba. His jaw caught her knee; his teeth clashed together. He cursed.

The world stilled.

His heart beat. He breathed. He lifted his head.

"Alba?" he said. Put a hand on her knee. She slumped over one arm of the chair.

He forced himself to his feet, though his legs trembled, and gently lifted her so that she sat upright. Her head lolled onto her chest.

Was she breathing?

His fingers found the soft skin of her wrist, seeking her pulse. For a long moment, too long, *too fucking long*, nothing happened.

Then: a beat.

Relief flooded him. Her chest rose and fell. She lived. She would be all right.

He wanted to gather her into his arms and cradle her to his chest, to sweep her away from this torment.

He couldn't, not before Bartolomé and Carlos, whom he became aware of again as their footsteps approached. He wanted to shove them away from Alba, to protect her from them. His ribs could crack from the ache of it.

"What on earth . . . ?" Carlos whispered hoarsely.

Elías shot him a sharp look, but Carlos was not looking at him.

He and Bartolomé were looking at the floor around Elías and Alba. At the black marks that scored the ground around the chair.

At Elías's hands, which he had quickly lifted off Alba at the others' approach.

His fingertips were blackened, as if he had run them through soot. A soft smoke rose from them.

What had he done?

XXXI

Alba

THE WINDOW IN her room was open. She knew this before she opened her eyes. The cluck of chickens from the courtyard seemed crisp, and there was a freshness to the room, a brush of chilly breeze against her cheeks. The insides of her eyelids glowed red.

Sun.

What time was it?

What—

She tried to thrust herself upright. Failed.

She was tied down to the bed with rope. Ropes at her wrists, around her ankles...

Memories swept up like nausea and struck her in the front of her skull, dizzying her. Sparks scattered across her vision.

Elías.

His face was the last thing she saw in the midst of the exorcism. He had thrust Bartolomé aside, sending the priest splaying on the ground, and approached. His hands were black, as if he had dipped them in ink. A delicate vapor rose off them like mist from a field at dawn—

Then blackness. Nothing. A still room, a ringing in her ears. An emptiness in her, a sense of vacancy. She was hollow as a drum. She felt weak, but she felt ... alone.

"Mija, lie back down."

Mamá was at her bedside, dabbing a cloth in a bowl of steaming water. So, not alone in the room. But alone in her body.

What had Elías done?

The work of Bartolomé left her feeling like the skin of an animal carcass stripped from its flesh and dumped in the dirt. But Elías—he had *done* something.

The emptiness that hummed white and rhythmic in her head was proof of that.

"Let me put this compress back on your poor head," Mamá said.

The light hinted at late afternoon. Where was Elías?

"Mamá, what are you doing here?" she said. With a jolt, she realized that for the first time in days, her voice felt like her own. It was not muscling past something else. It had no dissonant notes. It felt like it was *hers*. "I don't want you to fall ill."

Mamá laughed, but it was a dry laugh, partially forced. The kind of laugh that she gave when she wanted someone to know that the jig was up. "Padre Bartolomé has assured me that your condition is far from contagious," she said, "provided that I say my prayers and guard against evil."

Alba stared at her as she tried to force her aching mind to process the information. Mamá dabbed the compress on her forehead. Warm water ran down her temples.

"Your father and I know all about what torments you have been through now," she said. "I am so sorry. I didn't see. And it happened right under our very noses." Her eyes glistened like fine crystal in sunlight. "To think that sorcerer would curse you," she said, her voice shaking with emotion, "when all his family ever did was offer him a new life here in the Indies."

Dread was a stone rolling down a hill: a gentle push, and it rolled faster, and faster, and faster—

"I can't even say his name." Mamá shuddered theatrically and crossed herself, the compress sending droplets of water across the silk of her dress. The holy motion sent a steep sweep of nausea through Alba's head. "That devil. To think that we broke bread with him."

"That isn't true," Alba said. "He helped me. If it were not for Elías, I—"

"Hush, mija, I know you're confused," Mamá said. "Padre Bartolomé said that you would be."

"No," Alba said. "Mamá, if it were not for Elías, I could be dead. Who is calling him a sorcerer? Where is he?"

Mamá frowned. "I see I have upset you. I have said too much. I am so sorry, mija." She turned to the door to the sitting room. "Padre Horacio," she called.

Alba whipped her head to the door as a strange man entered. His hair was salt-and-pepper, his beard fully white. He had the long face of a dog and a tired, sloped bend of the back. His eyes, however, were dark, so dark they could have been black, and when they fell on Alba, an urge to recoil crept under her skin.

"Padre, she is awake, but she is confused," Mamá said, placing the compress in the bowl. She stood.

Mamá should stay. The impulse lit in Alba like a child's plea, urgent and swift. She did not want to be left alone with this man.

"Mamá," she said. "Who is that?"

"Padre Horacio, mija," Mamá said. "He arrived last night from the capital. He and the others will be helping Padre Bartolomé look after you."

Alba's mouth was dry as sand. "Others?"

"The other Inquisitors, of course. Thanks be to God," Mamá said, and nodded at Padre Horacio. "Won't you sit, Padre?"

Alba reached for her mother's arm, for her skirts, but they slipped out of her reach. Reality slid through her fingers, slick as oil, tilting and tripping her no matter how she fought to find her footing.

Her pulse thrummed like a rabbit's as Padre Horacio pulled the chair beneath the window and—without so much as greeting her—began to pray the rosary in a low voice.

"Mamá," Alba said, her voice low and urgent. "These people will hurt me. You can't leave me with them. They will *hurt me*."

Pity swept over Mamá's face. "Mija," she said, her voice softening as she put the compress down. "You can't see what we see. You are hurting now. Your papá and I . . . we know that this is necessary. You will understand, when you are well."

She stood.

"No," Alba cried. "Don't leave!"

Mamá shut the door softly, as if she didn't want to disturb Alba.

Alba was greatly disturbed.

The capital was several days' journey from Zacatecas, and that was without the hours-long climb into the mountains.

If this man arrived last night . . .

They had only been at Mina San Gabriel for a little over a week. Bartolomé must have written to them many days ago. Perhaps after they first arrived. Perhaps even before.

He had never said a word. Never warned them. Had he meant to dupe them?

Was the exorcism a trap set for Elías? Even if it wasn't, he had walked right into the jaws of the beast. He had seen how she suffered, and he had done *something*—though Alba knew not what—in front of Padre Bartolomé and Carlos that had condemned him.

Her head was quiet. Was it this priest droning on in the corner of her room, or was it what Elías had done at the end of the exorcism?

What *had* he done?

Where was he?

In danger, that was where he was. And she was in bed, God knew how many hours after the fact. Abandoned here by her mother.

Left here to die.

She did not want to die, and so she would not.

Abandoned, again. Not worth fighting for. You were the worst thing to happen to her.

She was the worst thing to happen to the woman she was born to, and she was the worst thing to happen to her mother now. She had ruined Mamá and Papá's chance at happiness, for when they received their child at last, it was a monster.

You are a monster.

She was a monster.

So act like one.

A freezing spray of water; Alba hissed in pain as the droplets struck her face like needles.

The priest was praying loudly. Oh, she wanted to rip his fat face off, to toss it out the window and watch the chickens make sport of it—

"Are you hungry, señorita?"

María Victoriana stood at the doorway Mamá had disappeared through, holding a tray.

"I hope I am not interrupting," she said, casting a look between Alba and the priest who stood over her, flinging more droplets of holy water at her face. "It sounded like an argument."

"Come in, girl," the priest said.

A bowl of soup steamed on the tray, its aromas of calabaza and puerco wafting into the room.

No, Alba was not hungry. But she was desperate for an ally. If one could be found in María Victoriana, then yes, she was hungry.

She remained obediently still as María Victoriana placed the bowl on the table at her bedside and slowly began feeding her spoonfuls.

"Where is Elías?" Alba asked.

María Victoriana looked as if she hadn't heard her. Perhaps she hadn't. Perhaps Alba's faculties of speech had vanished, and though she screamed, no one would hear her, no one would save her from this torment—

"Where is he?" she asked, louder, testing her speech.

María Victoriana hushed her sharply. "Let me feed you as I have been ordered, señorita."

That tone cut like acid. The girl would not tell Alba anything. She would be trapped here forever, until the priests saw fit to torture her, and then there would be no Elías to intervene, there would be nothing but the demon and the priests and her strung between, flaccid meat, powerless to save herself.

Heat seared her chest. She gasped, and instinctively flung herself upward. She hit the restraints of the ropes and fell back, but the burning on her chest remained—

"Oh no, it spilled!" María Victoriana cried out.

There was puerco con calabaza all over Alba's chest, in her hair, on the sheets. Hot broth burned her skin. There was too much of it everywhere, and she could not escape the smell; she wanted to vomit.

"I have to clean this up!" María Victoriana declared, louder and more obviously than was necessary. She immediately set to stripping the bed, pulling broth-soaked sheets out from under Alba.

"Your nightgown," she said. "It's soaked. I am so sorry, señorita. I must change it."

The priest was on his feet and huffing nonsense, holy water in hand, as María Victoriana scurried to the chest of clothing at the foot of Alba's bed and began pawing through it. When she emerged with a clean white nightgown, she turned to the priest.

"I need to change her clothing, Padre," she said. "I was frightened, and my clumsiness led to this, and I will be punished if I don't clean it all up. Please." Her voice pitched sharply toward tears. "I don't want to be punished, Padre!"

"So clean it up!" the priest snapped. "I don't want you here a moment longer."

"But Padre," María Victoriana said, her eyes growing theatrically wide, "I cannot change her with you watching. She will be naked."

Color rose in the priest's face; he blustered, wordless, then snarled, "I shall not leave."

María Victoriana had found the weak spot in the tendon; she took a firm thumb and pressed on it. Hard.

"For shame, Padre!" she breathed. "The indecency! I'll go directly to Padre Bartolomé and say—"

"Basta," the priest spat. "If you can change her without untying anything, you are free to. But if you are harmed"—here his voice became the equivalent of a wagging, warning finger—"it is your own fault."

When he stepped out the door, María Victoriana began changing Alba's soup-soaked white dress. There was no pulling it over her head with her tied to the bed; María Victoriana took a glinting dinner knife from the tray she had brought and began to rip the dress along the seams to remove it.

"Where is he? He needs to get away from here immediately," Alba said. "He did too much in front of Padre Bartolomé. They're going to hurt him unless—"

"They already have," María Victoriana snapped. "Save me your tears," she added harshly, seeing that Alba's mouth had dropped open in horror. "You're not the one who can hear him screaming."

"Where is he?"

"The stables," María Victoriana said. "The priests intend to exorcise you in the morning and then leave with him for the capital for trial. They'll probably kill him, and it's all your fault."

"We have to free him," Alba said. María Victoriana's fingers were cold as she wrenched cloth around her shoulders and over her chest. "If we can get him a horse and send him on the road to Acapulco, he'll—"

"You don't think I've tried?" María Victoriana snapped.

"I will fix this," Alba swore, low and passionate.

"It's no use," María Victoriana said. She had shoved the nightgown over Alba's head and buttoned it haphazardly, then tucked the sheets in around her tightly. Her eyes shone too bright, as full of repressed emotion as her shaking voice; her cheeks were flushed. "You did this. And I'm the one who'll have to bury him."

"Enough," the priest said. Alba startled; she had not realized the priest still hovered a step beyond the doorway. Had he been listening the whole time? "She is dressed, is she not?"

María Victoriana stood back sharply from Alba's side, brushing quickly at her eyes.

"She's dressed enough, Padre," she said. "You may continue. She is not hungry."

Without another look at Alba, she snatched the tray of spilled soup and left the room. The priest sat at his post. Fingertips over rosary; more droning prayers.

María Victoriana's words hung low over her, steady and swooping, a vulture over carrion. *You're not the one who can hear him screaming.*

María Victoriana was right: This was all her fault. They would continue to hurt Elías unless she did something. But she was tied to a bed, watched every moment. A sob wracked her body, and she let herself drown in helpless wretchedness and the acute knowledge that Elías was hurting and it was *all her fault*.

One wrist—her right wrist—brushed up against something cool.

Her breath caught. Her spine stiffened.

She shifted her wrist again, searching for that cool sensation.

It was metal.

ALBA WAITED FOR twilight.

Priests came in and examined her. Some wished to interrogate her; Padre Bartolomé restrained them. Not physically, no, but he was a dominant presence in the room whenever he entered. He made it clear that he had ownership of the situation.

She was *his*. He would lead the questioning, he would decide when they carried out the exorcism, he he *he*.

This resentment sparked a wan, distant flutter of delight from the demon. She felt it in her breast as Bartolomé stood over her speaking to the other priests, pointing at her face and explaining the appearance of bone and gristle. She saw his bone and gristle. She saw flaps of flesh hanging off his jaw as if a butcher had been interrupted mid-carving. She heard the buzz of fat, black flies when he drew near.

She shoved it all down. She would be her own tonight.

No one asked her if she was well. No one wondered if she was in pain. If she needed to relieve herself (she did) or if she was hungry (she was). The Inquisition was a famished snake in the presence of an unguarded egg. Priests circled her thorny nest, long tongues flicking between their teeth, beady eyes reptilian in their lust. They all looked the same. They all were the same: men who had been promised violence and denied it for years, who had finally found an object for their belligerence.

When the hovering circle of priests had broken up and left, herded by Bartolomé out of her rooms to dine with her parents, Alba looked within.

Nothing looked back.

It was like calling into a cavern and expecting an echo, only to have the words swallowed by darkness.

If Carolina's story that Elías had recounted was to be believed, she had been this way her whole life. Burdened by this parasite bound to her soul. Never alone. Never her *own*.

Elías was the only one who could fix that. They had been wrong to seek the help of Bartolomé. All he wanted was to use her for his own advancement.

How he had glowed in the esteem of the other priests! He was greedy, he was filth, she would sink her teeth into him, and—

A grim twitch of her lips as she fought to halt that line of thinking. It would be naive to think that she was fully free. But whatever Elías had done, he had weakened the demon substantially.

And María Victoriana had left a knife beneath the sheets.

She ensured her lips were pressed tightly together and her face was as blank as possible; she had been left with a guardian, another faceless priest deep in prayer, his rosary clicking in the corner of the room.

Freeing her first wrist took writhing and reaching. But she had never been bested by a knot in her embroidery, and she refused to be bested now.

She scored herself a dozen times before getting the rope off her right wrist; blood stained her sheets bright as poppies. The left was easier. At last, rope loosened and fell away from sore flesh. Light-headedness made the victory melt sweet on her tongue.

She shot the priest swift, apprehensive glances as she worked. His eyes were downcast as he rocked back and forth gently in the rhythm of meditation. She had to unbind her ankles next. But how to do so without alerting the priest?

There should be a key to the bedchamber on her desk. If she could unbind herself and flee the room fast enough, she could lock the door behind her, buying her precious time to escape the house.

But that would require speed and strength. Did she have enough of either? Only sitting up would tell her, and sitting up was the first step in a mad sprint to the stables. This could be a fool's errand. This could be madness.

She was going to try anyway.

She took the knife in her hand beneath the sheets and sat up.

"Señorita—"

She yanked off sheets. She reached for her ankles. The knife had been dulled by working on her wrists, but now she had been bitten by wildfire and worked as if possessed. The thought made a mad grin streak across her face.

Rope snapped. She yanked it away.

The skin at her ankles was open and wept, but she did not feel it. The priest had risen and was at her bedside. He put heavy hands on her arms to push her down to the bed, and suddenly she was in a dark hallway, she was a child, she was trapped by hot breath and grasping hands—

This time, she would not freeze. She would fight. For herself. For Elías.

We fight dirty.

She whirled up at the priest with a snarl, with a brandishing of teeth and knife right beneath his nose. He jerked back reflexively;

it was the only reason the blade did not slice his cheek open. Good. Let him know she was not defenseless. She would not be a virgin in a white dress waiting to be sacrificed. She loosed a warning hiss and jabbed the knife toward him as she flung herself from the bed and landed on her feet.

They were numb. She had barely eaten. Her throat was dry. Didn't matter. She felt only victory, a pure, drunken bubble of elation, as she half fell toward the door.

"Don't you dare—"

She ducked his outstretched hands. She was an animal, twisting and crawling and untouchable, and she was through the door. She slammed it shut behind her. Held it back with her own body. The priest tried to open it; a shudder through the door, through her chest. Once, twice.

He was bigger. Heavier.

She cast a wild look at her writing desk. Key, key, where was the key—

She spotted it.

She lurched forward, snatched it, then spun, and as the priest emerged through the door, she threw her whole weight against the wood and caught his hand in the doorframe.

A feral cry; a thick crunching of fingers. She released the door; the hand withdrew with a yelp. She slammed it shut and locked it with a violently shaking hand.

She was barely clothed. Buttons of her nightdress unbound and no shoes. A howling priest pounding on the door behind her.

She snatched a rebozo cast haphazardly over one chair and flung herself toward the door, dinner knife still in hand.

Through the door, down the hall. She yearned for the brilliant blue of Acapulco, for the salty taste of freedom stinging her lips as she stepped onto the deck of a ship, but she had no supplies, nothing. Not even shoes. She might have to release that dream to the night and weep as it slipped away.

But so long as it rode on a swift wind with Elías in tow? So be it.

"Alba!"

A hand caught her by the upper arm. She whirled and brandished the knife, ready to snarl, but—

Carlos lurched back from the knife. His face was openly shocked, streaked with salt as if he had been weeping. His grip was firm on her arm, pinioning her to the spot. She was but steps from the door to the patio. She was so close.

She lowered the knife. "Let me go," she whispered.

From behind her came the low thumping of a fist on a wooden door. A muffled cry. The priest—and her disappearance—would not go undiscovered for long.

She tugged at her arm; Carlos did not release it.

"Where on earth are you going?" he asked, voice low. "You're not supposed to be—"

She had heard the demon humiliate him. And now that she had, it was glaringly obvious: He was in love with Bartolomé, or had been infatuated, and he, too, had been betrayed by the arrival of the Inquisition. If he did not spin the story carefully, the priests' presence could cast the Monterrubios into ruin—their reputations and business had only a slim chance of surviving such a scandal. He was wounded. He was alone.

But he was her oldest friend. She had placed her life in his hands, for among all her acquaintances in Zacatecas, he was the only one she trusted to treat it with dignity.

Perhaps he still would.

"They're going to kill him," she said, low and urgent. "It's all my fault. I have to get him out. Let me go. Please."

"Alba," he said. "You must go back to your room. Bartolomé will—"

"You saw him hurt me," Alba cut him off, her voice cracking. She yanked at her arm again. Damn Carlos for being stronger than he appeared. She did not want to resort to threatening him with the knife, but if he didn't let her go, she would.

His frown deepened. "He is trying to help."

"And Elías actually *can*!" she cried.

A low rumble of displeasure in her chest. Its resonance felt foreign as it rattled against her ribs. She shoved it down. The demon was weak. And it would *stay* weak, so help her God.

Carlos hushed her harshly, casting a look over his shoulder. There were too many people in this house, too many enemies. She tugged at her arm; still he did not release her.

"I want him to live," she pleaded.

"You want him," Carlos interrupted, voice bitter.

Alba opened her mouth to defend herself, but Carlos held up his other hand.

"I don't want to hear why," he said. "I know that we don't love each other as a married couple should. Probably never would. But I like to think I could have given you a safe life. Perhaps even a happy one."

A sob thickened in Alba's throat. She had chosen her future husband well.

"You still can," she whispered. Her voice was shredded: from weeping, from screaming, from the way this felt like the most permanent goodbye she had ever voiced. "You're a good man. You deserve more than a mutually beneficial marriage. You should have someone who loves you, who will come here with you and make you laugh. That is not me."

He met her eyes and held them for a long moment. His grip on her arm loosened, and then dropped entirely.

"Bartolomé won't stop," he said. "And I fear . . . he hasn't been listening to me. If it came to it, he would let you die before he gave up the chase." He inhaled deeply. "I will help, but only if you promise to run too."

Relief threatened to make her knees weak. "Carlos—"

Shouts rose from the direction of her bedroom. The priest had broken free; or others had joined him. They would find her. She had to run.

Carlos, too, looked like a hare who had heard hunters: alert, alight, trembling with the need to flee. "He's in the stables." He reached into his pocket and withdrew a key, then pressed it into her palm. "I'll hold them off as long as I can and meet you there with supplies. And shoes," he added, glancing down at her bare feet. "Now go."

XXXII

Elías

ELÍAS LAY ON his back on the cold floor. Floor was, perhaps, a generous term; it was hard-packed dirt, and it had the chill of the earth in winter. It seeped up through his bones and into his throbbing skull. His hands were bound before him and his feet at the ankles, but he could roll onto his side and press his throbbing cheek to the dirt. A shift of liquid in his nose; it was bleeding. That he could tell without looking.

After everything he had done—communicating with an unholy, terrifying power that some called *goddess*, performing occult rituals, challenging a demon—he could not loosen rope around his wrists. His hands had tingled from bloodlessness; now, they had settled into a dull throb. He doubted he would be able to feel them at all soon.

All he had wanted was to come, get rich, and leave. And here he was. All because he was too soft to let a woman suffer.

His greed had failed him. Was that not the true downfall of a

Monterrubio? To be presented with riches—and all the security and freedom that entailed—and choose a woman instead?

Would he die for that choice?

A gentle thump of metal against wood at the door. He squinted through the gloom; a shadow appeared at the side of the door, then yawned wider as the door opened with a pained creak.

Long black hair falling into a pale, thin face; a white nightdress, wrists red with blood . . . and a knife clutched in one hand.

Alarm struck him like a flash flood. If he hadn't been prone on the ground, he might have jumped back with a cry.

But when she slipped inside and shut the door, it was her commanding her movements. He swore it was true. It was not the jerky, agitated steps of the demon that brought her across the room and to his side. She fell to her knees smoothly. Her face was her own. Her voice, when she began to exclaim at his state, was her own.

The blood on her was fresh.

Dread pooled anew in his belly.

"How did you get here?" he asked.

"There has to be something sharper than this in here," Alba muttered, working with the knife at the knots in the rope that bound his wrists. Her face lacked color; her cheeks looked drawn and exhausted. She had grown thinner in the weeks since he first saw her in Zacatecas, and never had it been more apparent than now: Her cheekbones were too sharp, the bones of her chest pressing against her skin as if they were determined to emerge. It was as if the demon's skeleton and Alba's flesh were fusing, becoming inseparable, but no, that could not be. He would separate them. He would.

"Ha!" With a cry of victory, Alba yanked on the rope binding his wrists. Blood rushed to his digits with stiffening pins and needles; he grimaced as he shook his hands out.

She immediately set to work on his ankles. Her fingertips, too, were splattered with darkening blood.

His stomach turned.

"How did you escape?" he asked.

"Acapulco," Alba said, ignoring the question. "Someone is getting horses for us. If we rush, we can make the fleet, can't we?"

"We need supplies," he said, heart picking up speed. They weren't getting out of this, were they? It couldn't be real. She couldn't actually be here, dressed in nothing but a bloodied nightgown, talking about fleeing tonight. This had to be a dream.

Let it not be a nightmare.

Alba rose sharply and whirled, looking about the room. "There has to be something sharp in here—" Her gaze caught on a shelf. When she sprang for it, the movement set his stiffening muscles crying to life—that was a predator's movement, and it was unlike her. He set to working the rope at his ankles himself. He could not be bound if the demon seized her.

It would be a death sentence.

If only they had time. Privacy. What he was able to accomplish in the chapel had brought her so close to freedom he could taste it. In a perfect scenario, they would leave this place without the demon. Flee everything. Be truly free.

This was not a perfect scenario. But it might just work.

"Yes, perfect," Alba hissed. She turned on him, a hoof pick in one hand, a fey light in her eye.

The movement was too quick; Elías fought the urge to fling himself back from her. Who was guiding her body now? Whose idea was it to flee?

He searched her face, but there was no sign of the skull.

Could he trust her?

He had to. He was laid out before her, vulnerable, as unable to defend himself as she had been when he bound her with ropes the other night. Until he was unbound, he had to trust that she was in command of her body. And that no fresh blood would thicken the patchy coating already on her raw, rope-bitten wrists.

His pulse quickened as she raised the hoof pick; his imagination supplying vivid, gruesome images of how the tool could be lifted up high overhead and brought down toward the soft flesh of his eyes—

Though his heart remained at the well of this throat, thrumming like a panicked rabbit's, all she did with the hoof pick was work at the knot. She pried rope loose. They were almost free, almost—

The door creaked a second time.

His heart stopped when Carlos stepped into the room.

No. No, it was not fair, Elías was almost on his feet. He could fight, he could—

Carlos did not look surprised to see Alba in here, working at freeing Elías's bindings. He held a burlap bag that was lumpy with items. A thick sarape was thrown over one arm.

His stance, on second glance, did not read *attack*, no . . .

Carlos had *helped* Alba? There was no other explanation: Carlos watched, waiting, as Alba unwound the rope from Elías's ankles with a pleased, victorious sound and helped him to his feet.

"There are two horses saddled in the stable aisle," Carlos said, his voice low. "Supplies in bags on their saddles. Here." He tossed the bag he held to Elías; when he caught it, it was heavier than he anticipated and hit his chest with a metallic sound.

Silver.

"Give my name at Casa Alfonso in Acapulco. They'll charge the room to my account," Carlos said, putting a pair of women's boots on the ground and handing the sarape to Alba, who immediately dropped her thin rebozo and yanked the thicker wool over her head. She reached for the boots and thrust her feet into them, barely stooping to tie them. "I'll do my best to direct everyone here to search in the capital."

Alba and Elías followed Carlos. Elías's feet could barely feel the ground beneath them—they were sharp with blood rushing back into them but also weightless with disbelief.

He caught the bridle Carlos tossed him and quickly put it on the larger of the two horses. Carlos helped Alba mount the smaller horse—a bay mare, one Elías did not recognize, perhaps one of her family's horses.

"Hurry," she hissed at Elías.

Carlos had turned to leave; Elías caught him by the elbow. "Why are you helping?"

Carlos shrugged his hand off roughly.

"I don't think I like you," he said, tone acrid, "but I don't want to watch you die."

First María Victoriana, then Carlos. Why did people keep saying that to him?

"Now get the hell out of here," Carlos said as Elías mounted. A shadow of grief crossed his face as he lifted a hand in farewell to Alba.

"Vaya con Dios," he said.

He turned away rather than watch them leave.

HEELS TO HIDE; a snap of leather reins. The clatter of shod hooves on stone. They were off like phantoms in the night.

Elías barely remembered the way they came into Mina San Gabriel, but there was only one way out, and his horse seemed to know it well enough. Once out of sight of the valley, he brought them to a trot, listening for any sign that they were being followed. The moon was high and cast long, gray shadows; the ground and the mountains around them seemed doused in molten silver.

They had supplies, money, horses, a destination. It was his to ruin.

He would not. He was not going to fuck up this one chance they had. Not when the mirage of Alba in the azoguería lingered in the back of his mind, thickening like mist: the shine of sunlight on her cheeks, the luster in her dark eyes as she wondered about Constantinople. How she had practically trembled with longing at the thought of a new world. A new chance.

They could have it all. All they had to do was run.

A gasp from behind him. A panicked, strangled sound.

He wrenched around in his saddle, tightening the reins to slow his horse. "Alba?"

His gut soured at the sight. She was a marionette drenched in moonlight, at the mercy of a mad puppeteer. Her arms were not her own but twisted at wrong angles. Her head jerked to one side, then to the other, then back, her throat white and exposed to him. Her horse had stalled but trembled as if it was preparing to bolt.

Alba's jaw opened wide, wider than it should, dropping down until her face seemed to be nothing but maw and a red tongue.

"Not *now*," Elías snapped.

Not if he had anything to do with it.

He dismounted and, keeping his horse's reins in one hand, lunged toward the mare. If he did not seize her bridle now, she would be gone, and they would be lost. The mare tossed her head up. Gravel crunched beneath her hooves as she backed away from Elías, her nostrils flaring, her ears flat to her skull.

"Shh," he hushed. It was pointless to try to communicate *calm* through body language; he felt no calm, the mare felt no calm. There was no lying about it either way. "Be still."

One step closer. One last reach, and Elías grasped the reins.

The demon flung Alba's body from the saddle.

She struck the ground. Instead of collapsing there in a heap of limbs, she skidded toward the edge of the road as if dragged by a great force.

She rose too quickly. Too jerkily. Her forearms and elbows were dark with blood and gravel; her nightdress and sarape were torn by rocks.

She turned to retrace their path to Mina San Gabriel.

Elías had the reins of both horses in his hands; he could not let them drop, not when one threatened to bolt. He could not lose Alba either. Jerkily, she made her way up the road, her feet barely touching the dirt. A phantom from a nightmare, moving farther and farther out of his reach.

He was trapped. He was paralyzed. No. He would not remain paralyzed.

Mercury in his blood. Mercury in his lungs. Wherever there was mercury, there was the thrumming power of whatever deity lived in these mountains.

Darkness can only be undone by its like.

He reached for the mercury that ran in his veins. With a chant from *El Libro de San Cipriano*, he took both reins in his left hand and flung his right toward Alba's turned back.

"Come back," he commanded.

The demon shuddered to a stop. Its whole body trembled violently, but it obeyed him. Pebbles struck against one another from the force of it being pulled toward him. Freedom was at their fingertips. He was not going to let it slip out of his grasp. This demon would not stand in his way.

Then, it whirled.

He expected the skeletal grin, the hollow pits, but his heart never did. It shrieked to a stop against his ribs and throbbed there, hysterical, as he met the demon's gaze. As the fetid vapor of brimstone rose to his nostrils and reached into his own skull.

"Begone," the demon growled.

Elías felt it like a blow to the chest. He stumbled a step back before righting himself. He dug his heels in and met the demon's gaze anew.

"I am not leaving her," he forced through gritted teeth.

The demon spat at him. A glob of something thick and dark and shining struck the ground at his feet.

"I am *sick* of you interfering."

Metal on stone, like a pickaxe pulled agonizingly slow along the wall of a mine tunnel. Elías clenched his teeth; the hairs on his arms stood on end. Alba's mare whinnied, high and sharp, and she tossed her head again, yanking at his left arm.

"You can't have her," he said, annunciating the words clearly and forcefully, feeling heat build in his fingertips as he poured sheer will into each syllable.

Darkness can only be undone by its like.

"Weakling. She is mine."

She was not. And he could prove it.

He inhaled deeply, and began to sing his mother's lullaby, the one thing that had soothed her terror in the mine.

The demon tilted Alba's head to the side, doglike, as if the sharpness of Elías's breathless notes disturbed it.

It was distracted. As he had planned.

Then, Elías flung out his right hand. His will reached out like an extension of that hand to seize the demon's throat.

He yanked; the demon batted him away with a furious snarl. But he did not relent. Once, twice, again. Finally, he found purchase, though the demon writhed and tried to slip through his grasp, slick as raw meat, but he held on with all his strength, ignoring the squelch of flesh, ignoring the warm drip of blood.

He would not let go.

With all his might, all his will, all the power burning through the mercury in his body, he pulled.

A dark cloud of smoke slipped out of Alba's body.

It shot across the space between them, as if released by a slingshot, and struck him full in the chest.

Sulfur and smoke. Stinging heat and clouded vision. His organs slipped and rearranged, wiggling as if of their own volition, meat shuddering and soft in all the wrong places in his gut.

He was on his knees. He was crawling forward. Backward. There was no up, no forward, no down, where was he? He heard his name; his shoulder struck the ground. He was clawing at his face. It was in him, it was under his skin, writhing like a thousand snakes. Beetles scurried over his bones, over his skin, up his nostrils, into his brain and out his eyes—

He balled his right hand into a fist. He would get to Acapulco, so help him God.

He struck the earth. Hard.

Mercury was heavy in his blood. Mercury would seize the demon and wrap it in gleaming chains. That was what he wanted; now he envisioned it happening. He crushed the smoke down; he bound it in a writhing quicksilver cage and locked it there.

Hands on his shoulders. They shook him.

"What did you do?"

Elías gasped for air. Wind struck his face like ice; his cheeks were slick with wet. Sweat or tears. Maybe blood.

Alba bent over him. She searched him for injury, checking his limbs, running warm fingertips over his skin. He shuddered. Moonlight frosted him. Shadows sank into his bones like stone.

He would deal with the consequences of what he had done later. For now, they did not have time to linger.

"Explain later," he grunted.

"Can you get up?"

He nodded. She took his arm and helped him to his feet; groaning in pain, he found his footing. Mercifully, the horses had not fled.

Claws rent at the inside of his face.

Weakling, weakling, I will suck your marrow—

Shut up, he snarled.

He shunted the voice to the side.

He walked with Alba to her horse. His limbs were numb, barely his own, as if he were feeling them through several layers of thick, rough cloth.

Alba tossed her mare's reins over the horse's neck. Elías interlaced his fingers and held his hands out to Alba, then assisted her into the saddle.

He felt as if there were a thick veil between him and the world, thicker than drink, thicker than opium. He shook his head. Bit the inside of his cheek. Pain would bring clarity, wouldn't it?

It brought metallic warmth to his tongue. That was it.

"Ready?" he said to Alba. "We need to make up lost time."

She nodded, gathering her reins.

One step at a time. The road to Acapulco was long. Once they were out of the mountains and found a place to rest and lick their wounds, he could assess their situation and decide what to do next about the demon that he now carried in his own breast.

Alba gasped; he turned.

THE POSSESSION OF ALBA DÍAZ

A horse had emerged from the side of the road, careening down the side of the mountain. A dark figure flung its leg over the horse's side and dismounted before the horse even came to a stop, and now stood between Elías and his own horse.

Padre Bartolomé drew a long knife from beneath his clothes and shifted his stance. He was crouched, on the offensive.

"In the name of God," he said, "you go no farther."

XXXIII

Elías

PADRE BARTOLOMÉ STOOD between them and their escape, and the demon delighted in this. A tingling rush skittered over Elías's skin; pleasure and anger grappled with each other in his throat.

Priestflesh.

Elías lifted his lip in a snarl, his hackles raised, as if he were a cur facing a foe in a dark alley.

"Get on the horse, Elías!" Alba cried. Her voice came from far away, farther than he expected—while the priest and Elías faced each other, she had already begun to bypass the men by leading her mare across the rocky, steep slope of the side of the road. "Run!"

But Bartolomé was directly between him and the saddle. Him and freedom.

Elías feinted left, then skid on loose gravel; he ducked around the streak of a knife in the moonlight. Then he leaped back, arms held wide to avoid a cut.

Bartolomé's sweat was acrid; the heave of his breath was not panicked but measured. Memories flashed like sparks in the corners of his awareness: Carlos gushing about Bartolomé's military career to Romero at the incorporadero; Alba's father commenting several times on the unpriestlike number of weapons Bartolomé traveled with.

Elías had killed a man while drunk in a back alley. It was a sin of rage and impulse. The give of fleshy throat beneath his thumbs left him screaming in his sleep, caught in the shackle of night terrors, for years.

Bartolomé had made killing his career.

Elías's heart flung itself to his throat as Bartolomé seized him by the shirt and brought the knife close to his throat.

Priestflesh.

The demon's presence shot through his face, stinging like saltwater through his nostrils. His eyes rolled back and saw black.

Judging from Bartolomé's strangled cry and the way he thrust Elías back in a shuddering, disgusted gesture, Bartolomé saw something different. Perhaps those black pits devoured his own eyes. Perhaps his skin had peeled away. Perhaps—

A flash of awareness: His hands were on the priest's neck. This had happened while his mind was distracted, wholly without his own accord. He discovered that he was pressing his thumbs into the soft valley of a throat, forcing Bartolomé down onto his knees—

Priestflesh.

Distantly, as if through a haze of far too much drink, Elías felt his jaw drop wide. He felt cold air on his teeth and tongue, he felt the pulse of delight as Bartolomé's eyes bulged from his face with fear, with the lack of air, with his death—

A spray of ice, burning ice, shot his face like a thousand needles. He dropped his prey with a howl, staggering back and pawing at his eyes.

With one hand, Bartolomé brandished a bottle of holy water. With his other, he clutched his throat—his breathing pulled dry and hoarse. He swayed on his feet.

"Elías! The horse!" Alba cried.

Now was the time to run.

Priestflesh.

Elías forced the demon down, down, then, as his vision cleared from the assault of holy water, he lurched toward his horse.

Priestflesh. Need—not his own, but a foreign, gut-deep lust—yanked him sideways. He staggered like a drunk. He fought to move forward past it; the demon fought to keep him back, close to Bartolomé.

I move with quicksilver . . . It is the road to me.

The mercury in his blood would kill him one day. Let it. So long as this demon did not drag him down toward death first.

"Obey me," he snarled thickly. The sensation of something foreign wrenching him back and forth weakened.

"Elías!" Alba shrieked. Her voice seemed as if it were coming from the wrong direction, from far away. Had she dismounted? "Behind you!"

He turned.

The demon bled sheer white delight: Bartolomé was upon them. Bartolomé and his knife—

Bartolomé ducked once, then twice—a solid *thunk* cut off his cursing. Alba had thrown a rock through the dark with admirable accuracy. A strangled cry of pain; Alba found her target again.

"Get on the horse!" Alba cried.

Elías turned to the horse. Mercury forced the demon back, far enough back that *he* was in command of his legs, his hands, and he reached for the saddle—

Bartolomé straightened. Raised his right hand, the one which held the knife, and made the sign of the cross.

"In nomine Patris, et Filii," he bellowed, the blade flashing up and down, side to side as it moved with the holy gestures. Elías could not stop the demon from jerking his body sideways at the sound of the prayer. His vision and hearing were dimmed as if he were underwater, fighting to see through the gloom.

Bartolomé swung the knife upward, its arc the perfect curvature of a wave rising from deep waters. "Et Spiritus Sancti."

A metallic glint; the whine of wind on a blade. A panicked cry, not his own. From far away: the crack of bone.

It was not from far away.

It was from here. At him; in him.

Bartolomé's knife sank into his chest, up to the hilt. The priest's hand slid away as he staggered back, arms raised, ready to defend himself. He thought to defend himself from the wrong threat, though—he ducked belatedly as a volley of angry stones struck him.

Elías's pulse thrummed in his ears. His chest felt tight, as if it were cramping.

The hilt was right over his heart.

How interesting.

Just as interesting: The demon had shrunk away somewhere and fallen silent.

"Leave him," Elías said to Alba. "Let's get out of here."

He turned to his horse, reaching for the reins.

He staggered. Blood throbbed in his ears.

The ground rose like a wave. It struck him in the face.

Waves of laughter rose in concert around him, brassy and dissonant and reeking of brimstone. He swatted them away. His arm hurt to move.

No breath in his lungs; he was coughing. Someone was pushing him. Lances of white pain spider-webbed his body.

Elías's ribs lifted, muscles tearing, ligaments crying out in protest, as Bartolomé wrenched the knife out of his chest—a sodden, slick sound, like the butchering of a hog—then, with a feral cry, brought it down again.

Compression. Popping. Searing white across his vision.

Blood splattered across Bartolomé's face, slick on his cheekbones. Wetting his eyebrows. He yanked the knife out and lifted it—

A dark figure appeared behind Bartolomé, its own weapon lifted high.

Alba brought the stone down hard against Bartolomé's temple. She shoved him aside and collapsed on her knees next to Elías, ignoring the howling of the priest.

Her fingertips danced over Elías's breast. Her breathing rasped, shallow and panicked; her cheeks were slick with silver. With mercury. The world was mercury, wet and silky, slipping through his fingers.

"Elías," she was saying. Over and over, like a prayer. "Don't leave me. Don't leave."

All you ever do is leave.

"I'm staying." His breath tasted wet. He grabbed her hands; his shook. He pulled in air. It sounded wheezing and weak. He could feel it whistling in places it shouldn't whistle, and he simply could not get enough. His mouth was full of mercury. He coughed around it. Too thick. Too heavy. He couldn't catch his breath.

Her hands were warm.

"I'm staying with you," he said.

XXXIV

Alba

SHE WOULD ALWAYS remember the exact moment Elías passed. It was viscerally tactile in her mind, more object than vision. It was as if she could lift it from under her hair, pull it through her scalp, and pin it, dripping, to velvet. She could put it behind glass, like a naturalist with luminously winged dead insects.

It was his sight.

His breathing had stopped, yes, but when his eyes went from looking at her, to past her, and beyond, and then went still—that was when he was gone.

She felt as if she hovered beyond her own shoulder, an impassive spectator. She could remember weeping, but it was as if she were watching someone else. Hot rasping sobs, wails of disbelief, fingers curled into the wet of his shredded, bloodied shirt, stiffening in the cold—these belonged to a stranger.

Then: Two shadows rose.

The first came from her left, where she had shoved Bartolomé.

His body lumbered upright with a curse and the grit of gravel, with an aura of rage shimmering over his bent shoulders like a red cloak.

The second: Before her, from Elías's grisly, wet chest, a curl of smoke lifted like the tail of a curious cat. It reeked of sulfur. It was looking at her when it spoke.

You know what happens now, it said.

And it plunged into her throat.

SHE WAS IN the mine. She was helpless, alone, abandoned. Cold. Weak. Ripped from warmth. From soft touch. Left to die.

But someone took her and led her forward. Upward. Elías walked before her, silhouetted by candlelight that bobbed several steps ahead of them.

He was singing her back. Back to the surface, to the light, to the air. It echoed all around her: that sad, lilting melody, rhythmic as a heartbeat, yearning like sweetness on the tongue. His hands on hers, guiding her out of the darkness.

IT WAS ALWAYS dark now. No one to lead her out. She could lead herself, she supposed, but why? To what end? What was waiting for her on the other side of the darkness?

Bartolomé was a constant at her bedside, praying, regaling anyone who would listen—most people at Casa Calavera, that is—with the struggle between him and the sorcerer. How Elías, powered by the might of his many deals with Satan, had almost brained him with a sharp stone to the head. That was why he had such an unsightly lump on the side of his skull and a black eye that turned yellow and green as it aged.

She could sneer at that. At the priest's vanity.

But what was the point?

No one would listen to her. No one would give credence to anything she shared, anything she felt, anything she thought. For was it not true that the sorcerer's presence had stalled, if not almost ruined, her recovery from the evil that afflicted her? Was it not true that he had cursed her to begin with? That was why they took him captive—to send him to the capital for a proper trial at the hands of the Inquisitors.

And now he was dead.

It did not matter. Elías would have been condemned to death anyway, for what he had done to Alba. The priests repeated this until it became as true as the prayers they chanted. God bless Padre Bartolomé for saving Señorita Alba. God bless Padre Bartolomé for his quick thinking and courage, God bless Padre Bartolomé's readiness to face danger and rescue the innocent maiden from that practitioner of the occult.

God bless the priests. And God damn Alba Díaz de Bolaños: Once again, she was the worst thing to ever happen to someone.

She was the cause of Elías's death. Everyone knew it.

María Victoriana flitted in and out of her room like a ghost, bringing things for the priests, her face puffy and red from crying. She would not even look at Alba.

EVERY NIGHT, SHE dreamed of the road. She dreamed of moonlight on the stark white bone of Elías's face, no—it was not his face but the face of a skull, with eyes like the pits of a mine.

His act was one of selflessness, one with which no one in Casa Calavera could ever compete, be they priest or layman or even her own mother. Elías had freed her, paying with his very soul.

For the first time in her life, she had felt free.

She felt vacant and quiet. In being emptied, she had become whole.

As if she wanted to lie down immediately and fall, weightless, into deep, pure sleep. A cold gray morning of pattering rain, a breeze on her face.

What she had not dared to hope had become truth: Elías had indeed been the cure. He was the one person—the only person—who could have freed her from her torment.

He had. He did.

Now he was gone.

She was white sheets on a line, drying in pure sunlight, snapping in the wind.

MAMÁ AND PAPÁ talked of a convent in Guadalajara. Endless droning, locked in the dark, kneeling as her whole body ached.

CARLOS SAT WITH her, carefully watched by an endless rotation of priests. He did not hold her hand. He did not speak. Perhaps it was a quarter of an hour. Perhaps it was many hours.

He snuck furtive glances at Bartolomé whenever the priest was present. How tragic, to be so ensorcelled by someone whose whole heart was steel and ambition, with no room for soft touch. How pathetic, to be the two of them, soul-broken and quiet in the twilight.

THE INQUISITION TORE Mina San Gabriel apart looking for the shrine Bartolomé was convinced still existed. For people to punish.

They could not find the shrine, but they found the latter.

And those souls were mere practice for what the Inquisitors had in store for her.

XXXV

Alba

"THIS WILL BE the final exorcism of Alba Díaz de Bolaños."

Bartolomé's pronouncement echoed through the chapel. Rain drummed on the ceiling and slicked the earth outside, turning it to clay and carving deep rivulets through the valley. The hem of Alba's white gown was wet and dark with mud. Her shoes and stockings were soaked from the walk to the chapel from Casa Calavera, but that did not matter—the priests had seen fit to have Mamá strip them off Alba's feet before she was laid down on the floor.

She lay atop a rough-hewn wooden cross constructed especially for this occasion. Her arms were splayed and bound in a pale imitation of Christ's. Splinters roughed her skin. No nails through feet; instead, more rope there. Of course. Always the rope. Always the chafing.

This was Hell: the brutal chafing, the disregard for her comfort or her safety. And this, too, was Hell: Mamá allowing it to happen. Mamá stood back, her mantilla shuddering as she shivered in the cold, the beads of her rosary clacking between her nails. Mamá stood by—every moment she did not protest was full-throated consent to her freezing, wet, and weak daughter being bound on a cross on the floor before her.

A pang of grief split Alba's ribs. From that moment on, she felt she had no mother. No friends, no defenders. Not even Carlos—for was it not he who had insisted that this final exorcism take place at Mina San Gabriel? Was it not he who was more preoccupied with rumors about her condition spreading in Zacatecas than by the sight of Alba bound to the cross?

She was alone.

With the priests now gathered in the chapel, Padre Bartolomé seized the reins and drew them tight. Among their number, the Inquisitors had brought an expert in exorcisms—some pale Galician with a strong lisp—but Padre Bartolomé had ordered him to stand at the back of the chapel, near Mamá and Carlos. Bartolomé, and only Bartolomé, would face down the devil in Alba's breast.

Her guts shifted. As if someone were pushing the blankets off the bed on a hot summer's night. Nausea stung the back of her throat; she caught it and swallowed it before it choked her. It was sour. It burned.

You're his creature, after all. A beckoning behind her ear, clear and coy as if it were mortal speech. *He discovered you. His pet. His prize.*

It began.

At every other exorcism, she had felt present. With Elías, especially, she felt involved. She did not simply observe; she lay in wait for the right moment to comb through herself, to pick out stitches as if from a swatch of embroidery. Knot by knot, stitch by stitch. She was devilishly good at embroidery. Better still at finding her work lacking and ripping it out to begin again.

But this time, her body reacted according to what *the demon* willed, not her. She was a foreigner in her own breast, a beast in a cage, limbless, barely a voice.

And so she retreated into her mind. She allowed the threads of her consciousness to become tangled, thick and snarled like matted hair. Buckets of cold water were thrown at her and went up her nose, choking her, making her gasp and weep, and she did not feel any of it. She did not care.

Romero slipped greasy and slick through her mind, the memories of another person. Hands sank into slurry, mercury and silver ore shining like the surface of the moon, like magic, as it poured into his ears and up his nose, into his gaping mouth, and his eyes, oh, how it slipped over his eyes like a funerary mask, how easy it was to hold him down even in liquid so thick, how satisfying the give of the body beneath the mud.

Pale hands—*mine*, she realized, *how odd*—on his shoulders, and a thrust, a push, a final condemnation. The lurch of a body. A trill of mad laughter—oh, it was hers too! She was mad! How freeing!

How foolish of her to dream of autonomy. Of control over her life. She had never had any. She had always been this: a mongrel of mortal and monster, her soul charred and crumbling, her life forfeit since the moment her wet body emerged from a stranger and met the icy mountain air.

She had never had anyone but the demon.

Do you know that Bartolomé sent for the Inquisition weeks ago?

That unearthly purr vibrated through her skull, soft and comforting, drowning out the droning, echoing Latin around her.

She was limp. She shut her eyes—or at least she thought she did. It did not seem to matter if they were open or closed, for she saw the same things: rage and spittle, billowing blackness.

He had decided to frame someone for witchcraft before you even left Zacatecas. He wants to be the exorcist of the Indies. Smash idols and shrines, spill blood, drink glory. So much ambition in the priestflesh, so much, so delicioussssssss.

Once upon a time, in a ballroom in Zacatecas, she had come face-to-face with Padre Bartolomé for the first time. She should have listened to how her gut had soured in the confessional. She should not have trusted Carlos nor Mamá.

For where were they now? They *watched*. They prayed along with the Inquisitors who burned with hatred at her so fiercely she felt she knew the scorch of hellfire.

Perhaps they loved her. Perhaps they cared. But not enough. They were cowards before the Church and slaves to Bartolomé's whims.

And for that, they would watch her be flayed alive. Perhaps even to death.

You provided him with an obvious target, the demon said. *The sorcerer did. It's your fault.*

The words throbbed. Her head was tender, too tender. Her arms ached. They might fall off. She might fall away, forever, forever—

"You mean *you* did." She meant for the words to have venom. They tasted weak and flat.

Behind her ear: a sound that brought to mind a delicate scoff.

I did not give the sorcerer his book. Nor his desire. The stupid man brought this upon himself.

"It's your fault he's dead!" Alba cried.

She did not know to whom she was speaking. The priests? The demon? Herself? The demon and her, her and the demon—were they one and the same? If she had spent her whole life with its menace stitched in her bones, was she even herself? What *was* herself?

Or is it your fault? the demon crooned.

"Damn you!" Alba shouted.

You were left to die, and I saved you, the demon said. *I raised you.*

We eat together, we drink together, we are together, together, together. Your body is mine and it will not die.

But what if she did?

Then I will pass to someone else here. Perhaps dear Carlosssss...

She knew she should feel something in response to this—temptation, perhaps, to inflict this upon someone else. Or anger that the demon was threatening her. Or even a desire to defend Carlos.

But she had no strength. She had not eaten in days. She had no muscle, no will.

"If I die then I am free of you, at least." The words came out thick, as if through blood. How had it gotten there? She did not know. Perhaps she had been struck again.

And then be released to a hundred thousand demons below, the demon snapped.

But did Alba believe that? Elías's use of the Lord's Prayer had caused the demon to shriek and writhe. Holy water stung and bit. But the priests' chanting, their droning—none of it was *fixing* her. None of it would ever fix her. The only person capable of that was Elías, who had looked at her and said *we fight dirty*. Elías, who sang her out of the dark. With whom she had shared one enchanted dance that sealed their fates, molten metal pouring gleaming into their ribs and setting around their hearts.

He was the one thing she had ever chosen for herself.

Her cheeks were wet. With blood, with tears, or with holy water—she could not tell. They all burned the same now.

You should believe me. Hell is real, the demon said.

"Have you seen it?" she murmured. Her lips were swollen and heavy. "Did you come from there?"

Silence.

And it was an odd sort of silence—the demon was not waiting

for dramatic effect, nor had it shifted its attention elsewhere. It did not have a reply.

Or rather, it did—and it did not want to say no.

Images flashed before her eyes. Burning embers. A man's face, lined and thin, framed by monkish, threadbare hair; a hand passing before its furrowed brow and pursed lips, midway through the sign of the cross. The inside of a ship. A brilliantly sunny coastline; swaying palms. The now-familiar stark line of the mountains that ringed Mina San Gabriel, timeless and ancient. A frisson of delight—that was not her own—coursed through her at the sight of men on their knees with dark heads bowed, men punished with whips and the booming chanting of a voice not unlike Bartolomé's reciting the Litany of the Saints.

Priestflessssh, the hum in her ear repeated. *Its juices are the most foul. So soaked in ambition.*

So that was how the demon came to these mountains: with the clergy.

But it had not come from Hell, at least not how Alba was taught to recognize such a place. The vision of embers could have been a cooking fire for all the suffering and dread it inspired.

Insolent human, the demon snapped. *Believe me, if you do not do as I say and live, the punishment you will receive—*

It tasted of bluster. Of bluffing. The truth was this: heaven, hell, gods, devils . . . the demon did not know.

She knew what kind of power worked against it. Prayers and holy water, yes, but most of all: Elías. Elías and sorcery.

"I don't think it's real." A whisper. An opening in her chest; a weight lifted, as if a thousand demons had been clustered at the base of her throat and had alighted, all at once, on loathsome black wings. "I think you're lying. I think the priests are lying. I think . . ." All she could see before her were Elías's sightless eyes, empty, glassy. "I think none of us know what happens after. You're manipulating me. You sound just like *them*."

The priests came into focus around her. She was aware that she lay on the rough wood of the cross, that her hands had gone bloodless and numb, that the water soaking her could have turned to ice in the air before striking her exposed arms and soaked dress.

There was no God in heaven, no fallen angel below.

The only fallen angel was Elías, aglow with infernal might not of this world, but not of Bartolomé's world nor the demon's either. He was the radiance of silver in the sun. He was freedom.

And he was gone.

Her one chance at freedom from both these chafing bonds and the darkness that slithered under her skin and hung thick in her mind—gone.

So what now?

Bartolomé stood over her, a cross in one hand, the burn of ambition filling him with an infernal light.

Her breast rose and fell, sharp, staccato. Her lungs burned. She could not feel her fingers. She could not feel her feet. She could not feel anything except, deep in her chest, a burning, powerful hatred for the priest at the front of this pack of salivating wolves.

We fight dirty.

She met his eyes. Perhaps he stumbled as he spoke; perhaps there was a shade of uncertainty behind those pale, uncanny irises. Perhaps it was because she could see him for what he was—and loathed him for it. Could he feel the burn of her hate? Could he recognize that it was not the demon's hate, but hers and hers alone?

Forgive her, Padre, for she had sinned, and would sin again.

"I will not be cured," she said. Liquid dripped thick out of the corner of her mouth and streaked down her cheek. "But neither will I be caged."

She had lived her whole life in cages built by the demon, built by her parents, built by all of Nueva España. She was expected to be nothing but a silent object moved from place to place. A puppet. A ghost among the living with no will. If she died, she might become free of the demon, free of its torment, free of weight and pain . . . but she would become a pawn in Bartolomé's story. Bound for eternity by the power of his narrative: the exorcist of the Indies, the beloved priest, the savior.

There had to be another way. If she could wrestle with the demon and bend it to her will . . . No, she was too weak. Forcing it down and following her will had not worked. It only had led to disaster. To losing Elías.

But what if she bargained with it?

"I . . . will . . . thwart you," she forced out, holding Bartolomé's gaze. "And you," she said to the demon, "will help me."

She was a curse on this land. An evil. People crossed themselves, spat on her, avoided her presence. She was the worst thing to ever happen to her birth mother. The worst thing to ever happen to Elías.

If it be with her dying breath, then may she be the worst thing to ever happen to Padre Bartolomé Verástegui Robles.

She felt the demon's assent rush through her like a flash flood, cold and bright and good. Her hands twitched and clenched, spasming and flexing, her bones lengthened and punched through her nails and—

She knew the perfect time to unleash her claws, and it was not now. The plan bloomed in her mind, measured stitches running together to form a thick, glorious tapestry. Perhaps this revenge might lead to her own death. So be it.

But not today. Not yet.

The first stitch in her plan: Let the demon do what it did best.

THE POSSESSION OF ALBA DÍAZ

She drank in one last vision of Bartolomé and the faceless mass of priests, then closed her eyes.

Priestflesh, the demon gurgled, rushing beneath her skin with renewed vigor.

Distantly, she heard ropes whine with strain and snap. She heard gasps. She heard a scream, thin and white and pointed enough to shatter glass. She drank it all in like cold water. She felt the demon lift her limbs, lift her chest, lift her wholly into the air.

"Yes," Alba said, and smiled down at the white faces of those assembled below, at those fleeing, at those crying out in fear. That was the price for the demon's collaboration, for its role in the brutal theater that the possession of Alba Díaz de Bolaños was about to become: "Priestflesh."

XXXVI

Alba

THREE MONTHS LATER

ZACATECAS BLOOMED IN the wake of the matlazahuatl. Lives had been lost to the plague, but that only served to burnish the existing lives brighter. Was it not a miracle, to have survived? Was life not precious? Must it not be celebrated?

"What better way to celebrate this miracle than a wedding?" Mamá cried, laying first one necklace, then another, over Alba's throat.

And what a miracle it was. After hours of battle with the demon that the sorcerer had unleashed on Alba, after hissing and spitting blood, after Alba levitated off the ground in a fit of the demon's rage, it was gone. Exorcised.

And was it not all thanks to Padre Bartolomé?

Alba was returned to her parents and Carlos, penitent and quiet. She was exhausted and ill, but it wasn't anything that rest and steaming bowls of caldo could not fix. The Inquisitors, exhausted but triumphant, softened their punishment of the people of Mina

San Gabriel for their idolatrous shrine. Work at the mine stopped for almost an entire week as every man, woman, and child said confession and carried out their penance.

And it rained. In the middle of the dry season, cleansing rain broke from the clouds and swept through the high mountain valley. How symbolic. How beautiful it all was. How clear the air was, shimmering like crystal lain on a dinner table, the day the Díaz family's belongings were packed onto the backs of mules and the family itself into a carriage for a muddy descent from the mountains.

Zacatecas welcomed them with sunlight glistening on puddles. With the gleaming pink spires of the cathedral and a pristine, azure sky spotted with faraway white tufts of clouds.

"I think the second. Or the first?" Mamá wondered.

Alba's wedding dress lay folded and complete in a chest at the foot of her bed; now it was up to Mamá to decide which jewels to adorn Alba with for the ceremony that Saturday. The second necklace lingered longer, its silver and pearls cold against her burning skin.

"Mija, you are so warm." Mamá set both necklaces aside and put the back of her other hand to Alba's cheek, then her forehead.

Alba dropped her gaze. "I am fine."

Satisfied with this answer, Mamá stepped away to cluck over the necklaces and solicit the opinion of one of the maids.

Alba lifted her eyes. She turned and reached for the hand mirror on the vanity to her left.

Her nails—left to grow too long—scratched against the silk on which it lay. She curled her fingers around the handle and lifted it, as if to examine the powder in her coiffure or the fashionable dark beauty mark that Mamá's maid had painted on her cheek.

She gazed at her reflection, appearing to all as a bride transfixed by her own beauty.

But they could not see what gazed back at her: dark pits, writhing blackness, boring out of a skull. A beauty mark, lurid against bone, affixed to one pale cheek.

Together, Alba and the demon grinned.

ORGAN MUSIC ROSE and filled the cathedral up to the rafters, reaching as if it could touch the very heavens. It swam around Alba in a fetid cloud, choking her as the high lace neck of her dress did. She walked slowly toward the altar. Each of her steps was weighed down by pounds of pure silver thread and jewels. She was pure silver. She was the fruit of the mine: born there, left to die there, born again.

The pews were thick with the lords of Zacatecas, dripping with silver and gemstones, powder from their hair and the coy, sickly sweet notes of their perfume melting together with the incense. A gag tugged, insistent, at the back of her mouth.

She swallowed it. She must press on. Toward the altar. Toward the groom and his golden hair and the bronze priest who stood before the altar. Other priests flanked them, fleshy white hands folded piously before them, eyes half-lidded as their Latin song joined the incense and the perfume and the reek of hundreds of bodies. The reek of blood coursing beneath skin in time with her footsteps.

Click. Click. Click.

The soles of her shoes struck tiled floor. They would have echoed, if not for the heaviness of her skirts dragging behind her and muffling the sound.

She had requested the presence of all the priests who had been present at her exorcism. To Carlos, she had explained that it made her feel safe. To Mamá and anyone else who asked, she batted her eyelashes and said, voice soft, that if it were not for them, only the Lord knew what could have become of her. Having them there was an expression of gratitude for all they had done.

Alba stared them down, all of them, as she walked toward the altar. Her strides became firmer. Determined. She unclenched her hands; they floated to her sides and slowly balled into fists.

Carlos's weight shifted forward to his toes. A muscle in his jaw flexed. His eyes flicked over Alba's head at the first pew where her parents sat, then narrowed. The gesture was almost imperceptible—only the faintest wrinkle of skin at his cheek and temple hinted that he was no longer the happy bridegroom awaiting her at the end of the aisle. His body had tensed. He was prey, ready to spring.

Perhaps that might save him. She did not care. It was no longer her business what he did.

She refocused on Bartolomé. His shoulders had stiffened, but his face did not shift. Not for the first time, she was struck by how his irises were like shallow water, transparent and untrustworthy. Pale as the flash of a knife in the moonlight before it was plunged into Elías's breast.

That was the last thing she thought before pain snaked through the backs of her hands, cramping and stiffening her fingers. Claws burst forth through the beds of her nails, carrying bright blood from beneath the skin to the surface.

She crouched and fastened her focus on Bartolomé.

"For Elías," she whispered. "For me."

A feral flush of pleasure filled her body from belly to the crown of her head.

Priestflesh.

Darkness curled at the corners of her vision. With a soft sigh,

Alba the woman, Alba the soul, Alba, who had battled and bathed and borne this body all her life, released her hold on its reins.

CLAWS FOUND THROATS and bellies under vestments. Pins from hair found eyes and cheeks and howling tongues. Screams were glass, shattering and filling her head with echoes that shivered down the insides of her skull. Awareness of the rush of bodies behind her, the panic, the flight. The panic, especially—it melted on the tongue like piloncillo, a textured, dark sweetness. She craved more. She craved salt, she craved warmth. She found it and lapped at it like a kitten, sinking her teeth into meat, relishing its rip as if she were a starving cur—

A hand on her arm. Firm, commanding.

It yanked at her.

She coughed, choking on hot liquid. She spat and pulled back as two hands wrenched her around.

"Enough." The command reverberated through her bones, rattling her as if the hands on her arms had shaken her bodily.

Smoke thinned. Color winked through the haze: gold, white. The pink walls of the cathedral, sharpening slowly. A glint of gold. Red, so much red—

Gold.

It was an earring.

Alba blinked. Her lashes were heavy with blood.

The hands that gripped her arms seemed to pour heat into her like liquid. Clarifying heat, metallic and good and bright on the tongue.

"Alba. Alba. Can you hear me?"

She was hallucinating. She was in the mine. Cold, moist, airless.

The flicker of candlelight, the glint of an earring. The lilting melody leading her out of the dark.

If it was a dream, a trick that the demon plied her with, she accepted it. It was too sweet not to. Not when she had been starved of that voice for weeks, grasping at it only in dreams and memories thick with grief.

"Elías," she said. Her voice was hoarse. It felt ripped. It cracked, weakened not by screaming but by a blooming, impossible hope. "Are you here?"

Elías looked down at her—at how she dripped with blood and the spoils of her savagery—and he grinned.

XXXVII

Elías

MONTHS AGO, MERCURY had filled his veins, slow and thick and sap-like, hardening as it cooled. As his body cooled.

There was a knife in his chest. Then it was gone. A hollow in its wake.

There was keening, far away, echoing through the cold night. Harsh chastisement, feet scrambling against gravel.

Retreating hoofbeats. Retreating weeping.

Silence.

He slept. Or perhaps that's what he thought it was—soft darkness, softer than the gravel and hard rocky earth at his back, cocooned him. Time ceased. He was aware of rhythm—breathing? A heartbeat? He was not sure. Simply that it was there, that it moved in time, keeping step with a slow-moving dance.

Mercury swam before him. Rich, silken waterfalls of it, as if it were gushing from a fountain. It swallowed him, lifting him from the earth, bearing him weightless, tilting him down—

THE POSSESSION OF ALBA DÍAZ

You're not finished yet.

He was not frowning—he had no body, no face to move, no expressions to command—but it was a similar flicker of confusion. A darting shadow across an otherwise spotless sky.

Then: a slap across the face.

"Joder." His voice. Wet, thick, through lips that felt like they were lined with wool.

His cheek stung. It burned.

He *felt*.

Once that thought trickled through him, it was followed by an avalanche of sensations. Bedding beneath him. Aching back. Aching arms. Aching legs. And, in his chest, a pain so acute he hissed.

"¡Tonto!" María Victoriana snapped. "I said don't move."

She slapped him again.

His eyes flew open.

Thatched roof. Adobe walls. Dark room, layered with gray shadows. The smell of pork and tomatoes roasting. A hint of comino. The crackle of a wood fireplace, but distantly, through a closed door.

"What," he said, "the—"

"What part of *don't move* do you not understand, you fat-headed idiot?" María Victoriana grumbled.

She then reached for his chest and resumed tightening bandages over a wet compress.

She was not a merciful nurse.

Elías hissed in pain. "Do you mind?" he snapped.

"It needs compression to heal," she replied, rocking back on her heels with a self-satisfied look on her face. "Señora Flores will be very pleased with me. That's the curandera," she added, somewhat pointedly, "to whom you owe your life."

Life.

Bartolomé's face flashed in his memory, splattered with blood. His own blood.

"Where's Alba?"

"Don't move," María Victoriana repeated, holding her hands out for emphasis. "I swear, I will tie you down if you don't listen."

"Where—"

"Gone," María Victoriana replied.

Dead? No, she couldn't be—

"Zacatecas," María Victoriana clarified, as if reading the panic that flooded his body with tingling pain. "They left yesterday morning after her exorcism. And no, before you ask, of course it didn't work." A shudder passed through her so viscerally it was as if someone had dropped a piece of ice down the back of her neck. "You could feel it when she walked past. I think it made it worse, somehow. She was . . . she seemed *feral*."

"I need to go to her." There was no question. His work was not done. "I'm not finished yet."

The words tasted like an echo.

"You are going to stay put until Señora Flores says you're well enough to leave," María Victoriana said sharply. "And then you're going to pay her handsomely for her silence." Perhaps confusion passed over his face, for she clarified, in a softer tone: "Everyone thinks you're dead, after all."

And so they did: After María Victoriana and Carolina carried his body back from where it had fallen on the road, no one looked to ensure it was buried. They took the women at their word. Prayers were said over a shallow filled-in hole in the ground, tidily arranged next to his father's.

Elías's death, it seemed, was too convenient to be challenged.

Weeks passed. The valley was broad enough that Elías went unnoticed on long crepuscular walks with María Victoriana, wheezing as his patched lungs fought to regain their strength. As he flexed his hands and recited passages from El Libro de San Cipriano to keep them fresh in his mind. He visited the shrine in the grotto, but only at night, with María Victoriana as his guide, so that no one saw or recognized him.

Thus hidden in plain sight, he knelt in the shrine.

Use quicksilver. This remained the only unholy revelation he received. It had helped him subdue the demon as they attempted to flee to Acapulco, had it not?

He planned. He prepared.

And when word came from the city that the former inhabitants of Casa Calavera were preparing for the wedding of the year in the grand cathedral of Zacatecas, he packed a bag, took a jar of mercury from the Inquisition-sacked ruins of his old workshop, and found himself mirrored, a doppelgänger on the opposite end of a nightmare. Here he was again, alone, nothing but mercury and a goal in his hands as he traveled toward the gleaming, opulent jewel of Nueva Galicia to meet his fate.

This time, however, he had a plan. He raced toward a defined end. Toward someone. And this time, he rode without El Libro de San Cipriano in his bag. He had left it in the rubble of the workshop. He had no need for it, after all—he bore it burned into his hands.

And he was ready to make use of it.

ELÍAS STOOD BEFORE Alba Díaz de Bolaños on the altar of the cathedral.

Bloodied priests lay scattered around them like fallen leaves, some groaning, some still. He had torn Alba off a man he believed was Bartolomé—he did not wish to verify this, for that would mean scrutinizing the exposed bone of the man's face. Skin had been peeled off cheeks as if by a paring knife.

He had arrived at the cathedral late, drenched in sweat and aching from the long ride from Mina San Gabriel, and dismounted just as wedding guests began pouring through the high, arched doors of the church. Screaming sent his horse's ears flat against her head.

He fought his way through the waves of people. Toward the altar. Perhaps he caught a glimpse of Carlos, right behind Alba's parents. Perhaps they met eyes; perhaps he had imagined it. It was over faster than he could blink as the sea of people swept them away.

He focused his attention forward, to the bride at the front of the church. His strides lengthened; he broke into a run. He raced down the center aisle of the cathedral, the soles of his boots echoing amid the agonized shrieks of priests, his bag thumping heavy against his thigh. He slipped on blood; he skid; he swore. Caught his balance. Took the steps up to the altar two at a time, skirting fallen priests with their arms akimbo.

Now here he was: face-to-face with Alba and her demon.

He stared down the dark pits. The lolling red tongue. The wash of hot brimstone breath. Was he too late? Was she anywhere to be found behind that blood-splattered skull?

Darkness can only be undone by its like.

There was only one thing to do: try.

"I made you a promise," he declared, the empty cathedral lifting the words high and filling them with light. "I'm here to keep it."

There, at the altar, beneath the crucifix, he began the final exorcism of Alba Díaz de Bolaños.

"Alba," he began, and the name was a prayer, an incantation all its own. "I need you to hold still. To hold the demon still. Can you do that?"

The demon hissed at him; spittle struck his cheekbone and stung like acid. He did not flinch. He did not falter.

He reached for that same lullaby he used when he led her out of the mine, out of the dark, and began to sing. It had distracted the demon while they were fleeing Mina San Gabriel; it would work again. His voice trembled, mangling the memory of how his mother had sung it, but it still tasted like quiet nights. Like peace.

Alba shuddered; the movement raced down her body like a wave, threatening to send her sprawling, collapsing under the weight of white fabric and silver.

She dropped her chin. Her head jerked violently to the side, but each time, she brought it back to center. Her chest rose and fell with sharp, heaving breaths, straining against a heavily embroidered brocade bodice. Perspiration shone on her neck and the curve of her bosom.

She was fighting.

He fumbled for his bag, still singing softly, and withdrew its prized contents: a jar of mercury. Quicksilver swirled and shone as he opened the jar—placing its cork lid within reach on the altar—and, without hesitating, dipped his fingers into the cool luster.

"Keep fighting," he said, "fight to be still."

He could not see her face beyond the skull, but her body shuddered a second time. She twitched once, twice—then was still.

He acted quickly.

He anointed Alba as if the mercury were holy oil. One long, deliberate swipe began between the hollow pits of blackness where her eyes ought to be and moved up the forehead. Another dip of fingers, a new location: this time on the insides of each wrist, following tracks of blue and green veins up the pallid inside of her forearms.

And finally, he dipped his fingers a third time and reached for her neck. He pressed the quicksilver gently against the well of her throat and brought the stroke down to where her clavicles met, slow and tender against her soft skin—for there was skin there. She was fighting the demon and she was *winning*.

Hope lit his skin aflame. Covered in blood and silver and mercury, she gleamed like an idol in the light of the empty cathedral.

This was what he had spent the last months planning, in the dark of the grotto shrine. This was what he had regained his strength for.

The mercury would enter her veins. It was not enough to poison her forever, but it was enough to pave paths, to be a conduit, to allow the terrifying, thrumming power of the goddess in the mountains to pass from him—through the mercury in his veins and in his lungs—to her. To rush from one to the other like a river.

He put the jar next to the cork lid on the altar, took her hands in his, and began to chant. Each time he had faced the demon, he had swung and fought for his life. This was different. This was poetry. This was a lullaby, sung in the dark of the mountain.

The mercury gleamed as if with its own light as Alba cried out. Black smoke poured forth from her chest. It was only then that Elías dropped her hands and snatched the jar from the altar.

As quickly as he could, he trapped the smoke within the jar's confines and slammed the lid shut. The jar shook violently from side to side; he set it down forcefully on the altar.

It was still.

When he turned back to Alba, he met her eyes. Her eyes.

Tears ran the blood on her cheeks pink; he stepped close to her and brushed the wetness away with his thumbs.

"How do you feel?"

She threw her arms around his neck and held him tightly. Silver and brocade pressed heavy against his humble clothes.

"You promised." Her voice shook. Her whole body shook, so he held her closer still, sliding one hand down her spine and pressing it against the low of her back. "You promised and you're here."

"I promise I will always be here," he said, his own voice rough. "Forever."

Thus was their oath, given at the altar, dripping in blood and wreathed in the black smoke of sorcery. Bound with a kiss.

Epilogue

MOST PEOPLE WHO share the story of the old Monterrubio mine will tell you that Alba Díaz de Bolaños stumbled down the steps of the cathedral alone that day, drenched in blood like a calf at slaughter. The wind carried her shrieks through all of the town, sending the people of Zacatecas fleeing inside to hide from her wrath. They say that she walked the whole way back to Mina San Gabriel, propelled by the strength of the demon she had sold her soul to.

By the time she reached the mine, her feet were bare and shredded and as bloodied as her wedding gown. It took her all night, and when the sun rose, she was spotted at the mouth of the mine: drenched in blood, thin enough to be a skeleton, her skin stark and pale against the dark, gore stiffening on her cheeks and against the black of her hair.

Sunlight glinted on the silver of her dress as she turned. She vanished into the mountain, never to be seen again—but often felt on nights when the moon is new and the mine is dark.

That's the better version of the tale, if you ask me.

THE POSSESSION OF ALBA DÍAZ

BUT THIS ONE has Elías facing me at the altar of the Zacatecas cathedral as a groom might his bride, his hands twisting in my hair, his mouth on mine. This one has us swept away in a burning reunion until the screech of the jar of mercury shuddering on the marble altar shocked us to attention.

Then there was a groan from the floor—whether it belonged to Bartolomé or another priest, I will never know.

For this version of the tale has Elías casting his sarape over my shoulders and spiriting me out of the cathedral. What sits on the altar and what lies before it, drenched in blood, are no longer our concern.

He leads me to a ramshackle hotel in the seedy outskirts of the city, where the single mattress is lumpy and thin, but a tub steams hot. This one has him wipe the salt of blood and tears from my face with an ineffably gentle hand and cut me free of the confines of my dress. It falls to the floor with a clatter of blood-encrusted silver.

My skin is left alight, bare and brilliant, my own. No longer a cage but a home.

"I promised I would touch you," he whispers, his voice hoarse and warm against my skin. And, with a reverence that could write the holy books of a new religion, he lowers me into the bath and holds true to his oath.

AND THAT IS the faithful version. I understand why it's less popular. A sorcerer who flaunted the priest's murderous knife and walked again? A woman who sought revenge and death but found, in the end, both freedom and belonging? It's fanciful.

But that is how it went: The sorcerer who had brought mercury to Nueva España left with me instead of with silver. After all, love was all San Cipriano had spun spells for, and love was what Elías had won, even as he, too, left the occult behind and fixed his sights on a new horizon.

Hand in hand, Elías and I board a galleon in Acapulco, our passage bought with bloodstained silver pried from my dress—the last we ever touch from Mina San Gabriel. We sail west, and farther west still, toward the final resting place of the sun.

There, this legend ends.

There, another begins.

Acknowledgments

My first thanks go always to my agent, Kari Sutherland, for helping me guide this ship through a tumultuous, exhausting year. The litany of things that went wrong and deadlines missed would last pages; suffice it to say that I don't know what I would do without you.

And second, of course, I thank Jen Monroe, editor extraordinaire, who helped me dig this idea out of a dark mine and refine it into the gleaming little book it has become. You are especially to thank for Elías making it out alive, and for that, we must all raise a glass to you and the brilliant Candice Coote.

I also raise a glass to Vi-An Nguyen for gracing me with a perfect trio of red dress covers. I am honored that my words are introduced to the world through your art. I thank the marketing, publicity, and production teams at Berkley, whose hard work puts my books into the hands of the readers who love them: Jessica Mangicaro, Kim-Salina I, Lauren Burnstein, Jennifer Myers, and

ACKNOWLEDGMENTS

Christine Legon, you guys make my world turn. I am indebted to the publishing team at Berkley, Clarie Zion, Jeanne-Marie Hudson, and Craig Burke, for their continued faith in my genre-bending ideas—here's to many more!

I extend a special shout-out to Sara Carminati for rigorous attention to historical detail and linguistic fidelity (across several languages and dialects, to boot!) in her copyedit: Your hard work made this book better. I am grateful for it.

Every one of my books takes a village of readers and cheerleaders; this one was no exception. I thank Rob, Honore (beloved violence adviser, who pummeled me with information about mercury poisoning the second she heard me say So I saw this thing on Grey's Anatomy . . .), Kara, Holly, Ben, and Christine, for early reads and ingenious plot and character troubleshooting. I also thank Aurora, Sam, Liam, and my mother for reading a later draft and giving me the energy to bring it over the finish line. I would lose my mind in publishing without the Berkletes, my Clarion West squad, and the brilliant writing friends (but especially my writing mom friends, to whom I am uniquely indebted) I have had the immense fortune of making over the course of my career and in the last year.

The support of friends like Debbie and Erin and of family—my parents, my sisters, my brother, my aunts and uncles and cousins, my in-laws—was vital this year. I must also shout out my daughter for providing indispensable perspective on my career and for teaching me the uncanny power of auditory hallucinations.

I especially thank Hailey for being the best caretaker Bean and I could ever ask for. I drafted tens of thousands of words when you were on deck (perhaps 90 percent of the book? If not all of it?). It simply wouldn't have happened without you.

Maple: You can't read, but goddamnit, I don't know what I

ACKNOWLEDGMENTS

would do without my sentient thunder blanket. Live forever, please and thanks.

I thank my grandparents, Arnulfo and Elvira, for making me the storyteller I am. I miss you. So much.

And finally, I thank Robert, my story doctor, my partner, the mast that I cling to through every storm: I write happy endings because with you, I'm living one.